'I could hardly put it down and was even reading during my work breaks. I love the author's poetic, bold and authentic writing style . . . From start to finish a simply breathtaking book that is a delight to read. You will love it! Highly recommend'

'Loved this book! Nilopar Uddin is an amazing writer and storyteller. Like the cover, the story was vibrant and intriguing'

'One of the best books I've read in recent times! Can't recommend it highly enough'

'This book has stayed with me and I can't remember feeling this way in a long time . . . I am amazed that as a debut novelist, Uddin has created a world where I have lost myself in. This is a unique voice and I'm excited to read more from her in the future'

'Beautifully told, well plotted, emotional, gripping and wonderfully cathartic. The characters brought to life in this novel are so incredibly human . . . An enchanting family saga that I adored'

'A stunning literary debut'

Nilopar Uddin was born in Shropshire to Sylheti parents who, like the fictional family in *The Halfways*, owned and ran an Indian restaurant in Wales. Every summer her family would travel for their holidays to Bangladesh to visit extended family, and this affection for the country has continued into adulthood.

Nilopar has had a successful career as a financial services lawyer practising in both London and New York, a city that she fell in love with. She now lives in London with her husband and two daughters. She has an MA in Creative Writing from City University where she first started working on *The Halfways*.

THE
HALFWAYS

NILOPAR UDDIN

ONE PLACE. MANY STORIES

HQ
An imprint of HarperCollins*Publishers* Ltd
1 London Bridge Street
London SE1 9GF

www.harpercollins.co.uk

HarperCollins*Publishers*
Macken House, 39/40 Mayor Street Upper,
Dublin 1, D01 C9W8, Ireland

This edition 2023

First published in Great Britain by
HQ, an imprint of HarperCollins*Publishers* Ltd 2022

Copyright © Nilopar Uddin 2022

Nilopar Uddin asserts the moral right to be
identified as the author of this work.
A catalogue record for this book is
available from the British Library.

ISBN: 978-0-00-847874-2

MIX
Paper | Supporting
responsible forestry
FSC
www.fsc.org   FSC™ C007454

This book is produced from independently certified FSC™ paper
to ensure responsible forest management.

For more information visit: www.harpercollins.co.uk/green

This book is set in 12.5/16 pt. Adobe Garamond Pro

Printed and Bound in the UK using 100% Renewable Electricity at
CPI Group (UK) Ltd, Croydon, CR0 4YY

Author's Note

I have chosen not to translate every Sylheti word and expression with equivalents in English, particularly where the meaning is adequately suggested by the context. The Glossary at the back has been compiled to assist the reader with a translation of a small selection of words where I hope it will be helpful to further the reader's understanding. In compiling this Glossary, I have transliterated the Sylheti phonetically into English and would like to note that these translations may not be a faithful representation but rather, they are underpinned by my experience of the language. Where verses from the Quran are referred to in this novel, I would also like to note that a literal translation of the words of the Quran is accepted by most Muslims to be impossible and that therefore the phrases used herein are explanatory translations.

A Sylheti's *matri basha* or mother tongue is not the standard Bangla they are formally taught to read and write at school, but Sylheti, which remains unrecognised as a language and is often referred to as a dialect of the standard Bangla. In the author's experience, speakers of Sylheti can be subjected to linguistic discrimination. Sylheti is principally spoken in the Sylhet Division in north-east Bangladesh and parts of India such as Assam and Manipur. It is also spoken by members of the diaspora around the world, including in England, where it is erroneously identified as 'Bangla' or 'Bengali'. Sylheti was written in a unique script called Siloti Nagri but this historical script appears to have fallen out of usage in the mid- to late twentieth century. It is experiencing a revival today.

Contents

PART I

The Humble Murta and the Graceful Pond Dancer 3

1 7

2 20

3 34

4 43

What Shamsur Saw Beneath the Tamarind Tree 53

5 59

6 65

7 71

Once When They Fought 76

8 83

9 94

PART II

1 111

2 114

Once During a Red-eye in the Bosom of the Cockpit . . 136

3 144

4 155

5 165

The Boy Deprived of a Braggable History 172

6 179

7 187

8 196
9 201
10 211
11 223
12 234
13 247
The Inauspiciousness of a Rainy Wedding 255
14 262
15 278
16 286
17 295
18 308
19 318
20 325
21 332
22 341
23 355
24 359
Once a Teacher's Pet 374
25 381
Lost in Low Cloud 384

PART III

1 389
2 398
3 404
One Summer Holiday 418
4 425
5 442
What Elias Saw Beneath the Tamarind Tree 444

Glossary 450
Acknowledgements 458
Permission Acknowledgement 460

For Ahmed

This land offered me
only dubious joys.
Where else could I go?
I found a broken boat
and spent my life
bailing out the water.

FAKIR LALAN SHAH

TRANSLATED BY DEBEN BHATTACHARYA

PART I

The Humble Murta and the Graceful Pond Dancer

Every few years, when his memory of his mother begins to fray, Elias makes his way to Sylhet as though on a pilgrimage to a place some part of her can be found. The mother he had known had always been fond of the brief summers she had spent there. She had believed herself attached to the place where the heart of her ancestry beat through the land. So, Elias makes the journey.

One year, on his way to his ancestral village, he takes a detour. He hires a nauka, a country boat, at a particularly solitary ghat of the Shari river. He holds the sides as the boatman manoeuvres them away from the river cliffs out towards the marshy fringes where, he has been informed, local villagers source shital bethi from the clusters of murta shrubs. He is curious to see what a murta plant looks like, a curiosity kindled by a thought his mother had shared with his aunt in one of her emails.

The boatman slows the nauka as they near the murtas curving around the shore. The plant that catches Elias's attention stands slightly apart from its brethren. Though this murta is taller and wider than the others, its languid leaves droop tragically into the water.

'They make the mats from the leaves?' he asks the boatman, thinking of the array of beautiful nokshi shital baskets and mats and trays adorning his grandmother's house in the Beacons.

The boatman shakes his head, and not a single well-oiled hair moves. 'Na, ba! Here, look!' The man drops the oar, grabs the nearest murta and pulls aside the leaves to reveal several wide stems that they are attached to. 'Ey, ta! Bucho? This is used for the mat – and the fans and the baskets. Everything!'

As the heat of the sun hammers down on his head, Elias rummages in his rucksack for his mother's old hand fan. The boat rocks from side to side with a sleepy softness as the boatman tries to keep it still. Elias finds the fan and shows it to the man, who nods without understanding what's being told to him. About the beauty of metamorphosis. About how the lime green plant has been sliced and dyed and deftly woven into this hand fan with its fading carmine border and its white shapla centre. How *this* comes from *that*. How *this* is, in essence, still *that*. Words his mother had written, words that have recently stirred in him a longing to be reunited with her.

Elias motions to the man to steer the boat back to shore. As the oar strokes softly through the water, the boatman begins to sing a bhatiyali, his voice travelling out over the horizon in search of the sun god. Elias suddenly reaches out to the last of the murta and pulls a leaf free as the boat passes by. He holds it to his nose – inhales the beloved old world that it carries in its fragrance, and in the cool of its touch. The feel of the murta appeases an ancient craving in Elias, a craving for stories. All the women who have mothered him have grappled with this greed, without fully grasping how each story has helped light his path: each bit of history a beam in a flood of darkness, revealing to him something of life's circularity, of its inherent wisdom and simplicity. Their stories are the bones of his being.

He arrives that evening at Nirashapur, his grandfather's ancestral village, the bruising sky quickening his footsteps towards the dots of turquoise blue glimpsed above the bamboo forest, the precious hand fan now in his rucksack, and the wilting leaf of the murta coiled in his pocket. The heat coaxed out by the darkness rises from the ground and blankets his legs. The shadows of the bamboo canes crisscross his path, as the Neel Bari, the Blue House, comes into view and the lights from the neighbouring doorways grow wide, and faces peer out.

A voice calls out: 'Khe beta? So late, who comes?'

'It is me,' Elias replies. The bamboo forest is alive with the sounds of crickets and frogs, the ghats, the breeze ruffling the leaves, and these sounds crowd in on him. 'It is me, Elias. Elias Suleiman Islam.'

The faces trickle out, mostly old but a few young. The people appear before him like ghosts from the darkness. They touch his face, rub his arms, run their fingers through his ponytail. He thinks he recognises his Nanabhai's fingers, and his high brow, and he sees Nani's shock of wavy hair on a young girl no more than five. Nani who had lived out the last years of her life in this village: long gone, but still lingering.

'Kitha re bhai?' his beloved Mustafa cries, stumbling across the courtyard to him. Mustafa's hair is a tuft of feathers, easily displaced by Elias's breath. Elias's shirt grows damp from the old man's tears, and he laughs as Mustafa, always so dramatic, says, over and over again, 'I never dreamed I would see you again! Never dreamed!'

Dream, Elias thinks – as they sit him on the old veranda and Mustafa hands him water – for Elias does not dream. Sleep is a darkness that swallows him and spits him out at the crack of dawn. All those stories he has collected rattle around, useless in his head, while he sleeps.

But that night, Elias dreams.

As the night deepens, and the sounds of the forest become a soothing percussion, Elias feels his supper of doodh bhat lying heavy in his stomach, tugging him towards sleep. He dreams of the murta and the shapla flowers, metamorphosed into long-limbed women. He thinks of the houris, and wonders if he has died – has somehow bypassed the summing up of deeds and misdeeds and ended up in Jannah. But then a banshee-scream tilts the world upside down, and suddenly the Bay of Bengal is a funnel, sucking in the murta and his shrieking shaplas along with the Ganges, the Brahmaputra and the Meghna. Elias watches in terror as the destructive force of the roaring tidal wave turns the Golden Bengal into a watery hell. He glimpses carcasses just visible beneath the surface, and leans forward, because the bodies are human, the faces on those bodies are recognisable, and he leans forward again, this time too far and then he is falling into the furious water, screaming until his lungs burst, before he wakes with a jolt.

And then for some moments in the quiet darkness, he feels that old fear of being on the brink of losing them all, and of losing his mother all over again.

1

On the last day of August, death could be observed everywhere in Nasrin's back garden.

She had stepped out onto the patio shortly after dropping Elias at his tennis lesson to find the colour wiped from her once beautiful refuge. They had only been away for four days – a last-minute trip to Istanbul, insisted upon by Richard – and she had even flouted the hosepipe ban on the morning of their departure (incurring the frowning disapproval of her neighbour, Mrs Humphreys). But the watering had been futile, Nasrin thought now, surveying the parched grass. The torrid heat had decimated her father's beloved rose bushes and her mother's rhododendrons. Only the marigolds emerged unscathed and Nasrin was moved by the plant's stubborn adaptability – they had been painstakingly transported from Sylhet to her small garden in Barnsbury, and even after such turbulent displacement and this recent heatwave, the diasporic genda continued to flourish.

Glancing up to the darkened windows of Mrs Humphreys's house, Nasrin sifted a fistful of dry, dusty soil through her fingers. Family lore had it that she had loved stuffing mud into her mouth as a toddler – 'mineral deficiency!' her father used to say, but it was more than that. Once, after a nasty fall in Nirashapur, instead of crying for help, Nasrin had lain there, surprised at how soothing the warmth of the sun-baked ground beneath her could be. As the sweet particles of dust tickled her nose and the bustle of Shabebarath took place behind her, she felt the urge to burrow deeper, to press herself further into the earth's embrace. There had been no tears when her mother finally found her, bleeding from a deep cut to her ankle, the thirsty soil drinking her up.

Nasrin stood up and reached decisively for the hosepipe.

The gushing water bought movement back to the leaves and stems. In the plum tree, a thrush twittered happily and Nasrin, elated by the sudden poetry of it, directed the hosepipe up towards the branches. Just as quickly, she brought it down, ashamed of her wastefulness.

The peal of the doorbell cut through the air. Frowning, Nasrin switched off the tap and dropped the hosepipe. The doorbell rang again.

'Coming, coming!' she called, running through the hallway.

Mrs Humphreys stood primly on Nasrin's doorstep, smiling at her from beneath a straw hat.

'Hello?' Nasrin blinked. Surely, she hadn't been caught with the hosepipe again?

'Naz!' The smile on her neighbour's face faded, and Mrs Humphreys's eyes darted from Nasrin's face to her gardening gloves. 'I am sorry to interrupt your gardening!'

'I was just … pruning the rose bushes. I don't usually, but my dad …'

'Oh, but those roses. La Tosca are very difficult to keep so late into the summer. Your father has good taste, though.' Her smile returned. 'How is he? Richard mentioned he's home now?'

'Yes, but not well enough to come visit and prune my roses,' Nasrin said.

'That can wait, I think.' Mrs Humphreys turned and nodded at her husband, who waited out on the street. 'I just wanted to check, Naz, whether you cooked something today … I mean something different?'

'Sorry?'

'Well,' Mrs Humphreys said, laughing self-consciously, 'I don't usually mind the cooking smells. I mean what can you do? But today

… It's just those lovely spices you use, they do have a rather strong smell that lingers. Perhaps you forgot to use the extractor fan?'

Nasrin frowned. 'I always use the extractor fan,' she said tightly.

Mrs Humphreys nodded. 'It comes into the house, you see, and nothing will eradicate it.'

'The fan just blows the odour outside anyway,' Nasrin said, feeling heat rise through her. 'It won't help remove odours "lingering" in your kitchen!'

Mrs Humphreys ignored the curtness in Nasrin's voice and nodded again, this time more eagerly. 'Oh, heavens, yes, of course, you're right, Naz. Of course you are. You know what might be an idea?' She leaned towards Nasrin as though the thought had only just occurred to her. 'Perhaps, when you're cooking, you know, the more *special* dishes, you could call me before you're about to start? And I can close all my windows beforehand?'

Nasrin stared at her. 'Call you before I cook?'

'Not always,' Mrs Humphreys said, with a voice thick with reproach, that blamed Nasrin for being unreasonable. 'It's so much more complicated in the summer – when the windows are always open. I was just telling William, I can't remember the last time it was this hot even in August! It's all this global warming! Well!' Mrs Humphreys smiled, patted Nasrin's gloved hand and stepped off the threshold. 'Say hello to Richard, Naz! He must be so busy at work, we barely see him! Bye, Naz!'

Nasrin watched the woman walk away, clicking the gate firmly shut behind her.

'And it's Nasrin to you,' she muttered. The Humphreyses, long-time residents of the square, had taken an instant liking to Richard when the Wilsons had bought number 34 over five years ago. 'My cousin's married to a Kiwi,' Suzanna Humphreys had told them upon hearing Richard's accent, and though Nasrin rolled her eyes, Richard had barely batted an eyelid, lapping up the older woman's attentions and ignoring the mistake. On weekends, as Nasrin tended her little garden, Suzanna and Richard discussed the *Sunday Times* and exchanged neighbourhood gossip over the garden fence and though the two were now on first-name terms, Nasrin continued to address her neighbours as Mr and Mrs Humphreys and found it condescending and overfamiliar that her neighbour addressed her as Naz.

She closed the door and sniffed the air. She supposed the dal she had cooked that morning did smell stronger than the grilled meat or fish dishes which made up most of their weekly suppers, and she had added a pinch of hing, even though she hated the dung stink – but she had used a chef's candle that promised to obliterate cooking odours and had even lit an expensive tuberose-scented pair as well.

'What a bitch!' she said, standing in the empty hallway. Then she roused herself and walked into the living room, where she lit another scented candle and placed it carefully on the sill of the window facing the Humphreyses' house. She opened all the windows again, closed the container of dal she had left to cool on the table, and shoved it to the back of the fridge.

She picked up her phone and rang Richard.

'What's up?'

'Is that any way to greet your wife?' she asked.

'Sorry. Tell me.'

'The dreaded Mrs Humphreys—'

'Suzanna?'

'Mrs Humphreys!' Nasrin tried to regulate the hysteria lurking behind her words.

'What about her, Naz?'

Nasrin was winded by his impatience.

'Nothing,' she said. 'Just forget it.'

She heard him sigh. 'Honey, sorry, I'm at work. What happened?'

'Nothing,' she repeated. Nothing, nothing, nothing.

'Naz, come on, don't be like that. I'm sorry. Just ignore her. It's just that generation. You know how they can be.'

'I've made dal for tonight,' she said, feeling sulky. 'I just fancied something spicy.'

'Mmm, good. Sounds good.'

'I think it's the hing that's offended her.'

'She'll get over it.'

'Will she, though? Apparently, I now have to call her before I cook! I mean … isn't that a bit offensive? I bet she hasn't asked her other neighbours to call her before they fry bacon or cook onion soup or make pickles or whatever! I mean, don't you think it's a tiny bit racist, Rich?'

Richard let out a guffaw, and Nasrin bristled.

'Racist? Suzanna? Naz, no – just look at the size of her – she probably eats nothing but salad, so she just doesn't like the smell of cooked food.'

Nasrin bit her lip. Richard continued after a short pause: 'Naz? So, what's your day like?'

'The garden's basically dead. And I still need to clean up inside.'

'Cleaner's here tomorrow, isn't she?'

'Yes, but she can't clean around piles of clothes on the floor and stacks of papers everywhere. I still need to unpack the suitcases.'

'Cleaning for the cleaner?'

'Then I have to pick up Eli.'

'Hey, the break was good, huh? We need to get away more.'

'It was good,' she agreed. 'Rich?'

'Hmm?'

'I was thinking, for our next trip, I want to take you and Eli to Sylhet. I want you to see Desh.'

There was a brief silence before Richard tentatively said, 'I mean is it safe, honey? Eli's still so young.'

Now it was Nasrin's turn to lapse into silence.

'Maybe,' Richard offered, 'we should do Sri Lanka instead? I mean just until he's a bit older … It's supposed to be pretty safe out there.'

Nasrin rolled her eyes.

'You know what you need to do today?' Richard asked, abruptly changing the subject. 'I mean, as a priority. The stuff we talked about?'

Nasrin bit her lip. 'Yep.'

'Naz, seriously. You need to do this for yourself. I don't mind you being at home – but like I said, I think it'll drive you nuts once Eli's at school.'

'I know.'

'Why don't you draft a CV at least and we can look over it tonight.'

Nasrin smiled, despite herself. 'Love you.'

'Love you. Just try to make a start, okay?'

'I was thinking maybe some volunteering somewhere, to start?'

'Sure. I mean don't sell yourself short – how many women have a first in bloody Engineering, huh? But sure, anything to get you out of the house.'

By the time she turned into the park and the tennis courts came into view, Richard's words were still ringing in her ears. *Anything to get you out of the house.* As though she drifted about from room to room like a dissatisfied spirit. How *had* she stumbled into this life, a replica of her own mother's? Wife, mum, housekeeper, cook, tailor, gardener, and general fixer of moods. Feminine will sacrificed at the altar of domestic harmony. She had always panicked at the thought of becoming her mother. Choosing to fly had been to avoid the stagnation of her mother's life lived in one place – and once she had chosen it, she had let nothing deter her; not pressure from her parents or her community or the shadows of a childhood of ill health. Obtaining an Engineering degree had been to appease her father, who demanded she had a good degree to fall back on *just in case*. When she had finally been awarded her Commercial Pilot Licence, Nasrin remembered her sense of relief that she had finally carved out for herself a life of frequent respite from all the relationships and worries that fettered her existence on earth. Just as the feel of the ground beneath her cheek had made her feel safe as a child, flying made her feel alive. And yet, by the time her son was four, Nasrin's short career as a First Officer was a distant memory and there was an edge of loneliness to her days that resembled her memories of her mother's isolation as an immigrant mother in the Brecon Beacons.

The arrival of Elias had brought with it the onslaught of disrupted sleep and the unending chores that characterise a young mother's life. Without complaint, she had woken at dawn for the tasks of feeding her colicky son, changing foul-smelling nappies and spending hours putting him down for naps, and most days she found contentment in his health and his wellbeing, but there were days, increasingly so now, when she yearned for the life that she had left far behind. She didn't just miss the flying, she missed the feel of the tarmac beneath the plane just before it took off, and even the faintly misogynistic camaraderie of the flight crew; she missed the freedom to drink three margaritas before dinner, to put on her trainers and run down to the park on a whim. She was tired of the inane connections made with other mothers from her old NCT antenatal class and Elias's nursery, and disappointed by the fragility of her older friendships that had not survived the disruption of motherhood. So, on one level, the prospect of Elias starting school was a welcome sighting of land.

Yet Richard's encouragement that she should find her way back out into the world of work felt more like a criticism of the years she had spent tending to their home than a supportive push towards freedom. More importantly, he was blind to her fears of all that had changed. Not simply that she found her younger self almost unrecognisable; the world itself was not the one she had left almost seven years ago. Whereas during her study and training, she had been able to focus single-mindedly on achieving her ambition to fly, now there was something manic in the itinerary of the modern woman, enlisted to be in so many places at once – in the boardroom, the school fundraiser, the yoga studios, holding placards out on the streets to protest for feminist causes. And yet through all of this they were still expected to make themselves available for on-demand breastfeeding (because breast is best!) and general round-the-clock care of their homes and families. And Richard made it sound … made it sound so offensively simple.

'Mummy!'

She had reached the courts. There was Elias, red and flustered – she'd told Richard he was too young for tennis lessons. What did a four-year-old know about hitting a ball with a racquet? Now, as she watched him miss every throw, she felt her son's exasperation flutter in her own chest.

'It's all right, Eli!' she called, rattling the gate. 'Just give it your best!'

His racquet made a satisfying thwack as it finally met with the ball, and Elias threw the implement into the air and flashed his mother a grin.

'Okay,' Nasrin laughed, 'no need to break it!'

She lifted the beaker of juice she had brought for Elias, and drank from it, watching her son, still grinning, skip across the court to retrieve his racket. When had she last experienced such unabashed joy or even an honest and ferocious outburst of emotion? Perhaps not since her baby had come wriggling and writhing out of her womb, her insides still covering him, when she had felt a burst of regret, for pushing him out into a harsh world. She had watched his face contorting with screams, and had understood his reluctance, how he might have wanted to stay inside his cocoon of fluid darkness. 'I'm so sorry, so sorry you had to come out,' she'd whispered to the roiling, shrivelled infant clinging to her breast, and Richard had watched her, aghast, mistaking her words as he so often did, even taking the doctor aside to ask whether she might not be suffering from a touch of postpartum depression.

'Mummy.' Elias had finished his game and was at her side, tugging at her jacket pocket. 'Angelica is crying.'

'Don't point, darling.'

'Can I go and say hello?'

'If you want to.' She watched him run down the pavement and called out, 'Don't run, you'll fall.' Then she smiled ruefully to herself; her poor son, caught between his mother's caution and his father's ridiculous catchphrases. Falling is Fun. Curiosity is King. Time for the Thinking Chair. Ludicrous modern-parenting malarkey. She smiled as she watched him walk over to his friend and offer up his pink dinosaur, Polly.

Later that evening, as he ate his supper, Nasrin sat beside her son with a cup of green tea and her laptop open before her.

'Are you writing to Khala-Amma?' Elias asked.

'Yes. Eat your food.' She opened an email from Sabrina, half a line at most, not even a full sentence.

'*Hey Didi, how were the hols? What's new in Old Blighty? X to munchkin.*' Nasrin clicked reply.

'Can I type something?'

'After you've finished everything on your plate,' she said, turning back to her screen.

'*All fine. Munchkin having his dinner.*' She looked at her son, who had asked specifically for sausages for dinner that evening. Unable to shrug off the years of pork prohibition in her parents' home, she had picked up some chicken sausages from Whole Foods, but they remained uneaten on the side of her son's plate. She raised her eyebrow. 'Finish them, please,' she told him. 'What does Nani say about wasting food?'

'Every dana wasted will be a snake that bites you,' Elias replied, taking a mouthful of his sausage. 'Can I have a story?'

'Eli! Finish your dinner first!'

'Tell me about the Rakkoshni one.'

'No.'

'Okay, tell me about when the Scaly Anteater came to the Neel Bari.'

'Eli …'

'Okay, then just Kajla Didi?'

'Eat!'

She turned back to her screen smiling, because Bagchi's popular poem had also been a favourite of her sister's.

'*I miss you, Sibby. How's the funny crypto deal going? You know Abba asked me to explain Bitcoin to him? I'm leaving that one to you! How is Daniel? Istanbul was amazing – we had a view of the Bhosporus! But back to life. Rich is still so busy. Just me and Eli tonight, and then when he's gone to bed, me and a nice glass of wine! Are you still stressing about missing my birthday? Don't worry! I know you're busy. I got the loveliest gift from Richard – remember I told you he was getting me Boodles earrings for my birthday, because I found that receipt? Well, he must have changed his mind because he gave me a Chanel bag. Anyway, long story short, I wanted to change it to the lambskin version, so I was queuing at Selfridges with all these Chinese and Arab women, and it made me remember going to Daleys with Amma when we were teenagers, to buy her underwear, and those bitches always served us last. Do you remember Sibby? And it used to make me cry, the way they used to reach over our shoulders to the customers behind us; the injustice of it, the burden of being a brown person in all that white.*'

Nasrin considered the last sentence. Was it too much? Her emails to her sister, Sabrina, were long, meandering strolls through her innermost thoughts. She wrote letters to her cousin Afroz too; but those letters, though tokens of her fondness for her, also reflected the gulf of differences that marked their lives. They were formal and well-wishing, worlds apart from the letters she wrote to Sabrina.

Nasrin stared at the last line again. She had forgotten what it was she had wanted to articulate. She was choked by the fact that these old injustices still swarmed her; that even though she could shop in London's most expensive shops, she still felt like an imposter. She opened her eyes, looked around and sniffed the air. Aside from the turmeric and the lentils, she was satisfied with the threads of tuberose and lime basil.

She hit send without signing off. Sabrina wouldn't read to the end anyway. Sabrina, who began riding a bicycle without stabilisers at the age of four – not just riding, but riding hands-free, and doing wheelies up and down the little square. Sabrina had no time for or interest in reading. It was Nasrin who had sat on their doorstep, poring through books by Blyton, Tolkien and C.S. Lewis, searching those imaginary realms for a world more relatable than her own. Nasrin had never learned to ride a bike. There hadn't seemed to be any point. When Richard once asked her if she was jealous of Sabrina, Nasrin marvelled how little he knew her even after almost a decade together.

Nasrin began a text on her phone.

'Sibby, forgot to say, Amma wants us home for Eid this year. She said Abba said he was up to it. Can you manage, do you think?'

She hit *Send*.

She looked down at Elias.

'You've hardly touched your food, Eli!' she said, eyeing the now cold sausage.

After some minutes of urging him, Nasrin relented and fetched him a glass of warm milk. She set it down on the counter, lips pursed in displeasure. 'You'd better drink every last drop,' she told him.

He picked up the glass. 'Mummy, is it bath time?'

She looked down at him, glad he had dropped the idea of a story. It was her fault. Her tales of Desh and its tribes and animals – stories which were littered with magical flowers that closed when touched, golden bears that could speak Sylheti and evil rakkoshnis that glared from behind scraggly mops of black hair – had bewitched her young son. She looked down at his dear face, his implacably thick, slippery hair, and the faint freckles about his nose. She smiled and tried to push his fringe out of his eyes, taking pleasure in her failure, and pressed her lips to his forehead as he squealed and wriggled.

'Mummy!' he shouted. 'Bath time! And then thel malish?'

She giggled at this pronunciation.

'Yes.'

'Mummy, Magnus says he doesn't know what thel malish is.'

'Because he is not Bengali, sweetheart. He doesn't understand Bangla.'

'Am I Bengali?'

'Yes.'

'But you said I was Welsh too.'

'Yes.'

'And Austrolalian.'

'Australian.'

'Because Daddy is Aus— That.'

'Australian.' She always felt constricted when he brought up questions like these. She wanted there to be a clean, linear logic to his identity, and she hated that she couldn't provide this.

'But am I American too?'

'Why would you be American?'

'Khala-Amma is American.'

The phone rang and Nasrin reached for it with relief. 'Hello? Amma?'

And just like that, as she listened to her mother deliver the news, Nasrin felt an old foe returning.

After an eight-year hiatus, she felt her bones tighten, heard the buzz in her temples. The kitchen began to spin, Elias's plate slipped out of her hand, and then the familiar aura crawled into her, possessing every inch, before the world turned black.

The only witness to the return of the seizures was Elias.

He dropped his spoon just as the vicious monster began to wrestle his mother. This was not, he realised with a sudden terror, some new game his mother was initiating. He jumped from his stool and sought refuge behind the door. He watched through the crack; the phone lay smashed against the leg of the stool, the batteries rolling out on the kitchen tiles. His mother's body had fallen heavily to the ground. The plate she had been holding had shattered into dangerous spikes of bone china.

'Mummy, Mummy, Mumma …' he cried, urging his mother to return to him, his small body shaking in terror, fearing that he was on the brink of losing her.

But on this August evening, Elias would not lose her. On this August evening, Elias eased out of his hiding place as the jerking of the monster ceased and released her from its clutches. He crawled into her arms and felt in her chest the judders of her grief, unfamiliar to him and all the more terrifying because of it.

2

Across the Atlantic, Nasrin's younger sister, Sabrina, was waking up. Her fingers searched for her phone even before her eyes had opened. Her first thought of the day, as always, was a continuation of her last thought the night before: work. It absorbed her waking hours and constricted her sleeping ones. She peered at the emails in her inbox, searching the rows for the sign-off on a trade that she had spent the last hours of yesterday chasing.

She showered and dressed with Tom Keene's raspy voice on the *Bloomberg Surveillance* programme following her about the apartment. The deafening sound of a jackhammer started up, drowning out Keene during a particularly interesting analysis of crypto-assets. Swearing to herself, Sabrina switched the TV off in defeat.

By the time she sauntered onto the trading floor, sipping cautiously from a cup of hot coffee, she had received her impatiently awaited sign-off, and was now preoccupied with thoughts of the impending conference call with a potential new client whose business would be useful in her new role as joint deputy in the Digital Assets team. She called out for the preliminary list of questions which Benjamin, her analyst, should have finished compiling by now. As if on cue, Benjamin sprinted up to her from the printer, stapling paper together and apologising because the conference call had started early. Her analyst was intelligent, a Yale graduate, but this did not prevent him from existing in a constant state of apology. It also irked Sabrina that he was prone to kicking off his stale-smelling Oxfords and running around the trading floor in greying socks as though he was out on the streets selling the *Big Issue*.

'Ben!' she shouted. 'If the call's started, why the hell aren't you on it?' Benjamin began apologising. 'Get the conference details and we'll dial in together. And hurry the fuck up!' He turned to go, and she called out to him, 'And put your frickin shoes back on, where the hell do you think you are?'

Just then, her phone pinged. A text from her sister.

'Sib, Mum's in hospital! Stung by a zillion bees!'

Sabrina smiled, shaking her head at her sister's propensity for exaggeration, a trait which Sabrina found endearing but which often misrepresented reality. Most likely it had been a single bee. She texted her father: *'Abba, is Amma ok?'*

'Ben!' she shouted, returning the phone to her bag. She stood and headed to C4. 'Where the hell are you?'

It was mid-week and the raucous, unbridled ambition on the trading floor was at a peak. The raised voices of the other traders, the fluorescent glow of the screens, and the eerie shadows of management that lurked behind blinds in the peripheral offices had once been overwhelming. Over the last seven years, however, she had learned to surf the frenzy of her nerves, allowing the chaos to carry her like a giant wave through to the end of the day. Through some process of psychological osmosis, once she entered the trading floor, in came Wall Street pandemonium and out went any sense of self.

That particular afternoon, after a busy morning negotiating a trade with numbers woefully prepared by Benjamin, she was ambushed by a late request from an old client. He wanted to sell his position in a collateralised debt obligation, a type of complex financial product which she had previously helped create. Though she and her boss, Ralph, had sought to distance themselves from these notorious products by moving into a new team, Sabrina often found herself embroiled in instructions to restructure or sell her old trades. Time was of the essence – rates and spreads were both moving wildly, and Sabrina had to aggressively brown-nose every trader she knew to get a mark on the position before it became too expensive. She tapped her fingers, paced the floor and shouted at Benjamin for his inefficiencies, as she waited for the compliance authorisations to come through.

At five-thirty, the post-deal paperwork completed, she made her way out of the office, high-fiving Jason, the trader responsible for her last-minute victory.

'You're the absolute best,' Sabrina told him, squeezing his shoulder. 'That screwball was up my ass the whole way through!' Sometimes, she heard herself, heard the Americanisms, the attempts at male camaraderie, and winced.

Jason laughed. 'I bet he enjoyed *that*!'

Sabrina shuddered inwardly and walked away. As she passed the Admin desk, Mercedes called out to her.

'Sabrina, do you want me to book you a cab for this evening?'

Sabrina pursed her lips.

'The barbeque …'

Sabrina let out a rushed breath. 'Oh! No, I'm good. Dan is driving us.'

As she rode the elevator down, Sabrina sent Daniel a message, reminding him of their evening plans.

'It's an oven out there, Miss Sabrina,' the security guard told her, opening the door to let her through. 'You keep cool now.'

'Thanks, Freddie,' she said, suddenly remembering her mother's bee sting.

Her father's reply sat in her inbox.

'Tipu re, no worry futh, I give amma epic penis. She ok now.'

Sabrina stood on the busy kerbside and snorted with laughter. Trying to collect herself, she forwarded the message to her sister and made her way to the subway. The only person with whom she maintained daily contact was her father, but these exchanges were impeded by her father's inability to use predictive text messaging. *'Ok Abba, hope she's feeling better. Heading home. Love you, miss you. PS. You mean epi-pen.'*

These messages were a redemptive act for Sabrina: akin to a brief prayer before bedtime or a morning's surya namaskar. He responded almost immediately. *'Ok my shunar Tipu, eat good, sleep good, be good re futh. What is ps?'*

Smiling, she slipped onto the subway, still texting instructions to Benjamin. Daniel responded to her message with a reminder that she had to pick up his navy linen suit from the dry cleaners so he could wear it that evening. By the time she departed the subway on 66th Street, she had forgotten this. She smiled at a woman struggling with a buggy and helped her up the stairs. The woman, who had curly hair that fell over her shoulders, reminded Sabrina of Nasrin. Thinking of her sister dampened Sabrina's mood: she missed her. She had forgotten to call Nasrin on her birthday the week before, and guilt only made Sabrina miss her sister more. If only there was an extra hour in the day, to reach out, to respond to the plethora of messages that her sister sent her. (How much time did the woman have on her hands?) And then there was the time difference. But she told herself she would call after her Bikram yoga class tomorrow. She ought to also call her mother, but the thought of her mother's overwrought anxiety, palpable even in a brief phone conversation, put her off. She could call her mother tomorrow, too.

The clouds were edged with violet as the sun began its descent. She hesitated, wondering if there was time for a walk through Central Park. It was a good evening for a walk. The late August humidity was beginning to relent beneath an early evening breeze. She could stroll uptown, stop at Magnolia on 72nd and pick up a banana pudding. When Nasrin and Richard had brought Elias to New York last summer, this had been Elias's favourite food – Sabrina smiled, thinking of Nasrin's dismayed face when she tried to take an unfinished container of it away from him and he had screamed and screamed. It delighted Sabrina that her nephew had inherited her sweet tooth.

Just then, an email from Benjamin lifted her spirits further. To her surprise, the misers at Rochdales were interested in doing a sizeable new trade.

Despite Ralph's conviction that digital assets could be a huge opportunity, Sabrina had privately worried about the difficulty of convincing her old institutional client base of this. But she had done it: this interest from Rochdales was significant, and it gave her an opportunity to make the firm almost ten million on a single trade. It was a huge positive, both for the viability of her new role and for the bonus. She wanted to top her million-dollar average over the last three years. It wasn't the money; she wasn't as reckless a spender as some in her profession, preferring to save and to ensure her family was financially secure – it was the validation of where she stood in this bell jar of egos. She intended much of this year's bonus to go to the Peacock, her father's restaurant, which had looked more dilapidated than usual during her last visit. Her parents would make a fuss accepting her money, but this time she would insist. She also wanted to wire a little extra into her sister's account this year. Though she was aware that Richard was a doting husband, Sabrina had been wiring several grand into Nasrin's savings account over the last few years, concerned that her sister had no income of her own as a stay-at-home mum. 'Sibby,' Nasrin protested every year, 'I still have all my BA savings, and Amma and Abba also keep giving me huge amounts of cash for birthdays and Eids!' But this year, Sabrina knew her sister was thinking about starting over once Elias started school, and she wanted to support her with enough to go back to college or to retrain if she wanted to.

Sabrina turned onto 64th and Columbus and joined the rushing stream of commuters. Ahead, a swarming crowd gathered at the Lincoln Center beneath billboards of the Bolshoi's ballerinas. As she watched a well-groomed woman in a floating dress get out of a battered taxi, Sabrina felt wistful. She too had once dressed with such care for every date; now, Daniel didn't notice if she wore track pants or if her hair was greasy and this lack of judgement was depressing. She watched the woman, clutching a beautiful magenta Dior purse, skip nimbly through the crowd in her needle-fine heels and disappear. Sabrina wondered who she was, that she could walk to the head of a queue and demand admission. Power did this. Not money. Money was overrated. It was only a ticket to the show.

She found no need to lament the fact that she had arrived in Manhattan with very little – as an upstart she was surprisingly attractive to the millennial world of finance, which fancied itself a pioneer of affirmative action. Sabrina was female. One tick. Ethnic minority background. Another tick. Non–Ivy League education (who cared that it was Cambridge?). Final and closing tick. Manhattan had taken in Sabrina because of her perceived weaknesses, and it had underestimated her. In fact, her background had made it easier for her because it made it look harder. And the universe had indulged her with exceptional good fortune. Newly graduated, Sabrina had landed a job in the sales and trading desk of a structured finance team at a time when the structured product market was in its heyday and then she had emerged miraculously unscathed when the same instrument became notorious for its part in the mortgage crisis. She had followed Ralph and Ashok into building a new team selling digital assets, and recently, Ashok had announced he would be moving to the Hedge Fund Sales Team, meaning there would be less competition for that top role when Ralph decided to retire. Like the legendary Tipu Sultan, to whom her father jokingly compared her, and which had become something of a family sobriquet, Sabrina lived with the tip of her sword poised, her toes constantly edging forward towards the next big thing.

Sabrina was proud of how far she had come. Her father was an immigrant who wore a balaclava even in the Welsh springtime, whose English was twanged with heavy t's and silent v's. Her grandfather had been a small-time landowner in a pretty corner of rural Bangladesh who had never stepped into the capital city of Dhaka, had never owned a passport and wore Bata flip-flops and a starched white lungi until the day he died. And yet here Sabrina was: eating, sleeping and rubbing shoulders with Manhattan's mighty. Prada, Pucci, Per Se, Pearl Room, a Central Park West postcode; the bonus money allowed her to partake in it all, and she felt like a king. Not a queen, but a king, because it was a man's world. There were still so few women at her level that she often forgot she was one herself. But behind the pride and the bursts of elation, there resided a deeper forboding that descended upon her in the sepulchral aftermath of losing a deal: it was the fear that it could all end in an instant. As Ashok had told her many times, 'In finance, if you're not winning, you're losing, there's no such thing as standing still' – and so, resisting the urge to look down and assess her progress, Sabrina was forced to focus on looking ahead and scouring for her next foothold so she could continue to scramble up.

Her phone buzzed. New emails – one from Nasrin. Sabrina saved it into the 'To Read' file to enjoy in the serenity of her apartment and scrolled down. There was one from Ralph's boss.

Her boss's boss!

She stood still beneath the yellow canopy of a hot dog stall to read it.

'Just bumped into Benjamin – Rochdales has been elusive for years, so great work, Sabrina. Exactly the sort of proactive, innovative thinking we need in our MD cohort next year. Can you call Melinda and schedule lunch next week?'

Sabrina felt a surge of joy, her ears buzzing. Managing Director!

To make MD at a bank like that at twenty-nine was virtually unheard of. It was the highest-ranking role below partnership in the banking world, and bestowed only to a limited number each year. The setting orange sun seemed to explode before her, swallow her, spin her around before putting her back on the pavement, dizzy and disorientated. Who should she call? The relationships she had built in Manhattan were mostly social ones, lacking the intimacy of any genuine friendship, and her family members were three and a half thousand miles away and probably asleep. But then who was there to witness this thrilling step in her ascent up the corporate ladder? Here she was, doing everything to live up to her sobriquet – she was Tipu himself, just as her father had named her – single-minded in a way that frightened her own mother, and so hungry for progression, so ambitious, that most on the trading floor tried their best to keep out of her way. She fed on New York just as New York fed on her. There were those, like Daniel, who were fascinated by this, and those, like Ashok, who were slightly repulsed but unable to turn away.

'Miss, you want hot dog?'

Sabrina shook her head, and walked away from the stall, towards a pedestrian crossing. She paced backwards and forwards on the same spot with people tutting around her. She tried to call Ralph but no answer. She tried Daniel and again no answer. It was torture not to be able to share this news. Since the financial crisis, the path to MD had become a long-drawn and onerous process of surveillance and interrogation, rarely reached before one's late thirties. Her mouth felt dry, her eyes wet, while her chest swelled with happiness. Finally, she made herself stand still, and focus on the uninterrupted view of Broadway, until her heart returned to a more regular rhythm.

She dialled Ashok's number.

Ashok's wife answered the call with a silky 'Hello?' and Sabrina, grinning sheepishly, hung up.

She ducked into Food Emporium and picked up a bottle of the Chilean Pinot Noir that Daniel loved, and as an afterthought, a packet of Trojans. She couldn't remember if they had run out or not – it had been a while; they'd been so busy.

She was embedded now, into this world that had once seemed so unattainable; she was a member of the entitled and distinguished, the sultana in a sea of sultans.

That evening, Sabrina showered quickly, the cold water startling her into a fresh level of wakefulness. She had come home to a sulking Daniel because, in the excitement of her anticipated promotion, she had forgotten to stop off at the dry cleaners. She rolled her eyes as he mooched about the apartment, holding fast to his sulk until she nudged him out of it; her hands, her lips working it out of him like a cramp in a muscle. She could hear him now, whistling away in the other bathroom as he shaved. So easily contented, like a child. Whereas she had so much left to do by tomorrow's 3 p.m. meeting with Rochdales, that she would need to get up at four the next morning.

As she unfurled the hairdryer, Daniel came into the room, a towel wrapped around his hips. He prised the dryer away from her and pulled her gently onto the bed, distracting her with kisses. She traced the contours of his biceps with her fingers and nudged him playfully onto his back, straddled his hips, pulling at the towel. 'We could just not go,' she whispered, sliding her lips along his jawline, and his lips parted with a trill of pleasure.

Then her phone pinged, and she sat up to reach for it. She walked away from Dan to read the message from Ashok: *'Heard you scored big with Rochdales, Sab! Told you, you've got what it takes. Proud of you.'* She bit her lip, an uncertain gratitude building inside her. She was unused to shows of sentimentality from Ashok. She looked back at Dan, who lay expectantly on the bed, and frowned.

'Hurry up!' she told him. 'You'll make us late!'

'That piece has been sold at just over one point three, but we have another lovely Gervex due to come in after the summer,' Daniel was telling Ralph as Sabrina extricated herself from the conversation and ambled towards the group near the oyster table. Sabrina loathed oysters. But the man who chaired the MD selection panel stood beside the oyster shack, talking to Fanni Delileo, a colleague of Sabrina's.

'Sabrina!'

'Hi, Monty! How are you? Fanni.' She accepted an oyster, holding it while the server squeezed a half lemon and tipped a dash of Tabasco into the gelatinous gloop. As inaudibly as she could, she took a deep breath and poured it into her mouth, swallowing immediately. The mossy saltiness made her grimace.

'We were just talking about all these grads wanting details of our corporate social responsibility programme,' Monty said. 'They have no idea just how much we spend on pro bono issues. And some of these new kids coming in from these lefty colleges think it's all about giving back to the community, and the thing is of course, A, we already do, and B, if you're into social justice, a bank isn't really the platform you choose to do it from.'

Sabrina joined Fanni in applauding this little speech with a gargle of appreciative laughter. She turned slightly towards a passing server, and took a glass of champagne, her fingers, sweaty from the heat, relieved by the immediate chill of the glass.

'Absolutely,' she heard herself saying. 'Someone needs to tell these kids: if you don't live and breathe money and markets, don't come here.'

'Money and markets!' Fanni scoffed. 'That's a tad old-school Gordon Gecko, isn't it, Sabrina?'

Sabrina, pretending not to detect the hint of spite in her colleague's tone, smiled in response and focused on the onyx ring on Fanni's pinkie blinking in the dusk.

'Talking of money and markets,' Monty turned to her, 'I heard about your win with Rochdales. Pretty amazing stuff, Sabrina, congratulations.'

Sabrina drank the small shot of victory in her glass, ignoring the way Fanni glowered beside her. A few feet away, she saw Ashok, with his gold-headed wife at his elbow. He seemed to sense her and turned to meet her gaze. She nodded at him, the back of her neck hot with the memory of him. He looked away, but not before delighting her with a quick appraising glance at the peacock-blue bodice of her Roksanda dress.

Ralph suddenly appeared beside her and led her to a group of his colleagues who had gathered around a young musician playing Mozart on her violin. One of them took the liberty of rearranging the girl's strap which had slipped of her shoulder. The girl glanced at him, her expression uncertain, but continued to play seamlessly.

'Hey, guys,' Ralph called, 'meet my Bitcoin babe!' The group turned to Sabrina as Ralph signalled a waiter to refill her glass, his fingers stroking Sabrina's bare back.

And Sabrina tried her best to rearrange her grimace into a smile, reminding herself that misogynistic belittlements such as these couldn't detract from her trajectory. Her parents' Manichean perception of the world didn't reach New York City where there was no evil, no good, just the conspicuous energy of consumption. Even so, at moments like this where a part of her wanted to shrug off Ralph's wandering hands, she had a twinge of nostalgia for the straightforward virtuosity of her parents' world: but then she would remind herself that to be here, one had to use every muscle, every nerve, every sinew to work towards affording better and winning more, because that meant mattering more, and justifying the square footage of prime real estate you stood upon. To attain such glories, a certain level of discomfort was to be expected.

The next evening, after a gruelling day full of calls and meetings, Sabrina shut down her computer and decided she would finish her outstanding tasks from home. As she passed by Admin on her way out of the office, Mercedes looked up.

'Bye, Sabrina!' Mercedes called out. 'Oh, your mother phoned a couple of hours ago. Said to please call her back.'

It occurred to Sabrina that her mother had never tried to reach her at the office before, usually calling her personal cell phone, and even then, rarely when Sabrina was at work unless it was an emergency. Sabrina opened her bag to find the battered iPhone she kept for personal use but couldn't find it inside the chaos of tissues, lipsticks and hand cream. She remembered sending her father a message that morning and setting it down on the kitchen counter. She had probably left it there. She would call her mother back when she got home.

She took a cab, unable to face the clammy, congested subway, and arrived home at just after seven. She let herself into an apartment swathed in darkness.

At first, she thought that perhaps Daniel wasn't home yet, and was still at Sotheby's. As her eyes adjusted to the light though, she saw him sitting on the armchair by the bookcases, staring straight ahead. The shadows diminished him. He had a way of never sitting up straight – he had once complained that his father would smack him on the small of his back to straighten him up – and now his head was sunk low on his chest.

Sabrina reached out and switched on the light.

'Hi!' She set her purse on the table.

Daniel seemed to be struggling to formulate words, his bottom lip twitched.

'Dan, are you okay?'

'I am not okay, actually.' His words entered the thick air of the apartment and fell like dense pebbles. 'I am so not okay. Because today. Today, I found a little something. A little something that was really very interesting.' He held up her iPhone.

'I was wondering where that was!'

'I'm sure you don't let it out of your sight.'

'I'm not following.'

'Oh, please, do follow. See, there are some interesting texts here,

31

I mean really very interesting – makes for some very illuminating reading.'

'You're reading my texts?' She was a little anxious, but she let her anger cut quickly through it. 'Does it occur to you that that's an invasion of privacy?'

'It's an invasion of privacy, sure.' He mimicked her soprano voice and British accent, churlishly nodding. 'What about, like, a breach of trust? What about infidelity? You're worried about an invasion of fucking privacy, and—'

'What else have you been through?' She took a glass out of the cupboard and banged the door shut. 'Oh wait, is my passport still in its place? Have you been reviewing my bank statements too? What the fuck is this?' Her anger wasn't rising fast enough to stem the haemorrhage of anxiety.

'Don't you dare get all moral on me. I picked up the phone because someone's been calling it, like, fucking incessantly. I just picked it up, and then I see this text come through from Ashok.' He held up the phone and proceeded to read from the screen. *'That dress is not fit for public consumption … wear it for me this Thursday, usual place?'* He looked up at her, blinking rapidly. 'Ashok? As in *work* Ashok?'

Daniel waited for her to react. When she didn't, he continued, 'And I thought to myself, well that's inappropriate. And, what's this, this usual place? Where is the usual place, and why would you wear a dress for him?'

'He's just messing about,' Sabrina said as airily as she could. 'Don't be such a girl about it.'

Daniel glared at her and then suddenly stood up and threw the phone down. He rubbed his face with both palms.

Sabrina stooped to pick up the phone.

'Dan.' She took a step closer to him. Despite the dread of being found out, she relished the fact that the six-hundred-dollar dress had done its job. Ashok had noticed it. Why wasn't she feeling more worried about what it meant for her and Daniel? Why didn't she feel more worried about losing him?

Daniel, hands still covering his face, shook his head, but it was a shake of resignation. If she insisted on either her innocence or her regret, she could lead him away from the edge. She took another step forward, reaching out for him, when the phone in her hand buzzed.

It was a text from Nasrin.

'Where ARE you? Call home NOW. It's Abba.'

Daniel let his hands hang by his sides as he watched Sabrina walk away, out onto the balcony, the phone cradled between her shoulder and ear.

Sabrina was so shocked by the news her hysterical sister was conveying to her that she did not notice her boyfriend take his coat and leave the apartment.

3

Nestled above the Bay of Bengal, antipodean to Sabrina's Manhattan bubble, Afroz was working in her kitchen. She spoke to a young girl, who stood outside and watched her through the railings of the window.

Afroz wiped her brow with her scarf. She had sent the two maids off to buy gual from the Biyanibazar fish market because their usual fishmonger had angered her mother-in-law by supplying a gual that smelled less than fresh. Meanwhile, Afroz was chopping the vegetables for lunch. Her neighbour's daughter, Munni, seemed uncharacteristically preoccupied, her mouth turned downward, and Afroz had to work extra hard to carry the conversation. The summer was slowly suffocating Sylhet. Afroz could hear the tinkling bells of the rickshaw drivers out on the streets, pulling their loads of two, three, sometimes four adult bodies, their calf muscles bulging obscenely, and she wondered how they were drawing breath in that inferno. Inside, beside the gas stove, her whole body seemed to be on fire, and the prickly heat rash on the small of Afroz's back, and along her forehead, stung sharply.

'Jamal!' she called out to the houseboy who was sweeping the back terrace. She heard him drop the broom and the soft pitter-patter of his run.

'Ji, Khala?'

'Ish, the heat today! Can you make me your lebu pani?'

'Khala, we are out of limes.'

'Ish, re.'

He smiled goofily at her, and she shook her head. He was a small boy for fourteen, the age he claimed to be, and it enraged her mother-in-law that he didn't wear a shirt when it was hot.

'Go on and put a shirt on before she sees you,' Afroz told him, resuming her slicing.

'Khala,' he said, 'there is Fanta. Shall I get you the Fanta?'

Afroz clicked her tongue as he rushed off, knowing he loved offering her Fanta, because she always offered him a glass too. Another thing that irritated her mother-in-law.

She looked up at Munni pressing her face against the window grille.

'Eh Munni!' she chided. 'Why don't you go home, get out of this heat? You're getting all black in the sun!'

The girl merely blinked at her, and Afroz wondered how her brow was so smooth and dry when her own was dripping with sweat. Her mother-in-law, a frightening widow with untold power within the household, refused to allow an air conditioner in the kitchen, believing it a waste to provide this luxury for the maids working there. The fact that Afroz had taken to spending much of her day in the kitchen along with the maids (cooking was a relief amid the monotony of married life) was something no one cared to acknowledge. She was not expected to do menial tasks like cooking and cleaning, and if she decided to do so, then she would not be given special treatment.

Jamal returned, cradling the bottle of Fanta in his arms like an adored infant. She took the glass he poured for her but was suddenly put off by its chemical orangeness, and told him to drink it instead. He did so with such speed that Afroz scolded him, to which he merely burped an incomprehensible reply. She chased him out of the kitchen, returning to her chopping board with a smile teasing the corners of her mouth.

Afroz had soaked chickpeas for her husband's lunch and chewed a few as she chopped the onions. One of the small pleasures of her married life was that her husband was fond of her cooking, and though her mother-in-law disapproved, he would praise her skill to anyone who cared to listen. But Humayun was a creature of habit and tradition – his love for her cooking extended only to the customary dishes, the shutki satni, the chops, the nali shag. And he preferred to have the same lunch day in, day out: a small chickpea salad followed by rice with gual fish stew. Its blandness bored her, and though she occasionally tried to vary it, Humayun was resistant. Any change, however small or successful, was met with grumbles of disappointment from her status-quo-loving husband.

Munni continued to sit on the partition wall, holding on to the window grille for stability, and Afroz passed her chickpeas to nibble on. Munni, who had been born severely hearing impaired, communicated with a combination of sign and sound, and Afroz liked the expressions she made to show her pleasure at the chickpeas. There was a marked absence of children in Afroz's own life. Her cousin Nasrin occasionally emailed photos of her son; photos which reminded Afroz of the Lladró figurines that had lined her English teacher's console table when she was a girl – lavish hair, huge eyes and a slightly upturned little nose.

'Afi?' Afroz looked up to see Humayun wander into the kitchen, holding the hem of his lungi in one hand and his tooth mug in the other. 'Can you warm some water for me? Damn generator is off too!'

'Ish, you need warm water on a day like this?' she asked, taking the mug from him.

'You can't wash your face with cold water! How do you talk such crazy talk, eh such fagol math?' Humayun watched her as she put a pan of water on the stove. He peered into the bowl of soaking chickpeas and helped himself to a handful.

'I'll bring your tea out,' she said, wishing him out of the kitchen.

'Eh, Munni,' he said, ignoring her and greeting the neighbour's daughter. 'Don't you have a home to be in? Thor kitha bari ghor nai ni?'

Afroz tutted behind him, and he laughed and sauntered out of the kitchen. 'No wonder there's never any Fanta in the fridge when you're feeding it to all the kids on the block.'

Afroz looked at the perplexed girl, who had understood very little of what had been said. She went to the fridge and fetched the bottle of Fanta and poured the last of it into a glass, passing it through the grille to the girl. Munni trilled with pleasure and Afroz continued her errands feeling satisfied that in all lives, even one as downtrodden as hers, there was always room for small victories.

When the buzzer rang, and Jamal ran to tell Afroz that her father was at the door, Afroz glanced up at the old wall clock and wondered why he would be visiting her so early. The late morning Sylhet sun was relentless, just like the searing breath of the Shoythan. She shooed the neighbour's daughter back home and wiped her hands on a tea towel. Humayun didn't look up as she passed him in the dining room.

'Don't you hear the doorbell?' she asked, indignant but taking care to keep her voice low. Humayun merely turned the page of his morning paper.

Outside the gate stood her father. Masoom's beard framed a face that was creased and translucent, like tracing paper, so delicate it made her heart ache. She embraced him, a low-level panic buzzing in her chest. As she ushered him into the reception room, he swatted away her offers of tea and biscuits, and perched on the end of the sofa. She saw with alarm the dust he had bought in on his heels and called Jamal to clean it. When there was no answer, she went to get the dustpan and brush before her mother-in-law came down and noticed it.

'What are you doing, Afi? Put that all down and come and sit with me.' He seemed so agitated that she dropped the brush and obediently sat down next to him.

'Is it you? Is it your health?' she asked him, her voice high and sharp. 'Tell me, Baba, what is it?'

Before her father could respond, Humayun appeared. Masoom stood up and greeted his son-in-law.

'How are you, Baba?' Humayun asked kindly. It was one of the few redeeming qualities in her husband, that he was kind to her father.

'Bhala, baba, and you?' Masoom replied. He glanced at Afroz. 'I came early because I have some sad news to share. Afroz's uncle, in Britain, you remember Sham Bhai? Well. He passed away this morning.'

'Inna lillahi wa inna ilayhi raji'un,' Humayun said, shaking his head.

Numb with shock, Afroz blinked at her father. 'What?' she said. 'How?'

'He had another heart attack, re futh,' Baba told her. He handed her an envelope from the pocket of his kurtha, just as Afroz's mother-in-law trailed in. Irritation blossomed across the older woman's face at the sight of the dust and the broom on the floor.

'Assalamualaikum afa, I was just imparting some sad news to our children,' Baba told her. 'You remember my Sham Bhai from bidesh? He passed away.'

'Inna lillahi wa inna ilayhi raji'un,' Afroz's mother-in-law said. She eyed the envelope in Afroz's hands.

'What is this?' Afroz asked her father.

'A ticket,' he replied, running a hand over his beard. 'One of us should go to your uncle's funeral, and I—'

'But, Baba—'

He held up his hand. 'Afi. Go and be with your Jahanara Fufu, and your cousins. They need you right now.'

That evening, while she packed, stunned by the news of her uncle's death, Humayun called to her from their bed, asking her to scratch his back. She ran her nails over the clammy skin. The house was in a state of offended stillness, unwilling to accept that she might have a life outside of it. Her father had had to intervene on her behalf, uncharacteristically raising his voice when Afroz's mother-in-law had objected. In the end, it had been Humayun, unwilling to strain his relationship with Masoom, who had given his reluctant consent.

'What time should we leave?' she asked timidly. 'To check in, I mean.'

'We'll leave when we leave,' her husband snapped.

'Can we go by the cemetery?'

She felt his body sag beneath her hands. Unlike her, Humayun hated to visit the tiny tombstone, near the north-western corner of the Id-Gah. But she wouldn't leave the country without going.

'I have to see her just once, before I leave,' she said.

'You make it sound like you're going forever!' Humayun scolded. 'It's only a week.'

He sighed and took her hand from his back and pulled her in. 'Okay, we will stop off there on the way to the airport.'

She lay back and he moved above her. She inhaled the scent of him, faint turmeric with the musk of his aftershave. He sought her lips with his, as he often did, and, as she always did, she turned her face away. She felt him tense momentarily. The ceiling fan whirred above, and she tried to focus on it, tried not to let her mind wander, as it often did, to Taseen. But it was harder today, in the wake of her father's visit and the anticipation of her impending journey. It seemed to unlock the nostalgia within her. She squeezed her eyes shut and tried to block the image of Taseen's laughing face. Taseen, who still occupied so many of her daydreams, how could she deny herself this moment to grieve him? She had heard that he had finally married, and moved to Dhaka with his new wife, to take up a position as an economics professor.

She also tried not to think of her child. The child whom she had loved from the moment she had fluttered in the swell of her belly. She felt in some way to blame for everything: so urgently had she wanted the baby in her arms, so desperately to run her lips over her nose and brow, to curl her tiny fingers around hers. The child had come too early, pummelled by Afroz's greed. She had held her barely breathing form for the hour that she lived, as Humayun anxiously hovered in the background. She had leaned close into the baby, her sobs vibrating inside her, even after the tears had finished. Then she had howled as they prised the baby away, along with Afroz's womb, wrenched from her along with her daughter. Humayun named her afterwards. Ruksana. And Afroz felt a wild regret for not whispering the name to the child while she had lived.

Her losses, freshly revived, now twisted and turned inside her and made her heart ache. She lay awake long after Humayun had fallen asleep.

In the end, she must have dozed, for the wail pulled her out of her sleep. A sound that was animal but human too.

'Afi!' Humayun whispered to her. They stared at each other, as another wail soared through the dark night.

'Stay here,' he ordered as he jumped from the bed. But the blackness of the night was frightening and so she got up and followed close behind. He tried the light. 'Electricity's out,' he said with a low voice. They emerged blinking onto the veranda, the darkness impenetrable without the light of the streetlamps. The wailing was now replaced by a low, loud moan.

'A fox?' Afroz whispered. Foxes, she knew, could make so many sounds, from infant-like cries to chilling screams. Humayun shook his head and she followed him to the gate.

'Let's go back,' she said, taking his arm. 'We'll call the police!'

'Afi, I told you to stay inside!' he snapped, shaking her off. Out on the road, the night seemed less dark, and everything was still: not a sound, not a movement. Afroz felt the spiky dust beneath her feet and realised she had left the house in bare feet. Humayun was already halfway down the alley that led to their neighbour's house and she scampered after him. Suddenly she felt as though she was in the eerie tunnel of a dream, with the low moans that she could suddenly hear drawing her closer. At the neighbour's gate, Humayun stopped.

There on the veranda, not twenty feet away from them, the neighbour's daughter lay on the ground being beaten with the buckle-end of a belt. In the darkness, Afroz made out that it was the girl's brother holding the belt.

Humayun leapt forward. 'Shumon!'

'Move, Humayun Bhai, don't interfere!'

'You'll kill her! Have you gone mad?'

'I tell you, Humayun Bhai, I am warning you, this is a family matter!'

'What did she do? Stop it, give that to me!'

'That construction worker from the Nori complex! I will kill her. I'll find him, and he is next!'

Afterwards, Afroz couldn't remember what made her throw herself between Munni and her brother's belt. She remembered how her heart had quaked with fear, but there was such malevolence in the beating of this vulnerable, deaf girl – a child barely into adolescence – that all of Afroz's fear had evaporated.

She glared at Shumon, daring him to throw the belt her way. Shumon advanced towards her, his boorish expression verging on the ludicrous.

'Shumon, khobordar!' Afroz shouted, surprising herself as her voice roared out into the darkness.

Shumon stopped, suddenly uncertain. He looked from Afroz to Humayun and then back to Afroz again. Afroz's heart thrashed in her chest. After a moment, Shumon threw the belt on the ground. 'Get on home,' he told her before turning away. 'This is the problem – when women don't stay at home, this is the root of the problem!'

Afroz turned to Munni, stroking the girl's hair away from her face: magnificent tresses that promised this girl's virtue to the world and shackled the girl to that promise. That was all they were as women, half a man's worth – a dimunitive value further restricted by their role as symbol of family honour. Munni shivered as Afroz led her back to the house and Afroz felt her anger spiking again. *Calm down*, she told herself, *you will be with your cousins soon*. The trip to Wales would be a short and temporary reprieve, but it was long overdue.

4

As the women readied themselves to make the journey to the Beacons, Shamsur's beloved restaurant stood silent in the night. Shabbier and shorter than its neighbours, the Peacock was also set apart by its colour – a deep ochre set against the magnolias and dove greys, and in these ways the old building bore a resemblance to its recent proprietor. It was as though, in the decades of diligent hours that Shamsur had spent in it, in each nail he had hammered into its walls, each sheet of wallpaper he had patiently replaced, each pane of glass he'd polished every morning, Shamsur had imbued a residue of himself.

In the staff cottage behind the Peacock, the newly orphaned staff mourned Shamsur's passing, huddled together on the only sofa, the dusty carom board pressed against their knees. Zee TV flickered mute in the corner as they looked out towards the Peacock, sensing his lingering presence there.

Next door in the town house in which Shamsur had lived with his family – furnished with its kitsch amalgamation of Bengali katha and Portmeirion pottery – his wife, Jahanara, nursed her grief alone. She stood at her window, watching a lunar eclipse with the patchwork quilt of the Beacons spread beneath it. She counted zikrs on her jade prayer beads, praying for the return of the silver moon from the belly of the greedy eclipse.

'SubhanAllah, SubhanAllah, SubhanAllah.'

She watched the tussle of the moon and sun as she prayed,

43

worrying the jade between her fingers. An eclipse was a sign of gordish – a time of struggle and misfortune – a sign that Shamsur's death wasn't enough and that there was yet more to come.

By the time she finished her duas, it was almost 5 a.m., and she sat on her janamaz, waiting for the dawn to rise out of the valley. Every morning for the last thirty-four years, Jahanara had woken at dawn for the Fajr prayer, only to be greeted by the eerie silence of a still-sleeping village, and she had yearned for the muezzin to burst into the call for prayer. In the early days she had missed the adhan as though it were a family member rather than a sound. Such yearnings had become fainter and less painful over the years. But this morning the nostalgia for Desh and all its sounds and smells was a wound split open again, and she felt heavy with its pain.

Shamsur had uprooted her to bring her to this strange land, had filled her with his affection for these sloping valleys, the enchanting shades of green, and the kindness of the Welsh people; and then, he had abandoned her with no warning. She was stranded here. She had little idea as to what the future held or how to navigate it: she had always been taught, first by her parents and then by her husband, that others were better placed to make decisions on her behalf. She trusted Shamsur had organised her future, just as he had managed her past. She knew that he had made a will, and that Riaz, the Peacock's head waiter, would manage the formalities. 'The girls are too far away,' Shamsur had explained, when she had expressed surprise at his decision to appoint Riaz executor. Jahanara regretted that her daughters were so far away, but she blamed Shamsur for their absenteeism: had she not warned him when he had argued with her to let Nasrin go to London for university, that allowing girls too much freedom would backfire? And she had been right – she and Shamsur had looked on in disappointment as the girls had gradually drawn away from them, freely choosing lives at a distance from their parents and their cultures.

She rolled up her prayer mat, hung her prayer beads around her lampshade, and with a corner of a cotton rag she kept hidden in a small basket beneath the bed, wiped away the layer of invisible dust that she was sure had settled on the bedside table. She then wiped the windowsill, and the door, the bed frame and the light switch, and finally the wardrobe, just as she had done the night before. Then she washed and dried her hands thoroughly, applied some cream to the patches of eczema on her knuckles and fingertips, and, shaking out her wet hair, took her comb and sat on the edge of the bed. As she untangled her hair, she tried to organise the day's arrivals in her head. Shamsur would be the first to arrive – from the hospital where he had taken his final breaths. She would gaze at him, her husband of almost thirty-five years; she would trace the beautiful arch of his nose with her index finger for the last time. Then her daughters would come to rescue her. Nasrin had promised to arrive in time for a late breakfast, and Sabrina would arrive in the late afternoon, provided her flight landed on time.

An old woman peered at her from the gilt wall mirror with darkness smeared beneath her eyes like ash. When had this woman last slept? Not for a while, and even then, not well. She tried to sit up straighter but the old woman in the mirror stayed stooped. She had worn white sarees for years now, had stopped wearing colour when Elias, her first and only grandchild, was born. She wanted him to have an image of her as a traditional Nani like her own had been – refined, with a neat silver bun, and always fresh in a crisp Jamdani saree with delicate strands of gold worn at her wrists. But this old woman's gold bangles had to go now. Jahanara slipped them off, and looking at her reflection, let out a pitiful cry.

'Fufu?' a voice called from the bottom of the stairs.

Jahanara started.

'Fufu, you up there?'

It was Riaz. She had not heard him let himself in, and she quickly wiped her face, and stood up. 'Riaz, come in, re baba.'

She walked to the dresser and returned the comb to a small drawer, pulling her hair into a bun at the nape of her neck.

'I thought we could make a start on clearing the living room,' Riaz called, leaping up the stairs and appearing in her doorway. 'Make space for Uncle – hearse arrives at nine-ish.' She glanced at him, saw the purple swell on his cheekbone.

'Ish, re Allah, why do you do this? That poor face of yours!' Both she and Shamsur had reluctantly accepted Riaz's penchant for mixed martial arts over the years, but it still upset her to see his face bruised in this way.

'Had a fight tonight, didn't I? Wasn't sure I wanted to do it, you know, out of respect for Uncle, but, then I had to, for him. I mean, out of respect, as he would have wanted that, I think? No, no, Fufu,' he said, waving her away from his face. 'It's nothing – that lad Lloyd snuck a jab in – I won it though, didn't I? Just for Sham Uncle, had to win it.'

There was a jitteriness in his usually calm, clear voice that made her turn again and look closely. 'Riaz,' she said, 'what have you been smoking?'

Riaz laughed, but she could see it was a sound that made no connection with his vague, watery eyes. 'Fufu, what!' He shook his head. 'See, no, I got back and they're all sitting in the living room, and I sat with them. Then J and I said we were going to bed, and well, I couldn't sleep. I was awake, couldn't sleep, brain was still buzzing you know, then I saw your light on and I knew you were awake doing namaz, and I thought …' He paused then, took a deep breath, unable to wipe the broad smile away from his face. 'I thought we could start.'

Jahanara watched him fidget with the button on his sleeve, watched him pick an object from her dresser and toss it from hand to hand. The acne-plagued, gangly boy of fourteen who had arrived at her doorstep had long gone and been replaced with the broad, smooth veneer of a man. But she realised with dismay that all it took was a few puffs of ganja to bring back the boy.

'Let us start then,' she said evenly. 'Accha.' She walked down the stairs, Riaz at her heels, and opened the kitchen door.

'Fufu,' Riaz said, his voice hesitant. 'I wonder … Did Sham Uncle mention anything … I mean about me?'

Jahanara turned in surprise. 'What about you, baba?'

Riaz looked flustered and embarrassed by the question. 'I mean, we were talking about my job … I wondered if he had mentioned anything to you?'

'You always have a job here, Riaz!' Jahanara exclaimed. 'Your Uncle loved you. You know that!'

Riaz nodded, but Jahanara could see her answer had not been what he was looking for.

'I know.' Riaz smiled. 'Forget it, I was … I'm going to make a start.'

She watched him leave the kitchen, wondering what he had meant. 'Riaz baba,' she called out to him, 'janosh, one of these days I will find that Junaid's stash and I will put it somewhere not very nice.'

Riaz let out a bellow of laughter followed by a sheepish giggle. Jahanara ignored him. 'Move the small tables to the side with the Ayatul Kursi, will you? I'll bring us some tea.' She heard him still chortling as he walked into the living room.

By a quarter past nine, Shamsur lay an arm's length away from his wife's Royal Doulton on display in her rosewood cabinet. Jahanara edged around him, humming a nasheed to herself, tiptoeing to and from the kitchen where frying onions and mustard seeds sputtered for her attention. She felt content to have these last moments with him, when she could imagine him suddenly sitting up and demanding his glasses or his balaclava or a cup of tea or asking her to check whether his toenails needed trimming. Every so often, members of staff appeared, never venturing further than the dining room door, where they stood speechless: Junaid with the whiff of marijuana about him; Lindsay with eyes pink from lack of sleep and sadness; and the briny-faced Mustafa rubbing his damp face in his palm, his turmeric-stained cuticles on show. He stayed the longest, nodding helplessly each time Jahanara passed by, until Riaz shooed him back to the restaurant, listing all the chores that had to be done before the guests arrived for the funeral prayers.

'Before I forget, Fufu,' Riaz told her, 'that lady from the health department called again this morning.'

Jahanara rushed to the kitchen doorway, her wooden spoon dripping hot oil. She tried to catch a drop to avoid it hitting the linoleum and scalded the palm of her hand. 'What did she say?'

'She wanted to come around, do a last inspection, you know, on the maggots.' He saw the alarm flare on her face and held up his hand. 'Listen, you don't worry about it, buccho? I'll meet her tomorrow. I mean what the hell. They ransacked the place and didn't find a thing the first time!'

Jahanara watched Riaz leave, feeling unsettled by the prospect that life at the Peacock would continue without Shamsur. She put down her spoon and brought out the Dettol spray and cloth to wipe the floor where she had dropped the oil, and then where Mustafa had sat crying. Then she sat down in the very same spot and gazed up at her husband, lost in reverie, until the smell of burnt onions sent her scurrying back into the kitchen.

Shamsur's coffin was being loaded into the hearse by the time Nasrin, Richard and Elias arrived, crumpled and travel weary. Nasrin took Elias out of his car seat, her eyes red and with a flush across her face.

Richard emerged from the driver's seat, struggling into his blazer. 'We've been driving for almost five hours!' he exclaimed. 'I just didn't take account of all this morning traffic!' His eyes flitted nervously from his wife's face to his mother-in-law's, but Nasrin kept her face averted, and Jahanara simply stood with her eyes glazed over. She looked down at her grandson and took his hand, letting out a shuddering sigh as the warmth of him pressed into her side.

The men and Elias accompanied Shamsur's body to the funeral parlour to perform the Islamic ghusl. Riaz translated instructions from Mustafa, directing an uncomfortable Richard around the body: upper right side, upper left side, lower right side, lower left side. And again. And again. The Sharia liked its things in threes. His eyes travelled the lines of Shamsur's face: the beautiful silver hair fanned around his head like a bloom around a clay pot. It was alive. He was dead, but that hair, so vibrant and shining, continued, perversely to live.

'Gently, gently!' Riaz exclaimed in a rushed whisper. 'They say the dead feel things more than we do!'

'Who says?' Richard asked. Holding Shamsur's ankle in one hand and a sponge in the other, he looked up at Riaz, irritation on his face. 'Who are *they*?'

'They! I don't know, man, the buzurg, the wise men. Like Mustafa Sasa here. They say even a breeze against a dead person's body feels like a thousand lashes!'

Richard stood. 'You do it then.'

'What? You know I can't, man! Has to be a close relative!'

'Close? Define "close".' Richard dropped the ankle, eliciting a sharp intake of breath from Riaz and Elias.

Mustafa tutted and Richard stared blankly at the older man. He felt Elias's hand clutch his knee.

'Daddy, I know you didn't mean to hurt him.'

Richard looked at his son, conflicting emotions contorting his features. 'He can't feel anything, monkey,' he told his son. 'He's not in there, buddy. He's gone. He can't feel anything.'

'But Riaz says he can,' Elias whispered, 'and it's like lashes.'

Richard glared at Riaz.

'Richard, please, come on!' Riaz held the sponge out at Richard from a safe distance. 'You're still the closest thing he had to a son! You can't hold things against the dead. You've got to do this.'

It occurred to Richard that this was why they wanted sons so badly, these Asian men, it was for moments like this.

'You know what? I don't, I can't do this, I'm sorry.' Richard walked over to the taps and began to wash his hands. The others sensed his dejection and watched in silence.

Richard's heart beat hard in his chest. He thought about how, when he had arrived home the night before, his wife had been sitting on the stairs with bloody cuts decorating her arms, reeking of TCP. He had been so disappointed that the epilepsy had returned, and he was angry that she didn't want to go straight to A and E. 'I need to get home,' she had said, and he had winced at the fact that she still referred to the Beacons as her home, but he had shrugged it away and reached out to her, only to have her turn stonily away. She gave him the news of her father's death with an air of accusation that had stunned him. He hadn't known what to address first – the fact that she had had a seizure, or that his father-in-law had died. His indecision had frozen him just for a few seconds, and she had given him a look that he would never forget. He no longer knew what it was he was supposed to be doing.

'Richard, man, we have to do this properly. Tik kore kortham rebo. Please?' Riaz pleaded, approaching him.

Richard looked up at him, feeling a stab of pity for this man who was always the bystander, unsure of his role or his place. It was clear to Richard that Riaz had been more a son to Shamsur than Richard had ever been – but there was one lesson he had learned about the Sylhetis after observing their ways over the course of his marriage and it was that their obedience to the *correct way* was unquestioning. Richard had not had the privilege of learning who the final arbiter of this *correct way*, or *tik kore kora*, was but he did know that for the sake of his intelligent, educated wife, who still refused to let him kiss her in front of her elders, he too succumbed to this unquestioning obedience. The *tik* way to proceed was for him to conduct the intimate washing of a man he had never been close to, even when there were far better friends present in the room.

Richard, despite his irritation, didn't forsake his father-in-law that afternoon. Perhaps, he felt, a simple act such as this could redeem their relationship. That, after years of being sidelined, disapproved of and dismissed, he could finally be the son-in-law that performed his duty. His mind remained heavy with the image of his wife's condemnation, as he washed every inch of skin with the studied tenderness of a child caring for his parent. Together with Riaz, he wrapped Shamsur in the white shroud, a uniform that made equals of the rich and the poor in the afterlife, and he helped to bear his coffin to the cemetery.

Back inside the Islams' house, Jahanara, who had sedated her grief and waited until she was alone, bawled purgatively into her janamaz. Though women were forbidden from attending the Janazah, Jahanara had followed the men to the cemetery, watching from afar as the rain cut through the air. As the coffin was lowered into the earth, she had tried to console herself that Shamsur would have been pleased with this resting place where there was nothing but the grey, bare branches of a few ash trees between him and an undisturbed view of the green ocean of the Usk that had always delighted him.

But still, she wept as she prostrated on her janamaz – *he will never see the old country again!* A place that had lived so vividly in their memories, a homeland that was intricately bound to their marriage. 'Shaath shomudhro, thero nodir paare, re Jani' had been the constant motto for his sense of adventure, but Jahanara knew that he had always been torn between Desh and bilath. She prayed that his Jannah brought together these two severed halves of his life; that it gave him the best of what lay on both sides of those seven seas and thirteen rivers.

Her heart heavy and dense with pain, Jahanara finished her prayers and went down to the kitchen. She transferred the biryani and roast she had cooked into casserole dishes and was about to leave for the

Peacock when she noticed through the patio door, the sparrows sitting on her rose arch. There were three of them, hopping and fluttering erratically in the rain. One of them flew up to the roof of the shed and disappeared. The other two followed.

Jahanara went outside to investigate and found the nest wedged into the eaves at the back of the shed. She went back inside the house and rummaged in a cupboard, where she found a tray constructed in a traditional shital weave; a kaleidoscope of purples and pinks which brightened as she shook the dust off. She placed a variety of seeds onto the tray, mixing it with her fingers, and stepped outside with it. Stretching up onto her toes, she placed it on the roof of the shed, a perfect makeshift bird feeder. She wondered if the birds had migrated, like she had, from a land where women sat to weave and made the tin roofs echo with the ring of their collective laughter.

What Shamsur Saw Beneath
the Tamarind Tree

In his short decade of life, Shamsur has not yet experienced this sort of darkness. The darkness of this particular night, bereft of clouds, stars and moon, is dense enough for his imagination to form hallucinations, and grey enough for his young eyes to believe he can make them out.

A wick dances in the kerosene lantern but manages only to make a shadowy penetration into the darkness as Shamsur peeks out from beneath Dadu's chador, searching the corners of the veranda where the light does not reach. Dadu's chador is gradually sliding off her shoulder as Shamsur, lying beside her, pulls at it, incrementally stealing an inch more with each step that fear takes towards him. He can hear it – his *dor*, his own fear: it is a muffled ululation and wafts around the compound, staking out its approach. His dor lives in the bot gas, the tamarind tree, which stopped bearing fruit many decades before Shamsur's birth. Now the mammoth silhouette of the tamarind tree sprawls across the night horizon beyond the guesthouse, indifferent to its barrenness, perhaps frightening because of it.

Shamsur's dor has been kept at bay only by Dadu's presence, and it waits patiently for her to leave for the toilet or her ablutions or her prayers. But for now, he is safe here by Dadu's side as she contentedly cracks betel nuts with a silver nutcracker – its edges decorated over time with rust and scratches. At Shamsur's insistence she is telling him stories. In fact, she is always so bored with the retelling of these stories that she often omits or glosses over certain parts in her haste to get to the ending.

'No, Dadu,' Shamsur whines. 'There weren't thousands of fish: there was just one! Tolla was his name, don't you remember? That's the whole point! The dacoit gets to heaven just by feeding one tiny, teeny koi!'

'You mean to say,' Dadu replies testily, bearing the weight of her palm and shoulder into cracking a stubborn betel, 'you mean to say that's how little it really takes? I get up at the crack of dawn and pray and fast and do tilawat, and a scoundrel manages to get in by feeding a fish? One tiny koi?'

'That's what *you* said!' Shamsur insists, jumping up to face her, still clutching her chador, one eye still on the shadow of the guest house about fifty yards from where they sit, beyond which lie the tamarind tree's unfathomable dangers. But stories are sacrosanct. Fear cannot impinge on the correcting of narrative detail. 'That's how benevolent God is, remember? You said so!'

'Accha re, Dadu,' she assents.

Dadu likes to call Shamsur, *Dadu*. Probably because she can't remember his name; he is after all the youngest of thirty-four grand-children. You can't remind a woman who calls you by her own name of the minutiae of fables she had thought up in her twenties. Shamsur lies back down and tells the story to himself, because listening to the sound of his own voice is better than listening to the sound of his dor. His words become slower and more slurred as sleep draws near, because stories have that soporific effect on him, part lullaby, part mother's caress, weaving their magic of diversion and forgetfulness, throwing him into worlds where darkness can't paralyse him.

The ground between the main house in which they sit and the guesthouse is an unpaved, muddy stretch of land that seasonal labourers have patted down with a mixture of cow dung and clay. During the day, you can make out the circles they have made with their palms – the larger ones of Subud's, and his daughter's fainter, smaller ones. Footsteps on this ground are so muted that only a soft, dull thud can be heard, as though the approaching feet are socked, or …

Or not of this world.

It is this noise that Shamsur suddenly hears, and which thrusts him upright from the periphery of slumber.

'Dadu!' he exclaims. 'Someone's there!'

Dadu yelps in pain: his sudden movement has caused her to trap her thumb in the nutcracker. She smacks her grandson's head. 'Gadhar bacha!'

'It is just I, Kamal Miah. No need for fear, Sham!' The voice laughs, and the laugh scampers through the darkness to them.

There is a pause before the footsteps came closer.

'Kamal Miah? Is that you? So late?' Dadu calls out. Shamsur's heart begins to relax. It is indeed Kamal Miah, whose feet emerge out of the darkness first, owing to their proximity to the kerosene lantern set on the floor. Kamal Miah goes around barefoot except during the winter months, when he squeaks around in Shamsur's grandfather's old plastic mules. His two large toes stare out at Shamsur from the gloom. The rest of him comes into view as he squats down onto his haunches.

'Yes, Mai, so late …' He waits humbly for some indication from Dadu that despite the lateness of hour, he is invited to sit. Dadu offers him some betel nut and he takes it, grunting with gratitude and re-settles himself on his haunches, his lungi folded neatly and modestly under him. The two of them chew noisily and the air is redolent with the cloying scent of zarda. Kamal Miah sways to and fro; Dadu continues to crack her nuts. The night begins to fold around Shamsur again.

He wakes abruptly to find Dadu and Kamal Miah immersed in conversation. It is perhaps the heat that woke him. Or perhaps it is a change of tone in Kamal Miah's voice – Kamal Miah's usual hoarseness is peppered with a certain acerbity tonight that makes Shamsur draw Dadu's chador tighter around him.

'You should send her away. Maybe to her maternal grandparents. Let her have it there. Or otherwise, just tell me, I know a place,' Dadu says. She has stopped cracking nuts and is sifting her fingers through the chopped pieces in her silver paandan. She watches the betel slivers slip through her fingers and drop delicately back into the paandan and she chews, slowly, thoughtfully.

'I should slit her throat is what I should do.' Kamal Miah spits to his side after he says this; he flicks a veiny wrist out into the darkness.

'Don't be so childish, Kamal Miah. Violence in this instance will do no good.' Dadu's fingers continue to sift deliberately through the chopped betel nuts. 'I have told you time and again to watch your daughters; too much education spoils the female mind. You didn't listen to me, and now look.' And Kamal Miah spits out a swear word reflecting his self-repugnance. Crickets out near the tamarind tree seem excited by something; they are louder, and the air is alive with their gargling. The kerosene lamp has been turned low and the darkness seems on the verge of some victory. Shamsur's skin beneath the chador is stinging from the heat, but he refuses to release this last totem of protection.

'What you do need to do, Kamal Miah, what you do need to do is to teach her a lesson. For the sake of the others, because of course it is too late for her. You need to give them all a lesson.'

Dadu loves lessons.

She is the self-appointed matriarch of the village; she will survive her spouse, and four of her five hot-blooded, ruthlessly ambitious sons, and many of her equally barbarous grandsons. She has marched to a position of great power in the patriarchy on the back of many a chilling lesson which she has been responsible for meting out: sentences of guilt and punishment upon the abstractly convicted.

Shamsur is wide awake now, and his phasmophobia is suddenly nothing compared with the fear he feels of the woman who sits next to him: the sinister way in which that plump, dimpled old lady sifts her fingers through chopped betel nuts as she considers an apt punishment. Shamsur wants – no – *needs* his mother, who is in the back of the house standing at the outside stove, making fish stew for the adults' late supper. He needs to be there, near her feet, burying his head into her attar-smelling saree, as she blows on her bamboo tube to unsettle the ash that forms around her cooking fuel. He wants not to be here, but the abyss of dor that separates him from his mother is impossible for him to navigate alone.

'Mai … I value your counsel …' Kamal Miah's voice is low. 'Tell me what to do.'

Dadu stops sifting and stares into the distance. The shadow of the tamarind tree looms beyond the guesthouse. Shamsur has heard that a jinn sits cross-legged under it, reciting his thasbih and watching the sins that are committed around him. It is said that if you look him in the eyes, an invisible hand will squeeze your heart until it stops beating.

And you will join him.

Under the tamarind tree.

For eternity.

Dadu stares out at the tamarind tree. Shamsur, sweating under the chador, looks out at it too.

'Send her away to have it, and then put it up for adoption. After that you can't let her come home. She has disgraced you. My meju khala in Chittagong is looking for a girl—'

'But Mai, she – in Chittagong?'

'What? She is too good for Chittagong with her education? Think of your other daughters, Kamal Miah! The rest is up to you!'

'You are always right, Mai.'

'When they ask where she is, tell them she is dead—'

'She is already dead to me, Mai.'

'And for Allah's sake, Kamal Miah, make the rest of those shameless daughters of yours human! Manush koro!'

'Yes, Mai, how unblessed I have been to have daughters. How will I marry them off after this?'

'Marry them off you must. It is your duty.'

'Sham Baba! What's wrong?'

Shamsur barely hears them call out to him. He leaps off the veranda, and runs over the compound, his footsteps making scampering, ghostly thuds. He sprints over the circles made by Subud and his daughter in the dust. His dor doesn't hold him back – in fact it has become a force propelling him towards the tamarind tree. Behind him, Kamal Miah runs too, his kerosene lamp swinging violently, making the earth, the shadows, the guesthouse all quiver around them. Shamsur stops underneath the tamarind tree and faces the cross-legged shadow with its blazing eyes.

Beside him sits Kamal Miah's condemned young daughter. She stares at Shamsur, a stillness in her eyes, a stillness that speaks to him of imprisonment, of no escape, of an eternity of dor. Something claws inside his chest and squeezes and squeezes, until he sinks to the ground.

5

A few hours after arriving at the Beacons, Nasrin sat behind the bar at the Peacock in the gloom of the accumulating rain clouds and reflected on the fact of her father's death. The news of it had been so sudden – like a punch to the jaw – but the realisation was slow, the gradual discoloration of an emerging bruise.

Her father was gone.

As the men returned from the Janazah, her mother accepted their condolences with an incline of her head and waved them towards the tables, laid with bowls of biryani and raita. The women were already huddled in tight groups, serving each other steaming spoonfuls of food. They had spent the morning completing a Quran Khatm to lead her father's soul to his maker, and a few of them were still wrapped up in their scarves, swaying back and forth, finishing the surahs allocated to them. Nasrin had been mortified when she had opened her own Quran and been hard pressed to read the beautiful script. This scripture, so significant during her childhood, had been thoroughly wiped from her adult life, and now she could not even participate in a Khatm for her own father.

She sat in his favourite spot just behind the bar. All about her were traces of him: a figurine of an extra-terrestrial which a customer had given him in jest and her old hand fan that he had hung up after she left for university. Amid the sour, warm aroma of spilt beer, she detected some lingering scent of him: that smell she had so loved, of poppadums and the tandoor laced with the muskiness of his Old Spice.

She watched every headlight that passed the restaurant window, but none belonged to her sister. She tried Sabrina's number again and again, each unanswered call increasing her agitation.

When Richard approached her from behind and placed his hand on her waist, it took effort not to shake him off. The women in front of her, sipping J2O from bottles with straws, tugged at their hijabs and looked away, affronted by the public display of affection. Nasrin stiffened, and Richard let out an exasperated exhalation before walking away, a bottle of iced Diet Coke swinging between his fingers.

There had been a time when he had been accommodating of all these idiosyncrasies as part of her cultural baggage and she had been apologetic. Somehow, his understanding had diminished, and her apologies had morphed into a low-level anger.

Riaz appeared before her and offered her a tentative smile. She watched as he stacked the plates on his forearm and nimbly picked up six glasses. He pushed open the door to the kitchen, exactly how her father had done it, the thrust of a shoulder along with the kick of a foot. The resemblance brought a lump to her throat. She realised that Riaz had had plenty of time to learn her father's mannerisms – he had spent more time with her father, in these last years of his life, than either Nasrin or Sabrina. When Riaz returned and came to stand beside her, she felt consoled by this thought, and smiled inwardly as he rolled down his shirt sleeves only to roll them up more neatly. Just as her father had.

'You're stressing about Sibby, aren't you?' he asked her.

The intimacy of this question took Nasrin by surprise, and she found herself giving a vague shrug. In the years since her marriage their old friendship had dwindled, and she had exchanged only brief conversations with Riaz in her short visits home, exchanges that were tritely formal, as was customary for a bachelor engaging with a married Bengali woman. That he could still read her mind was discomfiting.

'Stressing about it won't get her here any sooner,' he said, reaching for more bottles of J2O and placing them in front of the women at the bar, who watched them with side glances. 'The Tipu makes her own time.'

Nasrin smiled ruefully at the truth of this statement and watched Riaz do another round of the restaurant and return with used glasses pinched between his fingers.

She sighed. 'I'm just worried for her – I mean, she's going to have to live with herself, missing the funeral of the person she loved the most in the world.' The women looked over at her, smiling in compassion and irritating her even more. She caught sight of Mustafa poking his head around the kitchen door, and she called out to him. 'Mustafa sasa! Can you come help Riaz clear this?' She watched him disappear. 'What's wrong with him?'

'You know he was attached to your dad.'

Nasrin didn't have the reserves of compassion her father had had for his staff. Her father's legacy was a restaurant full of immigrants – the worst kind – who refused to become part of the fabric of the society they lived in, preferring instead to play their obsequious, colonial role, serving from the margins. She felt burdened by that legacy. They had never discussed, even after the first heart attack, what would happen to the Peacock in the case of her father's demise, partly because her mother panicked about tempting fate. Her father had surely left the Peacock to her mother, but would she want to sell or would she manage with Riaz's help?

She watched her mother walk around the different groups of people who had come to commiserate; locals who had lived all their lives in this town, and Bangladeshis, Pakistanis and Indians from neighbouring cities that her father had befriended or done business with. Her mother had become so thin, so hunchbacked and defeated-looking, that Nasrin felt the worry kneading her as she watched. How would Amma survive? How would she live her life without Abba?

Nasrin turned to find Elias by her side, pleading with her to play

Lego, his voice tired and whiny, until Riaz distracted him with the prospect of a J2O. Over by the window, Richard was on a phone call: he caught her eye briefly before turning away, still offended.

She suddenly felt claustrophobic, everyone else's needs crowding in on her.

Then it began: that tingling in her right hand.

She leapt up and rushed into the kitchen. Blinking beneath the glare of the halogens, she felt ten years old again – her father was swooping her up onto the worktop where she could reach the poppadum box and a younger Mustafa was handing her a tablespoon of desiccated coconut from his palette of spices.

The sounds of the kitchen shook Nasrin out of her reverie. She looked up to see Lindsay's rosy face, her hat sliding down one side of her head, her apron stained with the yellows and reds of turmeric and paprika.

'Are you all right, Naz?' Lindsay asked, glancing up from her chopping board. Nasrin nodded before fleeing through the kitchen door, through the gate and up her parents' driveway, her heart palpitating with fear. Finally, she was inside the house, reaching for her handbag where her new prescription pills lay.

She slipped the yellow pill into her mouth and lowered herself into her father's Queen Anne chair. Nasrin's forehead felt prickly with perspiration and the tingling had spread everywhere. She felt it the most just below her earlobes. She grasped the arm of the chair with one hand and clawed at an ear with the other, afraid the seizure was about to consume her, with no one to witness it.

But then, just as suddenly as it had appeared, the tingling began to dissipate. She rested her head back and breathed deeply. Her father had always sat here with the afternoon sun brightening the faded red leather, a plate of rich tea biscuits by his side and a cup of tea warming his gloved hands. Even in the summer, his hands had felt cold.

Around her, the paraphernalia of her childhood was on display.

The furniture was pushed up against the walls, as though a cyclone had hit the centre of the room. The disarray made familiar objects startlingly new: her father's reading glasses that had hung from his neck on a leather band were not black, as she had always thought. They were a dark tortoiseshell with a black rim, and a tiny strip of masking tape holding together one hinge, a totem of his parsimony. Next to it stood his tall pint glass, from which he used to drink tepid water. It was now bone dry, and Nasrin was sure her mother, a compulsive cleaner, had washed it that morning only to place it back on the mantelpiece as though her father would reach for it again. Nasrin's heart contracted. And there was the little canister of fennel seeds which Abba had chewed as an after-dinner digestive. She reached for it, letting the liquorice aroma bring back the memory of her father's generous laughter and his embraces. She realised she was sitting on something and fished out her father's balaclava. They had all laughed at him wearing this in the house, never understanding how the cold gnawed at him, when everyone else sweltered in the heat of the radiators. It occurred to her that this balaclava would never be funny again. That those glasses, which had been touched daily for the last few years of his life, were never to be used again. Death wasn't just the end of a man's life: it was the end of a whole microcosm that supported a man, a whole world of relationships and attachments.

She heard a crackling sound from the hallway.

'Amma?' she called out. When there was no response, she wasn't sure what she had heard. Was it the door? Did something fall? And then she heard it again.

'Richard? Eli, is that you?'

Again, there was no response.

'Riaz?' she called, tentatively.

The tingling in her arm, so recently in abeyance, began to pick up speed like simmering water on the verge of boiling. It made its way up through her body, closing in on her temples. Simultaneously, the delicate crackling in the hallway morphed into a hollow hissing and grew louder, crowding her ears with its menacing din. The proportions of the room began to do a macabre war jive, and then she saw him, standing unsmiling beside the mantelpiece: he held out his arms.

Nasrin made a little bleating sound as she tried to call out to him – 'Abba!' – before she slipped beneath the waves of the seizure.

6

Although the flight was a red-eye, Sabrina barely slept. Keeping thoughts of her father at bay was a task that required monumental effort. Every so often, his face appeared in her mind – the beaming expression he welcomed her with at every homecoming – and she would have to blink hard and drink quickly to push the picture away. Added to this she had had to fend off work queries until the very last minute when the air hostess had politely asked her to switch off her phone.

As the flight wore on, vivid memories slipped in unbidden, for long-haul flights were intimately connected with her family and their annual trips to Bangladesh, always so anticipated and joyous. Amma with her tinkling gold bangles hugging Nasrin and Sabrina to her as she shushed them to sleep. Abba with his cold hands asking for another blanket, worrying if Mustafa would remember to lock the wine cellar door. With a sudden start, Sabrina remembered Abba's pride during Nasrin's virgin commercial flight. The way he had held Sabrina's arm when they were led to the cockpit to meet the captain and first mate (her big sister!) as a special favour, and he had been heartbreakingly shy as Nasrin, looking splendid in her uniform, had explained some of the procedures and switches she would use during the flight. By Sabrina's second glass of wine, the memories had burst the floodgates, and as she dozed, they mixed freely with dreams of Ralph and Daniel and the trading room. She woke in a cold sweat as the plane passed through a patch of turbulence and asked for a glass of wine to calm her nerves.

By the time the flight had landed, Sabrina was so agitated that she decided to stop at the Café Rouge in the airport for a coffee and to check her emails. Her phone was on its last bar and she searched her bags in vain for the charger. It seemed that chaos had descended on the desk as her plane had made its way east. Ralph had sent a string of emails asking about the Altieri deal they had traded last summer – one of her last trades before she started her current role. His last email was sent, rather worryingly, from his personal account. She dialled his office number and it cut straight to voicemail. By the time she tried his cell, her phone finally died, leaving her phoneless and facing the long drive to the Beacons.

When she turned into Calbot Square, she was grateful for the distraction of an ambulance blocking the entrance of the Peacock. She was late – the familiar route to the Beacons had proved difficult in the torrential rain, and she had been hindered by missed turns and the need for frequent toilet breaks.

She parked up as carefully as she could and noticed a taxi pulling up behind the ambulance. A woman in a tight black hijab and abaya emerged from the car, adjusting the scarf near her chin and brushing a hand across her cheek. Something about her hand was familiar to Sabrina but her face was not visible. Perhaps it was one of her mother's friends or distant relatives from London or the North. Each time Sabrina returned for visits, she felt that her mother's circle became more and more religious. First the legs, then the arms, then the neck, and finally every inch of hair was hidden from view. Wahhabi Islam was invading England by swallowing its women, inch by black inch.

Sabrina squeezed her way past the funeral guests in the Peacock eating biryani and sipping on straws from orange bottles but couldn't spot her mother or sister and headed back out. She tugged at her skirt as she walked down her parents' driveway and finding the front door open, made her way through the narrow hallway that always smelled of coriander and agar batthi. A small crowd of people shifted slightly to let her pass, and she entered the living room to find her sister lying on the floor by her father's old chair, flanked by two paramedics and her mother.

'What happened?' she asked, stumbling to where her sister lay and dropping down beside her. She felt a seam of her skirt tear but ignored it as she searched her sister's damp and swollen face.

'The seizures?' she asked, touching the dressing close to her sister's eye.

Nasrin stared at her, her brow furrowed, and Sabrina was surprised by the hostility emanating from her.

Then a lone sob escaped their mother, and Sabrina, hearing it, was reminded of why she was here. Her chest swelled as she stood to take her mother in her arms, feeling her fragile form tremble with her loss. She was surprised that her hands sank further than they used to and met with bones that felt brittle. Sabrina thought of the many phone calls she had avoided, and the visits she had delayed. She swallowed her regret and turned back to her sister.

'Dids,' she croaked, still holding her mother with one hand, 'is it the epilepsy?'

Her sister nodded.

'It came back?'

Nasrin did not respond.

There were several people standing around them, more standing in the hallway and through to the kitchen. Beneath their sympathetic smiles, Sabrina detected disapproval and judgement and found herself unable to shrug these away as she would normally do. She watched the paramedics help Nasrin up and towards the sofa. Richard, rummaging in Nasrin's bag for her pills, led them out. Sabrina saw the gash on her sister's arm. 'Doesn't that need stitches?' she asked no one in particular. She stood for a few moments, wanting desperately for the room to stop contracting and expanding before her. Suddenly she felt Nasrin's fingers on her wrist pulling her onto the sofa. Her sister hugged her. They clutched each other for longer than they needed.

'When did the fits come back?' Sabrina asked, her voice so loud it made her jump.

'Oh Sibby!' Nasrin whispered, frowning. 'You need to drink some water.'

'Why didn't you say anything?'

Nasrin turned to her son. 'Eli, can you go and ask Nani for some water?'

Sabrina swallowed the irritation that gathered at her throat and reached for her nephew, inhaling the familiar smell of him as she embraced him.

'You got so big,' she whispered to him before his mother pulled him away and dispatched him to the kitchen for water.

Sabrina played with the fabric of her sister's kameez – soft from overwashing, the familiar scent of lavender making her feel like a child.

Richard emerged with the pills, looking puzzled. 'Are these the ones?' he asked Nasrin. 'Have they always been yellow?'

Nasrin ignored him and looked at her sister. 'You should go and be with Amma; go into the kitchen.' But Sabrina didn't think she could stand, so when their mother reappeared with glasses of water, she grabbed her hand and tried to pull her down on the sofa.

'Amma,' she said, 'why have you lost so much weight?' But her mother waved her away with a distant look on her face. Sabrina watched her shuffle back to the kitchen almost expecting her father to walk in. But of course he would not. The realisation made Sabrina feel like her insides were being hollowed out and she squeezed her eyes shut.

'You missed the funeral, Sib,' Nasrin said quietly, taking Sabrina's hand. Sabrina reached inside herself but there was no response to be found in all the emptiness.

'Hey, Sibby!' Richard said, passing a pill and a glass of water to Nasrin. 'How long's it been? Donkey's years, right?'

His accent suddenly made Sabrina giggle with badly-timed hilarity.

Her vacant body vibrated with laughter. Nasrin swallowed her pill dry and passed the water to Sabrina, hissing, 'Down it, now!'

Sabrina sipped her water, sharing a look with her brother-in-law, who rolled his eyes quickly before glancing cautiously at his wife.

'Have you been drinking?' Nasrin whispered.

'Ages ago,' Sabrina said, holding up a finger. 'Just one.'

'I can still smell it. Everyone can smell it. Is that why you're late?'

Sabrina looked away, annoyed. Her sister had not always been like this – fighting to get to Imperial and then on to the BA training scheme had seemed to transform Nasrin from dutiful older sibling to a surprising source of inspiration to Sabrina. But then, at the very first hurdle, Nasrin had retreated deeper into her old shell, donning again the role not only of obedient daughter, but also deferential wife and devoted mother. Sabrina found it disappointing, but now wasn't the time to complain about Nasrin's guilt-tripping. Sabrina hadn't meant to be late. It wasn't her fault that their religion required an immediate burial. It was unreasonable to expect one to miraculously travel over three thousand miles in less than a day. She looked up and saw a woman in a dark blue shalwar kameez standing near the window, staring at Sabrina's bare legs. Sabrina dared the woman to meet her gaze, but the woman turned away.

'Sibby,' Nasrin said, and Sabrina sighed and looked away. Nasrin took the blanket from the armrest and threw it across Sabrina's legs. Sabrina looked at her sister and let out a short laugh of ridicule.

When her mother returned with a dish of steaming biryani, Sabrina reached for it, desperate to fill the growing void inside her. She ate quickly, sharing it with her nephew, who had materialised by her side. She watched him eat as she ate, enjoying his appetite. His curls had grown lavish, so like her own he looked almost like a girl.

'You're turning out to be a pretty little girl,' she told him as she scooped another spoonful in his mouth.

'Boy,' he said, his mouth sputtering rice.

'Pretty little boy, then,' she said, winking at him. He blinked both eyes in return.

There was a shuffling by the door.

'Fufu.'

A woman in an abaya stood for a moment at the door before falling into Jahanara's arms. The same woman Sabrina had seen outside.

'Oh gosh!' Nasrin exclaimed as she sprang up.

Sabrina, spooning pilau into her mouth, watched the three women hugging. Finally, recognition dawned on her.

It was her cousin, Afroz.

The guests began to leave soon after, and Jahanara, accompanied by Sabrina, went back to the restaurant for final commiserations and farewells. Though Sabrina seemed oblivious to the disapproving glances thrown at her stockinged legs and short skirt, Afroz was uncomfortably aware. She felt hurt for her aunt and Nasrin as they visibly squirmed in discomfort at the accumulating whispers. She watched Jahanara nervously twist a corner of her white achol around and around her index finger.

In the wake of the day's events, the house now fell into stillness. Afroz perched on the corner of the sofa, practically sliding off the slippery leather, and blinked into the afternoon's greying light. Richard excused himself to take a call and Nasrin smiled uncertainly from the other end of the sofa. Afroz, who had not seen her cousin for almost five years, was amazed at Nasrin's youthful face. Looking at her unlined, unblemished features made Afroz sink lower into the folds of her abaya. She felt weighed down, not just by the folds of the silky black cloth that swathed her from top to toe, but by the knowledge that others had fared so much better. Others, who had sprung from the same earth, had lived a life that had not tarnished their youth.

Nasrin leaned over and took her hand. 'How is Humayun Bhaiya? You didn't bring him?' But Afroz, mesmerised by her cousin's nails painted a translucent caramel and shaped in neat squares, was tongue-tied. She slipped her hand out of Nasrin's and rubbed her fingers, suddenly aware of the overwhelming pungency of the attar she had put on.

'Who is Humayoo?' Elias asked, rolling off his mother's lap and coming to stand beside Afroz.

'Humayun Bhaiya,' his mother explained, 'is Khalu to you, and he is married to Afroz Khala.'

Elias rested his elbows on Afroz's knees and peered up into her face. She reached down and touched the soft down of his cheek with the tip of one finger. 'Do you know who I am, baba?' she asked. 'Has your Ammu ever told you about me? I am your aunt, your khala Afroz.'

The child stared up at her a moment, and then, without answering, he reached up and pulled her hijab off. Afroz shrieked.

'Eli!' Nasrin cried, pulling him away.

Afroz felt the prick of tears in her eyes.

'Eli, for goodness sake!' his mother shouted. 'What are you doing?'

'Everything okay?' Richard called from the hall.

'I just wanted to see Khala Afroz's hair,' Elias said.

'What?'

'I wanted to see why she hided it.' His voice was small.

Afroz let out a shaky laugh.

'That is absolutely no way to behave,' his mother told him. 'You apologise to Khala right now. Right now.'

Elias took a step towards Afroz.

'No, no, he is absolutely right, Naju, don't shout at him!' she said. 'There is nothing to hide re Khala, I like my hair. But you see, I also love Allah-ji, and out of my love for him, I do not be vain. Yes?'

'What is wain?' Elias asked. Afroz's heart sank again. With his one question, the little boy had highlighted the gulfs that separated her from this part of her family. Even their English sounded different. She reached up and ran her fingers through her flattened hair.

He ran his small palms over the folds of her abaya. 'Is this a special saree?' he asked.

Afroz smiled. 'This is an abaya. I wore it today out of respect for your Nanabhai, for his Janazah. You see underneath, I wear my normal clothes.'

Elias nodded sagely. 'Like a coat,' he said, and picked up the hijab she had set aside and placed it on his own head.

'I wear it for namaz time,' he told her, 'with my Nani.'

She was delighted by this. 'You do namaz, re baba? With this? But girls wear this! You need a topi! A cap!'

'Like my Spiderman cap?'

'Spiderman? Na, I will get you a special namaz cap, moyna-faki ekta!'

He showed her his rendition of an adhan, pushing his thumbs into his ears and bellowing out, 'Allah hu Akbar, Allahhhhh hu Akbar!' And she gathered him into her long arms and hugged him, her chest shaking with laughter.

Suddenly Nasrin, who had been watching, sat forward and pulled them both into a fierce embrace.

'I'm sorry I haven't brought him to meet you,' her muffled voice whispered into Afroz's ear. 'I'm sorry, but I'm so glad you're here now.'

Afroz pulled away, overhwhelmed by emotion. She smiled and took her cousin's hand. 'I had to come, Naju,' she said, 'of course I would come at a time like this.' Nasrin nodded. Richard returned, and took his place on the sofa beside his wife and son. Afroz, embarrassed by the way he nuzzled into Nasrin's neck, muttered about needing to take a bath and left them. She dragged her suitcase upstairs, into the spare room and closed the door.

The room was warm, so she peeled off her abaya, and opened the window. It faced out onto a little square, where a statue that she knew from her cousins' stories to be the Duke of Wellington was visible in profile. Beyond him was a short row of shops and cafés, and then the sleeping Beacons, which lay with their backs to the sun. Afroz had heard so much about Wales. The highlight of every year had been the monsoon season, when Afroz's Fufu and Fufa would bring Nasrin and Sabrina to Bangladesh. Wherever they travelled during their visit, Afroz accompanied them, running along the brooks of Shamsur's ancestral village or swimming in the ghat behind Jahanara's (and her own Baba's) childhood home. It was only Wales that separated their shared childhood memories, but even there, she did not feel totally excluded: through her cousins' stories of the faraway Beacons, Afroz felt as though she too roamed freely through the village with them, buying penny sweets from Mr Ruane's corner shop, pinching poppadums from the Peacock kitchen and racing with Riaz to the edge of Llewid's Pond.

And now that she was here, how different it was! The photos had never shown that the restaurant seemed to stand in the darkest corner of the town square. Or that its facade, an ageing ochre, was lacklustre next to its cream-coloured neighbours. It didn't disappoint her – far from it, she felt an instant connection with the Peacock and its air of humility put her completely at ease.

She crept quietly out of the room and heard Richard in the kitchen speaking on the phone. In the living room, she found Elias and Nasrin had dozed off on the sofa and she picked up the blanket that had fallen to the floor and pulled it up around them. She watched their sleeping forms as she slowly unbraided the thick snake of her hair, her scalp aching with how tight it had been pulled. She observed the graceful ease with which the limbs of mother and son found the perfect nooks and crannies to rest against. A yin and yang of maternal love. The sort of bond that she had experienced for only the briefest of moments before the shock of death. Her daughter would have been three now, Afroz thought as she bent to kiss her nephew.

As she showered, she allowed her spirits to lift. It was good to be here, with Naju, and Fufu. And this darling, Elias. But then she remembered Sabrina's cool welcome, and her stomach tightened. Not for the first time in her life, Afroz found herself hoping that her cousin would play nice.

* * *

Back at the Peacock, Jahanara stood at the entrance staring out into the empty car park. Behind her, Riaz and the other waiters were busy acting on Sabrina's orders to get the restaurant ready for the dinner shift. 'Business as usual!' Sabrina said. Jahanara did not say anything. She watched Sabrina giggle loudly at something Riaz said and caught the waitstaff snatching nervous glances at her daughter. She walked back to the bar and reached over the whisky shelf to grab Nasrin's old hand fan that hung beneath the elaborate cornices.

'What's wrong?' Sabrina asked. 'Why are you taking it down?'

'Because,' Jahanara said quietly, hugging it to her chest. 'Because your Abba loved it.'

Jahanara walked slowly back to the house with the hand fan pressed against her chest, feeling sorry for her daughter. She knew it was only a delay, and that the pain would rush in soon, all the more furious for being held at bay.

Once When They Fought

Bangladesh lies deluged beneath a rapacious monsoon. Nasrin and Sabrina step giddily off the plane and let the familiar humidity settle over them like a second skin. They wave at the throngs of relatives who lean over the yellow concrete barrier that separates Osmani Airport terminal from its runway.

'Naju! Omuka ao!'

'Sibby re futh, bala ni re moyna?'

'Jani, otho dhin phore dekha hoylo!'

The greetings are masked accusations, for the Islams rarely reach out to their Bangladeshi brethren while they live their lives in the UK. At the Arrivals lounge, an assortment of aunts and uncles crowd around them for embraces, clutching at their arms with possessive vehemence. They are ushered through the clamouring crowds to the exit where their Mamu's white Corolla awaits them.

'Afi is making a trifle for you girls!' their Mamu tells them as the driver reverses the car. 'Remember her trifles? Ha, Naju?'

Weariness descends on the girls, and they nod absently and settle back into their seats. The warm air blows on their faces from the open window, and through half-closed eyes they gaze out at the kaleidoscope of green rice paddies and silver corrugated roofs. As they turn into Chokidikhi, their car joins a traffic jam, adding its aggressive horn and their driver's curses to the chaos. Motorcyclists pick their way through the gridlock, ogling the girls as their car passes; some smile suggestively, others whistle or break into a Bollywood song.

Their Mamu closes their windows. The girls beg for air until he opens them again, and they salivate at the offerings of brown peanuts and sticks of raw mango sprinkled with chilli powder.

'Na,' their mother says, each time, waving the sellers away.

They finally turn into a driveway, flanked by Chinese hibiscus and marigolds, and bookended by two shefali trees. It is still early enough in the morning that the perfume of the sheuli flowers lingers in the air as they are rushed out of the car and into the house.

'Oh,' cries Nasrin, running over to the swinging birdcage in the hallway. 'Chinthamoni!'

'Salam, ruza nai ni?' And they all laugh as the impertinent myna cocks its flame-coloured beak at them.

'Chup re dhushta!' Afroz chides the bird as she rushes in and takes her cousins into her arms.

It isn't until they are seated at the table, in front of plates of limp trifle, that they realise how oppressive the heat is. They gaze up at Afroz, bewildered at the pink scarf that she has wrapped around her head.

'Why are you wearing that?' Sabrina asks, and Nasrin kicks her under the table.

Afroz's mother swallows her paan juice so she can speak. 'Y'Allah! Afi is a hafiza now!' she tells them.

'What's that?'

'Hafiza!' Their Mamu is aghast at their ignorance. 'Hafiza means memoriser of the Quran! Afi knows the whole Quaran by heart!'

Afroz serves trifle in silence and avoids their glances. Sabrina and Nasrin look up at the lethargic ceiling fan, as they spoon trifle into their mouths, wishing it were raw mango instead. Sprinkled with chilli.

'Does it taste like trifles in England?' asks Afroz. Nasrin answers quickly in the affirmative, aware of the contemptuous flare of Sabrina's nostrils.

The heat becomes increasingly oppressive over the next week and the incessant rain holds them prisoners in Mamu's home. There are days that echo the contentment of past summers: they make a foray into the tea gardens when the rain temporarily abates, accompanied by an entourage of driver, maids and Afroz's neighbour, Taseen, and they congregate with relatives in the cavernous cool of the dining room to indulge in adda, feasting on an assortment of fried handesh, phitha and a plethora of fruits their Mamu has had brought in from their village.

'Amar desher phol, re go!' their Mamu boasts, his pride in the food's provenance embellished by the clear enjoyment displayed around the table. The girls are delighted to see Amma reaching for more jackfruit: they sense that these fruits from her ancestral land satiate a more deep-rooted craving than meets the eye.

'Suto Miah has brought us some bhet from the village murta,' Mamu tells them. 'Our Kuki weaves good pankhas – girls, tell your designs to Kuki and she will make them. Kuki!' he calls, and the girl comes tripping out of the kitchen. 'Afa era will tell you their designs and you make them some pankhas.' The girls are captivated as Kuki explains how she dyes the murta leaves and weaves them, holding them down with her toes as her fingers push and cajole the bhets into place. Afroz chooses a pankha in the form of the Bangladeshi flag; Sabrina rolls her eyes and, to Kuki's dismay, opts for a black design with a white skull. Nasrin wants a red fan with a white waterlily like the one on the Bangladeshi coins. 'A shapla,' her father explains to Kuki, unable to hide his pride. The girls hole up in the living room, talking and listening to Mamu's Rabindra sangeet records as Kuki crouches over her designs, fingers working deftly.

But as the days go on, the humidity wears down the vestiges of their good humour and they begin to bicker between themselves. Their moodiness spreads like an infestation into their interactions with their parents, their aunt and uncle, and even the maids.

'Didi,' says Kuki to Sabrina, who lies on the living room rug listening to a Skunk Anansie album. 'What is this you listen to?

What are they saying? Is it a love song? Is it romantic? Do you think of someone special when you listen?'

'Hedonism is not romantic, Kuki!' cries Sabrina. 'It's angry!'

Afroz and Nasrin watch Kuki lose the coquettish tilt of her head.

Annoyed at the interruption and cognisant of the look her cousin and sister exchange, Sabrina gets up and switches the music off before walking out of the room, muttering in English, 'Why can't people mind their own bloody business?'

'Bloody business, bloody business,' mimics Chinthamoni from the hallway and repeats these words for the next few days, until Afroz's mother bashes the bird cage with a bamboo cane and threatens a beating.

'Naju, Sibby,' Afroz asks every afternoon, 'tell me, what shall I make for dessert today? Something English? What are you missing?'

One afternoon, Sabrina responds, 'Why are you so obsessed with English desserts? No one eats trifles and jam roly-polies anymore! We're not living in the Victorian times – besides, why are we eating dessert every day? It's so unhealthy!'

Afroz looks at Nasrin and Nasrin looks down.

'Bloody business!' Chinthamoni calls as Sabrina leaves the room, and Afroz's mother brings the bamboo cane and places it in sight of the myna in a corner of the hallway.

One evening, as the rain thrums the flat roof only a few feet above their heads, Nasrin, Sabrina and Afroz stand in the kitchen, a place none of them usually venture into. It is the domain of the three maids, under the supervision of Afroz's mother. But the monsoon is driving them to ever stranger places.

'Sibby,' Nasrin's voice quivers. 'Just put them back where you found them.'

'No,' Sabrina replies. In her fist, she holds a scrunched-up pair of knickers. She slowly, deliberately lifts them up and lets the black lace dangle in front of her. 'I told you she'd nicked them.'

Kuki, from whose room the overused pants have been recovered, snivels from beneath her veil. She stands hugging the doorway, as though she wants to be swallowed by its frame.

Afroz stands by the window and watches Sabrina.

Even when Nasrin speaks, and Kuki interjects in pitiful self-defence, Afroz continues to watch Sabrina. She has always, like her uncle and Nasrin, justified Sabrina's unkindnesses as rooted in a need to defend herself from some unseen injury; but today, after weeks of bearing witnesss to Sabrina's contempt, Afroz is temporarily overwhelmed by her own sense of injustice. This cousin, her wild curls flowing down her back, Medusa-like, who comes from a life of relative privilege, seeks retribution for a pair of old knickers that a deprived servant has stolen. It defies belief, and yet, Afroz watches Sabrina continue to goad Kuki with the evidence of her crime.

They're approaching a stalemate when Nasrin, the self-proclaimed judge, demands an apology.

'You had no right,' Nasrin says, her voice constricted by her fear of confrontation. 'No right to go through someone's things!'

'I think she's pinched other things – I've noticed my Rimmel eyeliner's missing.'

'Sib, what's got into you! Stop it! Apologise now! And put the knickers back where you found them!'

'You know it, Didi. She stole them.' Sabrina lets the word *stole* linger on her tongue, as though the roundness of it confirms Kuki's guilt.

'Please,' Nasrin says as she shoves a strand of her hair behind her ear. 'Please just put them back.'

The three remain motionless for a moment, letting the sounds move around them. There is the ceaseless hiss of the rain and the whimpering of Kuki. Suddenly, Afroz feels a sharp breeze through the open window, and it enters her lungs with the next breath she takes. She rushes towards Sabrina, tripping over the older maid who sits on the floor.

Who would have thought that Afroz, sweet, submissive Afroz,

who hardly ever shows great empathy towards the servants, would have the nerve to pin the much taller, broader Sabrina against the kitchen door? She draws back her arm and slams a balled fist into Sabrina's left eye, and then another at her jaw.

Sabrina grunts and wrestles back. She takes a handful of Afroz's hair and slams her cousin's head against the rusting window grille. She kicks. She spits. But through it all, she holds the knickers high above her head, an offering to the monsoon, a prayer for the heat to end.

There are now other noises; hissing and shrieking and scratching that almost drown out the percussion of the rain clouds. Afroz is injected with an unprecedented strength; Sabrina, slow to react, regains her composure and releases her wrath upon the thin frame of her cousin, throwing punches and kicks without pausing for breath. Kuki follows the fighters around the room, taking one step forward, summoning the courage to intervene, and then two steps out of the way.

To Nasrin, conflict is abhorrent. Conflict is asphyxiating. For some moments, she stands and watches in suffocating silence, but then, she takes a deep breath and she throws herself in.

She does so to stop the fight, to wrestle them away from one another.

But, as in all wars, the hearts that suffer the most belong to the innocent.

It is Nasrin that falls upon a broken glass vase, which the fighters have knocked to the floor, cutting open her thigh. It is Nasrin who succumbs to the tingling in her arm and falls into one of her seizures in the middle of the cold kitchen floor and the scattered broken glass.

The sight of her blood silences everyone and makes the rain clouds slink away. They watch the blood spatter about her, as her body grapples with its terrific convulsions; the seizures command her thin frame into ludicrous bends and lurches, and everywhere they look on that stone kitchen floor, is the blood of Nasrin.

Then the spell breaks, and they run to her, offering their hands, their caresses, and the blood soaks into their clothes, and into the black lace of the knickers that Sabrina has finally dropped.

Later Afroz sits on the veranda steps as the headlights of the ambulance disappear beyond the grille of the gate. The muezzin's call to prayer rises up from the local mosque, and the town slows under its spell. Afroz hears muted footsteps, and senses Sabrina dropping heavily onto the step beside her.

They are both so consumed with animosity that they do not exchange a single word.

It is Nasrin alone who nurses feelings of guilt. She feels responsible for Kuki's poverty, for Sabrina's arrogance, and for not preventing Afroz from dealing the first blow. As the muezzin's adhan unfurls across the city, Nasrin's disappointment sinks deeper within herself.

In the hospital waiting room, she watches a line of ants, which rush up and down the lime-washed walls. She follows them with her fingers, the tips of which come away with a white residue. Then she takes a white-powdered finger and presses down on an ant, until she feels the pop of its life. The brown ant blood stains the wall and she smears an angry graffiti with it. When she hears her name being called, she limps into the doctor's office, heavy with guilt.

Later that evening, she returns home and is surprised that Sabrina and Afroz have already made their peace. The speediness of their ceasefire makes her time at the hospital, her twenty-three stitches and drugged-up grogginess, feel unnecessary and extravagant. It doesn't occur to her that their truce has been orchestrated for her sake alone.

8

The day after the Janazah, Sabrina got up long after everyone else. She shuffled down the hallway and stood at the kitchen door, blinking in the bright halogens, aching from her hangover.

Her mother stood at the kitchen hob, frying her spicy eggs; the smell of caramelised onions, green chillies and coriander which had coaxed Sabrina out of bed now made her stomach rumble in anticipation. Afroz stood beside her mother mixing dough for more handesh and Nasrin, Riaz and Elias sat shivering around the table. It was a cold morning and the sky, visible through the window, seemed to survey the scene with hostility.

'I suppose,' Sabrina said, eyeing the milky tea which Afroz had put on the table, 'there's no chance of a good cup of coffee?'

Nasrin snorted, but Riaz turned to Sabrina. 'Chez Jones has a proper barista now – want me to go and grab you one?'

Sabrina sighed and shook her head. She was desperate for a few cups of good coffee, but she could go there herself later and have some quiet time to catch up on her work emails. She had barely slept and was yet to make contact with Ralph and discover the reasons for his rush of questions, followed by the worrying radio silence. Her restlessness was exacerbated by the discovery that her childhood home had been transformed in the wake of Abba's death. Walking through the sleeping house the night before, in search of painkillers, she had sensed the sadness and gloom that gathered like dustballs in the shadowy corners. She realised, sadly, that it had become less of a home and more of mausoleum to her father – a place where she, like a pilgrim, would visit every so often to grieve for him. And this mausoleum, like other places of worship she had visited, seemed omniscient – it seemed to know and disapprove of the life she lived in Manhattan and that it was antithetical to the moral standards of her parents. Abba's steadfast dedication to Bulleh Shah's axiom, which he had recited often to his two daughters, seemed to have formed a soul of its own which now resounded within the walls of the house like a haunting mantra. *Tear down temples, smash down mosques – but never break a human heart for that's where God resides.*

She watched her mother, frying eggs in the grey morning light, heeding the silver of her hair, the way in which the flesh around Amma's gaunt neck drooped around her clavicle. She turned to gaze at her sister, to verify the lines she'd noticed yesterday that clawed at the corners of her didi's mouth and eyes, the cuts from her seizures, that old foe they thought had been vanquished. Sabrina felt an old fear try to claw itself back into her. So many changes in both of them, as though her father had sucked a little bit of youth out of each on his way to the world beyond.

She edged past Afroz who stood at Jahanara's side frying handesh, the little pancakes made of molasses and rice flour: empty calories, peasant food. What, she wondered, was Afroz doing in the Beacons? Afroz looked up and smiled as Sabrina grabbed a finger full of the scrambled eggs straight from her mother's frying pan. Sabrina gave a small smile back, but then Nasrin approached for more handesh.

'These are so delicious, Afi!' Nasrin said, helping herself to another. 'Teach me how to make them before you go!'

Sabrina made her way over to the breakfast table, her sister's affection for their cousin reviving her age-old resentment. Her sister didn't even like handesh much! Sabrina sat down next to Elias.

'Where's Richard?' she asked.

'He had to go back to London,' Nasrin said, rejoining them at the table. 'Work.'

Sabrina watched her sister closely, but she seemed untroubled.

'Riaz will drop Eli and me off at the train station later, after his meeting with the lawyer to go through the details of the will.'

Sabrina snorted. 'What the hell is that about? Why isn't Amma the executor?'

'Since when do I understand such things?' her mother sniffed. She stirred grated cheese into her eggs. 'It's up to you children to decide what will become of me now.'

Sabrina glanced at her sister. Their mother's fatalism was equally oppressive to both of them. She tapped her nails on the table. 'And I hate that lawyer! That guy is the most obnoxious bastard—'

'Sibby!' Nasrin exclaimed. 'Not in front of Eli!'

'You know what I mean. The guy's a liar – remember when he billed three hours for a fifteen-minute call when the lease was being extended! Lying a-hole.'

'What's that, Mummy?'

'See?'

'He'll learn these words, anyway! Jesus—'

'Sib, can—'

'Okay, he's a lying kuthar bachcha—'

'What does that mean, Mummy?'

'It just means,' answered Riaz, 'that lawyers are liars! Course, Khala-Amma would know because it takes one to know one! If lawyers are liars, what are bankers? Right, Tipu?'

Elias shook his arm. 'My daddy is not a liar!'

'Shit, I forgot!' Riaz said.

'Riaz!' Nasrin exclaimed.

Riaz clapped his hand over his mouth. 'Sorry!'

'Of course it's okay when Riaz swears!' Sabrina muttered, rolling her eyes.

'You've not forgotten how to take a joke, Sib?' Riaz asked, smiling at her. But Sabrina did not smile back. She found his use of her nickname and his tabloid references to the vices of her profession annoying. But then she remembered how there had been a time when they'd shared spliffs in the corner of the green near Llewid's Pond. An age ago when life had been about gaining small victories over her mother.

She watched him help himself to the handesh Afroz offered to him.

'Your sister can't take a joke anymore!' he told Nasrin.

'Course she can,' Nasrin said, smiling at Sabrina and slipping seamlessly into the role of peacemaker. 'I bet Abba's will details who his Lalon verses are going to,' she said, changing the subject as Sabrina refused the plate of handesh. Riaz began to sing the opening lines of 'lokhe bole' and Nasrin joined in. The giddiness of the two grated on Sabrina.

Riaz, arriving at the Peacock at the age of fourteen, had been a fixture of their adolescent life: the three of them had spent every weekend together waiting on customers at the Peacock and delivering food in the battered Vauxhall Nova. Sabrina remembered how they had had to jump-start it in cold weather: she and Riaz pushing the car, their Doc Martens slipping on the icy road, as Nasrin called out to them from the wheel, 'Faster, weaklings! Put your back into it!' Growing up had been a shared experience. But then Nasrin had left for university and Sabrina and Riaz had discovered that without her, their friendship felt hollow, their banter boring and meaningless. To save them both from embarrassment, she had made excuses and he had found new friendships amid the Peacock staff. Nasrin's departure had signified the end of Sabrina's childhood. She had always thought the Beacons the most isolated place in the world, but she had never felt alone. When her sister left, however, it became a grey and oppressive place she could not wait to escape.

She watched Nasrin and Riaz now, bent over his phone, giggling like teenagers. He was showing Nasrin a video of one of his mixed martial arts matches, and she couldn't help but feel annoyed that Riaz and Nasrin could slip back into their friendship, without her. When Nasrin turned to adjust the belt on Elias's robe, Sabrina noted the way Riaz watched her: the heightened colour in his cheeks, the light in his eyes. She was aware there was a strain in Nasrin's marriage, but nonetheless they were a strong couple that had overcome their cultural differences. Even she, Sabrina, the only promiscuous, emotionally irresponsible person in her family, aspired to be part of a couple like that, one day.

'Didi,' she said, taking Elias onto her lap and kissing the top of his head, 'when did the seizures come back? Why didn't you tell me?'

'It came back when Amma called. About Abba,' Nasrin told her, shrugging as though this was to be expected.

Sabrina frowned. 'So, you haven't managed to see your doctor yet?'

Nasrin nodded. 'We did a quick visit en route to the Beacons. He upped my dosage.' She smiled reassuringly and held out the plate of handesh to Sabrina. Sabrina took one. 'Remember,' said Nasrin, 'when I used to get the fits when we were kids?' She turned to Afroz. 'You know, Afi, Sibby always seemed to know, and she'd come running over and hold my hand.'

'Well,' Sabrina said, 'I always remembered your old doctor, who was it? Doctor Park? I remember her saying how epilepsy – it's a *disease born of insecurity* – she said to make sure you always had someone to hold on to. So I always wanted to make sure you did.' Feeling embarrassed at the look Nasrin gave her, Sabrina tickled Elias until he squealed. 'You know what,' she said taking another handesh, 'these aren't as bad as I remembered!'

'You gotta eat them with hot milk, Tipu man.' Riaz laughed. 'You're forgetting all the old ways!'

'I can't think of anything more gross.' Sabrina made a face at Elias, who laughed.

'This daughter of mine has always rebelled against old ways, re Riaz,' Amma said, coming up behind Sabrina. 'And just look at your hair.' Jahanara yanked out Sabrina's hairband. 'What have you done to it? So dry, it feels like fish netting! Maasor jaal!' Sabrina's crinkly hair spilled out over her shoulders. She shivered at the thought that anyone from New York should ever see her like this, before she'd smoothed her straighteners over it.

She saw the bottle of coconut oil her mother was unscrewing.

'Oh, no way! Come on! Amma, no!'

But Jahanara, it seemed, had enough strength to wrestle her youngest back to her chair, and when she was done, the kitchen windows fogged up with everyone's laughter, and the usual curl in the middle of Sabrina's forehead had been pulled into a tight bun.

'I like it,' teased Riaz. 'It's the wet look, trending right now!'

'Very demure! You look like a nun!' Nasrin giggled.

Even Afroz hid a smile behind her palm. Sabrina scowled. There was no way she would venture out to get a cup of coffee looking and smelling as she did. But her sister had other plans.

'Come on, Sib,' Nasrin said, standing up and taking Elias's coat.

'What! Looking like this?' Sabrina protested, but the look on her sister's face made her stand.

'We'll be back in time to eat Afi's next batch of handesh.' Nasrin smiled.

Outside, the sky was a dispiriting shade of grey, and as Sabrina walked with Nasrin the short distance to the cemetery, she felt the return of the sensation that she was slowly being hollowed out, all energy and feeling were being replaced with a numb dread. *I don't want to see this,* Sabrina wanted to tell her sister. *I don't want our father to be reduced to a tombstone.* But she deferred to Nasrin, who, like their father, had always seemed to know Sabrina better than she knew herself. Elias, walking between them, dragged her forward, his small legs trying to keep up with his mother's determined march.

In front of a barely marked patch of earth, she and Elias watched Nasrin kneel down.

'It's started raining, Mummy!' Elias called to her but his mother ignored him and began to recite the Ayatul Kursi. As Elias stood with his aunt, the rain became heavier and his mother's recitation became interspersed with her soft sobbing. He watched her turn and reach for Sabrina, wrapping her arms around her sister's waist. It was what Elias would remember in the years to come: the wet that spread inside his shoes, and around his collar, and the smell of dry earth soaking up the rain, the scent he would later discover the word for, petrichor, that settled over them and both comforted and smothered. He would remember the slow flush rising through Sabrina's damp face, drawn up tight to contain something just barely suppressible, and the ache in his chest as he realised that he had never seen the Tipu cry before.

Later that afternoon, Sabrina tried Ralph's number again.

He answered immediately. He had news and none of it was good.

'If they've been on you about it for weeks, why am I hearing about it only now?' Sabrina felt winded. She lay on her single bed and watched the gentle movement of a cobweb dangling from the ceiling. She needed to focus on the conversation, on what Ralph was saying, but instead she felt she was watching the scene from up there, feeling the dread rise up in her as she tried to make sense of it all. There had been a client complaint about the Altieri deal. Due to multiple downgrades of investment grade companies into high yield companies, the Altieri trade's BBB rating had reduced to BB, leaving the client out of pocket by thirty million dollars. And alleging mis-selling.

'This is serious, right? I mean, mis-selling? That's like a serious conduct issue, right? I mean, why do they think we mis-sold to them?' She didn't mean her words to be accusatory, but she couldn't help herself.

'Look,' Ralph sighed, 'the thing to focus on is that we didn't know. We didn't know that this shit was going to get downgraded, and so it was just human error, Sabrina.'

Sabrina frowned. She got up from her bed and opened the window a crack to let some air in.

'But Ralph, you're the one who's always telling us, there can't be errors in what we do, right? I thought we always check that shit! Right? We always check ratings!'

'Yes, but look, it's never been a problem before, Sabrina! The ratings hardly ever move!'

She thought about the lunch invitation from Monty slotted in next Tuesday between the departmental meeting and her closing session with Benjamin. The lunch where they would talk about her promotion. Her gut ached with dread.

'Ralph? You there?' She wanted him to reassure her that this hadn't affected her prospects. 'I mean we could all get fired for this, right? This is a lot of money and the reputational risks … What the hell is going to happen now? What should we do?'

Ralph sighed again. 'Look, Sabrina, what we do, is we calm down, okay?' He sounded tired.

For a moment Sabrina did feel bad. He was a good boss, a good mentor.

'Now, Compliance or Legal will call you,' he continued, 'because they have to investigate everything – the client is saying that we deliberately omitted to give them key information – but we didn't – that's what we need to focus on is that we didn't. They found nothing in my emails, nothing in the recorded calls. It's all just conjecture on their part.'

'But then, why have they suspended you?'

Ralph did not reply and before Sabrina could speak, there was a knock at the door. She opened it.

'Sib, those people from the Powys health department are here.' Nasrin smiled tightly. 'Can you come down with me?'

Sabrina put a hand over her phone. 'I'm on a work call.'

'Oh …' Nasrin bit her lip.

'Didi, come on! It's just some local officials, just be assertive!'

Nasrin closed the door, and Sabrina rushed to open it and called out to her. 'I'll be really quick, and come down when I'm done?'

She put the phone back to her ear. 'Have you told Ashok?' she asked. Sabrina was sure he had been involved in the Altieri deal.

'He's fine.' Ralph sighed. 'No point embroiling him in this.'

Sabrina rolled her eyes and wandered back to the window. Of course Ralph would defend his son-in-law. The gentle slope of Pen y Fan rose before her, both her jailer and confidante throughout her childhood. When she had urgently needed to leave this life that was starkly segregated between the Bengali at home and the British at school, New York had offered Sabrina not only a home of her own choosing but also an escape from being trapped in the crevices between two cultures. Away from the disapproving eyes of her parents and community, it had welcomed and recreated her as a fully assimilated Manhattanite. She couldn't have anything stand in the way of becoming a New Yorker, especially as her pending naturalisation application was only a matter of months away from being successful.

'Are you there? Sabrina?'

'Yes. Sorry. I don't mean to … it's stress, that's all, a bit of stress.'

'I know. It's just a process. We need to let them do their jobs, and I'll be back in no time.'

'I just …' She rubbed her eyes. 'I don't understand, I mean, was it really a mistake? I mean, we would have talked about the downgrade possibilities with the clients, wouldn't we?'

She shouldn't have pushed it. At least not at that moment. Not to a man who fired associates and analysts on a whim, because their breath was offensive, or their telephone manner too abrupt, or because they slipped their hand beneath their shirts to adjust their bra straps. The question slipped out before she thought about it.

'Are you for real?' His voice was smooth and barely audible but the danger that lurked beneath was palpable.

'I'm just saying—'

'And I'm just saying,' Ralph cut in with a sinister tone, 'when the numbers were good, I never heard you complaining? I'm pretty sure you were looking after this deal for me. You were running with it, and if there is something you knew that the rest of us didn't—'

Terror lurked in the rapid beating of Sabrina's heart. 'What does that mean?'

But Ralph had hung up.

She stood on her bed and reached up to pull the cobweb from the ceiling. She watched the tiny spider scrabble around her palm.

He was right. She had managed most of those later deals herself because Ralph and Ashok, smug in the knowledge that their new roles in the Digital Assets team had been confirmed, took to leaving early for squash and cocktails each day and sauntered in late and hungover each morning. Even so, Sabrina would remember if the Altieri deal was one of hers – and she had always been conscientious with her due diligence and would have considered any downgrade potentials and warned her clients if there was a problem. But the client was alleging that someone knew about the potential downgrade and deliberately kept it from them to get the trade done, and she knew the only people implicated were her old team, including herself. She also knew that the firm was never going to ignore a claim such as this one from an important client.

Ralph seemed to have already decided she was at fault.

And Ralph was powerful; temporarily suspended though he was, his word counted. He would protect Ashok who was family and so that left only Sabrina as dispensable.

Fury pumped through her. She began to pace around, ramming her shoulder against the mirrored cabinet to vent her anger. *That bastard!* Why had she provoked him by asking that stupid question? She sat down and tried to think clearly. What did they have on her? She logged into her computer and over the next forty minutes reread every item in the file, trying to find something to support her.

Forgetting that she had promised her sister that she would help at the Peacock, Sabrina stared out of the window, hatching a plan, letting her rage embolden her.

Then she sat down on the corner of her bed, cracked her knuckles and placed her fingers on the keyboard.

She began to draft an email to the Head of Compliance. Time was of the essence. The whole point of whistleblowing, after all, was to be the first to do it. She was not going to have this pinned on her.

9

That afternoon, Afroz had been about to call Humayun when Nasrin asked her to join her at the Peacock – 'Kichu nai, Afi,' her cousin implored, 'these officers from the council are coming to inspect, and I can do with some moral support!'

'Is it serious?' Afroz asked, noticing Nasrin's nervousness.

'I hope not – but you know these things turn into a big deal if they find something!'

As they arrived, Riaz was ushering in two middle-aged men and a woman of indeterminable age, and Afroz spent the next half-hour trailing behind Nasrin and Riaz as they led the trio through the restaurant kitchen, around the maze of stainless-steel worktops, opening the fridge freezers, the cupboards and containers, and answering questions. One of the men asked Mustafa questions about the organisation of meat and dairy and he answered in Bengali, answers which Nasrin softened in her translation. Afroz, wondering how to be more helpful, suddenly felt a small hand slip into hers and found Elias pulling her towards one of the freezers.

'There's kulfi in there,' he whispered into Afroz's ear.

Smiling, Afroz took an ice out of the freezer and unwrapped it, before sitting Elias on top of the counter to eat it. Behind her, the man who had been questioning Mustafa was now asking Nasrin if he could inspect the staff quarters.

'Khala Afroz,' Elias said, pointing at the floor where his kulfi had begun to drip, and Afroz rushed to find something to wipe it with.

'Baba,' she told Elias, 'hold it like this so it doesn't drip.'

The woman who had been inspecting the oil canisters stood and called for Nasrin. 'Thank you for letting us have a look around,' she said, closing her notebook. 'I don't have any concerns, you seem to have a good, clean place here. If you only knew the places I've seen.' Afroz saw her cousin's relief wash over her. 'I'll send the paperwork over to you shortly, but I'd say there's nothing for you to worry about.'

Before Nasrin could respond, a pyjama-clad Junaid appeared at the kitchen door. Holding a tissue under Elias's ice, Afroz watched as Junaid told Nasrin that one of the male inspectors was at the staff cottage, asking to see everyone's work documents.

'Okay,' said Nasrin, looking perplexed.

'Afa, he's going to Mustafa's room,' Junaid said again, his face stretched with anxiety.

That was when they heard the raised voices.

Nasrin and Junaid rushed outside and Afroz grabbed Elias to follow them. They found Mustafa standing outside the staff cottage, clutching a bag to his chest as the two men from the council cornered him. Afroz felt Elias slip off her hip and run to Mustafa.

'I only asked him to show me his documents,' one of the men told Nasrin. 'He disappeared into his room to get them and next thing I know, he's climbing out the window with a bag!'

It seemed only moments passed before Afroz heard Riaz calling over the fence for her aunt, saw Sabrina and her mother rushing down the steps. Nasrin stood between Mustafa and the two men, trying to reassure him. But Mustafa was inconsolable: he sank to the floor, shaking his head and muttering quietly words which Afroz could not hear. Beside him, Elias was bent over Mustafa's duffel bag which had fallen open, thrusting items back into it with his kulfi-sticky fingers – an old silver razor set, some clothes and several photos. The half-eaten kulfi discarded on the ground made an ugly orange pool behind him.

'Sasa,' Nasrin was saying, dropping to her knees and taking his hand, 'you must have something? A passport? A visa?'

'Na re go, nai nai!' Mustafa cried, swiping furiously at his cheeks. 'I have nothing re go! Don't let them take me re futh! Don't let them!'

Afroz sat down beside Nasrin and took Mustafa's other hand. She did not know him well, but the fear on his face tore at her.

Nasrin looked at her, her expression pleading.

'Don't worry, Sasa, everything will be all right,' Afroz said, trying to reassure him.

'Futh, re! Tell them I have nothing! Tell them I am sorry! I worked hard! I am a poor man, where will I go?'

'Afi is right,' Sabrina said, appearing beside them, 'you'll be okay, Sasa.'

'We're going to have to take him with us,' one of the men from the council told Sabrina. Sabrina took his elbow and led him a few feet away, speaking in a low voice. Mustafa took the bag that Elias held up to him, and then he turned to the Peacock.

'Sasa,' Nasrin said, 'did you leave something? Don't worry, one of us will get it for you later?'

'Hai re futh,' the old man wheezed. 'I leave behind a life. That old restaurant. I will never set foot in it again!'

Nasrin and Afroz stared helplessly.

'When Sham Bhai left us,' Mustafa said, leaning back against the stone wall of his only home for decades, 'I knew that it is the time of gordish.' The little specks of white stubble on his chin trembled as a sigh escaped him. 'Gordish, re! I am indebted to your Abba. All his life he has protected me. But God has claimed him now.'

Nasrin dropped Mustafa's hand. 'Abba knew?'

Mustafa stared at her, his eyes round and mortified.

Nasrin turned to Sabrina who was approaching them. 'I've spoken to them,' Sabrina said, 'and they'll let me ride to the station with him.'

Nasrin shook her head. 'Sib, he knew. Abba knew Mustafa Sasa was an illegal!'

'Okay. So, he knew.' Sabrina frowned.

Nasrin shook her head. 'But he risked his business to hide him.'

Sabrina turned towards the trio from the council who waited near the gate for them. 'Well, Abba just wanted to help him.'

'It's illegal! And it was actually unkind – what sort of life has Sasa had? What sort of life will he have now?'

'No, na re go!' Mustafa whimpered.

She leaned over Mustafa. 'No, Sasa, I didn't mean that … I just – it will be all right. You will be all right.'

And Afroz watched as Mustafa deferred to Nasrin as he had probably once deferred to her father, small tears running down the side of his face as he gazed up at his beloved Peacock.

The house descended through many levels of silence and gloom after Mustafa's departure. Jahanara muttered as she went about the house, tidying, cleaning, cooking, worrying, with Elias at her heels. Mustafa had been Shamsur's right-hand man; the two buzurgs – the elders – whose presence had been so reassuring. Both gone.

Outside, the wet weather took a turn for the worse, becoming a full summer storm. A funfair, on its way to the village, was forced to stop, and Afroz, standing at the window of the guest room, looked out at the splashes of colour their caravans made on the horizon, noting how the rain softened the foreignness of the valley, bringing to mind the sounds and smells of the monsoon so recently left behind in Sylhet. She felt the foreboding all around her; she sensed that the family suffered, and though she herself was protected from the weight of it, she worried about Mustafa's misgivings that a time of gordish had arrived. It was difficult not to be affected by such superstitiousness growing up in Desh.

The only other sounds she heard were her aunt's soft murmurs entreating her grandson to finish his lunch in the kitchen, and she went down to join them there.

'I'm full though, Nani.'

'Eli! Remember what happens when you waste food?'

As her aunt spoke, Afroz watched her face; a round moon of a face that provoked in her the emotions of a homecoming after a long absence. Every summer Afroz had looked forward to seeing her Fufu; and even after she had returned to England, Jahanara continued to be a source of reassurance, someone to whom she often confided her many grievances and few contentments through both letters and phone calls. The contours of her face felt more familiar to her than her own mother's. A long-forgotten memory suddenly dropped into her like a coin in a slot machine: Afroz, aged nine or ten, lying on her bed with a broken leg and this aunt of hers by her side, wiping her face, while tiny, subdued sobs escaped her lips.

Afroz looked at the delicate arch of her Fufu's brows, at the way she pursed her lips as she coaxed her grandson to eat. Jahanara caught her staring and smiled kindly.

'Here, try this,' she said, placing a plate of brown paste in front of Afroz.

Afroz put a little in her mouth, delighted by the sweet and the sour heat that spread over her tongue.

'Chutney,' her aunt explained. 'Made from last summer's figs. Naju eats jars of it when she comes, but she won't take it to London.' She sniffed. 'That's what happens when you marry outside of your own – you leave half of yourself behind.'

Afroz looked up at her aunt, trying to decipher the mixed emotions displayed there. It had never occurred to her that her Fufu and Fufa were displeased with Nasrin's choice of husband. She had always assumed that they had fully assimilated; that they had found an easy cohabitation with the ways of their adopted homeland and the ways they wished to retain of their old one.

'Not like you,' her aunt continued. 'Such a good daughter, so obedient, so respectful, and look at you now.' She smiled. 'Happy.

And why shouldn't you be? Happiness, they say, resides in obedience to God and to your parents.'

Afroz flushed and looked away in pain. She wondered how much of her relationship with Taseen had been known to Fufu and Fufa.

Her aunt suddenly took Afroz's face in her hands and brought her own face down to meet it. She rubbed her nose tenderly against Afroz's, and Afroz closed her eyes. Fufu's skin was velveteen.

'I have missed you so much, my little Afi,' she told her, making Afroz look down with embarrassment. 'I'll put some chutney aside for you,' her aunt said. 'Take it when you go back. Humayun likes his sweet and sours, doesn't he?'

Afroz nodded. 'It's been almost five years since you last came home, Fufu,' she said, timidly. 'I've missed you all so much. At least when we were children, every year you would come.'

Jahanara's face darkened with sadness. 'After you were married, there seemed less and less reason to go.'

'I was still there!' Afroz protested.

Her aunt shook her head. 'You are no longer ours, Afi. A daughter is only a guest in her father's home, until she goes to her true home.'

'I thought perhaps you would come, when Ruksana ... when I lost Ruksana.'

There was a sudden silence.

Elias looked up from his Lego. 'Who is Sana?'

His grandmother wiped the table around him, stacking his Lego bricks to one side. Afroz watched the cloth go back and forth. The table was clean, but still her aunt polished.

'There is nothing, re moyna,' her Fufu told her gently, so gently that the hairs on the back of Afroz's neck stood up, 'that I could have done that would have lessened *that* pain.' She looked at Afroz's curled fist on her lap and placed her own hand on it. 'To lose a child ...' For a moment her aunt's lips quivered, but quickly she composed herself. 'We phoned – every day we phoned when you were in hospital, but that mother-in-law of yours – ish!'

Afroz smiled ruefully. 'I don't mean that you didn't reach out, Fufu,' she said softly. 'I mean – I mean that I really missed seeing you all. I miss those summer visits. That's all.'

Afroz picked up the spoon and continued to eat the chutney in silence. As the rain slowed to give way to the gentle moan of the wind, Afroz reflected, not for the first time, how her marriage had built a barrier between her and those she loved.

When her iPhone began to buzz, she leapt up to answer it.

It was Humayun.

'When are you coming home?' he asked her as soon as she answered. 'Ma is asking.' Humayun paused for a moment, giving the impression, as he always did, that Afroz could reply if she wished. But, as she always did, she took refuge in her silence, saying all the things that she wanted to say, into the blank space in her head.

'Has Ma taken her blood pressure medication?' she asked, hoping to divert his attention.

'Afi, you can't sit on the other side of the world and ask if she has taken her medication. The ticket man phoned.'

Afroz swallowed the lump in her throat.

'He said,' Humayun continued, 'you had messaged him asking about extending your stay. Why didn't you speak to me about this first?'

She sighed, and he mistook her sigh for intransigence, and began to reprimand her sulking and her attitude.

'Humayun, please. It's been such a difficult morning. I just wanted to stay a few extra days – to help my aunt.'

He was silent.

At moments like these, Humayun's silent displeasure was reminiscent of her own mother's stubborn disapproval, which along with that ever-ready cane, had overshadowed Afroz's childhood. She didn't believe people were born wanting dominion over others and she doubted that Humayun set out to bully her, but did he have to be so like her own mother? That voice, so accusing and demeaning, and ignoring her every need. She sometimes wondered if it was her that made people resort to the more selfish and caustic parts of their humanity.

'Okay, okay,' Humayun relented. 'Tik ache, stay a few days longer. But not too long, mind! What will people say? A wife should be home with her husband. That is the correct way. Your timing is terrible, Afi, Ma is very upset. That Munni, next door? They are looking for a groom.'

'She is underage!'

'I know that!'

'Humayun, they can't!'

'Ish, but what can we do? Ma is getting herself involved – she's been there since this morning to talk sense into them. She's wasting her time – do these people seem like sensible sorts to you?'

'But Humayun, why don't you do something—'

'Ish, why do I tell you these things? All this drama I have to deal with, Ma here and you over there!' He must have heard the frustrated sigh she emitted, for his voice softened. 'Forget that,' he said. 'Accha tell me, Afi, what is it like there?'

Afroz, frustrated by his apathy, caught the desire in his voice, spiked not only with natural curiosity but also with such an audacious wish to covet that it made her feelings of resentment and fury rally. She blurted out with a curtness she had never dared before, 'None of your business!'

There was a moment's silence before she heard him hang up. Which was just as well, because she had the urge to physically reach into the receiver and shove him out of the conversation.

How dare you? she heard her dead mother's voice ask her.

Afroz heard her mother's admonishments at the end of every terse conversation with Humayun, every refusal she made to his demands at night (which in any case were not many, because she had found early on that it was easier to simply take the discomfort of it than to hold back and make him angry), every dinner not sufficiently to his taste, or shirt not ironed in accordance with his requirements. Sometimes at home in Sylhet, an overwhelming desperation would descend on her, and with it those words from her dead mother. 'Thumi kitha,' she would ask her, over and over, flushing out Afroz's anger and frustration and replacing them with the anguish of not being able to answer the question: *who do you think you are?* But her mother's voice answered it for her. She was a nothing, a stain upon her family's honour, and she was not good enough for even this soul-destroying life.

And then God gave her this temporary respite: this family that she already loved, this child that she was falling hard for, and this place of delicious quiet. That very dawn, she had watched the beautiful valley rise out of the darkness, like some primordial creature stretching up and swallowing half the sky. She yearned to hold on to it, not as a memory, but as her reality.

Temporary though it was, this place was hers alone. She would not allow Humayun's curiosity and needs to sully it.

She returned to the table and watched her aunt chatting with her grandson as she tidied. How different this woman was to the woman who had brought her up. She radiated maternal affection, and gentle grace. A sudden resentment sliced through Afroz. Here in this house, where Naju and Sibby had grown up pampered by this loving mother, it was hard for Afroz to ignore the disparities between their childhoods.

She excused herself and went up to her room to do her namaz.

A few hours later, the rain had abated, and a weak shaft of sunlight emerged through a crack in the sky. The house was filled with the smell of Jahanara's cauliflower cumin shobzi, and Afroz, who had used up her reserve of stories to entertain Elias, now sat with him at the kitchen table, laughing as the child divulged some family secrets.

'My favourite drink is Ribena. Mummy drinks Ribena too, in

a special glass, and it's a special Ribena, which I'm not allowed to have,' he told her. He pressed the nib of his orange felt pen into the soft flesh of his finger. He held it up to her, and she rubbed at it. 'But I'm not allowed to tell Nani. About Mummy's Ribena.' He looked at her and then suddenly grinned. 'But you're not Nani, so it's okay!'

She surpressed a giggle. 'And what is your favourite TV programme?'

'That's really hard,' he told her seriously. 'There's *Topsy and Tim*, there's—'

The door opened and banged in the hallway, and Afroz and Elias fell silent. They looked up as Nasrin came into the kitchen with Riaz trailing her.

'Amma,' Nasrin said, her face pale. Jahanara finished her prayer and looked up from her janamaz.

She nodded at her daughter. 'How is Mustafa? What will they do to him?'

'Amma, where is Sabrina?'

Afroz was taken aback by the anxiety in her cousin's voice. She set her crayon down on the table and watched as Nasrin rushed into the hallway. Riaz stood in the middle of the room with a pinched expression.

'Sibby,' Nasrin bellowed up the stairs, 'get down here, now!'

'What is it?' Jahanara asked, folding her prayer mat, her voice sharp with anxiety.

'Riaz has been to see the solicitors,' Nasrin said, returning to the kitchen and pacing back and forth. 'Sabrina!'

Sabrina walked into the room, looking preoccupied. She joined them around the table.

Riaz traced the groove in the table with his fingers before laying his hands determinedly down. 'I've spoken to Dillon, and there's, um,' he looked at Afroz with a searching look that panicked her, 'a few surprises.'

'What?'

'Yeh … so there's no easy way to say this.'

'Come on, Riaz,' Sabrina laughed nervously, 'you're scaring everyone!'

'Just say it,' Nasrin said.

'Your dad,' Riaz said, his voice tremulous, 'he … okay, let's start with the simple things … he left the house to your mum.' He smiled uncertainly at Jahanara, who had found her thasbih beads and was softly praying on them. 'He left the holiday let in Bala to you girls.' Riaz paused then and looked down at his fidgeting fingers. 'Dillon says, he left the Peacock to his eldest daughter.'

'I don't mind!' Sabrina said with a relieved laugh. 'Jesus Christ, is that all? I don't mind at all! She's my sister, and I don't need it. Right, Didi?' She laughed again, a heady, rushed laugh.

'No, Sibby,' Riaz said, looking up across the polished mahogany at Afroz. 'He named Afroz as his eldest daughter.'

Sabrina laughed. Nasrin stared at Riaz and then at her mother.

'He's left the Peacock to Afroz,' Riaz said.

The silence in the room was filled by their shock. As all eyes turned to Afroz, she looked from one face to another, eyes wide in terror and her heart thudding in her throat.

His eldest daughter? Had she really heard those words?

'Is this a fucking joke?' Sabrina's voice was glacial.

'What?'

'Are you sure, that's what it says? Let me have a look!'

'Sib, no, this letter's for your mum. Here, Fufu!' Riaz handed a sealed envelope to Jahanara, who tore it open with shaking fingers.

'Amma, is that really what it says?'

'It's a joke! Obviously.' Sabrina was standing then, towering over them, glowering around the room, her eyebrows high on her forehead.

Jahanara opened the letter. There was a moment's silence as her eyes followed the lines. She paled and folded it quickly.

'What?' Nasrin whispered.

Beside her, Sabrina stepped back from the table, knocking the chair to the floor with a clatter. 'What is going on?'

'Sabrina, calm down,' Riaz said, but his voice wavered with uncertainty, and was no match for Sabrina.

'Don't tell me what to do! Why should we believe you? Why are you the executor and not one of us?'

'Because you weren't here,' Riaz said quietly.

This only served to inflame Sabrina more. 'I know your kind. Sticking around, constantly wanting fucking handouts.'

'Sibby!' Nasrin said, standing too. 'Shut up!'

'Really? You're having a go at me?' Sabrina demanded of her sister.

'Sib,' Riaz was out of his chair now at Sabrina's side, 'look at me. I'm not lying. There are no handouts, not for me,' he turned to Afroz, 'and not for her.'

The gesture quietened Sabrina, and she looked at Riaz, her eyes brimming. 'Riaz, though! We know our dad! We know him.'

'I know,' Riaz said firmly. 'We do. And we got the chance to know him and we bloody loved him.' He looked over at Afroz. 'But Sib, you see, right? Not all of us had that chance, you see that?'

Afroz stared blankly back at him.

'I mean,' Sabrina asked, her face tight with confusion, 'did he have an affair?'

'Is that why you came?' Nasrin asked Afroz, her eyes not leaving the table, and her fingers pulling at the skin of her elbows. 'Did you know?'

'No!' Afroz said, shaking her head in fervent denial. 'I mean, yes, I knew I was adopted but—'

'Adopted! You *did* know!' Sabrina hissed.

'No – please, I knew I was adopted, but not who my birth parents were – I came because my Baba told me to come,' Afroz stuttered, panic making her voice barely audible.

'No!' Sabrina shook her head, her voice raised. 'I don't believe it. It's not true, I don't believe it. You're a liar! Your father sent you here to spread these lies!'

'Don't you dare bring Baba into this,' Afroz commanded, rising from her own chair, a corner of her hijab catching on the armrest and tearing.

'We just – we're trying to understand if that's why you came?' Nasrin said quietly, looking up with dismay. Above their heads, the heavens opened, and the sound of rain filled the room.

'She came,' Jahanara said, in a distant croak, and everyone became still to hear her. 'She came because she has as much right as any of you to be here.'

'You're not angry? Why – so you knew?' Sabrina said, approaching her mother, but her mother shook her head, waving her away. 'You knew, Amma? Do you know who her mother is? Who is it?'

'Was he having an affair, Amma?' Nasrin asked, turning to her mother. Their voices were those of pleading children. Jahanara clasped her hands to her forehead, her thasbih beads swinging against her temples. 'Oh my God,' Nasrin whined, 'did you know? Did any of you know? I mean he … what else is there? I feel like I never really knew – wait, oh God, was Afroz's mum – Mamani and Abba, were they, oh God, Amma, were they—'

But she got no further, for at that moment Jahanara reached up and slapped her.

The thasbih snapped and jade beads scattered in every direction.

'Have I taught you nothing?' Jahanara sputtered. 'You dare speak ill of your father and of your aunt? They were not adulterers. They were not sinful like you ungrateful children!'

Nasrin, her face red and wet, ran out of the room.

The rest of them watched Jahanara stand up, the jade balls of her thasbih spilling from her lap and rolling about in every direction. She stared for a moment, and then stooped to gather them. No one helped, frozen as they were in shock. Afroz watched as her aunt rose to her feet – too suddenly, it seemed, for she swayed a little, and her hands reached out for something to hold. Riaz rushed to her.

'Help me to bed, Riaz re,' she said.

* * *

Elias crouched at the foot of Afroz's chair. A neglected jade bead rolled to a standstill by his foot. He picked it up, rolled it around between his fingers and looked up at Afroz. He watched her face, so empty of all the laughter and energy he had witnessed just hours before. He looked down at her feet and the way she curled up her toes. He squeezed the jade ball tighter in his palm.

'They just need time, Afa.'

Afroz turned to see Riaz standing by the door. She stared at him blankly.

'Did you know?' she asked him.

Riaz shook his head. 'Not until an hour ago.' He picked up his jacket and put it on. Before he left, he turned towards her, his voice despondent. 'The thing is, Afa: these Bong men love to disappoint us, don't they? But this one, at least he tried to do the right thing in the end, didn't he?'

Afroz looked towards the hallway through which her cousins and aunt, whom she held so dear, had left. When she heard the soft click of Riaz shutting the door behind him, she let her face collapse, and Elias climbed onto her lap, clasping his arms around her shoulders and burying his face into the folds of her scarf.

His embrace seemed to revive her. 'It's okay, Eli, shuna!' she said, her whispers shaking with the effort. 'It's nothing for you to worry about! Don't look so sad. Come now, show me what you have in your hand.'

He showed her the jade bead. 'It's mine. Finders keepers.'

She smiled. 'It's definitely yours. It came to you, didn't it? When things come to you like that, then you have to keep them.' And then she held him and continued to sit in silence, as the day settled into dusk and his soft snores were the only sound that she could hear.

PART II

1

In the moments after her mother abandoned them, Sabrina fled the house, her mother's mortified expression imprinted in her mind. Sabrina had always been reduced to a state of paralysis by the bouts of incomprehensible grief that her mother sometimes lapsed into, but this time was different. This time she understood the source of her mother's sobs, audible throughout the house, and she could not bear the wretchedness she felt in hearing it. She traced her father's daily trodden trail behind the village, through the kissing gates to cross the meadow to the long-abandoned St Teilo's Church, as though by tracing his steps, she might obtain some understanding of his last bequest. Before her, the lane split in two, and she took the rough track to the right to merge with the darker trail, letting the lengthening shadows edging out from the woods provoke her.

Afroz was her father's daughter. Afroz was her sister.

The thoughts whirled meaninglessly in her mind, unable to fit inside her. The descending nightfall added to her sense of incoherence as though a curtain was falling over every plausible moment of her life – how could it be? She had been the one who understood her father more than anyone else: he had confided matters to her which he had kept from her mother and sister – such as Mustafa's illegal status. 'Sometimes re futh, you have to let compassion dictate your actions,' he had responded when she reminded him that he was breaking the law. 'Law or no law – remember the words of our bidrohi kobi, re futh! Rest only when the world is free of *othachari*, of the oppressed, ha?' And he told her not only because she could stomach the truth, but also because she would agree with him.

But then why would he have kept this most important of truths from her?

Turning back towards the centre of the village, she wondered if it was because he knew she would judge him. Their relationship had been steeped in the roles they had played – the roles that Abba himself had dispensed: she was the daughter who had been brought up and encouraged to rebel against expectation and custom, and he was the father – the eternal do-gooder, the most morally compelled of men – who would protect her right to do so. But the contents of his will challenged those roles – now he seemed to be asking her to turn away from the very instincts he had nurtured in her by expecting her to give up her family and the Peacock without a fight.

Sitting alone inside the only pub still open, Sabrina's thoughts meandered through bizarre avenues – had her father been married before? Were there other children? How had Afroz come to be adopted by her Mamu? Exploring these questions alone was disconcerting and she wished she could talk it over with someone – not her sister who was easily mortified, and not her mother who was the most taciturn person Sabrina had ever known – no; Sabrina wished she could talk it over with her father. The ludicrousness of this caused her to snigger and spill the contents of her glass of wine onto the table.

'Are you okay, love?' The bartender loomed before her.

'I spilled my drink.' Sabrina waved her hand over the table. 'Sorry.'

The woman bent down to wipe the spilled wine, her expression softening. 'You're Sham's youngest, aren't you? Your dad was a good egg.'

'Thanks,' Sabrina muttered, placing a twenty on the table and grabbing her jacket.

Out in the night, the wind clawed at her face. Sabrina teetered slowly home, letting the darkness, the cold and her bewilderment congeal into something more comprehensible to her. There had always been something about Afroz that had grated on Sabrina – her capacity for self-pity, her acceptance of her downtrodden lot in life without lifting a finger to improve it had made Sabrina furious. It reminded her of her mother's unwillingness to challenge the old way of doing things – both women had marooned themselves away from any help or rescue, debilitated by their phobias of those twin imaginary terrors, dishonour and disrepute. Though she had spent her adolescence fighting against these tendencies in her mother, Sabrina had found it easiest to simply distance herself from Afroz's insipidness. Now there was no question of distancing herself because Afroz was here to claim everything – not just her family but the Peacock too.

2

Nasrin stood at her window, looking out at the silent shadows of the village and beyond it towards Pen y Fan. Elias was asleep, his eyelids flickering with dreams that Nasrin could not free him from. He made a whimpering sound, and Nasrin worried, stroked his hair before resuming her vigil by the window, watching the night spread.

A flurry of small cries fluttered intermittently from her mother's room. Two or three times, they became more like howls, sending Nasrin rushing to Jahanara's door. She spread her palms on the flimsy wood, pressed her nose against it until her mother's sobs died down. Each time she went back to her room, Nasrin felt the house sink lower into its despair. What could she do to stop the house from falling?

She spent the next few hours lying beside Elias, the heat of his body adding to her restlessness. Just after 4 a.m., she slipped out of bed to reclaim her place beside the window. Out on the square, she saw Riaz's solitary figure. He sat very straight on the bench beside the Wellington statue. In his fingers he held a cigarette, its feeble orange glow a firefly flickering in the darkness. For a moment, she considered going out to him to share his smoke and feel the warmth of him at her side. When she heard the creak of the floorboards, she turned to see the shadow of Sabrina, faltering and swaying down the hallway.

Her chest heavy with the mournfulness of the early hour, Nasrin tiptoed to bed and curled up beside her son, leaving the door wide open and the light on.

She woke to find Sabrina standing at the foot of the bed.

'You left the light on,' Sabrina told her.

'What time is it?' Nasrin croaked.

Sabrina shrugged. Nasrin rubbed her eyes, searching her sister's face. Sabrina looked like a woman who had been spurned by sleep. The shadow of her wild hair darkened her face like a demon in a comic strip. Sabrina yawned, a deep and painful yawn, then reached up and switched off the light. She crept beneath the duvet and tickled Elias's feet. Elias squealed in sleepy delight. But the smell of Sabrina suddenly closed around Nasrin. Stale smoke and alcohol. Her stomach turned.

With effort, Nasrin slipped out of bed and led them down to the gloomy kitchen.

'I'm cold!' Elias moaned, and Nasrin found a blanket to wrap around him. Sabrina filled her bowl with milk and then appeared to forget about it. She sat back and took out a cigarette. Nasrin bit her lip and looked away.

'Khala-Amma,' Elias said, 'did you know, the fair is here?'

Sabrina looked through him, smiled absently, the unlit cigarette in her fingers, the untouched bowl of milk before her. Nasrin noticed her sister's short nails, realising with a pang that she had bitten them until they were raw.

'She can't have it.'

'What?'

'She can't have the Peacock. If she had any respect, she'd leave.' Sabrina tapped her unlit cigarette on the table, squinted at it. 'I'll pay for it – taxi, airfare, boat.' Sabrina snorted miserably. 'Whatever she wants to take. Fucking Freshie.'

'Sabrina!' Nasrin hissed.

'The will …' Sabrina said, appearing not to have heard her sister. 'Maybe they made a mistake, when they were drafting it?' Sabrina threw her cigarette into her bowl. 'I mean why is everyone suddenly turning on him? Why is everyone just taking Riaz's word for it?'

'Because,' Nasrin said, closing her eyes, 'they're not his words, they're Abba's.'

Sabrina's chin trembled.

'Sibby—'

'It's not fucking true – there's something not quite right! I'm telling you now, that Afroz, she's always been scheming – always shimmying up to all the elders, acting like butter doesn't melt, following us around wherever we went, the attention-seeking little bitch.'

'Stop with the language! Can't you just please,' Nasrin put her hands before her on the table in entreaty, 'just stop fighting this.'

Sabrina stood up. 'You can't always play nice, Didi! Sometimes you've got to fight. Life's not about being nice. Jesus, why does everything have to look fucking perfect to you, whether it is or not!'

Nasrin stood too, making to leave the table, but within seconds Sabrina rushed to her side. 'Sorry, sorry, no, listen to me, Dids,' she pulled at her arm like a child, 'let her try and prove it's all kosher, the will and all that—'

Nasrin frowned, pulling her arm away. 'For God's sake, why her? Why are you making her the enemy?'

Sabrina stared at her in disbelief. 'She is the enemy.'

Nasrin shook her head.

'And she's trying to take everything away.'

'The will is real, Sibby. The will is real, the restaurant is hers.'

'Okay, fine.' Sabrina took a step back, narrowed her eyes and looked at Elias. 'So, we can buy it off her – in cash, I have the money, last year's bonus, right, we buy it off her.'

Nasrin sighed in frustration. 'And then what? You're going to move here and manage it, are you?'

Sabrina frowned, surprised by the heat in her sister's voice.

'What? You think I should leave London and do it? Is that what you're planning? Always old Didi here to look after things? 'Cos I don't have a life. I have too much time on my hands, sending you all those long, dull essays.'

Sabrina's face darkened. 'I never said they were long and dull.' She folded her arms across her chest. 'Amma can manage with Riaz's help.'

Nasrin touched her fingers to her temples. She reached out to take the soaking cigarette Elias had fished out of Sabrina's bowl.

'It's not just the Peacock, Sibby,' she said softly, turning to look at her sister. 'She's our sister. All this time she's been our sister.'

'But don't you see?' Sabrina pleaded. 'She's always done this – always tried to take everyone away – you and Amma and now Abba!'

'Eli?'

They looked up to the doorway where Afroz stood with an armful of wooden animals. Nasrin gasped. How long had she been standing there?

'I forgot about these, baba … I bought these for you.' Though her expression was blank, Afroz's voice shook as she lowered the animals to the floor, letting them spill out of her arms with a clatter. Nasrin pushed her son out of his chair and watched him approach the animals. He reached out to touch an elephant painted a wild orange with green eyes, and green tusks.

'Are we exchanging gifts?' Sabrina retorted. A chair screeched against the cold stone floor as she sat down on it, staking her ground. 'I thought you were just here to take?'

Nasrin sank into a chair and laid her face in her hands.

'Mummy?' Elias called, staring up at his mother in alarm, still clutching his new toys.

'You see?' Sabrina asked Afroz as she stooped to pick up her nephew. 'You're upsetting everyone.'

Nasrin willed herself to stop crying and say something, anything to stop Sabrina, to stop the wretchedness that spread across Afroz's face.

'I was wondering why you had come all this way,' Sabrina continued, talking over her sister's sniffles, her fingers soothing Elias's hair as he dug his head into her neck, 'and all along, it's because you wanted the restaurant, you wanted what's left of *my* father.'

Afroz shook her head, taking a step forward. 'Sibby, no, I came because you are my cousins and I wanted to be here for you.'

'Really? If we're that close, how is it you never mentioned you were adopted?' Sabrina snapped.

'Because I only found out myself three years ago ... and because you haven't been to Desh in so long. Naju,' Afroz said, taking a step forward, her voice timidly pleading. 'Don't cry, please? I wanted to say that I need to – I'm thinking of leaving sooner.'

Nasrin didn't say anything and looked up to see Afroz reaching out to touch Elias's head and Sabrina moving him away.

'Humayun wants me home, his mother is not feeling well, so—'

Sabrina raised an eyebrow. 'So, be a good little bouma and run on back?'

In the gloom of the early morning, Nasrin held her breath and watched Afroz.

The stillness was suffocating.

There was a flicker of change in Afroz's face.

'When I have decided,' Afroz turned finally to face Sabrina, and her voice had a dangerous clarity to it, 'when I have decided what I will do with my restaurant, then I will leave.'

She turned and walked out of the kitchen.

After Elias had finished his breakfast, Nasrin retreated to the living room, leaving Sabrina and Elias still sitting at the kitchen table.

'Khala-Amma,' she heard Elias say to his aunt. 'Can I keep them?'

Nasrin craned her neck to watch Sabrina take the elephant that Elias held out to her and give him a tremulous smile. 'They're lovely, aren't they?' she said. 'Of course you should keep them. Khala Afroz bought them for you. I just need to go out for a bit, Eli.'

Nasrin heard the chair scrape against the stone floor, and winced as her sister went out, banging the front door behind her.

Nasrin returned to the kitchen and watched her son play with his new animals in the grey morning light. She thought how different this morning was to every other she had ever had in this house. Mornings had belonged to her father. He had bustled into their rooms at the crack of dawn announcing, 'Fajr time!' and wrapped them in scratchy chadors, slipped their feet into thick socks, his own body already swathed in layers. As he made porridge, he regaled them with stories about Nirashapur; of the chitol fish, sometimes the length of his arm, about saddle-free horses, and kabaddi in the matt, his stories nostalgic for a life that he had long left behind. He poured his yearning for it into them, so that they too missed the sounds of the Pahela Baishakhmela, they too felt the urge to run into the compound when the first monsoon rains hit the hot soil with a hiss. In that hour or two before school, their world was not a conflicted one as it was outside. In this house, while their mother slept and their father plaited their hair, they were secure in the knowledge that they belonged. Not just to their father, or to their mother but to a beautiful Neel Bari in the shade of a splendid tamarind tree.

But then Abba had also fathered and abandoned a child. Where did that leave them? And to whom, then, did they really belong?

As the afternoon wore on, the guests came and went in waves: gangs of relatives offering well-meaning advice and prayers and containers of food. They were anxious to adhere to the custom of making sure the house of a recently departed was kept well-stocked for at least three days. Nasrin fried nashta and made tea with Afroz, which Sabrina reluctantly handed out on trays. At least, Nasrin thought to herself, the quiet in the house had been banished for a few hours. At least the three of them were working together.

But then the guests, at first sympathetically, then with more force, asked for her mother. Each time, Nasrin obligingly went up the stairs, and knocked.

'Amma,' she called, 'people are here. They are asking for you.'

But her mother's door remained obstinately shut. For all Nasrin knew, her mother might have died, nursing a broken heart, except that she heard the tap running at prayer times. She was grateful that at least Allah had managed to slip over the forbidden threshold, but the guests were difficult to console.

'But have you told her that I, Lal Bhai, am here?'

'Yes, Sasa, she is very poorly, I'm very sorry.'

'Let me go up and give her my condolences.'

'Sorry, Sasa, she is not accepting visitors.'

'The living cannot join the dead. Have you told her this? She must continue to live.'

'Yes, Dada, I will tell her.'

For hours she made these excuses, each guest seemingly more outraged than the one before. One elderly cousin of her father's hovered at her elbow before blurting out, 'Is it true about Sham – that he left everything to his wife's niece? I am not prying, goh ma, kinthu, is it true? Is that why your mother doesn't leave her room?'

A sharp snort escaped her and Nasrin glanced up from her pakura. 'And you are not prying?'

The woman moved away, shaking her head in disapproval. Nasrin looked down at her burnt pakura and switched the gas off. She wondered suddenly if the visitors had come only with the excuse of condolence – if they had come in fact to discover if there was any truth to the rumours. The thought peeved her. She was exhausted and hot, and she felt the remaining guests watching as she left the kitchen.

When Riaz arrived with an armful of tablecloths a few hours later, Nasrin was bidding farewell to two more guests.

'Can I use the washing machine? Damn Peacock one's conked out again.'

Nasrin closed the front door and followed him into the laundry room.

She watched as he bent to close the machine door.

'Is your mum ever coming out, you think?' Riaz asked. 'Has she been in there since yesterday?'

'She hasn't left the room once. I left some tea outside her door this morning. It's still out there.'

'She's like a desi Miss Havisham.'

She looked at him and frowned.

'You remember her? *I am tired*,' Riaz cried in a false soprano. '*I want diversion!*' He raised an arm to his forehead. '*I have done with men and women! Play!*'

'Oh my God!' she muttered, smiling in spite of herself.

'What is hasham, Riaz?' Elias asked, grinning.

'Play!' Riaz yelped again.

Nasrin laughed weakly, shaking her head. 'Stop!'

Riaz grinned.

Following him out to the kitchen, Nasrin felt some of the tension in her chest ease. 'I'd happily divert her attention if she just came out. I hope she comes out soon.'

'She will. She always does this – remember, when you first told them you wanted to become a pilot?'

'And when Sibby came home to tell them about her New York posting.'

'Then you told them about Richard. That was bad. She was up there for days. Where is the Tipu?'

Nasrin, remembering the morning's events, shook her head.

'She'll be okay, Naz. Everyone has their way of coping. When are you headed back to London?'

'I might stay a few weeks.'

'Richard will be okay without you?'

'Richard,' Nasrin replied, looking away, 'is busy with work. He won't mind.'

Richard. She needed to speak to him. Why hadn't he called back yet?

'What about Afa?' Riaz asked, nodding towards the living room where Afroz sat on the sofa, speaking in a low voice to her husband.

Nasrin shrugged. From the living room, Afroz looked up at them, the timidity of her expression suggesting that she knew they were discussing her.

'I'm not opening the Peacock at lunch today,' Riaz told her. 'Junaid has the afternoon off and I have to make a quick trip to Birmingham.'

'Now?' Nasrin asked, surprised. 'Can't it wait?'

Riaz picked up Elias and handed him a Chupa Chups. 'I'll be back before six. It's a family emergency.'

'Oh,' Nasrin said, searching his face, 'can I do anything?'

'Actually, yes – can you come and help out at the Peacock this evening?'

'What about Eli?' She looked at her son and smiled, taking him from Riaz.

'Ask Afroz. Or bring him along? I can't do a Friday night alone. Not with the main man missing in the kitchen!'

She nodded. 'Have you spoken to Mustafa Sasa?'

'He's pretty upset – they're deporting him.'

Nasrin nodded, wondering what Mustafa would think of her father once he found out about Afroz.

'Hey,' Riaz said, suddenly gentle, 'it's going to be all right.'

'Is it?' she whispered, the recent bravado leaving her. 'Is it? I can't reconcile it. Abba. Her father.'

'I don't know, Naz.' Riaz sighed. 'What I do know is that your dad was a good man, really, the best kind of man. You know? Great father, great husband, pious and upstanding member of the communities – both brown and white. I mean he made the Peacock a sort of haven for all us stragglers, and, well, whatever this stuff with Afa is – a bad decision, an old mistake, I don't know – but whatever it is, you can't let it give you amnesia about all the good he did.'

They both glanced out at the living room, where Afroz sat, still as a statue, with the phone on her lap.

'I have another sister,' Nasrin whispered, as though she had just discovered it. She had a sister in someone she already knew and loved, but who had been hidden from her for the sake of propriety. A sister brought up in such different circumstances on the other side of the world.

'Right?' Riaz shook his head.

When Nasrin reached the Peacock for the dinner shift, Riaz was already standing at the bar. She hadn't helped out in the restaurant since they had been teenagers together: giggling students, desperate for someone to order a delivery just so they could get a walk in along the river. She had been thirteen and Sabrina a precocious eleven when Riaz had arrived, an intense vulnerability lurking behind his Brummie street-boy facade which made them adopt him all the more fiercely. At first, he had been reticent, sharing little of the life he had left behind – which, according to Nasrin's mother, had been overshadowed by hardships she would not expound upon – and then their shared experiences had made that old life irrelevant. Riaz had become part of their present, part of their coming of age – an important character in their *bildungsroman*. And now, when he held up Panjabi MC's *Legalised*, she laughed because 'Mundian To Bach Ke' had been the soundtrack to their first forbidden taste of beer and a frequent score to the winter afternoons spent beside Llewid's Pond where they furtively planned their futures high on the weed supplied by Junaid.

As he busied himself around the bar, Nasrin searched Riaz's face for an indication of the emergency in Birmingham. She had been reluctant to ask him directly, concerned about appearing overfamiliar and interfering. But his expression belied nothing except his enjoyment of the familiar notes of the music which lifted her own spirits, and reassured, Nasrin went to flip the *Open* sign around and walked to the linen cupboard for an apron and hat. In the kitchen she was astonished to find Afroz, standing next to Lindsay in a loose shalwar kameez and her hijab.

'Your cousin's offering to help out,' Lindsay told her, her rosy cheeks loose with suspicion.

Sister, Nasrin should have corrected, and the way Afroz hastily looked away confirmed this.

'Where's Eli?' she asked instead.

'Sabrina took him for a walk,' Afroz replied.

They stared at each other, with only the sound of Hannan cracking and peeling boiled eggs. 'All right then!' Nasrin said in a too-loud voice. 'All hands on deck! Thanks!' She handed the apron and hat over to Afroz and backed out of the kitchen.

'What's she going to do? Can she peel an onion?' Riaz quipped when she told him. 'Isn't she married to some rich guy with several servants in the kitchen? I bet she can't even make tea.'

As it turned out, Afroz could definitely peel an onion.

She could slice, she could julienne, she could fillet. She knew her way round a chicken carcass, she knew how to cut a side of salmon and extricate the bones. In the frequent trips Nasrin made to the kitchen, during that busy Friday night, she was amazed at the grace of Afroz's hands as she sliced onions and chillies and peppers. Initially relegated to the periphery of the kitchen to dress the side salads, Afroz was soon promoted. At around nine o'clock, when Nasrin went into the kitchen armed with orders for a party of six, Afroz had taken Mustafa's old place next to Lindsay, bouncing about at the hob, tossing the contents of lamb balti in a frying pan.

'You kept this one a secret, didn't you?' Lindsay beamed at Nasrin, and Nasrin, overcome by the sudden unintended significance of Lindsay's comment, made a hasty exit.

At the bar, Riaz was snapping at Junaid for pouring gin freehand. 'I've told you a thousand times to measure it out, bebat!'

'Accha rebo! I was just trying to move us away from being in the jigger brigade! Place down the road's offering cocktails now!'

Nasrin stifled a giggle. Her pride over Afroz's kitchen skills had improved her mood. Riaz shook his head, smiled at her, and began to pull half pints for the two women waiting for a takeaway order.

'And what are you smiling about?'

Nasrin turned to find Sabrina standing in front of the bar in their father's green Barbour wax jacket, with Elias perched on her shoulders.

'Where've you been?' she asked, unable to keep the abrasiveness from her voice.

'Khala-Amma took me for a walk and ice cream,' Elias told her.

'I meant before that,' Nasrin said, directing her question to her sister.

Sabrina took Elias off her shoulders and waited for him to settle onto the old Chesterton with the Lego he had brought with him. She turned to Riaz. 'I'll have a gin and tonic.'

Riaz stared from Sabrina to Nasrin, and Nasrin felt the buzz of anger gathering in her. They didn't drink in the Peacock bar. It was a line they never crossed.

'Here you go, Sib,' Riaz said, pouring a Coke and placing it gently in front of her.

'That's a funny-looking gin and tonic.'

'We knocked on your door,' Nasrin said.

'Uh-huh. Did you knock on our mother's?' Sabrina responded, her voice cool and indifferent.

'Did you?' Nasrin asked, her voice shooting out of her.

Sabrina pushed the sweating Coke back towards Riaz. 'Gin.' The venom in her voice was unmistakeable. 'Please.'

Nasrin looked at Riaz, saw the way he bit his lip.

'You know we don't drink here, Sibby,' he said gently.

'Last I checked you were a waiter in my father's restaurant,' Sabrina said. 'Do your job. Wait.'

'Last I checked,' Riaz returned, coolly, 'it's not your father's restaurant anymore.'

Nasrin fled to the kitchen, her heart pounding in her chest. She ripped the new order from table nine and handed it, crumpled and damp, to Hannan.

'You know you can put the stems of the coriander into the pan when you're frying the onions,' Afroz was saying to Lindsay. 'It makes it flavourful.'

Nasrin watched as Lindsay ripped the stems off a bunch of coriander and washed it under the tap before throwing it into the pan. The same Lindsay who used to have screaming matches with Mustafa about when to add coconut milk to a pasanda!

'Naju!' Afroz called out, noticing Nasrin, and Nasrin melted beneath the affection in her call, in the pleasure of her sister's expression. 'Here, can you help me with this mutton? It's been simmering forever, and still so tough.'

Forgetting Sabrina, Nasrin peered down in the pan. 'Abba used baking soda, right, Linds?'

'What now? No! He used papaya!' Lindsay laughed. 'I thought you deshis eat goat curry all the time!'

'Yes,' agreed Afroz, 'but in Desh we like the toughness of the meat, we like it chewy, so it is harder to take off the bone, we want to fight for our food, see, it's more moza that way – more yummy?'

Lindsay laughed and Nasrin laughed too. She had never known Lindsay to be so easy around others. Something about Afroz seemed to elicit that ease in people. Except in Sabrina of course. The thought of her sister made her despondent again, for Sabrina would never forgive Nasrin's love for Afroz – suffering had turned Sabrina's mild dislike of her into an irrational hatred. She stood for some moments, watching Afroz peel away the translucent pink skin from several boiled tomatoes. As children, they'd loved playing restaurant; Sabrina had always wanted to be the chef, and Nasrin the head waiter, and poor Afroz, always the boring customer. Who would have known that she had been so ridiculously miscast! And not just denied her role as a chef in their childish games, but also denied in so many more important ways. The injustice and guilt burnt a hole in Nasrin's chest.

The next morning, Nasrin woke early.

There was no time for gloom today. It was the third day after her father's funeral when final prayers would be offered up for her father's soul. She slipped out of bed and shuffled along the hall to her mother's room, pressed her ear against the door.

'Amma?' she called softly. 'Amma, bara ay thay nay ni? Won't you come out now?'

For a moment it seemed that the room held its breath. But still her mother did not answer.

She took the white bedsheets from the linen cupboard and began to lay them out on the living room floor. She soaked the rice for the yakhni pulao and put the sipara and Qurans out on the windowsill, ready for guests to make their prayers. Elias sleepily followed her from room to room, until he became tired and lay down on the lower stair where Afroz found him as she came down.

'Y'Allah, re futh! Why do you lie here?' Nasrin heard Afroz ask him. 'Like a little beggar child?'

'What is a bigga chal?' Elias asked.

Nasrin watched Afroz carry Elias into the kitchen. 'Someone who is not Elias.'

'I'm hungry.'

'I'll make you porotha? With eggs?' Afroz asked him, taking the eggs out of the fridge.

Nasrin watched her, questions forming on her lips.

'Do you know how to make a good mutton pulao?' she finally asked.

Afroz nodded. 'For the third day khatam? Fufu won't come down?'

'I think we're on our own.'

Afroz handed the eggs to Nasrin and took the bowl of meat. She reached for the masalas and began to prepare a marinade of yoghurt, black cardamom, cloves, cinnamon and peppercorn.

'Are you all right?' Nasrin asked.

As she mixed the meat into the marinade, Afroz's face was drawn. Her eyes tired.

Afroz nodded. 'Yes.'

They heard the floor creak above their heads, the hiss and wheeze of the water running in Jahanara's bathroom. Nasrin's iPhone made them jump.

'Rich?' She walked into the living room, closing the door behind her. 'Where have you been?'

'Naz, you knew I was in Zurich!'

'I called you three times yesterday.'

'Yes, honey, it was an all-day conference.' Richard sighed. 'What do you want me to do?'

'What do I want you to do?' She heard her voice rise. 'I want you to fucking call me back!'

'Can you calm down please? What's wrong, Naz?'

She was silent.

'Come on, talk to me? I'm tired from all the travel and I've been up most of the night marking up a memo on litigation risk for a damn phone company. So, talk to me, what's up?'

And Nasrin wanted to tell him everything that had happened since the funeral, about Afroz, about her mother, her sister, but then she caught sight of her father's glasses on the mantelpiece. Already dusty, untouched, unused.

'I'm sorry,' she heard herself say gently into the phone. 'I'm fine.'

Richard paused. 'Are you sure?'

'Hmm.'

'Well, okay. So, honey, the card bill arrived this morning.'

'Okay.'

She heard him sigh again. In the kitchen, Afroz murmured softly to Elias and there was the hiss of the eggs hitting the hot frying pan.

'Two Gs in a month. Again. Why on earth do you need to spend a hundred quid on candles every week?'

The image of Mrs Humphreys's smirking face suddenly appeared in Nasrin's head, and she began to laugh. At first gently, but then picturing herself running from room to room lighting candles, she laughed even harder.

'Naz?' her husband said, his voice a tiny echo in the phone. 'Naz, what's going on?'

'Everything's fine!' she said. Her voice was someone else's: loud and sneering.

'It's so hard to even have a simple conversation with you these days.' Something hard had slipped into Richard's voice. Nasrin began to laugh again, unable to contain herself.

'Naz. Seriously, I don't know what's so fucking funny. Should I call back later or are you going to get a hold of yourself?'

'I'm sorry,' she rasped, breathing hard to control herself. 'My mother is a drama queen, my sister is a bull in a china shop – charging at the slightest provocation and—' She stopped. She wanted to add something derisive about Afroz just for the sake of consistency but what was there to say about her? That poor cousin slash sister, pitiful and subservient, unable to stand up to her own shadow?

'Fine. Don't take it out on me!' Richard said. 'I spent hours on the business plan yesterday and I have to hand it in on Friday. And I still have to do the day job. And the way you're spending these days, I need this promotion.'

She ignored this last. 'So, you're not going to make it today then?'

'Naz …'

'It's the third-day prayers,' she said, her voice breaking. 'The last time he sees us praying for him, sees how much we love him.' She wiped at her cheeks, feeling ridiculous about the pendulum of emotion swinging her from laughter to tears in moments.

'Honey,' Richard's voice was tender and torn, 'honey, please. You have to be strong. If it's important to you, I'll come.'

She wondered if she should test him on it. Wondered where she would be if she had tested him on all the many other occasions when he had made such promises to her during their life together.

For long seconds they listened to each other's breathing.

Then Richard asked, 'Is Eli there?'

'No,' Nasrin said. She would not test him on it because she suspected he would fail. She would fail. 'No, Richard, he's not,' she repeated before hanging up because why should he have that easy escape? Why should she let him live his part of the marriage through their son?

She felt the bubble of a blister forming inside her. She picked up her father's glasses, wiped the dust away with the edge of her pyjamas. She hadn't told Richard about Afroz and it wasn't the first time that she had kept something from him. She did it sometimes, just as a little *fuck you*. She guessed that it was for this same reason that she overspent on his Amex, to cause a little discomfort when the bill came.

Suddenly she thought of the ruby earrings. Why had he changed his mind and given her the bag instead of the earrings? Why had she never asked him about them? What was it she was afraid of?

She put on her father's glasses, let the world turn blurry around her. She was a daughter, sister, mother and wife, and she felt that she was slowly suffocating. She was all of those things, and they squeezed the Nasrin out of her. Who was she? She trod softly to the bookcase, took off the glasses and scanned the shelves for a sign of her father. She saw her old copy of Sylvia Plath's *Unabridged Journals*. She held it to her nose, inhaled the smell of her adolescence. The book fell open at a heavily annotated page, where a younger Nasrin had circled three, four times, the legendary words, 'custodian of emotions, watcher of the infants, feeder of the soul, body and pride of man?' How had she known?

* * *

It was only at sunset, when the women began assembling in lines to offer the Maghrib prayers and the air was thick with the smell of atthar, that Nasrin realised her sister was missing.

She slipped between the women and up the stairs to knock on Sabrina's door. There had been no sign of her sister all day – in fact she had not seen her since the night before at the Peacock.

There was no answer. 'Sibby?' she called.

She knocked again and pushed open the door.

She stared at the made bed and the empty rails of the open wardrobe. She stepped into the room and grabbed the duvet off the bed, hurling it to floor. 'Sibby,' she whispered, still in disbelief.

She leapt down the stairs two at a time and grabbed her iPhone and rang Sabrina.

'Hello?' Sabrina answered, her voice low and confused.

For a moment Nasrin couldn't reply.

'Hello?' Sabrina repeated.

'Did I just hear an international dial tone? Did you just fucking do that?'

'Didi, I just got in, I was going to call, but I'm so shattered—'

'Without saying a word, you boarded a flight?'

'Look,' Sabrina's voice was weary, 'I just—'

'A fucking flight? Without saying a word? You've been missing all day, we've been worried sick!' Nasrin was breathing hard.

'And who is we exactly?' Sabrina was wide-awake now.

'What?'

'I said, who is "we"? Amma dear wouldn't have noticed, Abba's gone to rest his soul after ditching his bastard onto us, and you? You're down in the restaurant playing happy families with your new sister.'

'Sibby—'

'The way I saw it, no one was going to notice if I left to return back to my real life.'

Nasrin was stunned. For a long moment, neither said anything.

'But it's the third day, today,' she stuttered. 'The third day Khatm. For Abba, Sibby.'

She listened to the dial tone for a few seconds before realising that Sabrina had hung up. The long beeps interspersed by the shots of silence were stupefying. She stood there for some time before she was able to break free of the spell.

What would she tell their mother? What would she tell Afroz? What would their father's spirit think, looking down to say his last goodbye, when he saw his Tipu, his golden moon, his unblemished last born, had fled before bidding him a final farewell? She realised with sudden dismay that this was her fault. Sabrina was hurting. She was jealous, and yes, she was also stupid, and rash. She was all of those things. But how many times had Abba told them, Sabrina was never cruel: if she was cruel it was because behind the facade there was a wound. And Nasrin had been too preoccupied to notice.

She sat down on the bottom step of the staircase and looked out of the frosted glass of the front door. Over the recitations, she could hear the warbling of pigeons outside.

'Naju, are you coming?' A middle-aged Auntie limped over to her. 'Let's try and finish the Khatm before Asr.'

'Yes, Khala,' she nodded, but she didn't move, and the woman, continuing her recitation, moved away.

During one of the last walks she'd had with Abba, a few days before she was married, they had walked up Pen y Fan with the wind whistling around them.

'Kitha re futh? Why so down?' her father had asked her, taking her hand in his, and trying to warm them in his gloved ones. 'Is it the flying? Is that what you worry about? Sintha khoriyo na re futh, you will fly again, InshAllah.'

She had slowed at the mention of her former profession because the remorse that shot through her was still spiked with pain. Her father slowed too, squeezing her fingers. 'It always surprised me,' he told her, 'that you wanted to fly. It was Sabrina who was always so restless, flitting about here and there like a junaki – how do you say – a firefly! But you, you were always so still, so peaceful and content. Amar moner manush!' He had hugged her to him, laughing. 'You have the stillness of Mother Earth, my little mud-eater!' And Nasrin had pulled away, feeling the familiar frustration of being misunderstood – for her stagnation and stillness had always been a silent form of desperation. Flying had been her escape, but he had never understood this.

'It's not that,' she had told him. 'I don't like it when Amma and Sabrina fight, Abba. It really gets to me. I especially hate it when they're fighting because of me. Can't you say something?'

'You are never their reason to fight, re futh,' Abba replied. 'You are the reason they always make up.'

And this was the story he, they, had always told her. They'd placed this mantle of responsibility on her as far back as she could remember, the first-born, the keeper of the peace. Let Sibby have the dress, Naju, just keep the peace; just wear the shalwar kameez Amma wants you to wear, Naju, just keep the peace.

'Allah tests us with only the things he knows we can handle. You are the peacemaker, because Allah deems you fully capable, more capable than your mother and sister.' Her father's words had washed over her as she looked out at the downward sweep of Pen y Fan, and wished that she could take flight and leave it all behind. She wanted to escape her father and these expectations of his that she felt she would always fall short of.

'I don't want to always be making peace, Abba! I just want them to stop bickering all the time. Do you even know what it's about this time? Amma found pills in Sabrina's room; they fell out when she was trying to take the spare roll-out mattress from her cupboard, and she thinks they are Sabrina's!'

'Is Sabrina ill?'

'No – not like that, ugh, contraceptive pills, Abba.' She saw her father about to protest and held up her hands. 'If they're hers, she's probably taking them for her skin or something.' She hadn't meant to stumble into an awkward conversation with her father about Sabrina's sex life. 'She says they're not. But even if they are, she says that Amma has no right to go rooting through her things! Now neither of them is talking to each other, and I'm getting married in three days!'

'It's okay. Give them time. And when you've done that, intervene.'

His certainty had infuriated her. His certainty that she, Nasrin, was happy to scurry round like a threaded needle repairing a rip here and a tear there, making sure the fabric of their family life wasn't damaged beyond repair. Then she had married Richard and her life had changed course. Her marriage had been like a strong wave that surged over her and swept her out, far away from her loved ones, far away even from the life she had intended to live.

But now from beyond the grave, her father was offering a role from the past. Did she have any of the old Nasrin left in her?

Upstairs in her room, Jahanara stood up from her janamaz, feeling lightheaded, her hip bone throbbing with pain. She clambered onto her bed and lay back, her fingers rummaging beneath her pillow for her prayer beads. Downstairs she could hear the voices crying out for God. As though God could be coaxed with such clamouring. *Lower your voices,* she wanted to say to them, *no need for such yowling. Allah hears the silent, for the silent, in their own way, are louder.* What was it her Lalon-loving husband used to recite? *Shob loke koy, Lalon ki jaat shongshare? Everyone asks, what is Lalon's faith? Lalon says, I've never seen the face of faith with these eyes of mine!* She smiled, picturing Shamsur singing Lalon geet with his eyes closed, his head swaying side to side. Her fingers felt something – not the prayer beads, but Naju's old hand fan that she had taken from the Peacock bar. Her Naju whom she had slapped and in front of so many people. Her Naju whom she had held close to her, like an amulet for protection, to bear the brunt sometimes of her own suffering. She stared at the waterlily at its centre. How her husband had loved this. How he had loved his daughters. How he had loved her. She clutched it to her chest and curled around it.

Once During a Red-eye in the Bosom of the Cockpit

It is a chilly evening in December, and Nasrin shivers beneath her flight jacket as she slips her cabin case onto the security belt next to Henri's. Henri is on her red-eye to Dubai and is mid-conversation with Captain Townsend, but, in customary fashion, he stops what he's doing to greet Nasrin, and waves her in front of him in the queue. He is rather cocky for a trainee in the Cadet Programme, but the crew likes him. Nasrin passes through the security line and the passengers smile at her as though she is someone remarkable. This makes her flush, even after a few years on the job. She is not remarkable but merely fortunate. Her three stripes are an accolade she feels undeserving of, and yet she is something of a poster child for the BA training scheme. She worries that in the glare of the spotlight she will be revealed as an impostor.

Once past security, she sidesteps trolley bags and children and orders an espresso and a bottle of water at Pret. Her phone vibrates in her pocket.

'I miss you already,' Richard tells her, and she feels as though he has handed her a hot water bottle, and the delicious warmth spreads through her. 'Did you tell them?'

Richard has proposed to her, leaving her no choice but to divulge his existence to her family. He has been her secret for the last two years, just like the beautiful yellow diamond she has hidden beneath her shirt, on a chain.

'Yes,' she says.

'Yes?'

'Hmm-hmm.' She takes the espresso and drops the coins into the cashier's hand. 'They need a bit of time to come around, but it's fine,' she lies. She follows it up with a laugh. It is a habit of hers, to punctuate nervousness or stress with bouts of sudden laughter. She looks round the lounge, feeling the glare of noise and light press upon her.

'Sure?' he presses. 'I can come up with you next weekend, maybe so they can meet me?'

'I have a flight next weekend, honey,' she lies again. 'I just found out. The weekend after, maybe?'

She bites her lips and listens half-heartedly to the plans he makes for Sunday.

'I love you,' he says, and she repeats the words into the phone before hanging up. She does. Love him. But suddenly, her love, buried for so long in secrecy, has emerged blinking, into the harsh spotlight of reality. It is waning in the face of her parents' disappointment that has torn through her since she told them the night before. Has she thought this through? she wonders now. Can she really do this?

Her chest is prickly with heat, so she undoes the buttons on her jacket. She thinks of Riaz. She thinks of the disappointment on his face and how wretched it made her feel. She felt scalded by her own guilt, but who was he to make such demands on her? He had been her staunchest supporter during her other battles with her parents – when she had revealed that she had selected Imperial, instead of Cardiff on her UCAS form and then when she had asked her father for the hefty deposit required for the BA training scheme. Unlike Sabrina's indignant demands which had always lacked credibility before her parents, Riaz's gentle appeals on Nasrin's behalf had always worked their charm. But he had withheld them this weekend when she had needed him most.

In the cockpit, Nasrin checks the weather reports and fuel guage again and begins her preparations. She thinks of Amma crying. 'Don't do this, Naju, don't do this re futh, it will be the death of me. It is not right. Itha tik nai! Think what people will say. You love Desh, you love your Neel Bari – do you think they will ever accept you if you marry a kafir? Will you cut your ties with that place and its people to be with just him?' Nasrin grabs a bottle of water and guzzles half of it in one go. Her mother's life has been guided by this one dogma: *What Will People Say?* She has grown up with this fear of her mother's, as though there is a world of spectators at the periphery of their lives that follow and judge their every move. Nasrin has never been sure who these spectators are and why their judgements are so absolute, but she is painfully aware of the power their disapproval exerts on her mother.

At Captain Townsend's request, Nasrin goes out to brief the cabin crew. Throughout these tasks she is distracted by her earlier conversation with her parents. As has been her habit since her very first flight, she had called her parents from the Operations Centre before she boarded. Each ring had wrenched her heart into her throat like a mad jack in the box. When finally, her father answered, her greeting was breathless.

'We're about to board, Abba.'

'Okay. Allah'r hawla,' he had replied, adhering to the customary greeting, but today his voice was so low that she barely heard him. She listened as he called her mother to the phone and hated the long moments of uncertainty before her mother picked up.

'We're about to board, Amma,' she had said.

Her mother had sighed before giving her the familiar reply, 'Accha. Be safe. Allah'r hawla.'

But the memory of her voice and the audible sigh still saps Nasrin's energy, and as she returns to the cockpit, her legs feel as though they are wading through water. Henri and Captain Townsend are in their seats, and she buckles herself into her own seat as the cockpit door is closed behind her.

It is only when they are preparing to taxi down the runway, and Nasrin picks up her phone to switch it off, that she sees the text from Riaz.

'Naz, are you sure about this?'

She is so angry that she wants to throw the phone on the floor and stamp on it. Who was Riaz to ask her such questions?

Suddenly, all the emotions she has held at bay thunder open within her. As the plane throttles down the runway and sprints into the air, dread flattens itself against her just as the gravity pushes her back against her seat.

Marrying Richard is freedom. It is release, from the brown in her life. Since university, Nasrin had been living a dual life; white in London, brown in Wales. By picking Richard, she is confirming her allegiance to a stable identity.

But she thinks of her mother's words, how she will be exiled from her community, and no longer welcome in Desh. She will miss the sight of those turquoise tiles every summer, the delicious tart of the first kala jams, the call for prayer soaring over the bamboo forest, the sounds of crickets lulling her to sleep ... how will she make up for losing all of this? How will she fill the gap it will leave behind?

She stares out at the layered night, and the swathes of grey cloud. The familiar vista that usually fills her with awe constricts her tonight.

'Ladies and gentlemen, we have now reached our cruising altitude of thirty-three thousand feet. I'll go ahead and turn off the seat belt sign ...' She hears Captain Townsend say, and she checks the autopilot settings and gives him the thumbs up.

As the flight wears on, her restlessness increases. 'Will he convert?' her parents had asked, and she couldn't tell them that Richard did not believe in any God, much less believe in The One. 'You're going to give up your parents, your upbringing, even God, Naz, is he worth it?' Riaz had asked. She was unable to respond that when she watches Richard's boyish face light up, she feels a surge of joy within herself. When he is proud of being an Aussie who has successfully infiltrated the old boys' network at his English law firm she feels the pride warm her own chest as though these achievements are hers. She wants this synchronised existence. The friendships and hook-ups from university have not lasted into this phase of her nomadic lifestyle, and Richard, along with her family, is her only constant. But unlike her family, there is a sense of freedom in her relationship with Richard. He is both foreign to her and as foreign as her. In their relationship, Nasrin thinks that she has finally glimpsed an acceptable place to call home.

And yet, as the flight draws near to its destination, she feels farther from her own journey's end than when she boarded the plane. She thinks again of all that she will lose, and distress gnaws at her. There is a sudden tingling in her shoulders and Nasrin stretches her neck this way and that.

Henri and the Captain are discussing the approach sequence, but Nasrin hears the exchange as if from beneath a crashing wave.

The tingling in her shoulders is an old but familiar sensation. Its unyielding force brings with it a deafening buzz that crescendos down her arms and her torso. Nasrin sits up. *It cannot be!* she whispers to herself, as though this will stop it from being. *It cannot be!*

But even as she thinks this, she feels herself jerk. It has been so many years since her last seizure that she feels she could laugh. How it has fooled her! How stupid she has been for thinking it gone! Then she feels control draining out of her. Her body is a puppet, played by a cruel puppeteer, crashing her about on the apparatus around her.

'Nasrin, what's wrong? Captain!'

'Jesus, she's fallen on the control column, Henri, move her!'

'I'll get the crew!'

'Speedbird,' the radio crackles, 'BA flight 109, do you copy? Why are you descending?'

And somewhere in that exchange, Nasrin loses herself.

* * *

A week later, Nasrin sits up in bed. Her T-shirt is soaked with sweat and her throat is parched. She has woken every morning in this way since that terrible flight, with the sun, already high, stubbornly pushing through the gap in the curtains. She hears her mother downstairs in the kitchen, moving about her tasks, singing a melancholy nasheed. The one about following the prophet (pbuh) to heaven. Read namaz. Do your fasts. Give Zakath. And then follow the faithful to heaven. Nasrin closes her eyes and lets the familiar melody bounce off her. Something about the simplicity of it soothes her soul. She wishes she believed in it.

'Naju,' her father calls as he comes up the stairs. 'It's after midday, re futh, come and have lunch with us.'

She refuses to engage, as she has done the last several days. He opens the curtains and moves the duvet gently away from her face.

'Come, come,' he says as he pulls on her arm gently. 'Life is long. There are many mistakes we will have to make before we can rest.' He is so sure of this that Nasrin lets him guide her down the stairs, lets her mother place a plate in front of her. They talk over her, enticing her to believe that nothing has changed. They talk of Sabrina's first Thanksgiving in New York, the fact that she would like the family there with her. They talk of Afroz's impending nuptials and that they should book their flights. Lindsay arrives, smelling of marmalade, and goes into the garden to call over the fence to Riaz and Mustafa.

'I've brought homemade amber pudding,' she hollers and comes back inside to slice it. Nasrin eyes the pudding; she is aware of the effort they are all making for her, but she is deep inside a cave of her own mortification, and their efforts are in vain. Snippets of the interview with BA Human Resources whittle away at her.

'In the screening report, you specifically wrote Not Applicable against history of seizures, Ms Islam.'

Yes, she had.

'But at the time, you were aware that you'd had approximately twelve epileptic seizures from the age of seven to the age of thirteen.'

Yes, she had been.

She lacked the words to explain why she had lied: how the emotionally draining years of study and struggle against her parents' expectations pressed in on her as her fingers quivered over the questions on her medical history. These questions had been the only barrier between her and the life she wanted for herself, of airports, planes and passport controls. *This is not lying,* she had told herself: *I haven't had a seizure in almost a decade, it's gone for good now.*

'Naz,' Lindsay says, 'aren't you going to try some? You love my amber pudding.'

'She has eaten hardly anything in the last week,' Nasrin's mother says. 'I am watching my child shrink in front of my eyes.'

'You children make mountains out of molehills,' her father says in English, a language he rarely uses with his daughters except in moments of indulgence.

'Eh, Naju!' Mustafa places his hand on her head. 'This is nothing. When it is over, you will laugh, hai? The English and their bureaucracy!'

'The English and their silly bureaucracy,' Lindsay agrees.

Nasrin bursts into tears.

They are all silent as her sobs fill the room. The incongruousness of the cloying smell of marmalade against the smell of her mother's fish curry seems somehow to accentuate everyone's disquiet. They sit still for long minutes, afraid to look at each other, even at Nasrin.

Then, suddenly Riaz speaks: 'Richard's been calling you, hasn't he?' Nasrin looks up at him in surprise. 'Have you called him back? Think how worried he must be.' Riaz swallows hard, looks from her mother to her father, shakes his head at them encouragingly.

After a moment's silence, her father clears his throat. 'Oy, oy, call him. Tell him to come for lunch tomorrow.'

Mustafa claps his hands. 'Tik kotha. Bhabhi!' he says. 'Lunch!'

'Can't wait to meet him, man! Shame Sibby can't be here.' Nasrin stares at Riaz, and then looks down at her pudding. She looks up at her mother, who turns away.

'I don't have anything in the house to make for a good lunch,' Jahanara says, getting out of her chair. 'Riaz, when you do the cash-and-carry tomorrow, get me a mutton leg.'

'Oh, Fufu, I love your mutton roast!' Lindsay says.

Nasrin takes the forkful of pudding Mustafa smilingly holds out to her, and watches her parents exchange meaningful looks.

Later that afternoon, she follows Riaz and her father into the Peacock, and begins to lay out the salmon-coloured tablecloths. She sets the tables, slipping the silverware into place, polishing the glasses and folding the napkins into peacocks. It is only four o'clock, but the wintry night is beginning to fall. The passing headlights give temporary respite. Nasrin moves to the bar and begins to clean the ashtrays, stacking them up next to a copy of the *Daily Mail*. In between cleaning, she flips the pages. Suddenly she stops dead.

BA First Officer jeopardises lives of 283 passengers by lying about epilepsy.

The ashtray she holds drops out of her hands and falls on top of the stack she has yet to clean. A cascade of ashtrays hurtles to the ground, but she is unable to tear her eyes away from the newspaper. She stands amid the debris of ash-smeared porcelain and reads and rereads the short article, reliving the pain of its quick condemnation. The pins and needles of her epilepsy tingle at her elbow. No more flying. It is a loss made all the heavier with shame, and it sinks heavily into her. She looks around, wide-eyed with panic, and realises that there is no way for her to escape any of this anymore.

Her trembling fingers undo the clasp of the chain she is wearing around her neck.

By the time Riaz finds her, cleaning the broken ashtrays, he immediately notices the yellow diamond that glints malevolently from her ring finger.

He silently untangles the hoover lead, and watches as Nasrin telephones Richard.

3

Just after 6 p.m. on the day of the Khatm, shortly before Nasrin found her sister's room vacant, Afroz sat in the middle of a room full of swaying women, all reciting verses from the Quran in feathery murmurs. She had been allotted Chapter 13, but her Quran Sharif stood open before her in its ornate rehal. Though she knew the verse by heart, she sat mutely. Her mind, too full to focus, was stuck in a painful loop of the night before.

It had been past midnight when Afroz had stepped out of the Peacock's kitchen into the calm night. The square was deserted and Afroz had turned her face up to the smooth indigo velvet of the sky, letting it soothe the adrenaline that still pumped through her from the night's exertions. She felt a surge of inexplicable happiness. She had never cooked like this – with such fanfare, to such acclaim – and the unexpected experience of it had been thrilling.

But as she approached her aunt's house, the forbidding darkness of its windows reminded her of the morning's argument with Sabrina and of spending the afternoon vacillating between her shock and her urge to flee back to Desh. Anxious about entering a house that unsurprisingly wanted to spit her out, Afroz sat for a while on the wall outside, watching the cars pass. A man locking up his café across the road waved at her and Afroz lifted her hand uncertainly. It occurred to her how unexpected this experience was; sitting outside in the middle of the night, on full display to the world, without any disapproving glares or blasts of car horns to disturb her solitude. How worlds apart her and her cousins' – sisters' – lives had been. Why had she been singled out as the one to miss out on this way of life where every action was not measured against the yardstick of honour and reputation, izzath and shomman? Why only her and not them?

She heard the Peacock's kitchen door open and bang shut, the shuffle of a plastic bag being dragged across the tarmac, and Lindsay came into view. Afroz watched as she bent over to pick up chicken bones from the ground.

'Which idiot leaves raw meat out for the bleeding foxes to find?' Lindsay asked her, and Afroz, surprised that she was noticed at all, was at a loss for words. 'You must be shattered. You're coming tomorrow too, right?'

Afroz nodded mutely and watched Lindsay heave the bag into the wheelie bin and stalk back to the kitchen. This time, the door was left open, and the sounds that escaped it reminded Afroz of all the Eid al Bakhrs of her childhood, when lungi-ed workmen would stir gigantic industrial saucepans with metre-long bamboo spatulas, and the smell of Eid beef curry lingered in the night air. She remembered the clamminess of Nasrin and Sabrina's arms against her own as they sat huddled together on the little footbridge, batting away mosquitos, their faces bathed in the amber glow of the gasoline lamp that the cooks used.

Cheered by this memory, Afroz jumped carefully off the wall, and walked into her aunt's house. Not wanting to disturb the sleeping household, she closed the door as softly as she could and groped her way up the stairs in the darkness. Suddenly, she heard a sharp zipping noise as she came to Sabrina's room. She stopped, gazing down at the cut of light at the bottom of the closed door. She reached out and knocked on Sabrina's door.

Without waiting for an answer, she opened it.

She wasn't sure what she would do once she saw Sabrina, except that she wanted to do something, share a word, or a smile, to show her awareness that she was the cause of all this distress, that she would never ask for more than they had already given her. She wanted Sabrina to know that she was fond of her. That Sabrina was important to her. And part of Afroz, the greedy, idiotic part of her, wanted Sabrina to return that affection. As children they had been friends one moment, and enemies the next, but they had always been bonded in some incomprehensible but tangible way. And she wanted Sabrina to acknowledge that bond – for Sabrina to say *yes, we are sisters!*

But her dreams had sped way ahead of her, and Afroz stood for a moment, blinking in the lamplight, trying to register what she saw. In front of her stood Sabrina in her coat, and a pair of pristine tan loafers. Her suitcase stood next to her, while behind her the open wardrobe revealed rows of shelves.

Empty shelves.

'Are you leaving?' Afroz asked, but even as she said the words, she understood that her question was a rhetorical one.

Sabrina wanted nothing more to do with her.

She looked at Sabrina and Sabrina looked back at her.

Neither said a word.

What more need Sabrina say, when she showed it so well in the way that she pushed past Afroz, dragging her suitcase down the hallway and stairs without so much as a glance back.

And now, seated in front of her open Quran Sharif, Afroz brooded on the cocktail of joy and pain that the night before had delivered to her. From the corner of her eye she saw a shadow on the stairs. Thinking it might be her aunt, she looked up in earnest only to see Nasrin bound down the stairs, two at a time, her brow lined in distress, her beautiful tresses unfurling from the loose bun at the nape of her neck. She had obviously just discovered Sabrina's disappearance for herself.

Why was it, Afroz wondered, that some women are given such beauty, such grace. And that this beauty and grace then deliver the world to their feet: a marriage of love, a beautiful child and home, and all the freedom one could ever want. Afroz raised her hand and touched the edge of her hijab.

For the first time, she wondered what her adult life might have been like if she had grown up in the Beacons like Sabrina and Nasrin, without this piece of cloth. She had worn a scarf since she had been a child, she couldn't remember her exact age – eleven or twelve – but she remembered the morning her veiled life began. It had been one of those cold winter mornings that Bangladeshis are never prepared for. She had walked to her Islamic studies, hugging her exercise book to her chest, trying to warm herself. But it hadn't worked. The teacher had noticed and called her to his desk. In low, even tones, he berated Afroz and reminded her of the importance of Islamic modesty. She felt the eyes of her classmates digging into the very core of her more than the sting of her teacher's words. Shame was being watched: shame was exposing yourself to voyeurs waiting to observe all the ways in which a woman could stumble into dishonour and ignominy.

She couldn't now remember the name of the teacher, even his face was a blur, but she remembered his words: shame, shoythan, sinful, repeated again and again.

And all because of the small protrusions of her chest, and the fact that the silhouette of her kameez was no longer smooth and flat, but offensively voluptuous.

When she reached home, still red-faced and mortified, Ma had been surprisingly sympathetic, showing her how to tie a thin muslin cloth around her head so that the edges trickled delicately over the chest.

'The trick is to hide the hair. There's no point if the hair shows.'
'Is hair sinful too, Ma?' Afroz had asked.
What she had really wanted to ask was about the sinfulness of

147

breasts. But those moments of camaraderie with Ma had been so rare that Afroz anxiously avoided any words that might bring back that other Ma, who was constantly on the brink of rage.

'So many things are sinful these days,' Ma had complained, her lips swimming in the harsh blood-orange of the betel juice from the paan she chewed. 'But see, you use your dupatta to cover both your hair and your breasts, so people can't shame you, like this teacher did today.'

As she stared at the Quran before her, Afroz realised that even though she had spent her life learning to keep shame at bay, it now overshadowed her: she was a bastard, born outside of a legitimate marriage, to parents who hadn't wanted to keep her. What bigger shame could there be when her entire existence was steeped in it?

It had only been three years since Baba had turned up at her house, unannounced, and hesitantly unravelled her childhood. She had not been shocked by what he told her – the news that she had been adopted seemed, in some way, the last piece in a jigsaw she had long ago started putting together.

There had been many signs over the years. Masoom had never raised his hand to her, but it was different with her mother. Afroz's childhood had been dominated by the bamboo cane that Amina kept behind the kitchen door: it was used to administer punishments ranging from whippings that merely stung to beatings that drew blood.

Her mother's hand reaching out to touch her, in any capacity, had always made Afroz's heart palpitate in fear. Amina could be whacking her with the rod of the vacuum cleaner or plaiting her hair for school, but it would make Afroz sit up rod-straight, attentive to any sign of the injury that may come her way.

During Ramadan, that month of sacrifice and devotion, Amina's bad temper, propelled by thirst and hunger, flared at the slightest provocation. Afroz helped her mother in the kitchen, kneading her devotion into the pale-yellow dough peppered with black nigella seeds and rolling out perfect moons to be filled with fried lamb. Then Amina would pack the samosas into foil trays for Masoom to take for Iftar at the mosque. With empty stomach and paan-less mouth, Amina's temper boiled like the hot oil in the fryer.

The day it happened, Afroz had forgotten to take off the pretty gold sandals that Jahanara had gifted her and they were covered with a fine layer of flour. Fufu lavished her with gifts on every visit, toys and clothes she had also bought for her daughters throughout the year. But this year, despite the identical gifts, Afroz had been surprised by the growing gulf between her cousins' world and her own. Far from donning the hijab as she had, Sibby and Naju now wore their hair short, their nails coloured and long, their clothes figure-hugging and low-cut, inflaming Ma's ire. 'If I see you taking the ways of these *noshto,* ruined cousins of yours – you'll see!' Ma reminded her every day. Afroz envied the liberated worlds of her cousins and felt increasingly constricted by the complex collective social structures that gave her parents, neighbours, extended family and teachers control of how she lived her life. She had watched in awe as her assertive cousins challenged everything – why should they not go for a run outside wearing shorts? Why should they lower their voices when their uncle entertained male friends in the house? Afroz herself was permitted to share their liberties occasionally: dancing with them into the wee hours at a family wedding and accompanying her cousins on a trip to Fakir Lalon Shah's Mazaar in Kustia with only Fufa as chaperone instead of the usual contingent of overbearing elders. But otherwise, her cousins' freedoms remained firmly out of reach.

Afroz was so caught up in these memories that she produced just over fifty moon-shaped pancakes that day. And, unthinking, she had piled them on top of each other into neat towers.

It wasn't until her mother came and stood before the tower that Afroz realised her mistake. The icy clamp of dread closed over her, making her tremble in spite of the heat. She watched Amina try to peel the top pancake off the one below. She couldn't. All the pancakes were stuck to each other, useless, wasted. Afroz had forgotten to put sheets of baking paper between them. She had wasted the last hour and they were never going to make samosas in time for Iftar.

Her mother brought her hands down upon Afroz's head in a storm of slaps. In her own hands, Afroz held the remainder of the dough, squidgy and sticky, and in the onslaught, she lost her balance and toppled the bowl of fried lamb onto the floor. Samosas and slaps, samosas and slaps, she thought to herself. Like a mantra in her head. Her arms tried to act as a shield, but they were thrust away. She emitted a low moan, but Amina, whose hands had begun to tire, took renewed offence. She turned around looking for something to use, a stick or a wooden spoon. She picked up the thing that was nearest to hand: the draining spoon in the hot fryer where she was frying the daler bola. Afroz shrieked, and her shriek came from a place outside of her, and her cheek, where the spoon was thwacking, felt uncomfortable, and when she reached up to scratch it the skin came away in her hand.

'How could you!' her father had cried. 'How could you do such a thing, Amina?' And her mother had cried too, massaged Afroz's hands with remorse. 'How could you do this to a child? Any child? But you'd never have done such a thing if she'd been—'

Afroz wished that she could hear those last words in the whispered ranting her father made at his wife over his daughter's bandaged face. He stroked her hair, and as young as she was, Afroz had known deep inside her what those unspoken words were.

And then, just three years ago, months after Ma had passed away from deep vein thrombosis, her father, Mohammad Bilal Khan, commonly known as Masoom, had finally confirmed it.

She had been adopted.

She had not known from whom, and at that moment, it had not mattered. At that moment, what had mattered was that she was not really her Baba's. Not really her Ma's. She was still Afroz but it no longer meant what it had once meant.

Masoom had broken her reverie by clutching her arm and she had gazed at him, an old man now, with a silvering beard trimmed to the religiously instructed four inches, his beloved Fulton umbrella across his knees, and was overwhelmed with gratitude. All the kindnesses he had lavished on her; from expensive chanderi silk kameezes to the bad-for-her-tummy sweet tamarind chutneys and the hours he had spent reviewing her homework with the assiduous patience of a saint – suddenly she saw that these indulgences were not acts of self-gratification by a parent to his offspring, but a generosity of spirit that was so much more praiseworthy. She had understood too why he had held himself slightly aloof throughout her childhood, had not fully owned his fatherhood, holding it at a distance as though she were a borrowed possession, soon to be returned.

'But Baba, who are they?' she had asked him, pleaded with him, for where else would she ever discover the secret to who she was? It had been almost eight months since Ma had passed away, taking with her all that she knew. Afroz saw her father's face clamp shut. 'Who were my parents?' she had pleaded. 'Are they alive?'

But Baba had shaken his head. 'I have been a good parent to you, haven't I?' he asked her, his voice thick with emotion.

'But can't I know who they are?' Her voice rose, but she couldn't control it. 'Then why did you tell me?'

'Because,' he had said, looking around the room anxiously, as though the answer might be lurking somewhere. 'Because I thought you should know.'

'Know what?' Afroz asked, her voice shrill. 'Know that I'm not yours?'

Her father had pursed his lips and began to refold his umbrella. Afroz watched him, letting her anger lapse, for she knew her father. If he had chosen not to tell her, nothing she could do or say would make a difference.

'That is not …' Baba had said suddenly, clipping the umbrella folds back in place. 'I am your father, and you are my daughter. What I wanted you to know was that you have other parents too.'

And now, years later, she finally understood the full significance of his words. This was why Masoom had urged her to come for her uncle's funeral. Her *father's* funeral. Her father, who had kept Nasrin and Sabrina, and had given them a life Afroz had been denied. In that other life, her Ruksana might have lived. Taseen might have remained hers. Perhaps in a life such as the one her sisters lived, her own tresses might be flowing about her face, unhindered by this hijab.

'O-go, Afroz, haven't you started yet?'

Afroz looked up to find the woman sitting beside her pointing at her Quran. 'We have to finish before four! How will you manage?' She adjusted her seated position. 'Shall I take half of the verse for you?'

'Na. I can do it – I know it by heart.' Afroz closed the Quran Sharif, and clutched it to her chest as she began to recite Surah 13 from memory. 'Alif, laam, meem, ra,' and slowly, she too became one of the softly swaying figures, moving side to side with the cadence of the verse. But the Quran still clutched tight at her chest was soon damp from her tears. She had no gripe with God – no, her resentment was towards a man who was no longer here to answer her questions.

For the last two days she had alternated between feeling nothing and feeling bursts of rage at the injustice meted out to her: but throughout she had devoutly, dutifully prayed for his soul. She had beseeched Allah to forgive him. He had tried, in the end, to give her back what was hers. Her sisters. Her family. This restaurant. But his efforts had been in vain. Having glimpsed Sabrina's hatred and disgust, Afroz realised that there were some things that simply could not be undone. The restaurant was poor recompense for what Afroz needed, which was a sense of belonging. And belonging required knowledge of who she really was, and why she had been cast off.

Afroz stopped reciting.

It occurred to her that that locked bedroom door may be keeping her from that which she needed to know.

She stood and began to tread carefully through the swaying bodies, her lips continuing to recite Chapter 13. She came to the foot of the stairs and looked up at her aunt's bedroom door.

There at the top of the stairs was Nasrin, ramming her entire body against her mother's door. Afroz fell silent and watched Nasrin, her face contorted in pain as the force of her body slammed again and again into the door. Then suddenly her sister was falling down the stairs, her body a lifeless rag doll, her eyes wide open as she made her descent and Afroz stumbled forward, hands held out.

'Fufu!' Afroz screamed above the clamour of voices behind her, the 'Y'Allahs' and the 'Thowwas thoghphirs'. 'Fufu!' she shouted as loud as she could, crouching over her sister, trying to protect Nasrin's head from the violent jerking of her body. 'Fufu, Naju's having a fit! Please!'

The door opened.

Without saying a word, her aunt flew down the stairs, and crouched over her daughter. She took Nasrin's hand and curled the hyperextended fingers around her thumb, holding it with her other hand for reinforcement.

'Shall I call an ambulance?' Afroz whispered, but her Fufu shook her head. She was still in the same pale blue saree from two days before, her hair matted against her head like a stiff cap. Her lips moved as she read an inaudible prayer and blew it on Nasrin's head.

'Please go back and continue your recitals,' Afroz told the guests, her voice shaking, 'Please!' They began to return to their places, straining their heads towards Nasrin even as they took their seats.

Nasrin was bleeding from a cut at her elbow, and her eyes rolled so far back that Afroz was afraid they would pop out of their sockets. A little head burrowed into her side, and Afroz took her nephew onto her lap, and shielded his eyes with her palm. A sudden memory forced its way in as she performed this simple act of protection. She recalled how, when they had been younger, Shamsur had similarly clamped his hands over Sabrina's eyes and instructed Afroz to look away, as he tried to calm his daughter's body. This man she had grown up believing was her uncle.

The vibrating in her pocket cut through her thoughts.

'Ji, it's me.'

'I was worried, Afi! I haven't heard from you since yesterday morning. You're not answering your phone. Ma has been worried sick! I called the landline before and one of your cousins said you were out! Where were you out? Alone?'

Afroz closed her eyes. 'Now is not a good time,' she said.

'What?'

'It's just that Naju has had a seizure, I'm here with her.'

'Oh, bucchi.' He was silent for a moment. 'Will she be all right?'

'Yes, she's had them since she was a child. She'll be all right, I think. Shall I call you in a few hours?'

'It's already late here,' he said, but then reconsidered. 'Call me on my mobile.'

'Before you go,' she squeezed the words out with immense effort, 'tell Ma not to worry. I am going to change my ticket and fly back early.'

Leaving, she decided as she swept Nasrin's hair back from her damp face, was the only way to make amends for the pain she had caused, the suffering that she was still causing.

4

As she snuck away, Sabrina knew she was cruel to leave Afroz restless and uneasy in the knowledge that there would be no peace between them. And she knew too, that it made no sense to blame Afroz for her father's betrayal, or her mother's abandonment of them, or Nasrin's increasing closeness to her new-found sister – but, unable to free herself from the ensuing rage and pain, she found that blaming Afroz was the only sense anything made, along with departing. So, she held fast to her anger and left the Beacons trusting that New York would deliver her from all the complications of the Islam family and return her to a world of order.

Yet here she was, and neither the glorious morning sky nor the shimmering Hudson would help her. Fragments of the memories she had tried to leave behind in the Beacons had escaped with her, and now clung to the avenues and the sidewalks, to the facades of the townhouses that she passed on the Upper West. The memory of Afroz's bewildered expression, which had given Sabrina a kick of satisfaction at the time, now became a sort of torture. Lurching about in the cab as it swerved through traffic, Sabrina tried to avoid thinking of her father, but the harder she tried, the more easily she pictured his gentle smile. Her erstwhile bondhu. Defender of his clan. Pretender to great virtue. Her fallen hero.

By early afternoon, she was dog-tired and crept into bed, her hair still wet from her shower. She imagined she could hear the faint echo of the Quran recitations, picturing the mourners in their uniform of white chadors, swaying to the murmured verses in her mother's living room, and she suppressed a shudder of regret.

She woke with a start to the phone ringing loudly. It was Nasrin, and as soon as she answered the call, her sister's accusations started to fly. How could she abandon them on the eve of their father's third-day prayers? As Nasrin spoke, Sabrina replayed the memory of her sister with Afroz at the Peacock the night before, acting like they were teenagers again, always the best of friends, making Sabrina feel like a third wheel. After she hung up, Sabrina bit the pillow with rage, and wiped at her wet cheeks.

In the days that followed, Sabrina found no relief. News of her sister's seizure conveyed by her newly emerged, furious mother only made her feel worse.

'How could you just leave like that?' her mother vented. 'Not to even stay for your father's third-day prayers – after all he has done for you, how much he has loved you! How we have been cursed with such ungrateful children! Hun re ni? Are you listening? Thor kuno math nai?'

Sabrina, unable to convey the chaos of pain and anger that engulfed her, found it easier to simply hang up. But the fact that her sister had had yet another seizure – one that had required stitches in a hospital – only added a layer of anxiety to the cloud of emotion that overshadowed her.

And of course, Abba would not call her to sift through and organise her emotions for her and demand that she put aside her anger. She would now have to do without his counselling, which had always sought out the better side of her nature. She would have to do without his advocacy in making that better side of her nature more visible to the world. Abba who had been her Kiraman Katibin, keeping tally of her good deeds and misdeeds, and who had cared enough to read them back to her. His death hadn't made sense to her in the Beacons where Afroz's presence sullied it, but here in New York, she felt the loss of him with harrowing clarity.

That first week, Sabrina felt cut off from everything, as though she had woken from a deep sleep and was struggling to shake off the torpor. By day, she made her way to work as though she were wading through water, but at night, she struggled to sleep, unable to grasp the things that tortured her. Even Ashok, who was generally able to improve her mood, grew exasperated with her.

'You don't seem like you're in the mood to hang out today,' he muttered. It was a warm day, and they had opened the window. Broadway traffic roared its way uptown. 'If you want to take a rain-check, then just say so.'

She took a cigarette from her drawer and gazed out of the window. 'What part of "my father passed away" did you not understand?' she asked.

'You didn't seem that close,' he said.

She turned to glare at him. 'I suppose you are an expert on family closeness?'

'Chill, Sab. It wasn't an attack; it was an observation. You're always complaining about how different your folks are from you, how religious and all.'

She watched him sink back into the bed. *When did we become so cruel to one another?* she wanted to ask him. He met her gaze and seemed to understand.

'Sorry,' he muttered. 'That's not even relevant … I don't even know why …' he trailed off, but she remained silent.

He lay down next to her and kissed her shoulder. 'Sorry,' he said again.

She ignored him, staring out of the window. She wondered what Afroz would make of this. A married man. This nakedness. These soiled sheets.

'Sab? Come on, I said I was sorry.'

She nodded. 'I'm just stressed at the moment. Work.'

'So, tell me? Maybe I can help.'

'It's this Altieri deal—'

'I remember that one – they changed the ratings last minute.'

Sabrina blinked at him, surprise flooding through her. She sat up. 'You were on that deal?' she asked him.

'So were you,' he said without missing a beat.

'No. I looked after it for a day while you guys were away. But, you *knew* the ratings had moved?'

'No …'

'You *just* said!'

'Well, it wasn't my problem, I left the team before it closed.'

'No, I specifically remember you left a few weeks later, because we celebrated up in the Catskills!' She shook her head in disbelief. 'It closed before you left! It was yours! AND you knew!'

'Sab.'

She stared at the top of his head, a realisation suddenly making her stand up. The tip of her cigarette caught on his shoulder and he yelped.

'What the fuck!'

'All along,' she said, the answer dawning on her, 'it was you! Compliance has been investigating Ralph for signing off on it knowing it got downgraded – but all along it was you.'

'Sabrina. He did know, and he—'

'Your own father-in-law!'

'Well, sweetheart, you're the one that emailed Compliance.'

'Because he was about to crucify *me* for it! I wouldn't have needed to if you had come clean in the first place!'

He flashed her an angry look, and then relented, taking the cigarette from her. 'Look, he did know, okay? So did I. It was just a mistake and he's about to retire anyway. Why are you so worked up? Are you worried about the promotion? Because you know I won't let this affect you.'

'As if,' she said, but the familiar feeling stirred within Sabrina and she took relief in its promise to divert her from Abba and Afroz. Now that the promotion had been dangled before her, Sabrina realised how desperately she wanted to make MD. The lunch invitation from Monty's secretary had mysteriously disappeared from her inbox soon after she had emailed Compliance from the Beacons alleging that Ralph had known about the downgrade before he had signed off and asked her to close the deal.

'You'll get the lunch invite,' Ashok said, reading her mind, 'once this has blown over.'

'But you *lied*, Ash,' she said, peering down at him. 'You know how it is in this industry – you told me yourself – any little mistake can be securities fraud.'

'Sab, what the fuck. It was just an oversight – the damn trade was closing the next day – we knew the downgrades were possible, but nothing was certain—'

'You knew the downgrades were *likely*,' she interrupted, 'which means you should have disclosed it to the client before the deal closed.'

He shook his head. 'I promise, I won't let any of this touch you.'

'It doesn't touch me because I'm not involved,' she told him, taking a step away. 'Don't make out you'll do anything for me.'

'We don't do anything for each other, remember? That's what we're about.'

After he left, Sabrina cleaned the apartment. Even though the surfaces had been polished and floors mopped by the cleaner the day before, Sabrina felt that there was a grittiness in the air she breathed and on the surface of all the objects she touched. Ashok's admission that he knew about the downgrade inflamed her. His comment about her closeness to her father grated on her. Who was he to pass judgement on her relationship with her father?

But avoiding Ashok over the next few days only made her lonelier. The lack of contact from her mother and from Nasrin made her feel abandoned – she checked her phone for an email or a text or a missed call and grew increasingly bereft as none arrived. Instead she sought out old friends and drinking buddies and over the next week, alcohol, loud music and the fatigue she found on a dance floor alleviated the solitariness and the silence of her apartment with its phantom layers of filth. On her way home from one of these clubbing nights she even called Daniel. She was not surprised when he did not answer.

It took the Flash Crash to plunge her back into her life.

September 10th started like any other day. Sabrina gazed at her calendar: it was full of pointless, soul-destroyingly dull meetings. Each morning she opened her calendar to find them encroaching on the white space, the boxes often overlapping each other so that she was always supposed to be at the next meeting before she had finished the one she was in.

September 10th looked like it was going to be one of those days.

'Boss?'

She turned to find Benjamin standing behind her. Shoeless.

'That was Dylan on the phone asking if we can dial into a call with the Goldstein team right now?'

'It's not even eight yet!' she yelped. She yanked her hair into a band, swallowed a Xenadrine Plus to give her a boost, and then slipped her headphones over her ears. She waved Benjamin back to his desk.

The conference had already begun, and she listened quietly, scribbling notes, getting a sense of the conversation until she was ready to announce herself with a comment or two. Fanni's voice monopolised the line for some minutes, as others tried to interject and were blithely ignored. Sabrina could see the back of Fanni's head three rows ahead of her, her blonde bob shimmying beneath the fluorescent lights.

'... and it's imperative, absolutely imperative, that we don't do that!' Fanni hollered. 'Just think about how it looks for a second, think about how it looks to the client. I mean, I don't even know what Jeff told them, and I'm on the line with the guy, trying to second guess—'

'Wait a minute—' Jeff interrupted.

'Please don't interrupt me while I'm talking.'

'I'm not—' Jeff struggled to find his words. 'I just, if a client calls me, I mean sure he's your client, but he's the firm's client, right?'

'He's my fucking client, not the firm's, I brought him in, so you don't get to—'

'Fanni, look.' Phillipe, the MD in Jeff's team, sounded the death knell. 'Why don't you and Jeff catch up, after this call? We can't tell the client not to call other people on the team, we just need to make sure everyone's communicating with each other.'

Fanni made an indecipherable comment. Sabrina watched as, three rows in front of her, Fanni's hand rose deliberately upwards, her middle finger stabbing up towards where Phillipe and Jeff sat, a floor up. Something glinted on Fanni's fingers, and Sabrina sat up in her seat to get a better look.

'Actually, Fanni,' Sabrina said softly, adjusting her headphones, 'I'm sorry, everyone, I just joined, but if you're talking about Mo Goldstein, well, he left Benjamin a message to call him back on Friday too. Right, Ben? It looks like he's calling everyone but Fanni …' She paused. 'Happy for Benjamin to get involved, I mean he's busy on other stuff for me, but he can squeeze it in. Thing is though, I think the onus is on Fanni to let us know what she's doing. You know, so we're all prepared? As a team?'

There was a moment's silence.

Then, a few rows ahead, Fanni twisted around, and mouthed *Fuck you* at Sabrina, before turning back.

Sabrina looked over to her left and grinned at Benjamin, who sat shaking his head.

'Right,' Phillipe said, 'so I think we can move on. Fanni? You're going to sit down with Jeff and Benjamin, maybe draft a memo or something to get the rest of us up to speed?'

'Memo!' Fanni exclaimed, and Sabrina had to cover her mouthpiece to muffle her laughter.

Throughout the remainder of the call, Sabrina thought about the ring on Fanni's finger, the way the diamond slid about, slightly loose, so that Fanni had to keep readjusting it. How does it happen, Sabrina wondered, that these undesirable, scarily insufferable women find men who want to spend their lives with them?

At lunch, she retreated to the bathroom where she examined her own bare fingers as they grew pale under the running water. She felt something settle within her; something hard like that rock of Fanni's: brilliant and sharp. The fact that she felt this sting of envy surprised Sabrina. For the last several years, her mother had frequently raised the question of marriage, and Sabrina had taken refuge in her work or had sought out her father or sister to placate her mother, for marriage was not in her game plan. So why should it bother her that Fanni had found someone?

When she returned to her desk, she pulled up Daniel's number on her cell phone and stared at it, tapping the screen with her nail. She wanted to see him, but at the same time, she wondered if there was a place for Daniel in this emotionally convoluted life of hers. Was it Daniel she missed, or the life she had when he had happened to be in it? She put her phone back in her bag.

'Boss?' She looked up to see Benjamin staring at her, his eyes wide and round. 'Have you seen what's happening to your Bitcoin?'

'What?' She swivelled around, switching to her Bloomberg screen. They both stared at it for a long moment. 'Eight thousand points? What the fuck!'

She stood up, her heart thudding in her chest. Bitcoin was one of the most important digital currencies her team worked with.

'Fanni,' she called, suddenly noticing the noise on the floor, the shouts of shock and outrage that vied for attention. 'Fanni!' she yelled louder. 'What's going on with the US stock market?'

She watched as Fanni checked on her screen. Fanni stood and walked briskly over to her.

'Fuck that. Fuck it.'

Sabrina thumped Jeff's extension into her phone. 'Hey, Jeff, since when does the market fall nine hundred points? Nine hundred fucking points?'

It took thirty-six minutes of nail-biting anxiety, a storm of cursing and stamping and slamming of pens and notebooks, and phone calls to other banks, and management appearing from the shadows sagely nodding as the numbers fell – until the stocks started to rebound.

But Sabrina rode those minutes like she was on a rollercoaster, and when it came to a stop, it delivered her back to the platform of her former life, leaving her shaky but revitalised.

The Flash Crash returned all her senses to her and suddenly it was as though Sabrina could smell again, see again and feel again. She rejoined her Wall Street brethren as they quickened their pace through the last sprint to Bonus-season. She stayed in the office until midnight, and when the markets closed, unable to wind down, she found herself at the gym, working off the adrenaline with an hour on the elliptical trainer.

When she finally reached home, the loneliness that she had kept at bay all day would threaten to draw her in and her thoughts invariably returned to the Beacons. She wondered what her mother and sister were doing, imagining the two of them laughing at something Afroz had said, all of them wedged on the living room sofa, drinking tea and eating handesh without her. She found herself wishing she was standing at the bar in the Peacock, breathing in the familiar smell of spilt beer and tandoor as the music of her father's sitar compilation poured in around her. The Peacock was a manifestation of her girlhood and her best memories of her father. The thought of growing old without it made her feel like she was mourning yet another death. She couldn't give it up without a fight. It was this thought that made her dial Humayun's number.

'Assalamualaikum, Sabrina.' Sabrina could hear the surprise in his voice.

'Assalam, Humayun Bhai.'

'You call from New York?'

'Yes.'

'Oye. Everything is okay?'

'Yes, yes, sorry, Humayun Bhai.' She sat down on her sofa. 'I wanted to speak to you about the Peacock. Afroz won't listen to me. But I want to make you an offer.'

5

After Jahanara's emergence the women were shy and awkward with one another, trying to accommodate their new relationships while also grappling with the voids left by Shamsur and Sabrina. Each morning Jahanara awoke with her husband's death dawning on her anew. It took great effort to shuffle out of bed and down the stairs. She sat silently at the kitchen table as Afroz took sugar and vermicelli from the cupboard, insisting on cooking a lavish shemai breakfast. Beside her, Nasrin begged Elias to finish his cereal in a dramatically hushed voice. It was as though they were afraid she would lock herself in her room again.

They did not understand that her bedroom was her place of refuge where she had sought safety from the demons that prowled the hallway. Demons who tormented her about the loss of izzath and shomman and who would strip her of honour should she step outside. Crouching on her janamaz, she had clutched the letter containing her husband's last words to her. Each reading of it bought him back for an instant – his moon-shaped face with its perpetual childlike quality, the cold delight of his toes seeking hers under the duvet on a winter's night. Then she thought of Afroz and grew afraid again of the demons hissing outside her door and she threw herself on her janamaz, whimpering and begging for Allah's mercy. This torment continued for three long days until Naju, always Naju, reached for her and pulled her free of her delusions.

At first, she spoke only when spoken to, her voice barely more than a murmur. She was afraid of the questions forming on the girls' faces, could not bear to speak of the will and its contents. But she saw how they held back their questions and navigated carefully through their interactions with her as though she were a delicate, breakable thing, and for their sake, she willed herself to reclaim her home. She began with the garden, cleaning the debris of cigarettes and cans that had accumulated in her absence, and then moved on to the kitchen. She restocked her freezer with kobabs and chicken curry and cleaned the tiles and work surfaces until they shone. These activities weaned her back into the world, and the relief on the girls' faces was all too apparent.

Only her youngest eluded her. So headstrong, so wilful; Sabrina had always been difficult to control. When Sabrina was a child, Jahanara had indulged these traits as characteristics which the baby of the family would eventually outgrow. But she had been wrong and Jahanara continually struggled with her daughter's resistance to everything Islamic and Bengali, including and especially her own mother. Where Nasrin had accepted the codes of modesty and deference that Jahanara had tried to inculcate in them, Sabrina flagrantly discarded such expectations with feisty rebelliousness. 'Amma, that's just so backward,' was her constant refrain, or 'Amma, for goodness sake, please just get with the times!'

'Afa,' Masoom once laughed, 'that sharp tongue of hers, it reminds me of that younger you! That know-it-all paaka-ness!' and this had only served to exacerbate Jahanara's disquiet. It was Shamsur that Sabrina had deferred to, and so over the years, it had been easier to let him handle her. But now Sabrina would have to make do with the less beloved parent who embodied the opposite of all that was modern and sophisticated.

There were moments when things felt as they had before. In the evenings after Maghrib, Jahanara would come into the living room to find Naju and Afroz lying on their stomachs in front of the TV, giggling as her grandson rolled from one to the other, and in those small moments, she could believe that nothing had changed.

Except that it had.

By mid-September, the last vestiges of summer were disappearing, and the village was invigorated by the changing of the season. In the first few hours of morning, the air held promising notes of autumn and the high-pitched chirrups of redwings could be heard in the trees. But inside the Peacock, business was sluggish, and time seemed at a standstill. The smattering of tourists cycling through the square were uninterested and the regulars stayed away, only pausing as they passed by, to gaze in curiosity at the state of things inside.

'All right, Steve?' Riaz called out to one of them.

The man waved, grinning sheepishly.

'Only a bit of illegitimacy,' Riaz shouted. 'No need to stay away. Pass it on, we're open for business.'

'You'd think that all this palaver about Afroz would be good for business,' Lindsay muttered. 'Rob from the cash-and-carry asked me if the old Boss had a second wife back home.'

'This *is* his home,' Riaz replied, scowling. 'Bloody idiots, seriously.'

'It's over, man,' Junaid said, exhaling smoke through his nostrils. 'The old Boss *was* the Peacock. He's dead, it's dead. Start looking now.' He turned to Riaz. 'This is when you go back to uni, get that damn degree.'

'I never got into uni.'

'Get in now. Right, Lins?' Junaid reached out to tug at Riaz's jacket. 'You see the way you-know-who was checking him out day of the funeral? Problems in paradise, man, I'm telling you, now's the time.'

'J, shut up,' Lindsay said, watching Riaz from the corner of her eye.

'What's that book you're always going on about?' Junaid continued. 'Ha? Do the whole Pippy thing and win Stella, right!'

'How is it you're such a prat?' Lindsay asked, huddling into the wall against a sudden breeze.

'Pip doesn't win Estella,' observed Riaz.

'Obviously I don't spend my time reading Shakespeare,' Junaid said, leaning back against the wall.

Lindsay giggled, before nodding sagely. 'It is all a bit Shakespearean.'

'I say, we should all get out, before they kick us out.'

'I need my salary,' Riaz said gloomily, jingling the keys in his pocket.

'Yeah?' Lindsay asked, curious. 'Where does it all go with you? You haven't bought a round in ages!'

He shook his head, unable to answer.

They turned as the door of the Islam house opened, and the women spilled out: Nasrin holding Elias's hand, then Jahanara, stooped and shuffling, and Afroz. They watched Afroz as she paused to take in a lungful of air before turning to lock the door. Her salmon-coloured hijab shivered in the breeze like the tail of a kite. This was their new boss, wearing trainers with her multi-coloured shalwar kameez. Carrying handkerchiefs in her hand.

Riaz glanced at Lindsay and grinned. 'At least she's not wearing that big black tent thing she arrived in. We'd never live that down in this village.'

Lindsay shrugged. 'I actually like her. I like that she wears her stuff and doesn't care what we all think.'

'Riaz re,' Jahanara called out to him, 'if Mustafa calls again tell him I will call back later. Tell him not to worry. I will find him something back home.'

Riaz nodded. As he watched the trio of women guide Elias down the path, he wondered about the fate of the Peacock. Despite Shamsur's encouragement that Riaz aspire to more, the Peacock was all that he had known, all that he had ever wanted, and it had also been, at least until Shamsur passed, a place that wanted him. Recovering from his first heart attack, Shamsur had reminded Riaz to think about his future, that the curry industry was not what it had once been. 'I know you struggle re futh,' Shamsur had said, 'I know he has started his gambling again and you are sending your money home. I will help for now with a raise, but you must think of the long term. Go out into the world, be more, earn more – we can't think like farmers anymore, Riaz! This West is what do they call it? This 'knowledge intensive' huncho? – education is what you need to get on. In the end that will help your family more. Buccho?' Remembering this now, Riaz felt a lump in his throat. His own grief had been eclipsed by the sorrow of the women Shamsur had left behind, but it was no less intense. He alone could appreciate how different this man had been from others in his community – who had found spiritual solace outside of the rigid bounds of orthodoxy, who encouraged aspirations in boys like him when his own parents had none. He realised with an ache now that Shamsur was gone, there would be no raise. There would be no hand on his shoulder to steady him and prevent him from falling back into the darkness of his childhood poverty.

He thought of the lunch he had at his mother's when he had visited the week before on his day off.

'This fish has a funny smell to it, Amma,' he said, grimacing at the fish curry she placed before him.

'It's fine, just eat it!' she said testily. 'We can't afford to buy fresh fish every day, not like your Islams. We do what we can.' She sniffed, poured him a glass of water. 'Do you have it?'

Riaz handed his father the brown envelope stuffed with his month's wages. 'Why have they cut it again?'

'Who knows?' his father grumbled. 'They say they sent a letter asking for something or other, who knows?'

'Abba!' Riaz raised his voice. 'Respond then! When they send you a letter, bloody respond!'

His father glared at him. 'Am I a barrister? Am I to know what is written in these things?'

'Every few months they cut the benefits, and I can't bail you out every time.'

'What? We placed a stone in our stomach to feed you, and now you are turning away?'

Riaz had eaten the fish, along with his sister and his father, and it was to sit heavily in his gut for days to come. As she dropped him at the station, his sister had asked him for money.

'Am I a bank?' he had shouted. 'What the fuck you need that much for?'

'We need to pay the rent, Bhaiya.'

'I just gave you my wages!'

'You gave it to him!' she said, her voice shrill. 'You know where it goes when you give it to him!'

He had turned away from the look on her face, the pit of his stomach filling with fear, for her and for himself.

That evening, when he went to fetch the Peacock's table linen that had been in the Islams' dryer, Riaz was feeling agitated. He found the girls in the kitchen, ready for work: Afroz looking ridiculous in a yolk-coloured kameez (turmeric can't stain yellow, she explained to him) and Nasrin resembling a younger, pre-Richard Naz. Like his old Naz. Her hair was pulled into a clasp, and the oversized shirt revealed her collar bones and the delicacy of her shoulders.

'You fools!' he said laughing, the sight of the girls diverting him, momentarily, from his family's worries. He saw how Nasrin suppressed her smile, scrunched up her nose: an old expression of hers that made his chest tighten. He nodded at Jahanara, picked up the neatly stacked linen and led the girls next door.

Jahanara stood with her arms around her grandson and watched Riaz. She had noticed the tension in him and how, when he smiled, it did not reach his eyes. Riaz's smile usually lit up his whole face. Elias led her to the fireplace where she helped him unload a shital basket of his toys onto the rug. As she watched him stack bricks of Lego, her fingers played with the tassels on the basket lid, tassels that were the deep green of the Bangladeshi flag. She remembered how proud her father had been of the Bangladeshi flag. 'Jani,' he used to say as he straightened his hat, 'this flag can bring a grown man to his knees,' and Jahanara had secretly wondered why that should be a good thing.

Shamsur had once told her that Riaz was a boy with many invisible ties binding him to duty, burdens that the boy's pride prevented him from sharing. Burdens as compelling as a flag to its country's youth. Shamsur had been one to notice such things: had broken the shackles of others to free them where he could. But there was no more Shamsur. Jahanara prayed that whatever weighed on this proud boy, he had the strength to shake himself free.

The Boy Deprived of a Braggable History

Sitting in the clammy living room of their terraced home in Lozells, Riaz's father delivers his verdict. Riaz will take a job in an Indian restaurant in the Beacons, far away from the scandal of the scantily-clad Janine next door, and the drug peddlers that trudge up and down the street delivering pot like they are neighbourhood milkmen.

Riaz is sceptical, but his scepticism barely penetrates his pot-induced haze. He knows from the agitated way his father moves about the house and the caustic way he has been rebuking them of late that he has ulterior motives. The bets have been more frequent, the stakes more than they can afford to lose. It is because of this that Riaz is being exiled to the middle of nowhere – an alien place, whose very remoteness, Riaz knows, means it will be full of white people and no brown. Lozells is a small brown world inside the big white one and Riaz doubts his ability to navigate outside it.

'You will go,' his father bellows, cutting through his son's reverie, 'and you will meet her. You have left me no face to show people. On the street people spit at me with disrespect. Do you know why?' He leans so close that Riaz can see the huge pores on the sides of his nostrils. 'Because I cannot control this family – my family! These drugs! These girls! I cannot control you!'

Riaz ponders his father's words, and despite himself, airs his curiosity.

'Her?'

'That's right,' interjects Riaz's mother, placing diced mangos in front of Riaz and his father, but ignoring his sister. 'Her. Sham Bhai's wife is a distant cousin of your father's and she is doing us a favour, so—'

'So, don't mess it up, you good for nothing son of a pig!' His father snatches the bowl of mango and begins to shove forkfuls into his mouth.

Sniggers squeeze through Riaz's lips, and within moments the contagious laughter spreads to his sister, who begins shaking beside him. Their mother leaps on them, smacking the sides of their heads; the majority of the blows, Riaz is aware, are borne by his poor sister. He lifts his hand to shield her, and this only emboldens his mother's rage.

'Don't you dare disrespect your father! Don't you dare!'

His father waits patiently for the beating to subside before he runs his hand down his beard. 'Don't think just because it's a she that the job's going to be easy. She comes from a good family. Izzaddar zaath. Father was a daroga in Biswanath district police.' He shakes his head. 'But be careful about that Sham Bhai, he's a bit too *mishook* with the whites – too much mixing with the locals, forgetting who he is—'

'You're going there to stay out of trouble and earn some money,' interrupts his mother. She is a woman who is silent unless she is interrupting her husband or interjecting on his behalf. 'So, don't get too friendly with them, keep your distance.'

When he finally meets her, Riaz finds that Jahanara lives up to his curiosity. She has a regal, almost numinous beauty that he has never observed in the other Sylheti women he has grown up around. She wears the same brightly hued polyester sarees, and she has the familiar glint of gold on her left nostril, but her lips are not stained with paan juice, and there is not a hair out of place on her head. The Peacock itself stands in the darkest corner of the tiny market town, and yet, upon closer inspection, has a certain distinction. As if it said to the square and the statue of the Duke of Wellington that it faced, *Yes, I'm different, but I can hold my own, I can stand here in this corner and hold my own.*

'Do you have any qualifications?' Jahanara asks him. Riaz laughs.

'Well, don't need a degree to be waiter, right, Mrs Islam?'

'Your father is related to my Abba's uncle on his maternal side,' she says evenly. Her words, so familiar to him, are enunciated in what he laughingly deduces is posh Sylheti. He says nothing, watches her count the cash in the till and carefully write it into a ledger. He notices how dry her hands are, notices the patches of skin inflamed with eczema. 'So, instead of being so Western,' she continues, 'you can call me Fufu. As for qualifications,' she looks up at him briefly, 'education is important. My daughters, they are your age, and they will also study, find a good job. No, you do not need a degree to serve customers, but education is important.'

She points behind Riaz to a wiry, bespectacled man in his forties, who is hovering near the entrance. 'Gul almost had a BA in commerce from the Dhaka University, and Junaid' – a stockily built youth not much older than Riaz appears behind her as if on cue – 'he was accepted into Sylhet Medical, but of course his studies were put on indefinite hold so he could come to England. Our assistant chef, Lindsay, who you will meet in a minute, has a Hospitality Management degree from Bala. And Hannan and Saleh take English-language lessons in town. And this,' she waves at a large, curly-haired man who nods at Riaz, 'is Mustafa, our chef.'

'Right.' Riaz coughs a little, abashed, and surprised at how much he suddenly wants this job. The prospect of being surrounded by a different type of Bangladeshi – a superior type – than the ones in Lozells is alluring. 'Suppose I'm a bit under-qualified.' He shrugs. 'Suppose the customers around here pay extra for their tikka masala, you know, to be served up by all your graduates here?'

Jahanara puts down her pen, draws closer to Riaz, looking him square in the face. 'It's a shame not to encourage a little aspiration in people as young as you. I have children too. I only tell you what we tell our children. Education is freedom, baba.'

Even in his defensiveness, Riaz recognises that Jahanara's words are borrowed ones. When he finally meets Shamsur, he realises that Jahanara has taken her words and her demeanour wholesale from him.

'Perhaps,' she remarks as she turns away, 'you might be better suited to the kitchen sink – you'll find that our dishwashers can say a single sentence in English between them: "Afa, can I have my pay check early?"'

Junaid chuckles, and Riaz joins in. He notices and is reassured by the whiff of marijuana that hovers about Junaid. When Lindsay is introduced to him, he notices and appreciates the low-cut T-shirt that reveals the delicate dip of her breasts. There is nothing in Birmingham that he would miss here.

Just a few days later, he once again takes the train from Birmingham New Street, this time clutching a holdall with most of his clothes, and a small container of curry and rice. He is conscious that even though he cannot smell it, others probably can. He watches the craggy yellow fields of the Midlands rush past, before the landscape starts to take on a gentler and greener hue.

At the station, a man with high cheekbones and a small, fragile frame who seems to be cowering from the cold is waiting on the platform. Riaz is surprised. He had expected Shamsur to be taller, and stronger. They shake hands in the Islamic way, touch one cheek and then the other during the embrace, the older man guiding the younger in the greeting as though the latter's education has just begun. Then Shamsur calls out to his daughters, tells them to welcome their cousin, and Riaz can see in Sabrina's eyes that she has been forewarned and is delighted by the prospect of all the trouble he is bringing with him from Birmingham. He glances at Nasrin, and then averts his eyes quickly. On the drive back to the Peacock, he is painfully aware that she sits inches away from him, and he is unable to shrug away the image of the slant of her eyes, and the dip of her upper lip. There is something fragile and transient about her. It makes him afraid to look again, for fear that his greed will dissolve her.

Those first few months, life is about waiting eagerly for the weekends when the girls present themselves at the Peacock, dressed charmingly in baggy black trousers, and white shirts with bow ties: his own workwear made sexy in their wearing. The girls slowly adopt him, and he's soon invited to their house next door for his breaks; he is singled out as blood, and he forgets all about his mother's warning to keep a distance.

He enrols into the school a year above Nasrin's and realises how far behind he is. There has never seemed to be anything important between the pages of a book – school has always been a necessity both he and his parents have resented. But the Islams revere learning, treating every book in the house as a Quran, every sentence as a surah. Jahanara and Shamsur, usually such mild-tempered people, fly into a rage if a book is mishandled.

In his own home, Riaz barely hears the voice of his sister, but around the Islams' dinner table laden with mouthwatering delights, female voices reign supreme. Jahanara's stories are as lavish as her food as she regales them with her childhood adventures with her brother, Masoom, and her myna, Chinthamoni. Shamsur favours the story of the turquoise tiles transported from Istanbul by his great-grandfather, that have given his ancestral home the name *Neel Bari*. Riaz listens to it all and marvels. These are a people with history.

Riaz has heard that even ordinary people have their own history. People like Riaz, who have tumbled out of the filthy ghetto of Lozells, where the walls are sticky with cooking oil and the air smells of cannabis and curry. People who venture out into the world bearing the nuisance of their rounded vowels. Even they, those unfortunate scramble-uppers, those people living hand to mouth, month to abysmal month, have their own history.

But the foundation of history is its transmission from one generation to another and Riaz's parents can't place a memory in the right decade, let alone the right year; both of them celebrate their birthdays on Christmas Day because they don't know their date of birth. Their lack of knowledge of their own heritage coupled with their shady childhood memories (which Riaz attributes to the chewing tobacco corroding their brains along with their teeth) makes it impossible for him to construct a family history. With recollections as vague as, 'I remember sitting on the bazaar wall as the army traipsed through with their guns, and someone said that we were at war with West Pakistan,' how can you build a history?

He has tried to construct a past by relying on his own memory, and this takes him back only as far as his fifth birthday, which he spent on his grandparents' farm in Sylhet. His grandparents tilled their own land, and reared their own cattle, and that summer Riaz saw a calf being born, its vibrant auburn coat slathered in slime. Given the privilege of naming it, Riaz honoured his favourite superhero, Batman, which the villagers mispronounced as Betaman, and he saw Batman again over the next three summers, until Batman was sacrificed during Bakra Eid. The animal's body jerked horrifically as Riaz ran around demented with grief, screaming, 'They're doing Allah hu Akbar on Batman, someone save him, they're doing Allah hu Akbar!' It is his first memory of loss and he remembers screaming until his father took a bamboo cane to his legs.

Riaz's grandmother tended to his bruised legs with the same hands she used to mix manure with clay to even out the porch after every rainy season. And when he recalls this, it is as though he can smell the manure, and he feels ashamed, because the stink of dung is the stench of poverty, and it is poverty that repels him, it is poverty that frightens him.

The thing about ordinary people like Riaz is not that they don't *have* history, it is that the history they do have lacks braggability. Where is the uncle that served his country, or an aunt who owned a textile mill, or a grandfather who worked with so-and-so in the Civil Service? None in his family. Menial paper rounds, homework done on a sticky kitchen counter and washed clothes that always smelled of onions and ginger-garlic paste: these are the memories of his childhood which sabotage his ability to construct a proud history. His pimply-faced adolescence was no better, peppered as it was with cannabis-induced sex with white girls in New Street Station and driving around the dirty streets with boy racers in souped-up BMWs. And now he must contend with all his father's gambling problems, his mother's tears, and his sister's terrified voice begging him to pay their rent. These are the burdens that deplete his young life, the burdens that deprive him of a braggable history.

No, Riaz denies his history until he can construct himself a worthier one. Here, sitting at the mahogany dining table, Riaz breathes in the history of the Islam family: a family with roots similar to his, but one that is neither struggling working class nor bored bourgeoise, residing somewhere halfway having broken free from the shackles of illiteracy and poverty. All around him is evidence of the Islams' uneasy sprint towards progress and their daughters' embrace of modernity. The walls hang with photos and degrees and awards and memorabilia, and he reads in them the narrative of a family that have rid themselves of an ignominious history. Riaz is inspired to reach for it himself, to write for himself a future that will be worth its pages in a glorious history.

6

A quarter of an hour before opening time, Nasrin was walking through the restaurant floor with a lighter in her hand. The wan light of the candles she lit flickered uneasily against the last sharp rays of the setting sun. Behind her, Junaid hummed as he restocked the bar with mixers and glassware. Riaz had sat Elias on the bar to finish the jalmuri chanasur snack that Afroz had made for him and the familiar smell of the mustard oil and chilli made Nasrin's mouth water. She called over to her son, 'Can I have a bite, Eli?'

Riaz laughed. 'I tried already, but this boy's not sharing!'

'It smells so good! We should add this to the menu—' Nasrin was cut off by her phone ringing.

It was Mrs Humphreys.

'Hello? Naz?'

'Hello.'

'I'm so so sorry to hear about your father.'

'Thank you,' Nasrin said. 'It was very sudden.'

'Oh, Naz. I can't imagine what you're feeling. And your poor mother. If I lost William … Shamsur seemed like such a nice man, always such a smiley face when I saw him in your garden, always so friendly.'

'Thank you,' Nasrin said, this time more sincerely. Mrs Humphreys had always been friendly if she caught her parents in her garden on the rare occasions they visited.

'You will have seen, we've been watering the geraniums in your window box while you've been away. We wouldn't want them to wither away.'

'Thank you for that.'

'I thought we could maybe pop by to see you later today?'

'Today?' Nasrin asked, frowning. 'No, I mean, I'm still in the Beacons.'

'But, didn't I see you this morning?'

'No …'

There was silence at the other end, so Nasrin ventured, 'Perhaps you saw Richard? He's back as he has work. I decided to stay a couple of weeks.'

'Well,' Mrs Humphreys said. 'It wasn't Richard.'

Nasrin laughed. 'Mrs Humphreys, I assure you, I'm not home yet! My cousin is here from Bangladesh, and I've begged her to extend her stay by a few weeks – we hardly get to see each other any more! So I'm staying a bit longer and taking the train back on Friday morning. Would you like to pop round then?'

'Oh?' Now it was Mrs Humphreys's turn to sound unsure. 'Well, I must be going gaga! But yes, Friday is good, Friday it is. See you soon, Naz, and please pass on my condolences to your poor mother.'

'I will do,' Nasrin replied as a small hand tugged at her shirt. 'I'll see you on Friday, Mrs Humphreys.'

She looked down to find Eli by her side offering her his bowl. 'I'm done, Mummy. You can have the rest.' As she took the bowl from him, empty but for a few pieces of puffed rice, she heard Riaz chuckling as he walked to the door to flick the sign to *Open*.

'All right, you cheeky monkey, time for Nani to give you a bath and then bedtime,' she told her son, leading him out through the door. Riaz was lighting a cigarette on the step and stood to the side to let them pass.

'Can I ask you something, Naz?' Riaz said. Nasrin turned to him. Behind him, the light was falling, and the grey sky was merging into the asphalt. 'Why did you hide the Afroz stuff from Mustafa Sasa?'

Nasrin knew that he was referring to their visit to the Immigration Removal Centre that morning to deliver home-cooked food to an anxious Mustafa, and the fact that despite all the pleasantries that had been exchanged, and the reassurances she had passed on from her mother that Mustafa would have work found for him in Desh, Nasrin had consciously hidden Afroz's parentage.

'It's not anyone else's business,' she said, looking away.

'Well …'

Elias tugged at her hand, and she shook him off.

'What?'

Riaz raised his eyebrows, pushed his tongue against his teeth. 'I don't … I mean, are you ashamed of her?'

Nasrin glared at him. She tried to speak but couldn't find the words.

'I don't know, I just mean that …' Riaz looked away from her, seemingly distressed by his own words. 'It just seems like you're ashamed to admit that she's your sister.'

'How can you say that?' She said this with great effort, squeezing the words out of herself.

He shook his head, as though she had misunderstood. There was an earnestness in his face that made her chest tighten.

'Sorry, Naz, I just meant … all my life, I've looked up to you! The Islams, the educated, liberated, going-places Islams.' He stepped back and frowned at her. 'But now – I mean, Sibby was so cruel to Afroz, and you … well, you're hiding her. And I can't think of a reason for that except that perhaps something about her makes you ashamed – I get it, I used to be the same … walking yards behind my mum because she's decked out in 22-carat gold and a hijab. But you're better than me …'

He waited for a moment, but when she remained silent, he took Elias's hand and walked him to the house. Nasrin watched as the door opened and her mother emerged to pick up Elias and take him inside. As Riaz walked back towards her, she fought the urge to lunge at him. Out by the road, she could hear the growl of evening traffic. Her rage danced about inside her, making her feel dizzy. How dare he say such things to her?

'You don't get to talk to me that way!' she called out to him, crossing her arms. 'I am not ashamed of her! And Sibby is not cruel, she's just hurting. And you – who are you?'

She watched him walk slowly up the steps. 'You're right,' he said. 'I'm nobody.'

His words silenced her. They stood there until Junaid popped his head out of the door. 'I'm going down to change the beer keg,' he told them, glancing from one to the other, 'all good up here?' Riaz followed Junaid back inside.

After some moments glaring at Riaz through the glass door, Nasrin opened it and went inside.

'Who Afroz is – that's no one's business,' she said flatly. 'Everyone's allowed their secrets. You have yours.'

He glanced at her.

'You're the "friend" Mustafa lent his savings to, aren't you?' When she had questioned Mustafa about his lack of any savings, Mustafa had intimated, glancing nervously at Riaz, that he had lent them to a friend.

'That's none of your business,' Riaz said, turning away from her.

'Oh?' She walked towards him.

'Okay,' he muttered, 'so, I'm skint. It's not a crime to be poor, Naz. At least I'm not pretending to be someone I'm not.'

'What is that supposed to mean?'

'It's supposed to mean that you're not the Naz I knew, not since you married Richard. I feel like the old Nasrin would have told Mustafa the truth.'

Behind them, the bell tinkled as the first customers arrived, and Nasrin, unable to shrug off her anger, turned to serve, Riaz's words still crowding her head. Returning from delivering the order to the kitchen, she sensed Riaz lingering behind her at the bar.

'Sorry,' he whispered. 'It's not my place to say any of that stuff.'

'Then why say it?'

She turned to look at him, watched his face turning soft. He shrugged. 'I don't know. I guess I just feel bad for Afroz, you know? And I don't like to see you unhappy. You seem unhappy. And not just about this Afroz stuff, you know?'

'I'm not ashamed of her!' Nasrin said.

'I know you're not – I actually don't know why I said that, I'm sorry. You always used to rave about her – about your summers in Desh with her, and I know you love her.'

'It's just that with Mustafa, you know, Amma's always been a bit reluctant with him—'

'Because she respects him – he's an elder—'

'No, more than that, Riaz, I mean when she talked about people watching, or people judging, I've always had the impression she's talking about Mustafa. It's weird, I know, because I know he's stern, but he's always been so affectionate to us all. So, I didn't want to tell him until she was ready to tell him. But I'm not ashamed of my sister! And Sibby – remember my wedding day, how she had that awful argument with Amma, and you found her afterwards at the Pond, crying because she thought she was going to lose me? That's just who she's always been – lashing out when she's hurting! She's not cruel!'

Riaz ran a hand over his head. 'I know! Of course you're not, neither of you are capable of that sort of cruelty. I just … Mustafa is like family and I feel like, haven't there been enough secrets? I mean it's stressful as it is – your dad's gone, the Peacock's doing badly, I just, I'm sorry, I spoke out of turn. It was probably just the stress.'

She frowned. 'What does that mean? Riaz, how badly is the Peacock doing?'

Riaz shrugged. 'Your dad drew in the punters. Maybe it's just a temporary lull, I hope so. But last couple of weeks, business is down.'

She nodded. Behind them, the doorbell pinged again.

'I got it,' Riaz said, and she nodded again and followed him out into the restaurant.

It was only when Richard called later that night that Nasrin remembered what Mrs Humphreys had said.

'How is it down there?' he asked, his voice sounding tired. 'Has Sabrina been in touch?'

'No.' She pondered telling him how she herself had not made contact since that awful call on the day of her father's third-day prayers. Every time she began an email, her anger at the way Sabrina had left resurfaced and her feelings of remorse about Afroz made her delete the draft. She hadn't called either, because any discussion would inevitably lead to Sabrina asking her to choose between herself and Afroz, and how could Nasrin make such a choice? But she could not tell any of this to Richard because she had still not told Richard that Afroz was her sister. She wondered now if there was some truth to what Riaz had said – was she ashamed? She would prove Riaz wrong by telling him now.

But before she could do so, he asked, 'How did the prison visit go?'

'Detention centre,' she corrected. 'It wasn't great, to be honest. Mustafa is in bad shape.'

'Poor guy. But you know, your dad shouldn't have hired an undocumented worker in the first place, really.'

Nasrin bristled. 'Is compassion a crime?'

'Well, in this case,' Richard said, uncertainly, 'it is.'

Nasrin shook her head. The reason she didn't tell Richard about Afroz had nothing to do with shame, but with the way he would use the disclosure against her father. When she didn't respond, Richard said, 'Naz, you there? Come on, I didn't call to argue, I'm sorry, okay?'

But to Nasrin, he didn't sound sorry. She said, 'Mrs Humphreys called.'

'Hmm-hmm?'

She toyed with the frayed end of the curtain tie as she stood in the living room. She looked through the doorway at Elias, who was sitting at the kitchen table giggling with pleasure as Afroz massaged oil onto his scalp.

'What did she say?'

'Nothing,' she lied. 'Nothing. Just wanted to say she was sorry about Dad.'

'That's good of her. She's all right really.'

'She is.'

Until a year ago, Richard had mentioned Fabienne frequently. The two of them shared an office, so every breakfast meeting, conference and lunch featured Fabienne. Nasrin had met her several times and had always felt uneasy. Then one day, after Richard returned from a lavish offsite in Barcelona, he simply stopped talking about her.

Nasrin had googled Fabienne every few weeks, zooming into her Facebook image, admiring the angular handsomeness of the other woman's face, the way her dark hair flowed about her shoulders, and the cornflower blue of her eyes.

She didn't blame Richard.

She blamed herself. She blamed the monotony of her own brownness, the darkness of her eyes and her hair and her knuckles and her knees. For her brownness had always set her apart, and it had never mattered that she felt exactly the same as her white friends, because the mirror told her otherwise, as did other people's behaviour towards her. She would never be allowed to forget that she was brown, and neither would Richard. Sometimes she would imagine Fabienne wearing some item of jewellery or clothing that Richard had gifted Nasrin, and instead of hating Richard or hating Fabienne, she would look in the mirror with utter self-loathing.

And then one day, almost six months ago, Richard came home with the news that Fabienne was leaving the firm to join a client.

And Nasrin had trembled with the relief of a calamity avoided. There was no need for confrontation, or conflict. What might have been was firmly in the past, and the future was hers. Hers and Richard's.

But now Mrs Humphreys had seen a woman with long hair in Nasrin's home, and Nasrin felt winded. Where, now, did the future lie?

7

One evening, midway through the dinner shift, Afroz felt her phone vibrating. It was Humayun. Panicking as to why he was calling when it was the middle of the night in Desh, she asked Lindsay to finish cooking the dhansak while she took the call.

'What's wrong?' she asked.

'You didn't even tell me! Any of it – about Sham Fufa, about the restaurant! Afroz, I had your own cousin waking me in the middle of the night to tell me what you're plotting!'

Afroz inhaled sharply. 'Who called you? Sabrina called you? From New York?'

'She told me everything. About Sham Uncle, I mean, who he is.' Humayun grew quiet for a moment, and then when he spoke again, his voice had softened. 'You didn't … why wouldn't you tell me about something like that, Afi?'

Afroz frowned, trying to find the words to explain to him that it had not seemed her secret to tell. The reputation of the other members of the Islam family was as entangled in it as her own.

'What did she want?' she asked Humayun instead. 'Sabrina, why did she call you?'

Humayun's voice took on a harsher tone. 'Sabrina said she had offered to buy the restaurant from you, and you refused. Have you forgotten, Afi? Have you forgotten that you are a married woman? Of course you must sell it! Sell it quickly and come home.'

'I won't sell it to *her*,' Afroz said quietly.

Humayun sighed. 'Afi, don't you see? Whatever the will said, you have to read between the lines. These people – if they wanted you, why would they keep it a secret? They don't want you, that's why she wants you to sell. Afi,' he said, his voice softer now, 'don't you see, you already have a home, and a family? Why stay where you are not welcome? How many times will you keep extending your visit? Just come home.'

After the call ended, Afroz stood clutching the wheelie bin for support as the truth of Humayun's words sank in. In a culture where having more than one wife was perfectly acceptable, Shamsur had kept her a secret. Which meant that his relationship with her biological mother was in some way unacceptable, shameful even. Of course they didn't want her, of course she would have to sell.

She wiped her face with her scarf and returned to the Peacock kitchen. She was determined to enjoy it for as long as she could.

The day before he and his mother were due to leave, Elias insisted that they visit the fair. It was a clear day with a light breeze and Afroz walked alongside Nasrin, watching as her nephew flitted between his mother and his grandmother and Riaz. They could already hear the shrieks coming from the direction of the fairground.

'I'm going to have candy floss first,' Elias announced, 'then those twirly, whirly string things, you know, the red ones?' He ran back towards Afroz. 'Then the bumper cars, then the merry go, then the scary house. Riaz, will you come with me to the scary house?'

'No way, man, that place scares me!'

'I'll come with you then, Riaz.'

'All right, if you promise to hold my hand.'

'I will. Then we'll go on the bumper cars and eat those red twirly thingies.'

'He's such a little moyna faki!' Afroz said to Nasrin. 'Do you remember my myna bird?'

'Chinthamoni? Oh, my goodness, she was so naughty! When did she pass?' Nasrin slowed to fall into step with her.

'The year before I got married. She lived a long time, for a myna bird. You know she used to be Fufu's?'

'Yes, Amma reminded us all the time! She loved that bird.' Nasrin took Afroz's arm. 'So,' she said, changing the subject. The cheer in her voice, Afroz thought, was forced. 'Have you spoken with Humayun Bhai? How is he? Missing you, I expect?'

Afroz smiled. These questions referring to a non-existent romantic connection between Humayun and herself compelled the politest of responses. How could she explain that her husband didn't miss her so much as feel outraged that she dared leave the matrimonial home? Hardly the romantic longing for an absent lover: more like the outrage of a warden when one of his prisoners absconds. It saddened her that, although she had once confided in Nasrin about Taseen, she was unable to confide in her on the subject of her leaden marriage.

'Amma,' Nasrin called out to her mother. 'Don't, just please don't let him have one of those.' Afroz saw that her aunt had pulled out a bag of yellow sherbets from her handbag. 'He's too young for boiled sweets!'

The sweets went back into the handbag, and Elias grumbled about his mother's meanness.

'But I'm hungry, Mummy,' he called back to her.

'I have some lovely apple slices in my bag if you're hungry.'

The look on his face made Afroz laugh, and he went to her, pressing himself into her side in a sulk.

'Just one sweetie, Mummy,' he moaned.

'He's not a rabbit,' Jahanara scoffed, commiserating with her grandson. 'You and Sibby had sweets and chocolates every day – I never denied you – and you turned out fine?'

'I wish to God you'd denied me, Amma. A mouth full of fillings – I don't call that fine.'

They walked on, the cool beneath the branches of the beech trees that lined the path making them shiver and draw closer to one another. Soon they reached the entrance. Elias ran ahead, returning to take Afroz's hand again and pulling her faster towards the gate.

Afroz stared all about her. The colours, though jewel-like, were more subdued than the melas in Desh, not helped at all by the paltry sunlight that ventured over the valley. The sounds, too, were muted. People didn't scream and shout out to one another, like people did in Sylhet melas, where voices vied to be heard. People spoke to one another in tones just above a hush, and they stood in queues with inches to spare between themselves and the next person. Yes, it lacked a certain energy that the melas had, but, Afroz thought to herself, smiling, there was an unexpected freedom in this restrained way of enjoyment, an unobtrusiveness that she appreciated.

'What do you think you will do?' Nasrin asked, appearing beside her. The merry-go-round began to move and Riaz and Elias yelped for their attention.

'What will I do?'

'About the restaurant.'

Afroz didn't reply, and Nasrin paused, biting her lip.

'I didn't know you were such a fantastic cook, Afi. Everyone's so impressed, the customers, I mean. And Linds,' Nasrin said.

Afroz allowed herself to be seduced by this. *Everyone's so impressed.*

'But I know that it will be hard to manage. All the way from Sylhet,' Nasrin continued.

Afroz remained silent.

'Afi?' Nasrin pressed. 'I haven't spoken to Sibby since she left, and I'm so angry at her … but she would buy it off you. You know, so you can get a clean break from it. If it's what you wanted.'

Afroz stared out at the merry-go-round. The sounds suddenly

magnified and even the colours seemed to roar at her. As much as she loved these Islam sisters, they would never love her back: not in the way they loved each other and not in the way she loved them.

'Sorry,' Nasrin said, squeezing her arm, 'I don't mean to pry. It's yours to do as you wish with. I just meant that I could help deal with the sale if you want to sell it.'

'You just want me to sell it,' Afroz said, snatching her arm away, her anger racing out of her. 'You just want me to do it because Sabrina wants me to do it. Why can't you think for yourself?'

Nasrin stopped in her tracks, and Afroz turned to her.

'She called my husband and offered to pay cash. She went behind my back and did that. Now it's no longer my decision. Is it? How is it my decision if you keep taking it out of my hands?'

'She did what? Look, Afi, I'm sorry—'

'No, Naju, I'm sorry. I am,' Afroz said again, her voice trembling. 'Who am I, anyway? Of course I need to sell. What choice is there?'

'No,' Nasrin said. 'I meant it when I said it. It is your choice.'

'In my world, there are not so many choices, Naju.'

'That's not true …' Nasrin began but she trailed off when she saw the look on Afroz's face. 'I'm sorry. Who am I to say that? Gosh, Afi. I'm sorry.'

There was something disconcerting about Nasrin's voice that made Afroz turn to look at her.

'You're right about me too,' Nasrin continued, 'I should think for myself – it's just that she holds me ransom sometimes too, you know? They all do!' Nasrin laughed, but it was a mirthless laugh. 'I have no fucking idea what I think, what I want. Nada!'

Afroz didn't understand. She took Nasrin's wrist. 'What's wrong?'

'No! Nothing. But you're wrong, you know? You're in the Beacons now, not in Desh. Here, you *do* have a choice. And you're perfect for the restaurant. You could do it! Stay here?'

'Humayun won't agree.'

'Well, if it's what you want, you can talk to him. He's your husband, he loves you,' Nasrin said, and Afroz felt a pang of envy for the sort of marriage that Nasrin obviously had. She looked away.

'I can't run a business.'

'Why not?' asked Nasrin and Afroz looked at her, wanting to believe in her enthusiasm but the sudden giddiness in Nasrin's voice grated on her. 'Your English is as good as mine; you have a degree! Abba had less, and he managed pretty well.'

Nasrin took Afroz's arm again and jiggled it playfully. 'I'm here,' she said softly, almost shyly. 'Amma is here.'

'I'm not wanted here.' Afroz shook her head. 'I know what people are saying about you all, and about me. I don't want to keep causing trouble for you or for Fufu.'

'Afi,' Nasrin's face was pink, 'I don't care. I'm not ashamed. You're my … my sister.'

Afroz looked away, feeling her heart thudding in her chest. She tried to restrain the gratitude that burst through her, but she wanted Nasrin to say it again. Sister!

Instead she smiled nervously. 'Richard must wonder what sort of family we have,' she said, trying to lighten the moment, but the expression on Nasrin's face made Afroz realise that she had not told Richard.

'I'll tell him soon,' Nasrin said, 'it's not you, Afi. It's just things between me and Rich … they've … anyway, the point is, you are my sister. And I want to be here for you.'

Disappointed, Afroz shook her head. 'Sabrina wants me gone.'

'She'll come round. I promise. Just think about what you want, okay?'

'Okay.' She paused and then asked, 'What about that woman? The one from the council. Will she back? I don't know how to deal with that sort of thing.'

'No.' Nasrin became gloomy for a moment. 'They got what they came for.'

'What?'

'Council fined us for employing an illegal. Twenty thousand.'

'Y'Allah!'

'Y'Allah, indeed.'

They watched a woman struggling to get her toddler out of his pushchair.

'But, look, don't worry about that stuff, Afi. Riaz does all the books and he'll manage that side of things.'

A few metres away Jahanara was leaning against the other side of the barrier with a queer, absent expression. In her hands she was twisting the bag of yellow sweets around and around. Her white saree billowed out beneath the hem of her cream mac, and little wisps of hair which had escaped from her bun flew about her face. She opened the bag and popped a sherbet in her mouth. She looked so funny sucking it that Afroz couldn't help but grin.

'What about Fufu?' she asked.

'We'll figure out something. When she's ready to talk about it.' Nasrin's smile didn't reach her eyes.

'If I sold, would she live with you? Or with Sabrina? She can't stay alone.'

Afroz saw that Nasrin had not considered this. Nasrin gave a shrug and led her to the nearest stall. There was an array of alphabetised key rings, and embroidered tea towels and pretty-patterned pencils with rubber ends. Nasrin picked up a hand warmer and showed it to Afroz, who had never seen one before. She slipped it into her pocket and pressed the button as the stall-owner instructed and felt the warmth gush beneath her fingers. She laughed at the simple joy of it.

It was only then that Afroz noticed her cousin's attention focused on something happening by the merry-go-round.

Several people stood crowded over someone on the floor.

Nasrin began to run and Afroz, the warmer still in her pocket, sprinted after her, her shalwar flapping awkwardly at her ankles.

They fought their way through the crowd where Riaz and Jahanara were crouched on the floor by Elias.

He was gasping, fighting for breath. His face was sticky and damp and his eyes were glass marbles.

Riaz was slamming his fist down on the small of Elias's back.

'I've tried that Heimlich manouevre, but it's stuck!' he shouted up at them. 'Can't get it out!'

Crouching next to him, her aunt was reciting the Ayatul Kursi, her fingers lifting the shirt from Elias's chest so she could blow the words at him, as though her breath making contact with his skin would somehow escalate God's mercy. Beside her, Nasrin was on the phone shrieking for an ambulance: 'No, not at the entrance of the fair, between the bumper cars and the merry-go-round, just send someone, please hurry!'

But Afroz knew it would be too late. They couldn't wait for an ambulance. The Ayatul Kursi was not meant for this. The crowd that had gathered around was too hesitant and afraid to help. It was up to her.

She pushed Riaz out of the way and fell to her knees. Dragging Elias onto her lap, she reached her fingers into the gaping wet hole of his mouth. She closed her eyes from fear. She didn't know which bits of muscle or flesh her fingers were sinking into, but she had to probe deeper and find it. The tip of her middle finger touched something hard. Elias had stopped moving, his body twitching as though he were dreaming in his sleep. Afroz panicked – she wouldn't lose another child, *please Allah-ji, not another child* – she thrust her hand further in, and he gagged. Her middle finger hooked around the object, and she pulled.

Out it flew. Yellow, and whole and covered in mucus.

There was silence. And into that silence, Elias poured his breaths.

The scratchy rasping was so slow and onerous. *Breathe harder,* she wanted to say, *breathe more!*

A force field of tension wrapped around him as he fought for each one of those first few inhalations. Each exhale was sharp and brief as though they were wasted seconds when he could be breathing in.

Afroz watched him, her heart clenched tight.

He breathed a few more times and then, finally, he began to whimper. And with the sound of his whimpering, all the other sounds to which Afroz had become oblivious poured in around her. Nasrin was breathing into a soggy paper bag, Jahanara was whispering prayers into the fold of her saree, while people around her offered her a coat, a glass of water.

Afroz looked down at the face on her lap, and the face looked back up at her. To think that they had almost lost him. How quickly it could all be over. Then when he began to cry, she began to laugh. She held him to her chest and laughed. And Nasrin was behind her, the bebat, hugging Afroz from behind, sobbing with relief into her hijab, and Riaz stood muttering profanities, fear still clinging to his face. And her aunt was now praying Ya Sin and blowing on all of them, moving her tiny face in big circles so the divine breath would reach them all. But Afroz sat there and she laughed. Like Nasrin had said, there was a choice here in the Beacons. For once in her life, Afroz had chosen to fight and had won. The shock of this brief moment of triumph made her wonder who she could be if she stayed a little longer. *Could places make people?* she asked herself. And if so, was there a self she could forge who would be more worthy of the Beacons, of this child and her Fufu?

She would call Humayun. She only had time to give them, after all, and she would give them that. Just a month or so.

8

As was her habit, Nasrin shed her Bangladeshi ways as soon as she crossed her parents' threshold and stepped back into her other life. It was liberating to get on a train and leave the valleys behind for the bustle of London and to turn the key in her lock and enter a space where she had the freedom to put on thigh-skimming shorts or relish that first glass of pinot after days of abstinence without worrying about offending her mother's religiosity. Inside the end-of-terrace Barnsbury property, Nasrin returned to being Mrs Wilson.

The orderliness and calm of her minimalist home were a relief after the emotional tumult of the Beacons. Here she could slip on the racially undetermined alter ego that had been her salvation after she had married Richard – a caricature of her school friends' seamlessly groomed mothers whom Nasrin had admired as a child. Unlike in her parents' home, there was no bodna in Mrs Wilson's house; there was a bidet. There was no da or narikel kuruni – there were an assortment of chef's knives, and if she needed to desiccate coconut, she bought it desiccated from the supermarket. Just like those school friends' mothers, Mrs Wilson was refreshingly, commitedly English in both language and manner.

But as the week passed by, Nasrin's thoughts returned to the Beacons and to her father. Abba had hardly visited her in London, but his absence seemed to haunt her home. She longed to hear his voice and her longing for him morphed into something insidious, lengthening the shadows inside her house, creating echoes to the slightest sounds. There was an edge to her pining that was compounded by her rift with Sabrina. She had tried calling Sabrina after Elias had almost choked, but the phone had cut straight to voicemail without ringing, and she had not wanted to leave a message. It was disorientating to live without that companionship – this was the longest she and Sabrina had ever been without talking, and it didn't help that she was called every morning and night by Afroz, who had extended her stay again. These conversations only made Nasrin feel guilty, as though she were betraying Sabrina. But her conversations with Afroz made Nasrin nostalgic for the world she had left behind – the world within a world in that house next door to the Peacock where her mother and half-sister were living in surprising harmony. Their daily calls stirred up her grief and her longing, and suddenly the two worlds she had painstakingly kept separate, began to collide.

Now, Mrs Wilson would trip on the corner of that darned hallway carpet, and she'd shriek, 'Y'Allah goh' out into the empty house, the way her mother yelped whenever in pain or in shock. Or Mrs Wilson would have a surprising need to feel the heat of a fried red chilli on her tongue or a craving for the dried fish shutki, the abominable pungency of which had made her father forbid her mother from ever cooking it for fear of offending their Welsh neighbours. Or Mrs Wilson would look up from her ironing board with a sudden desire to hear the language she was born to, the language of her first five years, reciting a Tagore verse that Afroz had taught her when they were children: *tal gas ek paye dariye, shob gach chariya, uki mare akashe*; or she'd reach for her iPhone and the small speaker would emit a little fragment of an old Bollywood song she'd find on YouTube, because a little was all she needed, all she desired.

'What's that?' Richard asked one afternoon, arriving home earlier than she had expected. Bally Sagoo crooned *churaliya hain thum ne jo dilko* out of the kitchen Bluetooth speaker. Nasrin almost tripped over in her rush to switch it off.

'Calm down!' Richard laughed, reaching out and taking the

iPhone from the docking station. He peered down at the screen. 'Bally Sagoo,' he said, holding the 'ooo' too long.

'It's Mummy's favourite song,' Elias told his father. 'She dances to it sometimes.'

'Since when?' Richard asked.

'Since always!' Elias said, shrugging with the confidence of a four-year-old who was certain about everything.

Richard put the phone down, made an *Is that right?* face and went upstairs to change.

Nasrin worried about this slip in front of Richard. She worried about revealing the details that she was slowly learning about herself. Because inside her parents' house, the house she had grown up in, lay a whole other world, galaxies away from Richard's. Yes, as a teenager she had loved Fleetwood Mac and laughed through *American Pie* and bruised her bottom with frequent falls in the local ice rink; but did Richard know never to pass in front of a praying person, or never to address someone older by their name? Did he know the Amitabh Bachchan catchphrases that every desi who couldn't speak a word of Hindi could still bellow out with glee, did he know the melancholic beauty of an old Lata Mangeshkar tune, or the pointless pleasure of adda?

One afternoon, bored of eating lightly seasoned meat and poultry with bland steamed vegetables, she texted Mrs Humphreys the obligatory warning and spent the afternoon cooking a five-dish Bengali meal, labouring over the kumro phul er bora batter so they tasted just like her memory of her mother's ones and taking particular care to balance the sweet and sour of the murgh roast. Richard had invited two partners and their wives for dinner. Instead of the usual coffee-shop jazz playlist, she played a Nitin Sawhney collection and wore a velvet black kurtha with bronzed kundan work on the chest and sleeves. When the guests and her husband arrived, there were trills of pleasure from the guests, but from Richard, she saw only surprise, and a slight reluctance.

She realised then how their common ground had been staked in his cultural territory, forcing her to abandon her own. She had tried so hard to buttress their mutuality and to create something substantial enough on which to build a family. But in spite of her best efforts, this house of theirs, which she had kept cleansed of all things Bengali, felt like it had become porous since she had returned to London. There were smells and visions seeping in that she thought she had eliminated over the years. She would stand at the little kitchen island preparing a rocket salad for dinner, and she would see things which shouldn't be there and hear things that couldn't be there.

Like the apparitions.

After seeing her father in the Beacons and dismissing it as some side effect of her grief and a presage of her seizure, Nasrin had seen him several more times. He was always still – even that time she had seen him standing in the garden beneath the fig tree, with the breeze clawing at everything in sight, he had stood with not a hair out of place, nor a flap of his shirt, as if he had been superimposed into the scene of a windy day. He had simply stared across the patio at Nasrin and Nasrin had stared back, until the overflowing sink and the running tap had distracted her. Was he a ghost? A vision? A memory formed by a grieving mind? Whatever he was, seeing him felt like a reprieve. To feel his quiet presence as she fed Elias or made the bed or cleaned the kitchen gave her comfort, like the warmth of the sun on a cold day.

Then, during the second week of her return home, Nasrin saw her seven-year-old self, standing at the bathroom door.

She had switched on the hallway light and made her way to the bathroom, and there it was standing by the open door, halfway between the light and the dark.

Nasrin wasn't afraid of the apparition. It had startled her, but when she thought about it, she realised she was more afraid of what she had become than of the seven-year-old she had once been.

She passed by, pretending that she didn't need the bathroom after all, and walked down the hallway to her room. By the time she looked back, there was nothing there except the towel Richard had left hanging on the doorknob that morning.

9

Manhattan sweltered beneath a freak heatwave in the last week of September and its inhabitants moved torturously, glugging on bottles of lukewarm water. The day Nasrin finally reached out to her, Sabrina had an unusually difficult morning commute. A sudden dearth of cabs meant she had to walk to work, already hot after a Bikram yoga session, feeling the city melting into her. As she walked, she wondered why she had not heard back from Humayun. Her sister had not called her either. Only her mother had begun to call her each night: their conversation brief and restricted to questions on food and sleep and wellbeing. By the time she reached her desk, Sabrina was panting heavily, the sound jostling with the unhealthy wheeze of the air conditioner in the empty trading room floor. Her blouse stuck to her front and back, and her hair was tangled with the straps of her handbag. Cursing under her breath, she extricated herself and heard footsteps behind her.

'Get your shit sorted, Islamio!' Fanni stopped for a moment, looking at Sabrina over her shoulders. 'You're letting the place down looking so shabby.'

Sabrina sat down heavily on her chair. She pursed her lips and called Benjamin over.

'Are you messing about?'

'Uh, sorry, Boss?'

'Where's that cash flow model I asked you for?'

'I'm just logging in. I'll send it to you now,' Benjamin said, retreating to his desk.

'When I ask for it to be at my desk at seven, I mean fucking seven!' she growled at him.

Sabrina logged in and there in front of her was an email from her sister. Three thousand two hundred words.

Sabrina felt her face break into a smile. Her sister had finally reached out to her. With three thousand two hundred words. *'Hey, little sis, I'm so sorry,'* it began, and Sabrina closed her eyes for a moment, tears pricking her eyelids and relished the relief that flooded her.

'Hey, Boss?'

Sabrina opened her eyes and closed Nasrin's email, saving it to read in the safety of her apartment, away from prying eyes.

'Oh, God, has someone died?' she asked, noticing the shoes on Benjamin's feet.

He grinned and shrugged. 'Seeing as it's my last week, I'm on my best behaviour.'

She took the model he handed her, swallowing her surprise. 'I should hope so too!' she said, grasping for words. 'I suppose you want to know where I'm taking you for your exit dinner?' She wondered whose arm she could twist to get a last-minute reservation somewhere.

Ben shrugged. 'Wherever. I'm a hole-in-the-wall sort. Um, so, Sunil Kapoor from Compliance came looking for you after you left on Friday.'

Her heart seemed to stop for a few seconds before it kicked back to life.

'What did he have to say for himself?'

'He said he'd come by this morning, but I thought you'd want to know.'

She experienced the next few hours as two human beings: the dominant one moved her along with her day, answered her emails, took her calls and corrected her pricing structures. The other person cowered inside her, scanning the floor for Sunil Kapoor and cringing every time the phone rang from an internal line. She stood in front of the mirror in the ladies' considering the questions that she thought Compliance might ask her. She practised answering questions in a steely but helpful demeanour, trying on different faces before settling on a face that said, *Do I look like I need to cut corners?* A face that said, *These deals are extremely complex, nothing is clear-cut, but I am trying to be as helpful as I can be.*

The call came just before lunch.

'Sabrina? Can you step into Conference room 68? We need to ask you a few questions about the Altieri deal.'

She pulled down her shirtsleeves and fastened her cufflinks. She put her jacket on and made her way over. Her heart thumped. But she tried to calm herself. She smiled at Mercedes as she passed her.

'M, can you do me a favour? Find someone who can get us a reservation for Per Se Friday night? For two?'

'Tall order!'

'If anyone can do it, Mercedes—'

'I know, I know, it's me!'

She was surprised at how level her voice sounded, and it gave her confidence. She had rehearsed this. She was prepared.

Sunil motioned her in. 'Sorry, Sabrina, looks like we'll need to reschedule for a bit later as James McGuffe is tied up. I gather that you and Ralph both report to him?'

'That's right, yes,' Sabrina replied, swallowing the urge to scream, *I'm available whenever.*

The next three hours and forty-six minutes were excruciating. It was either too loud or ominously quiet. She shivered from the air conditioning one minute, only to break out in a sweat the next. She couldn't concentrate. She opened Nasrin's email.

I can't explain why it's taken this long to reach out to you, Sib, except that things have felt quite overwhelming. I felt so crowded on all sides, and I just needed time. But I'm back in London now. Everything is the same but weirdly different too.' At that moment, Sabrina stopped, not wanting to spoil the pleasure of reading it until she was at home. Besides, her sister's affability didn't fit this moment. She turned off her phone and put it face down in front of her and tried again to concentrate. But she messed up a pricing proposal twice, making the same stupid mistake, and had to grovel to the client. Finally, Benjamin walked over to her.

'I can take care of things if you're sick, Boss?'

'Headache!' she said, waving him away. He stood blinking at her for a moment. She sighed.

'Hey, Ben, I sort of dropped the ball. I know you guys expect a grand exit dinner, at Per Se or somewhere, but I just plain forgot. With everything … I just …' She stared at him blankly.

Benjamin shrugged. 'Seriously, Boss, it's no big deal!'

'Mercedes managed to get us a booking at Crypt, though.'

He smiled. 'It's a good place. I prefer places I don't have to wear shoes though.'

She gave him a weak smile. 'McDonald's has officially been removed from the entertaining budget. Too expensive.'

She watched Benjamin walk back to his desk and wanted badly for the day to be over.

When James and Sunil finally buzzed for her, Sabrina felt so light-headed that she had to grasp the wall as she walked off the trading floor. Outside the conference room she stopped and composed herself, pinched the inside of her wrist. She willed herself to focus and took a few deep breaths before opening the door.

Sunil was already inside. He motioned for her to take a seat and continued to scribble in his notebook. A few minutes later, James entered the room, effervescent with smiles and goodwill. He grabbed Sabrina's shoulders as he passed by and shook her in awkward camaraderie.

'Pocahontas!' He beamed at her. 'How is our Pocahontas doing?' She shrugged in deference. He paused before taking a seat.

'We have a few questions for you, Sabrina,' Sunil began. 'These relate to the Altieri deal that your supervising manager, Ralph Miguel, was in charge of, and as I understand it you are aware of some inappropriate behaviour with regard to this, as you sent an email with some information about three weeks ago?'

She nodded throughout this introduction, remembering to hold her head up high. Beneath the table her knees had collapsed into jelly.

'Now during your email to my guys, you said you were suspicious that whoever closed this trade knew about the potential downgrade of the ratings? Can you please elaborate on this for us?'

Sabrina stared at him and then at James. Her mind was a blank.

'Why don't you begin with when your suspicions arose?' Sunil prompted. His pen poised above the notebook seemed to Sabrina the most threatening device she had ever seen.

'Yes,' she said carefully. 'I was in the Beacons, I mean in the UK, on compassionate leave. My father passed away, and Ralph called me to ask me if I remembered anything about the Altieri deal.'

'Were you aware at the time that he was being investigated?'

'Not at that time, no.'

'Go on.'

'I reminded him that I wasn't staffed on this deal with him, but that I did dip into it during the structuring stages. I couldn't remember anything, and I told him I would look back over my notes and call him back.' Her throat was dry but there was no water in sight. 'So, I checked back on it: as you know, this product was backed by a pool of assets that served as collateral, and basically I helped to pick that collateral.'

'Can you describe the collateral in it? Anything out of the ordinary?'

'Well, it was all the standard assets we'd always used for collateral on this type of deal, except there was one thing.'

'What's that?'

'Because of everything that happened in August, the ratings agents were already talking about downgrading the ratings on some of those assets, so those assets weren't as valuable as the client thought they were.'

'Did you make this clear to your supervisors?'

'Yes. Absolutely, I have an email alerting the team to this fact and reminding them to make the appropriate disclosure to the clients.'

'Did you have any further involvement?'

'No, I did not. I merely dipped into that trade to help collateralise it.'

'Did you do anything else with respect to this trade?'

'No.'

'Are you aware that the client is claiming that the firm misled them by failing to tell them about the potential downgrade?'

'I only became aware when Ralph told me about it. That's when I called you.'

'Do you know these are potential allegations of at least dishonesty, and maybe fraud, that can cause severe financial and reputational loss to the firm?'

She nodded.

'Ralph is claiming that though he was supervising this deal, one of his subordinates with knowledge of the possible downgrade signed off on it.'

Sabrina turned to ice. 'Like I said,' she said, holding her voice steady, 'I dipped into it for a day. There was no way I signed off on anything.'

'Who else was working on it? Do you remember?'

For a moment, Ashok's name lingered on her tongue. But it was a moment that passed swiftly. 'I think it was just the juniors and Ralph. He dealt with it top to bottom.'

The whole thing lasted maybe fifteen minutes at most but felt like hours. When James signalled the end of the session by clapping his hands together with an alarming thwack and bounced out of his chair, Sunil was still writing in his pad.

As they exited the door, James held her back.

'Hey, Pocahontas, my condolences about your father. I'm very sorry to hear it.'

She nodded weakly.

'The other thing I should tell you of course is that, the numbers are in for the year,' he continued, tapping his phone against the edge of the door. 'Obviously they're still being finalised, but I think you're going to be very pleased. Very good work this last quarter especially! Hmm?'

She smiled.

'Right, and Monty's been in touch, wants me to get some dates in the diary, do that lunch about the MD gig, say end of October? How does that sound?'

It sounded, amazing, absolutely thrilling!

So why, why did she ask, 'Is Ralph going to be okay?'

James regarded her silently.

'I don't mean to interfere …'

'Good. Because there's nothing I can do. You know that these are matters are out of my hands.' They both looked back through the glass walls of the CR68 where Sunil was still scribbling. 'I can't interfere with investigations; that's for the disciplinary committee to oversee.'

She nodded mutely.

'Sabrina.' He leaned forward and peered at her closely. 'As you said just now, Ralph booked all the trades, and priced this stuff himself. Right? He marketed it. You made him aware of the potential discrepancies in the ratings. So, you don't have anything to worry about, do you?'

'No.'

And it was the right answer. 'Then we're good. Once we find out who gave the sign-off on the deal, we'll pin Monty down and book your lunch meeting.'

Sabrina gawped at him. 'But I thought we'd established – Ralph was the only one working that deal.'

James nodded reassuringly, his fingers impatiently waving along the corridor. 'No, see if it was just Ralph's word, it would be fine, but the client says he spoke to someone other than Ralph the eve of the deal who assured him there was no change to the ratings. We've pored through the records, but it must have been on a personal cell.'

Afterwards, she sat inside one of the immaculate toilet cubicles just outside the client dining rooms, her stomach lurching frantically. They needed another scapegoat, and if they didn't find anyone, it was going to be her. She knew it.

The ledger on the door showed seventeen minutes until the next clean. She put her head in her hands and stayed there until she heard the cleaning lady burst through the door. Then Sabrina washed her hands, straightened her skirt and walked back out to her desk.

That night, exhausted and stretched out on her couch, Sabrina opened her sister's email. Glowing from the tiny screen, Nasrin's words whispered to her, warmed her and made her eyes fill up.

'Hey, little sis, I'm so sorry, I can't explain why it's taken this long to reach out to you, Sib, except that things have felt quite overwhelming. I felt so crowded on all sides, and I just needed time. But I'm back in London now. Everything is the same but weirdly different too. I feel like I can feel your anger from here, blowing across the Atlantic. But poor Afroz, Sibby. Can you see how unfair it all is? Don't be mad at me. I know I've disappointed you, but I promise I'll try harder. Just call me please.

I'm going through the motions here. Eli is at nursery in the mornings, and Richard has been entertaining at home more than usual, to help his chance at partnership. It's almost nicer when he's at work, and I can just be on my own. I'm pretty exhausted. Eli has been waking up at night, and coming into bed with us, and I find it so hard to sleep next to him.

He kicks and snores, and he talks in his sleep. Just this morning Rich sauntered in while I was giving Eli breakfast and says, "Bad night?" With no compassion or concern, like he's making an observation about the weather.

I don't remember Abba being so detached, you know? Remember Abba in the mornings, Sibby? He took command. He sang that Baul song in that weird wailey voice, Barir kache arshi nogor… And I keep listening to it on YouTube, and it takes me back to the mornings of our childhood. It's like the last time life made any sense to me was when I was a child.

At the pool today, I tried to persuade Eli to dip his head under the water. He's so terrified of water, Sibby – he clings to me the entire time and he won't let go until we get out of the pool. Remember what Abba used to say? Our people come from a land of nodis! River souls can't be afraid of water. So I told him to watch me, and I put my head under the water, just to show him it was safe. He began to cry! So I tried it again.

And I saw the weirdest thing, Sibby.

I saw us, when we were younger.

Do you remember, Sibby when we went to the ghat, the three of us? The steps all slippery after the rains, and we didn't tell anyone where we were going, because we knew we'd be stopped. What would have happened that day if the maid hadn't come to wash the rice at the ghat? If she hadn't seen those ripples on the surface of that calm green pond? What would have happened if she hadn't waded down those perilous steps, and pulled us out?'

Sabrina vividly remembered the time the three of them had fallen into the ghat. How indifferent the water had been. Amma had always tried to keep them away with stories of the jealous water spirits – but Amma had been wrong: there was no Manna in the water; the water was the Manna! How cold it had been, how curiously it had watched as they panicked and struggled and held each other down! Sabrina remembered the tiny bubbles that escaped the mouths of her cousin and sister … her sisters … as though their little lives were being squeezed out of them and she could hear the water Manna cackling with laughter, delighting in their pain.

She shuddered. Something about her sister's email unnerved her, but it was too late to call her now. She kept her bedside lamp on that night; the image of her sisters' panicked faces submerged in the water preyed on her, preventing her from sleeping.

10

Just over a week after Nasrin and Elias left the Beacons, Ramadan began.

For the first time since her arrival, Afroz missed Desh. There had been no 15th of Shaban night to herald the arrival of the holy month, for she had completely forgotten it. It had been Humayun who reminded her, during one of her dutiful morning calls to him.

'You sound tired,' she had said.

'Well what do you expect?'

His sullenness exhausted her. Since she had extended her stay, he had been trying to break down her resolve with his surliness.

'You didn't sleep well?' she asked.

'Who sleeps during Shabebarath?'

And she had felt a lurch in her stomach. 'The fifteenth night of Shaban has passed?'

'You forgot?' He sounded as shocked as she felt. Never in her life had she forgotten.

When she told her aunt, Jahanara had blinked at her, a slight frown creasing her face.

'I didn't forget, re moyna,' she said, 'I didn't say anything because you were working at the Peacock.'

'Fufu!' Afroz said, tearing up. 'I wish you had reminded me! I missed such a holy night. I have never missed it before.'

Since Nasrin's departure, Jahanara had been quiet in her presence, and Afroz had taken every opportunity to make herself scarce and not demand her attentions. But the intense disappointment of missing the holy night overcame her resolve and she began to cry.

'So no tusha shinni? I make tusha shinni every year – Baba loves it, and he always comes and he takes it to the mosque to hand out to the poor. I should have stayed up all night, and sought Allah's forgiveness, and prayed for Ammi and Ruksana.'

Her aunt watched, alarmed, as she hiccupped through her words. She drew closer to Afroz.

'Afi,' she consoled, 'Allah's ibadath needs no holy month – every moment you think of him is made holy.' Then she paused before leaning forward, through some barrier visible only to her, and touched Afroz's hair. It was the first time she had touched her since the will had been read. Afroz stopped crying and stared at her aunt, and her aunt stared back at her.

'Go on and read some nafal namaz now. And when you're finished, bring a comb and some oil – that hair of yours feels so brittle. What will your husband say? You can put some on me too.'

The night before the first fast, Afroz invited the staff to her aunt's house for sehri.

'I will make fresh puris and egg curry,' she said, 'and I have prepared a lot of mishti dhoy – sweet curd – for everyone. Lots of good protein to help you through your first fast.' She nodded at the blank faces gathered around the Peacock kitchen and then moved back to her place in front of the stove.

'I don't think any of them fast,' Lindsay whispered to her as the others shuffled away.

'But they are Muslims!' Afroz said, dropping the ladle back into the gravy pan and frowning at her friend.

'Yes, and so they don't eat pork. And I think they don't drink during Ramadan.'

'But they are not supposed to do that anyway!'

'Yeh,' Lindsay looked at her, sucked her bottom lip, 'they don't fast.'

Afroz nodded, disappointment dousing her. In Desh, the roads would be emptying of all the impoverished men, women and children who would head to the mosques that offered food and shelter for the month of Ramadan; the hoodlums on their motorcycles would be shouted off the squares by elderly men on their way home, for Ramadan was not a time of adda and catcalls. There would be delicious naaths spilling out of the loudspeakers, and families would be knuckling down, all manner of sins on hold, all tongues calmed, ears closed, hearts melted. Just for one month.

Here in this country, it was just another month.

'But Fufu fasts,' Afroz said, unable to drop the subject.

'Yes, but I don't think Sibby and Naz ever did.' Lindsay grinned. 'I'd catch them up on the flat roof, eating KitKats, and guzzling Cokes every ruza.'

Afroz stared at her in dismay and began to peel the onions.

That night she dreamed that she was up on the flat roof of the staff cottage, though she had never been up there. It was shrouded in darkness, and beyond Pen y Fan, a fierce battle raged between the sun and the moon.

'Chand goh!' she shouted to the moon. 'Thumar shawosh kitha! How dare you! Come down before you get burnt!'

But the dwarf moon didn't heed her; it continued to wrestle, and she watched in alarm as it began to melt under the sun's molten rage.

Then a small hand took hers. She looked down, and it was Elias.

'Why are they fighting?' he asked her.

'Afroz!' Down below, by her aunt's fig tree, Humayun stood shouting at her. 'Come down, now!'

'But Elias is here!' she shouted back.

'Forget him!' Humayun shouted. 'Come for your daughter.'

Afroz blinked, and there, sure enough, was Ruksana, lying on a blanket beside his feet. Afroz tried to let go of Elias's hand, but he held to it tighter.

'Why are they fighting?' Elias asked again.

She looked at him, feeling the despair buzz in her chest, and then she stared up at the flamingo-pink sky.

'Afroz?'

Afroz woke with a start.

It was her aunt calling to her. 'Afroz! Who could it be at this time?'

It was the doorbell ringing, and the clock on her bedside table showed it was almost time for sehri: 2.40 a.m.

Afroz opened the door and there they all were: Riaz, Junaid, Hannan, Gul and even Lindsay, yawning and shivering in the night breeze. Behind them, a slender crescent moon peered through a cloud. Afroz couldn't stop her smile from widening with each step they took towards the kitchen, their sleepy conversation filling the house.

'Everyone, sit down, let me fry the puris!' she said, aware of the quiver in her voice. She smiled at the surprise in her aunt's face. 'You too, Fufu!'

But none of them sat down as they'd been told. Instead they stood around her, becoming more awake as the smell of fried puris lifted out of the pan, and mingled with their chatter.

'Lins, are you going to fast then?'

'I might do, I survive on water and a fag most days anyways.'

'Oh man, you can't drink water, fool!'

'You can't smoke! You shouldn't smoke anyway.'

'Are you serious?'

'Nothing – no eating no drinking. Some people don't swallow their spit!'

'Oh, gross!'

'Not gross,' Jahanara said, 'this is people's love for the divine. They will deprive themselves of even—'

'Their own bodily fluids!'

'Dhur bodmash!'

'No tea!'

'Oh, then no, I'm not going to fast. Can't do without my Yorkshire blend! But I'm not missing the sehri party!'

Afroz's face hurt from all the smiling and her heart ached with gratitude.

'Afa goh,' Junaid said, swallowing a mouthful of puri, and holding out his hand for another. 'You can't just do sehri! What about iftari? Iftari party at yours too?'

She handed him a puri and looked around the room. She watched her aunt slicing lemons, and then sliding a sliver onto each plate. Afroz nodded at Junaid. 'Oy, of course, iftari here too.'

'Monthlong party,' Lindsay said, her mouth full. 'I love it.'

Each night, Afroz wept into her janamaz, her toes numb from the twenty rakaths of tarawih, the Ramadan prayers. *Ya Allah*, she cried, *thank you for your love, thank you for this love, for these people, for this place.* When had her life ever been this full? When had she ever felt such satisfaction as she did in the restaurant's kitchen – learning how to check supplies, measure food temperatures, the importance of thoyri kora, or preparation: the portioning and marinating of the cuts of meat, the peeling of vegetables and chopping of garnishes – life in a restaurant was about so much more than simply cooking. It was like setting a stage and putting on a performance night after night. And the staff were so good to her, their kindnesses morphing into more substantial relationships. Hannan seemed to think her the expert on all things Islamic and had begun to seek her opinion on certain hadiths. And Lindsay asked her to join her outside when she went for her smoke, for no other reason, that Afroz could see, than to chat to her. And she had begun to enjoy Riaz's company while helping out in the front, hoovering the maroon diamond-patterned carpet under the legs of the tables and chairs. Then she would join

Riaz behind the bar, where he showed her how to bundle the corner of a tea towel into the wine glasses and polish the inside and out in one swift movement.

'Some people just take them out the dishwasher and serve, but see, you don't get that shine unless you polish, right? Like the boss used to say, you've got to pay attention to all the little details!'

Afroz stiffened at the reference to Shamsur.

'Sorry, Afa,' Riaz offered, letting his arms hang. 'Sorry, I didn't mean—'

'It's okay,' she said, stuffing the corner of the cloth inside her glass. She found the movement difficult after a few glasses. Her wrist ached.

'It's all in the shoulder, see?' Riaz explained to her. He made a show of loosening his hips and bounced on his knees. 'Should be no tension anywhere but the shoulder. A bit like MMA?'

'MMA, abar kitha? What is that?' Afroz asked.

Riaz laughed. 'You never see any boxing, Afa? MMA is a kind of fighting – that's what I do – that's why I have these big guns, see?' Riaz leaned forward to show her his bulging biceps, and Afroz, mortified, took a step back, though Riaz didn't seem to notice. 'Just like MMA, see? You have to use your shoulder, otherwise your wrist will kill you tomorrow.'

One afternoon, midway through Ramadan, the few hours she spent at the restaurant with Riaz went swiftly by. By the time she left and walked the few steps next door, her limbs felt pleasantly weary. When she looked back, she saw that Riaz had joined Lindsay and Junaid, and the three of them were standing by the side entrance, puffing on cigarettes, watching her. She smiled, and they waved at her.

'Come join us!' Lindsay called.

She joined them, standing in the shade of the gate, shivering pleasantly in the afternoon breeze, letting their smoke warm the sides of her face, letting their strange, lilting chatter warm her heart. They watched the man from Chez Jones lace up his trainers, one foot on the door frame to steady himself.

'Off for your run, Tom?' Lindsay called.

The man nodded, grinned, held up a thumb.

'I used to love running,' Afroz heard herself say. She shrank into the wall, wondering what had possessed her to say it.

'Seriously?' Riaz looked dubious.

'You should go running here! Did you bring your trainers?' Lindsay asked her.

Afroz shook her head, smiled. 'No, I don't have any. I haven't run since I left school.'

'Oh, so like a couple of decades ago?' Riaz laughed, and she laughed too.

'What size are you?' Lindsay asked.

'UK five.'

'Same as me. I'll loan you a pair.'

'No, I couldn't.'

'Hey, Tom,' Lindsay called out, 'take our boss next time, won't you? She's new to the area.'

Tom began to run towards them. Afroz, numb with fear, watched the throbbing veins on his calf muscles.

'Yeah, no problem!' He smiled as he went past, gliding more than running. They watched as he passed the Islam house.

'He's a fit little thing, isn't he?' Lindsay muttered.

'Yes,' Afroz agreed. 'He is extremely fit, very athletic.'

She didn't understand the laughter erupting around her, and she didn't mind it either. Her eyes settled back on her aunt's house and reminded her that this was also a month of redemption.

Afroz would work hard for her redemption. She would cook and clean and organise the home she had wrecked, she would tend to Fufu, making the woman's meals, helping her in the garden and around the house and she would work harder than ever in the

Peacock. She would make amends through hard work and long prayers and her fasting body.

Fridays were cash-and-carry days, and on the Friday before Eid Afroz found herself dealing with the drink order by herself. She hoisted a six-pack of sparkling water into her shopping trolley and then pushed it down the aisle. It still galled her that people paid for water and that the tap water was relegated to mundane tasks like teeth cleaning and hair washing. Afroz guzzled litres after sunset, loving the way it poured out of the tap and into her glass, the taste of the mountains sharp on her tongue. She had boiled water for hours in Sylhet and had still never been able to obliterate the metallic taste.

She took a Biro from her pocket and put a tick next to the items she had collected. It was cold inside the cash-and-carry, even with her aunt's oversized angora cardigan and the exertion of pushing the heavy cart. It was the one thing that still plagued her after weeks of being in the country, as though her very bones had become damp.

'Just like Shamsur,' her aunt would say, whenever she shivered or complained of being cold. 'He felt the cold like a tiger in the Arctic!'

And Afroz would look away, ashamed of this genetic predisposition.

She soon reached the alcohol aisle and, as she had done the several times she had been there before, she paused between the rows of dull reds on one side and blanched whites on the other and she swallowed down the lump of guilt in her throat.

'Excuse me,' she called to an attendant stacking Tiger beer at the end of the aisle. If she could help it, she avoided touching the stuff directly. 'Could you help me, please?' She held the cart still as the man loaded it with the boxes she pointed out. She had raised the issue of alcohol with Riaz a few days before – suggested that, as good Muslims, they stop serving alcohol on the premises. She had been mortified by the way Riaz had laughed at her exclaiming, 'BYOB isn't going to work around here, Afa!' and, though she had not understood, she forbade herself from broaching the subject again.

She found her aunt near the haberdashery section where she had left her, still trying to choose between the poppers she wanted for the rose-patterned duvet cover she was making for Afroz. Fufu had resurfaced just as Afroz had begun to make friends and, in the company of the people Afroz invited to the house, Jahanara seemed to find it easier to slip into her old role of affectionate aunt. It was only in the quiet afternoons that Afroz would find her aunt silently watching her every move with an indecipherable expression on her face. Soon, Afroz began to invite not just Lindsay and Riaz and Junaid, but regulars at the restaurant too, as well as the neighbour from next door. Entertaining, it turned out, was Jahanara's forte – she plunged into cooking and cleaning with a new zest.

One morning, she called Afroz into Sabrina's room. The window seat from Nasrin's room had been moved into it, and the walls hung with white-framed pictures of garden abstracts and the Ayatul Kursi. 'I can't stay here!' Afroz gasped. 'It's Sabrina's room.'

Her aunt had shrugged. 'This room has the morning sun.'

Afroz had felt mortified, knowing that Sabrina would be aghast if she discovered it, but the little rug that had also been placed at the foot of the bed, round and soft beneath her feet, made her trill with pleasure. She pleaded with her aunt not to go to so much trouble when her visit was temporary, but Jahanara waved her away, reminding her that she was a daughter of the house, and as a daughter, she would have two homes, one in her husband's and one in the Beacons. Afroz didn't have the heart to tell her that Humayun was so enraged at the extension of her visit that it would be unlikely he would ever let her out of his sight again. Instead she said, 'That's kind of you, Fufu. After everything …' and Fufu had looked at her, puzzled, as though she had already forgotten the great secret that had been disclosed, and Afroz felt a fleeting flush of anger. 'Don't you know anything?' she asked suddenly. 'Don't you know why he kept me a secret? Or who my mother was?' And Jahanara had sat back, as though willing the backrest of her chair to open up and swallow her, the fear returning to her face like a purple shadow. Then she had abruptly stood and left.

When Afroz found her, several hours later, cleaning out weeds from the patio in the gentle sunshine, Jahanara called out to her. 'Afi, it's almost time for iftari! What shall we make with the kisuri today?' And Afroz realised that she would have to wait. She would have to wait, or she would have to forget, if she wanted the company of her aunt.

Afroz waited with the trolley as Jahanara weighed the packets in her hands. A child in a pair of zigzag leggings ran past them, her father calling after her, and Afroz was reminded of the story Nasrin had once told her, of the time she had lost her father and Sabrina in here. Afroz imagined a small Nasrin running wild with fear through these aisles, too high to look over. It was such a cold, unfriendly place for a child to get lost in. When the attendant had finally found her, Nasrin had been in the throes of an epileptic seizure.

'Fufu,' Afroz said, watching her compare one hue of lilac thread against another. 'Naju's epilepsy is getting bad now, na?'

'Ish, yes it is – she's promised to see the doctor this week.'

'Has she had it since she was born?'

Her aunt seemed surprised by the question, affronted even. 'Na! She was not born with it! Nothing in either of our families – it is not hereditary!' She put one of the shades of lilac back on the shelf and the other into her basket with the poppers. 'She was seven when she had her first. A classmate of hers, a Vicky, bodmash bacha, locked her in the cupboard in the school gym. Allah only knows. They say that trauma started it.'

Afroz couldn't stop thinking about this as she paid. The thought of her sister in the darkness, alone, grappling with her first seizure. It was unfair, she realised, to constantly envy her sisters for their good fortune. Nasrin, at least, had her fair share of woes.

Outside, one of the Stoney brothers, who owned the cash-and-carry, helped her load the boot of the old Volvo.

'How's business doing? The summer's always a good time for it, isn't it?' Afroz liked that he thought she was up to the task of making small talk about the state of trade. Taseen used to discuss his student politics with her, though she realised now that many of her opinions were, in fact, his. She had grown up conflicted over whether her voice should or should not be heard; learning finally that in the presence of her mother, it should not be, but in the presence of her father it could be, albeit in a censored way.

'The summertime always makes people hungry,' she offered, wishing that she had a less stolid response prepared. 'The heat makes people want spice, crave spice.'

'That's very true,' the man said, returning her smile. He deposited the last of the boxes and shut the boot. 'I hate to ask, Miss, but could you settle the outstanding bill? I know it must be taking time, the transfer of the business and all – my dad's told me you've got all these legal things to deal with – but …' His voice trailed away and she nodded vigorously through her surprise and confusion.

As she reversed out of the car park, her aunt inspecting the shopping beside her, Afroz wondered why Riaz hadn't paid the bill. It seemed unlike him.

'Humayun,' said her aunt, breaking into her reverie, holding up Afroz's phone in front of them. 'It's him.'

Afroz put her earphones in and answered it, her sandalled feet slowing the car down as her heart raced. 'Hello, assalamualaikum?' Hearing his words made her physically slouch. Words hard as pellets, loaded with bitter recrimination.

'You didn't call this morning.'

'Sorry, I woke up later, last night we worked until after two.'

Humayun sighed, and she felt wretched at the sound of his frustration. 'Why Afi? Why work until two? Ish, if Ma found out that a daughter-in-law of this house was working – kaj korche – she will be beside herself!'

'Is it a crime, Humayun,' Afroz asked quietly, 'to work?'

'Afi, please come home,' Humayun said after a brief silence. 'I don't understand what you are still doing out there.' And Afroz wished she could make him understand, but instead she said:

'What did you have for sehri? Did you eat well?'

'Who will make me sehri?'

'Isn't Minara there?'

'Pfft, you know how greasy she makes the porotha. Already I have so much acidity from the stress of all of this.'

'Please make sure she does the starch on your kurthas. She always forgets. Shall I speak to Ma?'

'I suppose you must go back soon?' her Fufu asked when the call ended, her voice sad and small.

Afroz nodded. But the idea of leaving her ageing aunt alone worried her. She had asked Nasrin on numerous occasions what was to be done with her mother, and Nasrin avoided the discussion. This indifference preyed on Afroz's mind. A few weeks before, Afroz had found Dorothy, her Fufu's nearest neighbour, whose house stood at the far side of the small field, getting drenched in the pouring rain because she had locked herself out. If Afroz left, who would make sure her Fufu was never so vulnerable?

11

There was barely a seat to be had at the doctor's surgery. The waiting room was a mess of mismatched sofas and armchairs, as tired as the patients that sat on them fussing with their coats and scarves. Nasrin spied a gap between two women; but it was an awkward space, one she would rather not squeeze into after having spent almost a quarter of an hour ironing the wrinkles out of her chiffon skirt. She escaped instead to the bathroom, and while washing her hands, inadvertently splashed water down the front of her skirt. Silly of her to wear it to the doctor's. The delicate material had started life as one of her mother's occasion sarees and had been refashioned by Nasrin into a skirt during her university days. Back when she thought she could find an accommodation halfway between being Bangladeshi and British. She had found it at the back of the closet this morning and held it out, letting the delicate strands of gold glint against the pale pink. It hadn't been the weather for it, but she had slipped it on and enjoyed the way it shimmied against her bare legs as she did her morning chores.

When her name was called, she followed the nurse to the office towards the back.

'Oh, no, I'm seeing Doctor Hardeep Junior,' Nasrin called out.

'No, no!' the nurse said, ushering her into the room. 'You're with Doctor Hardeep Senior today.'

Nasrin watched as the woman closed the door behind her.

'And what brings you here today, Mrs Wilson?'

The way Doctor Hardeep Senior emphasised *Wilson* always had the effect of making her feel disloyal for appropriating a name that didn't belong to someone like herself, a person as brown as a langsat. She smiled thinly, eyeing his navy turban.

'Is Doctor Kulwant Hardeep away today?' she asked as she took her seat. When he didn't answer, she sighed. 'The seizures came back, you see, when my father passed, and Doctor Kulwant gave me some new pills to try. Well, these new pills, I think they're making me sick.'

There were myriads of symptoms she wished to describe with that explanation. The fatigue. The nauseating taste of metal in her mouth. The visitations of things that shouldn't be there.

'Are they? Well, it's to be expected for a short stretch of time, you know, as your body begins to get used to them, but let's see.' Doctor Hardeep turned to his screen and typed her name with such agitating slowness that she had to fight the urge to lean over and snatch the keyboard away.

'And I don't think that they're making a difference, with the epilepsy,' she said, jiggling her right knee. 'The seizures are more frequent than they were before.'

'Well, you know Kulwant talked to you about getting a seizure dog,' the doctor said, glancing at her knee. She stopped shaking it. The doctor peered at the computer screen. 'It says here you were going to talk to your husband.'

Amma would never set foot in a house with a dog in it.

'It's not really an option for me,' she said, fidgeting with the folds of her skirt. 'Out of interest, doctor – are there any side effects to these pills?'

'Dizziness can be common in the early days.' Doctor Hardeep turned to her. 'Fatigue, a little nausea perhaps – are you experiencing any?'

What Nasirn wanted to ask about was hallucinations, but instead she shook her head, 'No. I just wanted to know what to expect.'

'Of course. Yes, I see that you have been on the new ones for several weeks now so any side effects should start to settle down soon.' He turned back and strapped her arm into a blood pressure cuff. 'How are you feeling yourself?'

'Sick,' she replied. She turned away from the little hairs poking out of his nose and looked at the far wall, where a large green poster demanded she take a flu vaccine if she were over sixty-five.

'Maybe time for a holiday, Mrs Wilson!'

'Yes, we do have one planned, but not until Christmas. Richard is so busy at work these days.'

'Very good, good to be busy. What does your husband do again, Mrs Wilson? I think he is in finance?'

'Law. He's a lawyer.'

'Your blood pressure is a little low.' He unstrapped the cuff and peered at her from beneath his huge eyebrows. She saw where Doctor Hardeep Junior got his hazel eyes. 'And when are you feeling the sickness, Mrs Wilson?'

'Nasrin, please, you can call me Nasrin. Throughout the day, it comes and goes.'

He pushed his chair back and reached for a urine sample container.

'Would you be able to provide a quick sample, Mrs Wilson? Even a little will do it.'

Nasrin retreated to the toilet. She returned with the container, wrapped in tissue, and handed it awkwardly over.

'So where is holiday this year?' Doctor Hardeep asked as he opened it without ceremony and plunged a strip into it.

'Antigua,' she replied, mortified by the deep amber colour of the liquid. She reached for the bottle of Evian in her bag.

'Not India? You are not Indian?'

'No,' she said hotly. This was not the first time Doctor Hardeep Senior had asked her this. He was always trying to interject India into the conversation wherever there seemed even the smallest opportunity for it. Like her father, who had done the same with Bangladesh. *Do you know Bangladeshis did this and Bangladeshis do that? Do they have*

anything like the Ilish maas here? Where do oranges come from, Nasrin?
She was fairly certain that oranges did not come from Bangladesh.
Not that she'd ever had the courage to openly contradict him on this.
But with Doctor Hardeep Senior, it was more than simply absentee
patriotism. Doctor Hardeep Senior seemed to be staking his claim
on her, trying to contain her within a brown box. India isn't the only
country with brown people in the world, she wanted to say. Have
you heard of Pakistan? Or Bangladesh? Or Brazil?

'Mrs Wilson, when was your last period?'

Nasrin peered at the two lines of pink on the strip the doctor
was holding.

'Antigua is in the Caribbean,' she told the doctor. Her face felt
unpleasantly hot, as though she had opened a hot oven and bent
over it. She reached up and touched her eyebrows. 'Not India. It's
nowhere near India.'

'I see.' Doctor Hardeep nodded, reaching on a shelf for a gown.
'Would you pop this on, Mrs Wilson?'

An hour or so later, she called Richard from the cab and his
PA picked up.

'Is Richard there, Di?' she asked.

'Naz! How are you? How is that beautiful baby of yours?'

'He's fine,' Nasrin answered. 'As am I. I thought I could pop in if
Richard's free for lunch? See you all?'

'His calendar looks open to me,' Diana replied. 'I saw him leave
a little earlier, probably to get a bite – I'll put you through to his
mobile if you hold just a moment.'

'I can't, sweetie,' Richard said when she asked if he had time for
lunch, 'I've got back-to-backs.'

Nasrin frowned. 'Oh.'

'Love you,' he said before hanging up.

She stared out at Bishopsgate, feeling the doubt build up inside
her. 'Sorry, change of plan,' she said to the cab driver. 'Islington
please.'

The cab pulled into a side street to turn around, and she saw the little deli Richard had taken her to a few times. She was so near the office now. She could pick up some pasta and salad from Ottolenghi and just pop it in. Accompanied by her news. That would be a nice way to tell him.

She leaned forward and rapped her knuckles against the glass. 'Sorry, I'll get out here.'

She ambled towards Artillery Lane for a few minutes before speeding up, abashed at the way others tutted as they swerved to pass her by. People walked fast in this part of the City; their legs were the only animated part about them. They moved like speedy automatons, jaws set in steel, gaze set mechanically ahead. She was an alien with her little Mulberry bucket, an unfashionable shade of tan, her silver leaf-drop earrings and this ridiculously inappropriate paisley skirt. She was an unravelling spool of thread in a row of neatly rolled bobbins.

Yards away from the restaurant, her heel caught in the crack of two paving stones, and she had to catch herself from saying 'Y'Allah!' as she bent down to release it. She straightened, looking up at the sky and noting, with a certain giddiness, that it was the colour of a newborn's fingernails – a hint of pink in its translucence. She bit her lip to stop herself from smiling and stepped giddily into the queue outside Ottolenghi's door. As she waited, she toyed with her phone, wanting to call Sabrina, but worried it would be inappropriate to share the news with anyone before she had shared it with Richard. A waitress with a ring in her upper lip swung the door open to ask if anyone was waiting for a table, and the queue shortened as several people stepped inside. Nasrin gazed after them. She shivered. She could go inside, get warm, eat some of that lovely aubergine with the crème fraiche and pine nut dip. She could order some for Richard and drop it off before she went home.

As she followed the waitress in, Nasrin saw them, both in profile.

Richard and Fabienne, facing each other, were deep in conversation over a shared plate of half-eaten raspberry meringue.

The rest of the day dripped away slowly. The memory of Richard's relaxed smile directed at another woman tore at her. How he had gazed at her once. All it took, she remembered reading somewhere – all it took to fall in love was a gaze. That gaze.

That evening, Richard came home in a loud, obnoxious mood. Barging in with his bundle of papers, which he refused to use a brief-case for, jiggling his phone in his hand. He dropped kisses on Elias's head and looked over and caught Nasrin's eye and smiled.

She laid the table, waiting for him to remark on her silence, to ask what the matter was, but he did not.

They ate bland poached salmon and stringy, soggy asparagus, and as he washed it down with yesterday's Sauvignon, she stuck to water, and still he noticed nothing. Her eyes wandered to Richard's fingers, to the band of ugly platinum digging into his flesh. She looked away and stood to clear the plates.

Richard picked up his papers from the hallway table, and with the bottle of wine tucked under his arm and his chipped Best Dad mug dangling from his finger, made his way up the stairs.

She watched him from the kitchen, thinking about the raspberry-sized foetus performing somersaults in her uterus during the ultrasound.

She looked at the plates left on the tabletop, at the crumbs beneath the stool, at the smudges of butter on the counter and the sprays of cooking oil on the splashback. She looked through the kitchen window with its smeared pane that needed cleaning from the outside, at the potted orchids that were resilient to her neglect. She looked at the rug on the white ceramic floor, once far too pretty to be in front of a hob, but now so stained that it would be useless anywhere else. As she took in all the details of her home, her prison, something in her howled to be released.

What had her life become? Was this what it was to be married? To have a child? Was this it? The half-baked attentions of a man she had once loved, and the half-formed affections of an over-coddled child.

And then that woman. That woman.

She leapt up the stairs two, three at a time.

She had a first in Engineering from Imperial. She'd flown at the helm of a Boeing 747. And that history translated to something. It did. It translated to more than being the mother of his child, the mistress of his house, a janitor and nurse and secretary revolving around him and facilitating his life. All while he was doing what? What was he doing with that woman?

She stood outside his study, her breaths tumbling out, one on top of the other.

She could hear him inside listening to Miles Davis. In his own space, sipping his wine, perusing those damn papers and oblivious to her.

She opened the door.

'Oh fuck! Nasrin, what the fuck!'

She closed it again. It was a measured response; a dignified response to the undignified posture of her husband, hunched over the lewd images on his screen.

She walked downstairs and sat at the kitchen table, staring at the blackening bananas in the fruit bowl as she waited for him to come down to her.

'How about knocking?'

'What?'

He sat down opposite her, rubbed his nose with his thumb and stared at the corner of the table.

'Look, Naz – it was porn, just some porn!'

She looked at him, tried her best to keep her voice even. 'I saw her with you. Eating raspberry meringue.'

She watched the blood drain from his face. She looked down, back at her knuckles. The rings on her fingers felt tight and she twisted them around.

He stood and walked round the table to sit on the chair beside her and this alone terrified her.

'It was a working lunch,' he said, but his consoling words were contradicted by the fact that his voice was tight. 'You know I've got the partnership stuff coming up at the end of the summer.'

She waited.

'I feel like I have to focus on this. I know you're finding it difficult since your dad—'

'Really? How is this about my dad?'

'You know what?' He leaned back and slammed his hand on the table. 'I don't understand it either, because you never seemed that close to him! Always found an excuse to get as far away from them as possible, and sure, don't deny it, I was your best excuse!'

She leaned forward, one hand bearing her weight on the table, and slapped him hard across the face with the other.

Her throat swelled with shame at what she had done.

She stood up. Behind her the chair teetered on two legs and she let it for a few seconds before pulling it back. He looked old in this yellow light. A half man in tracksuit bottoms that were too snug around the waist and with the light glinting off his exposed temples.

'This isn't about my father, Rich,' she said quietly. 'This is about us. About … About *her*.'

'Okay, Naz, you want to talk about us, let's do that.' Richard rubbed his face, his voice unnaturally shrill. 'You never want to have sex … It's been months, you know?'

'Not months,' she said, ruefully, thinking of her pregnancy test that afternoon. 'Not months.'

But he wasn't listening. 'And that's just not normal. You're constantly on the phone with your mother. You're always writing to your sister, who never seems to have any time for you, anyway. When I'm with you, you're not with me.' He turned to her. 'I don't mean just physically, but emotionally too, you're just not really here.'

A movement caught her eye. She turned to look past Richard to the rose bushes huddled in the garden as the night descended. Just beside them, sitting on the low brick wall was her seven-year-old self in her faded paisley nightie.

'You see?' His voice drew her back. 'You're gone already.'

'Are you sleeping with her, Rich?'

Her voice was so plaintive. Pleading. *Lie*, she silently willed him, *just lie to me. I want you to.* She watched his lips twitch, but there was only silence. It was the longest silence of her life.

'Oh, God.' She moved away from the table. 'Oh God, ohgodoh-god.'

Every part of her from her scalp to her toes felt like it was being twisted and rung out. She walked from the fireplace – she must get the marble man to come and see to that juice stain – over to the kitchen counter. And then back to the fireplace again. Behind her, still sitting at the table, Richard said something, words which were swallowed by the buzzing void around her. They couldn't reach her where she was, immersed in a sea of panic. She rubbed at the juice stain with her forefinger, and then thumped it with her fist. Marble was beautiful but so weak. Permeable to alien substances. She let out a gasp and laid her head onto the mantelpiece, letting the cool stone soothe her forehead.

Still he did not come to her. His words, whatever they were, did not reach her. She silenced him by turning and staring at him.

She remembered how seven years ago he sat in her room in the Beacons, wiping the tears that poured down her cheeks, as she hiccupped the tale of her shameful disciplinary and firing. She remembered how five years ago he laid his head on her lap as he sang 'Waltzing Matilda' to the bulge of their unborn child.

'*Once a jolly swagman camped by a Billabong,*' she whispered. He looked at her. 'Do you remember that?'

But he didn't answer and Nasrin realised that somehow, while she had not been looking, he had ceased to be the man she had married. It occurred to her that her mother probably felt the same about her husband since Afroz's paternity had been disclosed.

She let out a laugh. A wretched one that stopped abruptly. It was only right that the sins of the father fell on the child.

'Those ruby earrings?' she asked.

But she didn't hear Richard's response. There might have been a sorry, and an *I wish it hadn't happened*. But they didn't reach her. She was concentrating on the stain on the marble. She remembered clearly how it had happened. She had put down a cracked beaker with cranberry juice in it and had remembered too late that it was leaking. Hours later she had found the berry ring mark embedded in the grey marble.

'I gave up everything for you,' she said softly. 'My family, my community, my religion, all of it.'

'I gave up everything for you!' he said, his voice tight. 'My country. My family don't speak to me.'

'Because they're racist!'

'And yours aren't?'

'My family accepted you!'

'They did nothing of the sort! Doesn't it seem weird to you that they *chose* to live here and still have these backward customs from some bygone era from a country they chose to leave! Doesn't that seem weird to you?'

For a moment the air seemed to thin, and she surprised herself when she said, 'I'm going back to the Beacons.'

She wanted her mother. More than anything, she wanted her mother.

He stood looking out of the window and shook his head.

'It takes two to make a marriage work, Naz,' he said suddenly, turning to look at her. His words were scratchy with anger. 'You're blaming me, when you know, if you're honest, you checked out of it ages ago.'

He looked at her, challenging her to say something. But she merely stared back blankly.

'You don't need to go anywhere, Naz. This is your home. I'll go.'

Her heart sank to the floor. 'No,' she said.

'Okay.' He nodded. Was it her or did his eyes glisten? 'Go then. Do what you need to do.'

12

On Friday evening, Sabrina and Benjamin stood outside the office and tried to hail a cab. The evening air was warm and humid, and each wished that they were heading back to the privacy of their apartments rather than out for dinner at an overcrowded, stuffy restaurant. Sabrina's exhaustion was exacerbated by her anxiety, for her lunch meeting with Monty had been cancelled yet again and it was not unreasonable to connect this with the Altieri investigation. Compliance were still hunting for the person other than Ralph who had collaborated in hiding the potential ratings downgrade. On top of this stress, she was also feeling an old envy return at the news that Nasrin was returning to the Beacons.

'The Beacons?' Sabrina exclaimed when her sister had told her that morning. 'Again? Has something happened?'

There was a short almost imperceptible wobble in Nasrin's voice when she answered, 'Nothing's happened.'

'Dids. Are you sure?'

'Yes.'

'Okay, but you just got back!'

'I know,' Sabrina heard her sister sigh and when she spoke again, there was a feigned lightness in her tone that did nothing to convince Sabrina. 'I think I'm just missing Abba, Sibby … and maybe it would be good to be with Amma for a bit.'

You mean it would be good to be with Afroz, Sabrina had thought, feeling the familiar sting of envy.

Now though, as Benjamin tried to hail a cab, Sabrina found herself worrying again about the tightness in her sister's voice.

'Got one!' Benjamin called and she rushed to get in as he held the door open for her. The cab glided to the intersection, and then stopped short in front of a traffic jam.

'So, you're going to be one of the chosen ones!' Sabrina said, referring to his next placement in the firm's prestigious investment banking division. 'A trader! I think you might be my only analyst to have made it up there.'

The cab pulled up at the Crypt and Sabrina peeled out fifteen dollars and handed it over.

The driver glared at her. 'You give only a dollar tip!'

She ignored him and closed the door.

'Here,' Benjamin said lightly, as he rapped on the window to give the cabbie a five-dollar note.

When they were seated at the bar waiting for their table, Sabrina slid a glass across to him. 'The way I see it, if you only use one cab a month, then sure you should give a thirty per cent tip. But if you're using a trillion a day, then your custom is enough.'

'Okay, boss. You know how much these guys get paid, right?'

'I'm sure it's not very much.'

'Average is a hundred and sixty dollars a day. Out of that they pay a hundred for the medallion and probably about fifty on fuel. They live off your tip, not your custom.'

'What are you? The tip police?'

'My dad's a cabbie.'

There was an awkward silence, and Sabrina delivered a tiny, almost imperceptible burp into it.

'Oh my God! Excuse me!'

'Excuse you!'

'Champagne,' she explained, giggling.

'Do you tip your manicurist?' he asked, grabbing a handful of wasabi almonds from the silver bowl in front of them.

'Your mum works in a nail salon?'

'Actually, my cousin.'

The word *cousin* dampened her mood. The word echoed and magnified a thousandfold within her.

'I have a cousin,' she said, so softly that she barely heard herself over the the hum of conversation about them. 'Except, not anymore.'

Benjamin pursed his lips and looked about to say something when the front-of-house approached them.

'Sir, your table is ready.'

Sabrina picked up her glass and stepped off her stool. 'I hope we have a good table – facing the terrace would be nice.'

They were seated at a table near the window with a view of the terrace fountain, and Sabrina felt lightheaded and foolish. She should know better than to drink on an empty stomach, especially after such an exhausting week. She excused herself and walked past a table of women full of laughter and the sounds of chinking glasses. A tall woman in a red sequined dress rose from her seat and slipped in front of Sabrina on the way to the ladies'. The curves of the woman's body were the delicate sort that came from daily Pilates classes and a healthy diet, reminding her of Nasrin. Nasrin, who had sounded so strange that morning and who was going back to the Beacons to be with Afroz. Sabrina washed her hands and criticised the roundness of her shoulders and the bulge of her hips in the mirror. As she accepted the warm towel the attendant held out for her, she berated herself; she needed to exercise more, eat less, spend a little more on maintenance like one of those Upper East Side Pilates herbivores. As she turned to leave, she stopped, rummaged in her purse for a ten-dollar bill and slid it onto the tray.

'Thank you, ma'am, you have a nice evening, now!' the attendant exclaimed as Sabrina slipped out.

The room was twice as busy as when she had left it five minutes ago. She walked through a large group being seated and emerged on the other side to see Benjamin standing with his back towards her, speaking to a group of four people. She felt her throat tighten as she approached them, and she had to pull at the corners of her lips to form a smile.

'Hi, Ralph, wow! Fancy seeing you here!' she said, blindsided by his presence, her eyes searching his for clues as to whether he was pleased to see her.

'Sabrina!' Ralph gushed his introductions, his vowels slippery and uncontrolled. 'Rachel here wanted to come. And what the birthday girl wants, she gets,' he explained.

'Happy birthday, Rachel! That's a beautiful dress on you!' They touched cheeks with one another, and Rachel smiled vacantly, her bare arms held gracefully to her sides.

'Ah! There he is! The man of the hour!' Sabrina turned to find Ashok standing behind her. He held her gaze for a moment before slipping past her to stand by his wife. Sabrina felt a jolt of envy as Ralph smacked his son-in-law on the back and said with a theatrical whisper, 'We can tell the in-crowd, right?'

'Some good news?' Sabrina asked, turning to Rachel, a smile frozen on her face. 'A little one on the way?'

'Oh, God no!' Rachel returned, frowning.

'Haha, no, no!' Ralph chuckled. 'No, the news is that Big Guy here is getting promoted to acting head of the Digital Assets team, just, you know, while I'm out and they look into this stuff.'

'What?' Sabrina gaped at Ralph. Her thoughts scattered like marbles in her head. 'What?' she asked again, this time looking to Ashok. 'I thought you were moving to the Hedge Funds Sales team?'

Ashok opened his mouth to speak but then seemed to think better of it and threw Sabrina a wounded look before turning away. Ralph threw back his bald head and roared out a laugh. 'It's okay, Sabrina, I'll be back before you know it. This,' he said to his daughter and son-in-law, waving his arm expansively, 'is loyalty for you. Word of advice, Ash, always inspire loyalty in the trenches.' He looked at Sabrina and shook her shoulder. 'I'm sad you guys are doing the exit dinner without me,' he said, gesturing at their table set for two, 'but I guess we can do something belatedly when this whole fiasco is over. What say I get us a table at Per Se, Ben? Have you been? It's where I took Sabrina all those decades ago when she was a rotating analyst! Course,' he guffawed, 'Sabrina's too much of a cheapskate to take someone there herself! You'd think we don't pay her enough!'

'I don't think it was quite decades ago, Ralph,' Sabrina heard herself saying. 'Decades is rather overstating things. And actually, yes, it's true, you don't fucking pay me enough.' She tore her eyes away from Ashok's hand placed gently on the small curve of Rachel's back and instead gazed dumbly at Ralph's shiny hairless scalp, the tightness of his collar and the way his bumpy, rash-ridden neck spilled over the side. Anger swelled inside her.

Ralph let out a hoot of laughter, and pushed his family along to their table, mouthing at Sabrina as he passed by, 'Let's talk.'

'He's pretty sure he's coming back!' Benjamin whispered over to her as soon as they were out of earshot.

'Yes,' she said, trying to calm the fury within her. As they walked away, Ashok turned towards her with a look of concern, but Sabrina turned away.

'That Ashok Mehta,' Benjamin observed, still watching them, 'he's a smooth operator, huh? You can't see him coming.'

Sabrina felt a flash of irritation at this incomplete appraisal and did not reply. She watched a couple wander outside with their drinks, and slowly circle the fountain. They were young, probably in their late twenties like her, except they somehow looked younger than she felt. The woman stopped and stood with one leg crossed behind the other: so girlish and trusting, so whimsical. Had Sabrina ever stood or looked like that?

No, she had spent the years running like a lunatic towards the carrot strung up in front of her. She'd sprinted for all she was worth. She'd run straight past everyone she had once loved, treating them as though they were spectators, cheerleaders even. She had been so focused on the finishing line and on keeping track of where her competitors were, and yet it now appeared the line had moved, her competitors were gone and the rest of the racecourse was empty.

With sudden clarity, Sabrina realised that Ashok was the reason her invitation to lunch with Monty had mysteriously been cancelled without so much as an apology. The firm would not want two MDs in one team – if Ashok was being promoted to head, he would also be made MD, which meant she was not being promoted anytime soon. Ashok had taken it all. What the hell had she been doing, sleeping with her boss's son-in-law? This city had dirtied her. Far away from everyone and everything that was clean and good and wholesome, she was living a dirty life.

She accepted a refill from the waiter and downed it in one go.

She turned to Benjamin. 'You know how you said you were a hole-in-wall kind of guy?'

'Yes …'

'Let's get out of here, I know a place.'

They finished a bottle of champagne before they left and decided the evening was too lovely to waste in a cab. Benjamin had finally shaken off the last vestiges of his office restraint, and happily followed Sabrina as she meandered through the streets towards the Lower East Side. She nodded as he talked, but she was unable to shake the image of Ashok's hand on Rachel's back. The bastard. If they had promoted him, then they had certainly decided that she was the one they were pinning the Altieri mess on. She was the junior that was going to be fired along with Ralph. The evening's heat was suffocating, compounded by the fury unleashed within her. On her phone were messages from Ashok: *'I'll explain everything.'* And, *'I have your back Sab.'* She felt like slamming the phone into the bonnet of a passing car. But she also knew she would see him again. Not only was he going to be her new boss, but there had always been something that stopped her from ending the affair, some deep-seated attachment to him that left her feeling a strange paralysis if she tried to envisage an Ashok-less future. She needed a drink, quickly. She sped up, colliding with two women coming out of Bashir's falafel shop.

'Ya Allah! Sorry, sorry!' one said, taking a dramatic step out of Sabrina's way. The woman was dressed in a linen shalwar kameez, which was wrinkled around the midriff and an eye-popping lime green. The other was dressed, much like Sabrina, in Western clothes and had neat hair styled in a bob.

'Didi!' the bobbed one chided the older.

Sabrina, forgetting herself, responded in Bangla. 'Dekya cholo!'

The two women stared at her for a moment. Despite Sabrina's rudeness, the woman in the green shalwar seemed inordinately pleased.

'You're Bengali! You don't look Bengali!' she said to Sabrina.

Sabrina ignored her and swerved round to continue downtown.

'You're Bengali?' Benjamin asked, easily catching up with her. 'How did I not know that?'

'Because I don't need to shout it from the rooftops,' she said, 'like that foolish cow back there.'

Benjamin whistled. 'Harsh, boss.'

'I feel sorry for the other lady,' she continued, the words streaming out of her, as she quickened her pace. 'The woman with the bob, I mean, having to walk through a neighbourhood like this with a companion dressed for the tropics.' She knew she wasn't being politically correct, but she couldn't, didn't want to stop herself. 'Those sorts of people let me down, you know? There's people, like me, trying to assimilate, not just assimilate, but trying to rise above, you know, because you've got to be better than them just to be equal, and then there are people like that imbecile wearing a green shalwar kameez on the Lower East Side on a Friday night. Dragging us all down. Not just green, but fucking parrot green.'

'Wow,' Benjamin said and fell silent. She felt satisfied with the shock she had elicited. These women grated on her with their dogged resistance to progress and their reliance on superstitious, mythical beliefs that they deemed traditional. Never mind that those 'traditional' ways made them, in this modern world of atheism and science and technology, targets of ridicule. But they had done this to themselves, had they not? They had resigned themselves to these ignorant and diminutive lives.

She stopped and turned back to watch the woman and her dishevelled companion saunter away, and she suddenly felt a sliver of indignation, realising this could be her. She pictured herself walking down the Lower East Side accompanied by Afroz: a fresh-off-the-boat, old-fashioned woman mired in Islam and disturbingly obedient to the patriarchy.

How could they share a father? The same father who had raised her as a tenaciously independent Tipu, had failed to bequeath even a sliver of such empowerment to Afroz. When she recalled how Afroz had submitted to an unwanted arranged marriage, a flash of pity mixed with Sabrina's repugnance, adding to her wretchedness.

Being cousins had been a safe distance, but sisterhood was another matter. Sisterhood required meaningful connection and a promise to protect. How could Sabrina be expected to understand a woman like Afroz, who was the very embodiment of a breed of female Sabrina had railed against for years: a breed who incarcerated themselves inside the bounds of custom and orthodoxy, who believed it a sin to resist! How could she accept into the sorority she shared with Nasrin – with all its pledges of affection, safeguarding and esteem – someone she held in such disdain?

In her head, Nasrin's voice chided her for being cruel, but Sabrina protested that she had done her part. Every summer she had shared her sister, and her parents and their family income with Afroz – she couldn't forget how her mother had always made time for Afroz, especially that one summer, when she and Afroz had both contracted chicken pox, and Sabrina had constantly wanted her mother near her. But Afroz with her incessant whimpering had drawn Amma away. Sabrina had woken one night, the heat heavy on her chest, and had looked over to Afroz's bed to find her mother lying beside Afroz, her body curved around her, as though Afroz was a foetus inside Amma's womb. That was the image that, each time she thought of it, provided new fuel to Sabrina's dislike of Afroz. She had taken Amma, she had taken Abba, and now she was going to get the restaurant too. Sabrina thought of the Peacock, its yellowing facade, and the window boxes with the fuchsias, the heavy, pink blooms so dense during the summer. Would she ever see it again?

When they arrived at the bar, they found a table in the basement and Sabrina waited as Benjamin went to buy the drinks. Her thoughts returned to her sister again and the odd catch in Nasrin's voice that had made her seem further away than usual that morning. Perhaps her sister was tense because she knew that Sabrina would be envious. But what if it was something more? Sabrina had forgotten to ask Nasrin about the appointment she had scheduled with the doctor – could her sister be hiding new details about her epilepsy? She would call Nasrin tomorrow and make sure that all was well.

Benjamin returned with a tray of drinks and Sabrina forced a laugh.

'Lord, Ben, that's a tad excessive.'

'Well …' He seemed momentarily abashed before regaining his composure. 'I figured, seeing as you're paying,' he said, and patted his jacket pocket. 'I've kept the receipt.'

They knocked back the shots and margaritas, letting the rum and tequila soften them. They shared office gossip and shop talk, and Sabrina attempted to educate Benjamin's uninformed opinions on the rise of digital currencies and potential risks arising from their use. They talked about their career plans, their preferred Manhattan neighbourhoods, some friends and acquaintances they realised they had in common, and gradually Sabrina felt some of the venom within her lift away. This guy could be her friend, she thought as she gazed at him through heavy eyelids: when had she last hung out with some friends? Real friends? Did she even have any?

'Sabrina,' Benjamin said, sometime after midnight, leaning forward and placing his elbows on the sticky metal tabletop. Sabrina looked at him, wondering if she had ever heard him say her name. It tickled her, the vocalising of her name in a mouth unaccustomed to saying it. 'What did you mean back then,' she concentrated hard on his words, they were so slow and garbled, 'you know, when you said your cousin isn't a cousin anymore?'

Sabrina sipped her drink in silence, rolling the rock salt on her tongue.

'Did she pass away?' he pressed.

'Yes,' she said. The word slipped out and some grainy residue filtered into her soul. She finished the rest of her drink.

Before Benjamin could speak, she held up her hand and stood up, falling straight back down again.

'You okay, Boss?' he laughed, holding her steady. She felt his moist breath on her cheeks, and it made her stomach tighten.

She put her hand on the back of his neck and drew him close.

'Sabrina,' she said.

'What?'

'Not Boss,' she whispered. 'Just Sabrina.'

His arms tightened around her, and she sought out his mouth with hers.

Several hours later, Sabrina walked out onto Third Avenue. She searched up and down the street for a cab, shivering in the early morning breeze. The eerie stillness of the Lower East Side made it seem like a place she had never been before. She teetered down the street, passing huddled bags of trash and a cat that eyed her coolly. Her hair billowed about her face and refused to settle; strands tickled her chin and nose, but she was too cold to reach up to brush them away.

She was thirsty. She needed water. Desperately. Water to wash, to drink, to immerse herself in. The bottle of water in her fridge which her mother had transported all the way from the Well of Zamzam came to mind, and a wretched giggle escaped her lips; to think of her mother's Mecca pilgrimage and then this seedy, disgusting night Sabrina had just lived was absurd.

'Central Park West and 65th, please.' The tequila had disembodied her voice. Was it still her voice? Had the cabbie heard her? She slid onto the cold leather, wincing as the black tape that curled over the rips on the seat scratched her legs. She lay down, lifted her feet and curled up.

She thought of her father who had once told her – she had been so young that the memory of it was dreamlike – that when she was born, and they had laid her on the examining table to wipe her down and carry out the Apgar tests, she had turned and reached for his pinkie and had grasped it in her fist, demanding he take her home. It had become her favourite story, this creation myth, and had become the fuel with which she rode her childhood and then her youth: the idea of that mighty fist, the first-class Apgar score, the commanding tone of her infant wail, but first and foremost, that vice-like grip on her father's finger. Others had had role models, but not Sabrina. Sabrina had her father and his faith in her fortitude.

And yet how many times had she found herself, like this, curled up in the back of a cab after a night that had filled her with self-loathing? That creation myth was all consuming – she was powerful and strong and determined. So, when she was none of these, reduced like tonight, to an insipidly weak version of herself, too drunken and disorientated to find her way home, she felt herself a traitor to her father, and her father's version of her.

Back in her apartment, she switched the shower to its hottest setting, and although it was uncomfortable against her skin, she stood beneath it because the pain of it was nothing compared to the respectful way the doorman had averted his gaze as she had entered the building, or to the way the cab driver had got out of his car to open the door for her.

Other people's kindnesses.

She thought of her father, the kindest man she had ever met. The man who made them stop to pick up a hitch-hiker even when they were running late; the man who would give a forgetful pensioner a job to help him pay his rent; who should have died richer but had given away too much in his lifetime. She recalled the time he had driven four straight hours after closing the restaurant on a Friday night to pick her up from Oxford because she had had a bad interview.

'I just crumbled, Abba,' she had ranted to him in the car, ignoring the pink in his eyes and the jitteriness of his knuckles. 'I knew the answers, but I couldn't get my stupid words out, because I'm stupid.'

'Sibby.' He'd taken one of her hands and placed it on the steering wheel so he could hold it while he drove. She could still remember the feel of her father's hand on top of hers, making her guide the wheel. 'It's in Allah's hands. Put it behind you.' And she remembered the look on his face when he said this to her, because it was so at odds with his reassurances. He wore an expression of sudden and extreme self-doubt. From that day on her father transformed into a retreating, otherwise occupied figure, and instead of going to him with all her troubles as she had used to, Sabrina too retreated. She had progressed beyond the realm of his experiences, and he no longer knew how to help her. Sensing that they been distanced by their separate experiences, Sabrina had turned him into a near-deity, to be idealised and respected.

Then Afroz had come along and muddied it all.

She didn't know what to think of her father now. He had lived his life by such a strict moral code, one that he had impressed upon her and her sister every day. And now this was shown to be a lie.

She dried herself and crept into bed; she lay still as the thoughts milled about her head and the pillow grew damp from her wet hair.

Her cell phone beeped, and she saw that it was a message from Ashok.

'Sab, are you awake? Can you give me a call please? I need to know you're ok.'

She put the phone down and curled herself ever tighter into a ball.

13

It was Eid – the most low-key Eid-ul-Fitr that Afroz had ever experienced – and the day was disappointingly muggy with a single sheet of cloud that filled the sky. She was making her way to the bins with a bag full of feathery onion peel, recalling her run that morning. She had run alone – a sense of propriety had made her refuse Tom's invitation, and now that she knew the route, she found that the run was more soothing alone, giving her space to reflect on the thoughts crowding her, such as the troubling slur in Nasrin's voice during their telephone conversation the night before – presumably caused by the 'special Ribena' – and her argument with Humayun about when she would return to Desh. Her standoff with Humayun had lasted a few days now and she knew she would have to reach out to him before the matter escalated. As he refused to answer her calls on his mobile, she would have to call the landline and ask whoever picked up (most likely her mother-in-law) to pass the phone to her angry husband. She felt so weary of this struggle against him.

She reached up to open the bin and hurled the sack into it. It was at that moment that she noticed a grey Volvo pulling up to the restaurant.

She stood back to watch as it reversed into the Peacock's driveway. The passenger seats were occupied by men with white prayer caps.

She rushed back into the kitchen, scratching furiously at the prickles of heat beneath the edge of her headscarf. She suddenly wished that Lindsay was here, but it was a Tuesday, and Lindsay was off visiting her mother. Afroz wiped down the steel countertop. Then she did it again. There were only a handful of customers who were taking their time with their main courses. She wished they would hurry and order dessert and give her something to do.

Afroz could not make out the voices at the bar, muffled by the walls, but their intonation was without doubt Sylheti. She took out packets of turmeric and garam masala and proceeded to refill the canisters. Her breaths were sharp and loud and aggravated her panic. The turmeric she was decanting spilt onto the countertop and over her fingers, fine as talc.

She froze as she heard footsteps coming towards her and Riaz burst through the swinging doors so hard that they boomeranged back onto him.

'Afa!' he said in a loud whisper. 'Your hubby's here!'

'Kitha?'

'Your husband – Humayun – with a whole bloody gang of pakis!'

'Paki?'

'They're asking after you, I said you were next door …'

Afroz stared at him. Thoughts filled her head, weighing her down so she couldn't move.

'Afa?'

'Will you go and get my aunt?' she heard herself squeaking.

The minutes were thick and sticky, and Afroz felt each second of them as she stood cowering behind the door. Every so often, she squeezed the door handle for some relief from the panic. Hannan came down the stairs for a snack and stopped when he saw her. He turned slowly and retreated, empty-handed. Afroz glanced again at the wall clock. The voices at the bar ominously turned an octave lower. Afroz allowed her panic to swell: what if Fufu was not coming? What if they took her, right from this kitchen, like the immigration people had taken Mustafa? She began to count softly: ek, dhuy, thin, chayr, fas. With a start, she heard the kitchen doors swing, and the voices rushed at her through the opening. She stopped counting and listened with her heart in her mouth.

'Afi?'

'Fufu?'

She let go of the door, relief flooding through her, making her giddy. She hugged her aunt tight.

'What are you doing back here? Humayun is here with his uncles, and you didn't go and greet them?'

'They'll make me go back! I don't – they'll force me! That's why they're here!'

Afroz looked from Riaz to her aunt and wondered at the confusion in their faces. Did they not understand why these skull-capped men were here?

'Why would they do that?' Jahanara asked her, gently wiping Afroz's face.

Afroz dutifully followed them into the bar. She made her salams, making sure to keep her eyes rooted to the carpet.

'Eid Mubarak, ma,' one uncle said, holding his hand to her head, and pressing down on it with forceful blessing. 'We were so worried, Humayun was so worried! Humayun's mother was so worried. They claim they had no word from you, and we had to come and see you, make sure you are all right!'

'Eid Mubarak, Bhaisab, we are very happy that you have come,' her aunt insisted. 'Please, come and sit. Riaz, bring some drinks!' As Jahanara fussed over them, Afroz glanced over at Humayun, who stared fixedly away from her. It occurred to her that he was still trying to decide whether to be angry or sheepish, and the gall of his indecision enraged her.

'You could have just called,' she said quietly, leaning towards him. She did not mean for the words to come out in a hiss, but they did, and around her, the men fell silent.

They all stared at her until one of them spoke.

'If you had left opportunity for a call, that is what he would have done. You leave your husband and your husband's home, and there is no word for days – is that any way for a woman of a good household to behave?'

Another uncle piped in, clearing his throat and addressing only the first speaker. 'Girls these days, they know nothing of shomman, izzath, re bo. Should have just called, she says! It's a thing to hear.'

'This poor man was worried sick,' the first man went on, his voice tight and stern. 'He had no idea when you were coming back. How was he not to come?'

Afroz felt her panic swarming her. She looked at her aunt.

'The daughters of this house know about shomman,' her Fufu replied evenly. 'That is the way they have been brought up.' She looked up at Humayun. 'Baba, forgive me, maaf sai, I kept her back. With the girls gone, and their father … I didn't want to do Ramadan alone …'

She trailed off, and Humayun, who seemed relieved by this adoption of blame, pounced on it quickly before it was taken away.

'But of course, Fufu! Of course, you have every right to detain her!' For the first time, he looked at Afroz, searching her face in consternation. 'Why didn't you just say that Afi? You think I would not have understood this?'

Afroz glared at him, making him look away.

'Go, Afi,' her aunt entreated. 'Heat up the Eid phitha we made. Your guests will be hungry!'

'Fufu—'

Her aunt shook her head. 'Na! What am I saying! Why would we serve Humayun's family at the restaurant?' she chided herself. 'They should come to the house! Riaz, bring the drinks to the house!'

The men, coughing and nodding, allowed themselves to be mollified and followed her aunt out of the Peacock. Afroz watched them go, watched them point out the beauty of the village, this village that she was becoming so fond of. This village that was never meant for her.

'Afa,' Riaz said. 'If you want to stay in the restaurant, I can make an excuse about some customers.'

She looked up at him, unable to stop herself from welling up in a thick tumble of tears.

'Afa,' Riaz said, 'don't cry! Come on, nothing's going to happen.'

'For you,' she said, suddenly reverting to Bangla. 'For you, and for Naju and for Sibby – for all of you, nothing's going to happen! But bad luck follows me around – bad luck is reserved only for this abagha,' she smacked her forehead, 'only for unlucky, ill-fated me.'

Riaz stared at her, open-mouthed.

'They'll force me to go back, these men – and in Desh, they're everywhere. Being here, away from them, I felt like I could breathe again re Riaz! But in Desh, these people are the word of God, and they twist their tongues, so it comes out warped in a way that hurts us, binds us, confines us – all we do is be judged by what they deem reputable, honorable! A group of buzurgs with beards and namaz caps and long white kurthas, they've become those things for me now, *they* are izzath and shomman.' She stopped, her breaths coming out sharp and fast. She thought of the beating of Munni the night she had left and shuddered. Then she looked at Riaz. 'All my life, it's been about upholding honour – whose honour, Riaz re? Mine? My husband's? These men's? But you wouldn't know, how would you know? Even Fufu, I thought she would understand, but even she, living so long away from Desh, has forgotten.'

'Thing is,' Riaz said, in English, his voice tight, 'we've all got our problems. So, yours are invisible to me, but mine are invisible to you.' Afroz frowned. 'And the shomman thing,' he continued, 'believe me, those things, they've followed us all out here. Nobody's escaped all of that. Besides' – he turned to the tray he was stacking with glasses – 'isn't your dad – Masoom Uncle – he's like that too? Cap, beard, kurtha pyjama? But he's a good guy, right? You can't paint them all with the same brush.' He softened. 'Listen, if those men are here for trouble, we won't let them have any, will we?'

She remained silent, watching him.

'And who've you got on your side? Eh?' Riaz flexed his arms tightening his biceps. 'You've got the big guns on your side! They're coming out for you, Afa!'

She sighed, wiped her face. Then she pointed at the window. 'Did you see Fufu? She was practically sending me back with them.'

He shook his head, smiled ruefully. 'Na! She's just been around long enough to know how to deal with them. You've got to say "no" by looking like you're saying yes.' He handed her a tray and picked up the other and she followed him doubtfully out of the door.

Later that evening, Afroz sat at the window seat undoing her plait, while looking out at the speckled night and the Eid moon. Behind her, Humayun was unpacking his small suitcase as he spoke on his phone to his mother in a voice that was needlessly loud and sycophantic. Finally the conversation ended and he lay down on the bed, groaning as he clicked the bones in his hips and legs.

'The AC on that flight was too strong. I will be suffering with my arthritis tomorrow.'

She looked at the half-empty suitcase on the bed and began to finish putting away his things, nudging her shalwar kameezes to one side to make room for his trousers, begrudging the space he took up.

'Can you boil some water for me?' he asked her as he worked his teeth with a toothpick.

'You don't need to boil it here.'

'I don't like that metallic taste to it. It feels like there is something contaminating it. Better to be safe.'

She snorted. Turning to him, she said, 'Why did you bring those men?'

'They came to drop me!'

'They came to bully me!'

'Afroz,' he said, sitting up and throwing the toothpick to the floor. 'You have been gone for weeks. You haven't called me for five days. Five days! My mother was so worried, we were all so worried!'

Afroz picked up the toothpick he had thrown to the floor and jabbed the air in front of his face with it. 'Don't do that! There is no one here to look after your mess – no servants or houseboys, you understand? We all clean up after ourselves here.'

'I should be the one that is angry! You've been here weeks! And you wouldn't tell me when you're coming home! Of course I had to come! And I won't leave until you come home with me.'

She sat down on the window seat again, combing her hair with fury.

Humayun came and stood behind her. He gazed out of the window, resting his hand on her shoulder.

'What a beautiful Eid moon! You can really see the stars here, na?' he asked, his voice conciliatory.

They were still for a moment, staring up into the sky. Then Afroz stood abruptly.

'I'm going to do my Isha namaz.'

She left him standing by the window.

In her room, Jahanara stood by her door, listening and hoping for laughter, or some indication of easy chatter. But instead she heard tension in their voices and then silence. She heard the door open and close. She sat down on her prayer mat and stared at the weave of the shital pati, the tan colour murta entwined with maroon, and the steady etching of the Ka'bah in black. She had asked her brother many times if Afroz was happy. If Humayun was good to her. Each time her brother had nodded and reassured her. He was educated, from good stock, wealthy and they had many servants.

Afroz would never have cause to worry. Now Jahanara pressed her forehead against the Ka'bah until it hurt: *Ya Allah*, she whispered, *forgive us for being senseless to the pain of our children.* She sat up for a long time, reading her tasbih and listening in vain for a sound to break the silence of the house.

The Inauspiciousness of a Rainy Wedding

Afroz picks her way through a line of shy cousins, who sit uncomfortably in their jewel-coloured fineries. They fall into a reverent hush as she passes by, their eyes tracing her from head to toe and their fingers reaching out to brush the hem of her saree. She is a spectacle to behold and they hope that they too will walk with such demure grace when they are led to the place their own girlhoods shall be sacrificed.

Shamima, Afroz's second cousin, long relegated to a life of spinsterhood, sits by the window, one leg folded beneath her. Shamima is threading yellow and orange flowers for the garlands. She is always asked to make the garlands at weddings, as though the purity of her own unending virginity will braid into the garland a vividness of colour that the fingers of a married woman could not achieve. Afroz stands for a moment, mesmerised by the marigolds. Shamima holds one up to her and her smile makes Afroz well up.

Afroz locks the bathroom door behind her and turns on the shower, twisting the tap as far as it will go. She drops the toilet seat, pulls the flush and puts the phone to her ear.

He picks up within a few rings.

'Afroz!'

'Taseen!'

'Don't do this, Afi, I beg you, don't do—'

'I can't talk, I just wanted to—'

'Afroz, I can't hear you properly!'

'Taseen, huncho? I can't talk louder, they're all outside—'

'No. No, come out, I'll meet you at Englishman's Cemetery, like always.'

Afroz laughs, full of disbelief that he is still in denial. She could close her eyes and be convinced that his proposition was possible. But with her eyes open, she sees the marble tiles below her feet, scattered with hairs from the heads of the wedding guests who have showered and dressed here in order to celebrate her nikkah. 'I'm marrying him.'

Silence down the phone and so much noise all around. She stares at her henna-painted hand, lifts her fingers up to wipe her wet nose, and the smell of the mehndi hits her with force. The earthy pungency has always made her feel nauseous.

'You're not even going to let me talk you out of it? In person?'

'Is there a point, Taseen?' she asks quietly. 'I asked you, didn't I? Ami thumar fao forya, I asked you not to go. You weren't here.'

'Afi,' Taseen says, his voice crumbling like sawdust in the receiver. 'How many times can I explain? I had to go – Masud was in trouble, I had—'

'Then you have chosen,' Afroz says. 'You have chosen Masud, your Chhatra League, your politics.' More silence. 'Now you must let me go.'

'You've known forever who I am!' Taseen's voice seems far away. 'Forever. I've known you forever. My best friend.'

'I don't want to do this either.'

'Then why are you?'

Taseen's question is laden with accusation and the suggestion that somehow it is he who has been betrayed. That it was she that was at fault. Even though she had been the one to plead with her parents to meet with Taseen's. Baba had been willing, despite Ma's resistance, to entertain a proposal of marriage. They set aside their concerns about Taseen's involvement in the notorious Bangladesh Chhatra League, and had agreed to meet with Taseen's family several weeks ago, settling on the Friday before Shabebarath, and they had waited, having missed Baba's jummah prayers, and with the dining table ladened with murgh roast and homemade roshogolla and alur chop that had long since gone cold. But only Taseen's brother had arrived, with news of Taseen's embroilment in a new Chhatra League scandal. She could have forgiven him for exposing her to the slander and gossip hurled her way by their neighbours and friends, but she could not forgive him Baba's dismay. As he pulled off his silk kurtha later that night, Ma pelted Baba with words she had until then kept locked behind her lips. Her Baba had had to suffer such insults just so that Taseen could realise his political ambitions.

A part of her wants to hurt him, to tell him that her reluctance to marry Humayun is unrelated to any feelings for Taseen. But he has already hung up.

'Apu!' One of Afroz's cousins taps timidly on the door. Afroz opens it a few inches. 'Khala is asking if your blouse needed tightening?' Afroz's blouse, taken in only last week, was loose again when she tried it on this morning.

She hands her cousin the blouse. 'Quarter inch on the sides, including arms.'

It is strange that she can focus on these banalities. But the phone call has helped. Indignation has refuelled her. She lathers hersef in soap and applies conditioner to her hair. She is marrying someone she barely knows or likes; someone she doesn't feel attracted to. But this is no surprise in Desh. This is how things have always been. Her head has been filled with romantic notions by Taseen and her British cousins, and so for a time she had forgotten this. As the water falls on her, she washes herself free of those old delusions.

Everyone in the older generations has had their marriages arranged. She had just been naiye enough to dream that she was different. Taseen had made her believe this. He had held up a vision of a secular life where she could keep her God and he his atheism, a life where man and wife were true equals. He would continue to teach, and she would continue her business degree and find a job as a clerk somewhere. She had been seduced by that dream. She didn't want to spend her life indoors, with the whirring fans and the house geckos, rolling perfect moons of porothas and serving a husband and children who would outgrow her, while becoming obese on a diet of curries fried in rapeseed oil. There was something about Humayun that hinted that he was committed, in a very dedicated way, to a life she had long rejected, even though he did try to hide it, laughing away any questions about his views on religion and society.

She steps out of the bathroom in her robe and retraces her steps past her cousins to her room, where the make-up artist waits. She sits at her dressing table and glares at the reflection of her twenty-six-year-old self in the very same mirror that she had used as a little girl learning how to plait her own hair. She wishes suddenly that Baba had betrayed her sooner, had married her off at a younger age when dreams hadn't yet been committed to, and compromises came easier. The make-up artist transforms her into someone she doesn't recognise, with a layer of too-fair foundation painted over her yellow skin, and eyes elongated with thick, black kohl.

Draped in scarlet and gold, she makes her way down the stairs, past the women standing hushed in awe. She hears her bracelets tinkle, and her father outside shouting for the car to come closer to the front door. She hadn't realised it was raining. It's only now she notices that it is pelting down. She can hear it drumming on the roof. Her mother, surrounded by a gaggle of aunts, stands at the door and refuses to meet her eyes. She escorts Afroz out to the driveway and a strong wind flaps at her shawl and blows it into Afroz's face, so Afroz reaches the car as if blindfolded.

She is seated between her father and Jahanara, who arrived with her Fufa the night before, in time for the Mehndi ceremony. Her aunt kisses her hand, and Afroz feels the dampness of the kiss, and looks up to see her Fufu's face puffed up and red from crying. Her aunt has always shone a spotlight of love and reassurance on Afroz. Afroz's gratitude makes her own eyes tear up and she looks away.

She doesn't look at Baba, whose silence cuts through her. Since he rejected her wish to decline Humayun's proposal, he has avoided her; whether through guilt or anger, she does not know. Today he holds her refusal of Humayun against her, as though she has challenged his parental rights in some deplorable way. He sits stiffly next to her, the child whose education, diet, clothes he has fussed over. All those battles he has fought for her – and now he has undermined it all with this marriage.

As the car pulls up to the Nirbana's entrance, the wedding guests swarm her like bees around honey. She keeps her face lowered as she is expected to, nodding when spoken to and replying only in the lowest of voices.

Someone takes her hand and kisses her on the cheek, and she looks up. It is Nasrin, her eyes shining, and resplendent in a pink saree. Afroz forgets herself, slips out of the role of demure bride and exclaims in delight, kissing her cousin's cheek, and squeezes her hand. She turns instinctively and finds Sabrina standing next to her. Sabrina takes Afroz in her arms and kisses her forehead. Afroz suddenly feels ashamed of herself, in the gaze of her courageous, headstrong cousin. Sabrina would have fought to the death rather than succumb to an arranged marriage.

The maulvi arrives with Humayun, and Afroz feels her legs go numb. It happens very suddenly, and she lurches forward amid gasps from the guests standing beside her. Someone takes her to the window for some air.

The saree she wears weighs over twenty kilos, and the ornate bangles on her arms catch on anything they touch. She suddenly feels hungry, and it is a relief to feel it – the gnawing starvation of someone who has fasted. She sits sipping the water that Sabrina holds for her. Her cousin's face is full of questions – there is no space inside Afroz for more questions, so she averts her eyes. She already has so many she wants to ask. She wants to ask Humayun what he meant when he told her she had the best bloodline of anyone he had met, or why he wasn't more impressed by her degree. She wants to ask her aunt if she would ever do this to her own daughters, and if not, why she has not intervened on Afroz's behalf. She wants to ask the maulvi, with the thick beard that quivers as he recites the verses, does marriage have to be for life?

All these questions rock through her as the maulvi reads the wedding sermon. Then a hush falls and Afroz feels confused.

They all look at her: Humayun, his eyebrows raised, the maulvi, Baba, her cousins, her aunt. Her mother is suddenly before her, shoving Sabrina aside and pinching Afroz's arm beneath her achol and whispering in her ear. Afroz doesn't understand. She feels like she is in a dream and has come into the room stark naked. She turns to look at Nasrin, who takes her hand and squeezes it.

'They're waiting for you to say *Kobul*,' she whispers and Afroz holds Nasrin's gaze, and then her eye is caught by a skirmish taking place near the entrance. She searches over the heads of the seated wedding guests and glimpses Taseen's face. He wears same pained expression he'd had when he had once fallen off the school roof and broken his leg.

His brother holds him back and struggles to lead him away. As she sees the security guards approaching the brothers, Afroz begins to whimper. She does not know when her whimpering becomes hysterical, or when her veil is pulled forward by her mother, covering her distraught face.

Afterwards, Nasrin tells her that Humayun's family are outraged as they did not hear her say 'Kobul'. The whole point of the verbal consent is that the guests bear witness to the acceptance of the marriage. Afroz wonders at this, at the murky grey that conceals her recollection of this moment: had she consented? Had she made a sound that might have been interpreted as consent? The grey would persist, stubborn and unsolvable, and she would never know for sure. But at that moment, it did not matter: the maulvi was triumphant that the consent had been forthcoming, and he had stood so the congregated guests would witness the dramatic bite he took from the mejdool date handed to him to solemnise the marriage.

'You didn't consent, did you?' Sabrina asks her. They are in an airless room upstairs; Afroz's mother stands by the door, smiling away the concern of the guests – for even in a country of reluctant brides, this one seemed more distressed than most. They are taken aback by how she shakes, at the pallor of her skin. Sabrina shakes her head and is led away by her father. 'Abba, I was sitting right fucking there, she didn't consent! This is outrageous, are they forcing her? Do something!' Hearing her, Afroz smiles, because of all the people she loves, it was always going to be Sabrina, Tipu, her brave, unruly, headstrong cousin, who stood up for her.

When she and Humayun are walked out to the wedding car, Afroz sees her mother by the far wall, her face pale and tired. Afroz decides that even if this marriage works out, she will never become a mother. She could never betray a child that came from her womb the way these parents have betrayed theirs. But, by the time the car drives away, Afroz is looking back and she has already forgiven them. Feeling betrayed is too painful, and so she gives in to the grief of leaving them. She sees her mother crying. She sees her father wiping his damp face. She sees that her cousins, her aunt and uncle, standing at the window of a first-floor room, are dry-eyed, but their expression seems the most bereft of all.

14

On the 12th of October, Nasrin and Elias left London in a cab, quietly rolling through the streets while the city still slept, then onto a train, where Elias napped, occasionally waking to glance worriedly at his mother's pale, drawn face.

Riaz was already standing on the platform when the train pulled into the station. It was a cold day, but he wore nothing but a Superman T-shirt, bouncing up and down for warmth with his enormous bundle of keys dangling from one of his fingers. He smiled when he saw them and rushed towards the window, but Nasrin looked away, fussing with her mac and her bag.

Elias squealed with pleasure and jumped up and down in his seat as Riaz tapped the window and pulled a face.

'Elias, stop that,' Nasrin admonished as Elias hit the windowpane, leaving moist smudges from his palm. 'Here, put your coat on, come on!'

The wind hit them hard as soon as the train door opened. 'It's freezing,' Nasrin complained, letting Riaz take the suitcase from her.

'A bit of good Welsh weather for you!' He ruffled Elias's hair and Elias grabbed at the thin leather bands he wore on his wrist.

'I'm feeling cold just looking at you,' Nasrin muttered as they walked towards the car.

'Mummy, I want to take my coat off too.'

'I don't think so!'

'Let him!'

'He's a child, not an MMA gunda like you.'

This elicited a guffaw from Riaz.

They were diverted by road works near the Co-op and ended up taking a longer route into town. The sky was ashen and cut to shreds by the white lines of aeroplanes and pollution, and they passed through a small hamlet lined with thin terraced houses that seemed pitifully desolate. The hedges were a dismal brown and a few neglected wheelie bins added to the air of deprivation.

'How's London?' Riaz asked. 'How's Richard? How is all that partnership stuff going for him?'

Nasrin didn't reply. Riaz glanced at her profile, once, then twice. After some time, Nasrin said, 'Just imagine living here.'

Beside her, Riaz stiffened. He said, 'It's not like you do.'

'Well ...' Nasrin said and lapsed into silence again. Then, quite suddenly, she said, 'It was hell when I did.'

Riaz looked at her, and then back at the road. 'You've got some serious jiggling going on there.' He tapped her knee with his index finger. She stopped shaking it, moving away from his hand.

They drove on in silence, passing a long-neglected industrial estate, the listless buildings seeming to plunge Nasrin deeper into her gloom. Riaz watched her from the corner of his eyes.

'Why would they come here?' she finally asked.

'Who?'

'My parents. Why would they come *here*? Why wouldn't they go to places where there were more of them? As in, more Asians? Safety in numbers and stuff?'

'Your dad wanted to give you the best start, didn't he?' Riaz shook his head. 'You and your sister, always so bloody down on this place.' He swept his hand around. 'Look at how beautiful it is, would you? It must have taken so much courage to leave the fold and give you somewhere as special as this to grow up in. Think about the poor sods like me that had to learn to ride a bike on a shady street in Lozells because my parents weren't as brave as yours!'

Nasrin finally looked at him, a weak smile appearing on her face. 'You don't know how to ride a bike.'

'Exactly. Streets were too dangerous! Bloody knives everywhere!'

A chuckle escaped her, and she turned back to the window. 'I wonder why you do that.'

'What?'

'Create this ridiculous story about being a slumdog. Pledge allegiance to some gangster version of yourself.'

'Have you been to Lozells, Naz?' Riaz asked, his voice gentle, but Nasrin seemed not to notice.

'Streets of Lozells! Knives! Drugs! Those stories you used to tell us about mad men singing Michael Jackson songs on the street corners. All that violence with your MMA. And it's such nonsense, all of it, because actually you grew up here. With me and Sibby.'

Riaz considered this. 'I was fourteen when I came to the Peacock.'

'Exactly,' Nasrin said, 'only fourteen!'

'By then, the damage was done. I reckon the defining moments are the ones that happen when we're too young to know what's what. Besides,' he shrugged, 'none of it's pretence to me, you know, the stories about where I grew up and my martial arts. These things lift me up. I mean the Peacock … you guys … you all had an effect too … but where I'm from is important too. Knowing where we come from – that makes us stronger, right? Inspires us, reminds us of our journey, how far we've come and all that.'

Nasrin had turned in her seat to look at him, her eyes large and shining. 'I … I never looked at it that way.' She turned and looked back out of the window at the gathering clouds. 'That's deep.'

'Oh, get lost!' He laughed.

'No, seriously! I suppose I envy you. I don't really feel like I have anywhere I want to call home. Those trips to Bangladesh were good, you know, every summer: they were the closest I ever came to feeling like I belonged somewhere. But then something Afroz said made me realise that the Desh in my head isn't a real place. I haven't experienced the reality of it, not in the way she has – I hadn't really appreciated how restricted women are out there.'

'I agree, you wouldn't have lasted a day in the real Desh!' Riaz said, ducking as she swiped him. 'Anyway, you're confusing things – nativism and belonging – they aren't the same thing. The Beacons is my home and London is yours, simple as that.'

Nasrin glanced at him. 'London?'

'Yes, you know that place you live in with your husband and child?' Riaz laughed, then saw the expression on her face and fell silent. 'Is everything okay, Naz?' he asked after a few minutes.

Nasrin did not answer.

'The other thing you should know,' Riaz said, changing the subject, 'is that Afroz's husband is here.'

She turned to look at him. 'Here?'

'As in, at your mum's. He arrived with a small entourage of supporters yesterday. Think they were going to try to strong-arm Afroz into getting the plane back home. Poor woman was bloody scared!'

'Who were they?' Nasrin asked, a slow anger building inside her. She'd seen this before: the proliferation of dogma and testosterone to bully a woman into submission.

'They said they were Humayun's mother's relatives, all namaz caps and long white kurthas.' Riaz shook his head. 'I've seen those sorts in Birmingham, always interfering in other people's businesses. But man, Afi was so angry and upset.'

'Oh my God, poor Afi! How did she not know he was coming?'

'She definitely didn't know! She was so angry with him – sounded like they'd been quarrelling.'

Nasrin lapsed into silence until Riaz called her softly. 'Earth to Naz, you okay?'

'You see,' she said, her voice barely above a whisper, 'it wasn't really spoken about, but everyone knew that Afroz didn't want to marry him. There was someone else.'

'Shit, Naz,' Riaz said, 'that's sad.'

It occurred to Nasrin that if she had been having this conversation with Richard, she would be frustrated by now by the the accusatory questions he would have thrown at her to challenge a culture that treated women this way, forcing her to take a defensive position even through she didn't want to. Riaz though, slipped into a brief moment of silence in deference to the solemnity of her disclosure, understanding without being told that certain cultural legacies were too complex to take a dogmatic position on.

'Poor Afi,' she repeated, breaking the silence. 'So, they didn't force her back then? They just sat around the Peacock wearing their white caps, drinking tea like it was their baaper bari?'

Riaz laughed, throwing his head back against the headrest. 'Naz, that's not the right context for that term. Such a bounty bar, you are!'

She smiled, and turned to hide it, looking silently out of the window.

'I was teasing!' he said, thinking he had irritated her.

'You have a point though. I do have more English in me than you do. Is it right to say that? Can a brown person be English? Why is it that they allow us the Brit bit but not the English? British-Bangladeshi. Never English-Bangladeshi, never Welsh-Bengali. Why do you think that is?'

'It's just semantics, Naz,' Riaz laughed, 'why are you so obsessed with this stuff?'

'I feel like the language works to exclude us,' Nasrin said quietly. She pursed her lips and gazed out of the window. 'Have you noticed,' she asked, 'how Afroz always refers to herself as Sylheti, and not Bangladeshi? She says Sylhetis were different from the rest of the Bengalis, they – I mean we – have our own language and culture. She got really mad once when Sabrina said Sylheti was a dialect. She got so mad about it! Not like Afroz, is it?'

Riaz smiled. 'I can't imagine it, actually.'

'She was insistent that we have our own language, Nagri—'

'Nagiri,' Riaz corrected.

'You knew that?' Nasrin turned to him, eyes wide with surprise. 'How come you know all this stuff? Anyway, so now we can't even say we're Bangladeshi anymore. We're Sylheti. And even pinpointing that doesn't help, does it? I mean, we've been out of there for so long, that we can't really claim it in the same way as Afroz. Right? Even you and me? Members of the same diaspora. We're from the same place, and yet we're not?'

'What do you mean?'

'I mean, we're both British-Sylheti-Bangladeshi, but the choices our parents made makes our experiences as members of the same community so different!'

Riaz nodded. 'I understand what you're saying. But I don't put so much importance on all that, Naz.'

'Riaz, you just said *Knowing where we come from make us stronger!*'

Riaz shook his head. 'You come from the Beacons. Come on, Naz. You're so modern, so progressive. So you know race isn't the only thing that matters. The world's moved on from race – you know this better than anyone! You married a white guy for God's sake. It just doesn't matter.'

Nasrin did not respond. Riaz switched on the windscreen wipers as the first drops of rain hit the glass.

'I mean, sure,' Riaz continued, 'tribes still exist. Those tribes are just not along racial lines anymore. It's other stuff like class, religion, political leanings, veganism ... Those white skull caps that came to force Afroz home? That whole community pressure thing? It exists in different forms in all cultures. It's what humans do – this inbuilt tribal thing, from cavemen days when tribes kept us safe. Point is, even if we're different, we can still get along, right? We can still find the things that we have in common.'

She looked over at him. 'Where did you get that from? Have you been reading serious books again?'

'Yeah, we can't all have Daddy pay for a formal education, can we? Us ignorant Brummie Bongs, we have to go get our knowledge where we can find it.'

Nasrin remembered the time she and Sabrina had found a stack of library books in Riaz's room; aspirational works by Chomsky, Tolstoy and Omar Khayyam. When they'd laughed at him, for a moment he had looked like he had been slapped. She cringed at the memory. She couldn't even remember why she had laughed, except that she had. What bleak comedy had she seen in the story of a young Indian restaurant waiter trying to read great literature?

'As I was saying,' Riaz said, cutting through her thoughts. 'I managed to send them away.'

'They didn't try very hard then? To get Afroz on that plane?'

'They were more curious about why your dad left the restaurant to her.'

'Oh.' It had never occurred to her that it might still be fresh gossip in some quarters. 'So, they don't know?'

'Strangely enough, they did know. But they kept wanting me to confirm it.'

She nodded and looked out at the landscape and sighed. Here she was again, this hell on earth, where she was never anything but brown. Except this time, she had no idea when she would escape it.

She checked her phone and saw that Richard had not called or texted.

Her knee shook, thrumming against the dashboard all the way home.

When they arrived, Nasrin and Elias were hurried into the house by Jahanara. Afroz hugged Nasrin, grinning ear to ear. Jahanara rubbed her nose to Nasrin's, and then her grandson's, and then Nasrin again, her cheeks flushed pink.

'When you called to say you were coming, I didn't believe you!'

Jahanara told Elias, and Nasrin felt choked. The sentiment hovered in the room like pollen, making her eyes tear up.

It wasn't until she was seated in the kitchen that Nasrin was able to take in the changes in the house and its inhabitants. The kitchen's new additions included a nokshi katha tablecloth, an array of shital objects pinned to the wall, an oblong tray with the Bangladeshi flag, and some hand fans, among which Nasrin recognised her own with the familiar white shapla spread across its centre. Jahanara took a lunch of keema kobabs out of the freezer, and Afroz wiped Elias's face and hands with a damp flannel. Riaz stood beside Nasrin, pinching grapes from the fruit bowl and chattering away as he ate them.

Nasrin sat quietly letting the action unfold around her.

'Fufu,' Riaz was saying, settling himself onto the sofa next to Nasrin. 'That Aravis guy is killing me, yeah? He's just—'

'The chicken man?' Afroz interrupted him.

'Hiked up prices three times this year, and each time, only tells me after I put in an order! We've got to find another supplier.'

'Whatever you think is best, re futh,' Jahanara told him.

'I think he's fleecing us!'

'Fleecing?'

'As in, lemta khorilar, cheating the very shirts off our backs, like,' Riaz paused to find the right explanation, 'undressing us.'

'Y'Allah!' Afroz tutted.

Nasrin laughed. She felt a sudden surge of affection. She thought of their conversation in the car – how long had it been since she had voiced uncomfortable thoughts to someone who had listened and understood? It occurred to her that the ease and intimacy of their conversation ignored the many years of absence in each other's lives, and this made her smile. She turned slightly to look at him. Though Riaz's metamorphosis – from lanky, pimpled youth into this man with a generous presence whose voice boomed to the furthest reaches of any room – had occurred years ago, she found she had not fully appreciated it until now. His face had always had the shadow of a beard, but in the last few weeks he had grown it out, although it was kept neatly trimmed. It glistened like polished coal along his jawline and without thinking, she reached out to where his jaw met his ear and stroked it.

Silence swept over the kitchen.

Nasrin twisted her fingers and stood up.

'For goodness sake, Elias, don't touch the phitha, you haven't washed your hands yet,' she told her son. Frowning, she helped him wash his hands and filled herself a glass with water. She turned back to the still-stunned room, wondering how to escape. She reached for the hand fan. 'This is mine,' she said, hearing the petulance in her voice, and feeling even more ashamed. As she left the kitchen with her glass of water, she yelped as she collided with someone and felt the shock of the cold-water splash against her stomach. Stepping back, she came face to face with Humayun, an older man than she remembered, with greying hair above his ears.

'Assalamualaikum,' she said.

'Bala ni, Naju?'

'I am well,' she replied, swallowing her surprise. 'Apne?'

'Ji.' He shook his head and Nasrin watched him make his way into the kitchen, holding up his lungi with his left hand as though it were a ball gown and he was about to make a curtsy. She stood there for some minutes before she turned and took herself up to her room. She sat on her bed and checked her phone again. Still no word from Richard. She dialled Sabrina's number but it went straight to voicemail. She opened her inbox but found herself unable to write her usual email to her sister, not knowing how to articulate the chaos of emotions that tumbled through her.

Instead she leaned back and closed her eyes, trying not to think about the changed landscape of her life, and how completely she was lost in it.

* * *

Nasrin had never known this house to be so alive with the comings and goings of people. She had spent a childhood in this kitchen, sitting at this very table, with its starched-to-death tablecloth, aware of the lives that were being lived elsewhere – next door in the restaurant kitchen, or in the book in front of her, or on the television which was kept on constantly to alleviate the unearthly silence of the Beacons valley — but now it seemed the divisions between life at the Peacock and the house had been flung aside, and despite the bricks and mortar that still separated them, the rumpus of the restaurant had found its way in. Frequently she found a pot of loose-leaf tea brewing on the stove, and Junaid or Hannan or the not-so-new-boy whose name she never remembered, smoking a bidi just outside on the patio. Her mother's once tidy flowerbed had half-smoked cigarette butts strewn about it, and each afternoon her mother was heard muttering as she cleaned it up. Lindsay, who had been working at the restaurant for over a decade and had previously only visited the house on Eid or at Christmas, was now in and out three or four times a day, looking for Afroz.

'Isn't she in the restaurant, with you?' Nasrin would ask, perplexed. It surprised her that Afroz might be anywhere other than inside the house or in the restaurant. She looked out over the minuscule square – with the Chez Jones café, and Mr Ruane's newsagent, and a few gift shops that were closed out of season – and wondered where Afroz could have found to go? But Nasrin never asked, because Afroz was always in a state of flux, constantly moving from one thing to another as though she were fleeing something.

Each afternoon at five, just as Afroz and Jahanara finished their Asr prayers, their neighbour, Dorothy, rang the doorbell. Nasrin let her in and watched the old woman tread softly into the house in her brown house slippers, armed with some sort of pudding or cake. Dorothy hardly said a word, reserved as Nasrin had always known their neighbour to be, but she sat at the table and drank the milky tea Afroz made her, exchanged a few words with Elias and pressed her chin into her neck at his every response, as if giving it serious thought, and then she would slip out without saying goodbye.

'She's a bit odd,' Nasrin ventured to her mother after witnessing the first of these visits. 'Just invites herself around?'

'Afroz invited her one day, when she was in the garden putting out her washing,' her mother explained. 'Us widows, what else do we have to do? Just pop in and check on each other, make sure we haven't died in our sleep.'

'For goodness sake, Amma.'

But Dorothy's five o'clock cake visit quickly developed into a daily event as well as a free-for-all: Junaid, Hannan, Riaz, Linds dropped in for a quick cup of tea and a piece of cake, bringing their laughter and chatter into the tiny kitchen while Nasrin sat shell-shocked in the middle of it all.

Humayun also occupied the fringes of the bustling hive they resided in. Each morning she would find him, still in his lungi with a neat kurtha on top, sitting quietly in front of the breakfast that Afroz would have laid in front of him. Sometimes he read the *Beacons Star*, the boredom emanating from him, but mostly he asked her where Afroz was. She didn't know. It seemed that the world and its mother were searching for Afroz.

Often, Afroz sent Junaid or Hannan around to the house with plates of food for Nasrin and Humayun to try, followed by timid questions such as 'too salty?' or 'something missing?' texted to Nasrin's phone. Those were the only occasions during which Humayun and Nasrin had any sustained conversation.

'I can taste the cumin in them,' Humayun would say, chewing a salmon and spring onion bhajia with relish. 'She's definitely roasted them first.'

'I don't usually like salmon,' Nasrin said, taking another from the Tupperware.

'It has such an overpowering aroma,' Humayun agreed, fetching them glasses of water. 'Not like our deshi fish, so light that they will be good to any spice.'

'I used to love the ilish maasor jhol and keski mas with shatkora – but I hated the bones!' Nasrin said.

'Ooof! Those bones were edible, Naju, you don't dissect keski, you eat them whole!'

'I didn't know that!'

'Now you know.' Humayun laughed, finished his glass of water. 'You know, Naju, it has been nice talking to you and getting to know Elias. I find that when Richard Bhai is around, you are much more shy.'

Nasrin was about to protest before the truth of Humayun's observation slowly dawned on her.

Humayun smiled. 'Ekta mojhar jineesh, a funny thing, Naju, but our Sylheti women are like this – so formal around their husband and his family. My father used to say, if you want to see who your wife is, stay with her in her childhood home with her family and you will see the girl in her. Look now, in Desh, Afroz never cooks new foods.'

Nasrin, about to take a sip of water, paused and looked at him. 'Perhaps she thinks you wouldn't like to try anything new,' she said lightly.

'Perhaps,' Humayun said, a sudden steeliness in his expression as he picked up his newspaper again. 'Or perhaps this place has made her very adventurous.'

Dinnertime was like the Mad Hatter's tea party gone a few decibels madder. They ate late, usually around eleven or even midnight, and the kitchen was such a commotion of people (from restaurant staff to some regulars that Afroz would entice from the restaurant with the prospect of authentic Bengali food) that each night, Elias would wake up and run down the stairs, feverish with excitement. Nasrin felt her objections melt away as she watched him, reflecting sadly that to an only child, a populated room was a thrilling prospect. She watched as he was sent round the kitchen to pass the rice bowl or some plain yoghurt because someone had bitten into a chilli, and her hand flitted to her still flat abdomen, for it was difficult these days to think about her son without thinking of the life growing inside her.

Despite all these surprises and changes, Nasrin settled into the hubbub of her once silent family home with an unexpected sense of joy. She sometimes caught an image of herself in the dining room mirror, seated between Linds and Riaz, her hair piled high on her head, wearing one of Afroz's cotton kurthas on top of her jersey leggings, and she was surprised by the shine in her eyes, the gentle upturn of her lips. When Afroz offered her some more keski, Nasrin looked over at Humayun and held up a tiny fried fish before slipping it whole into her mouth, and Humayun smiled broadly and did his Sylheti head swoop to one side, which could mean so many things, but in this context meant pleasure. Nasrin smiled and mimicked him, and she wondered how she had never managed to reconcile the Sylheti with the Welsh, when Afroz had done so with such ease and grace.

But then at night when she was back in her room alone Nasrin felt like a patch of earth after a storm. Damply numb and eerily uninhabited. She realised then, how easily crowds were dispersed, and how the loneliness drew her back into its icy hold. She tried hard in those moments before sleep to work out if it was Richard that she missed, or the warmth of his feet against hers. Whether it was Richard's voice she missed, or his telling her that he missed her. She wondered if he was with Fabienne and the thought of them together curdled her insides. He called the landline each morning, spoke to her as though nothing was wrong, and then spoke to their son. But aside from those five-minute calls, nothing was normal between them, and the uncertainty frightened her when she allowed herself to think about it.

One night, the apparitions came to her room; her father and her seven-year-old self, accompanied by a chilling convoy of shadows that flickered about the walls and hid in the curtains. Heart in her throat, Nasrin ran out of the house, barefoot and shivering. She ran towards the Peacock, stopping only in the driveway to watch Riaz climbing the iron staircase to the flat roof of the staff cottage, where the old tandoor ovens had been thrown out. Nasrin had not been up on the flat roof since she was a teenager and following him up there, she was surprised by how much smaller it seemed. Riaz had placed a plank across the two ovens for a makeshift table, and over the next few weeks, the two of them lay on it, heads meeting in the middle.

Out on the roof, the distant light of the stars made the darkness less oppressive than in her room, and Riaz's easy conversation kept her darker thoughts at bay. The apparitions never made it onto the flat roof and so it became her nightly refuge, a place to watch the world open into daylight again, accompanied by a chatting, yawning, smoking Riaz. She was gratefully, guiltily aware that he sacrificed sleep only to keep her safe from the darkness.

A few days after her arrival, Nasrin finally got through to Sabrina.

'Hey,' she said, trying to keep her tone light, 'you've been a busy bee.'

'I'm sorry I didn't call – I meant to yesterday, but I had to unwind a trade last minute,' Sabrina replied. 'But you haven't emailed in days – thought you might be busy with *her* now you're back in the Beacons.'

'Sibby,' Nasrin sighed. 'I just needed a break.'

There was a pause before Sabrina asked, her voice less sullen, 'Didi, come on. Are you hiding something? Is something wrong?'

'Tell me about you first,' Nasrin said, 'did you have that lunch with your boss's boss? Did you talk about the promotion?'

'No!' Sabrina said. 'There's so much shit going on, Dids – all these issues with a trade I did last year, so the promotion is not happening. They gave it to Ash.'

Nasrin bit her lip. She knew how hard her sister worked for these victories, the gravity of which she herself did not fully appreciate. 'You'll get there, Sib, you're so smart!'

'I'll be lucky to keep my job at this rate,' Sabrina told her gloomily, 'they're still trying to pin the whole Altieri thing on me.'

'But if the worst happens,' Nasrin said, 'you'll get something somewhere else? Maybe back in England?'

'No, Didi,' Sabrina moaned, 'you don't understand. In an industry as regulated as finance – something like this can potentially bar me from working again. And you know I love New York! I'd never move!'

'I know. You love New York.' Nasrin smiled. 'I wish I had that.'

'You have London.'

'Not like you have New York. I don't really feel like I fit in London ...'

'Why do you need to fit there, Dids?' Sabrina asked. When Nasrin didn't answer, she continued, 'You don't need to fit into a city like London – that's what's great about them – they're not fussy about where you're from, it's about who you want to be that matters. Besides, you're overthinking it, Dids. I mean I love New York, but it's the connection that matters – you can just as easily find that connection with people or a career ... For you, finding your place isn't so much about London as it's about being with Richard and Eli – Didi, you still there? Why have you gone quiet – are you okay?'

Nasrin, who had been looking forward to the relief of confiding to her sister on the pregnancy and this uncertain separation with Richard, now hesitated. 'I'm fine!' she said, trying to sound it. 'Richard is travelling a lot, and well, I thought I may as well be here than be lonely in Islington!'

'Okay,' Sabrina said, sounding doubtful. 'And what about your seizures? Are you still having them? What did the doctor say?'

Her sister laughed. 'Sib, come on, I promise I'm fine. I haven't had an episode in ages. And Doc is happy with my meds.'

'Okay, but you'd tell me if it was anything else, right?'

Nasrin nodded, though she knew she could not worry her sister when Sabrina was worried about losing her job. To convince her, Nasrin offered up a smaller morsel of truth: 'Well, Mum and Afroz are annoying me.'

Sabrina perked up. 'How is that?'

'They're just behaving so oddly. Like, I'd expected Mum would still be a bit weird around Afi, like she was when I left, but now they seem inseparable.'

'Like you mean cooking together and stuff?'

'Cooking, cleaning, praying.' Nasrin laughed, though there was something not quite right about the growing closeness between her mother and Afroz. Five times a day, her mother and Afroz came together in the corner of the living room and did their namaz. After lunch, they read the Quran, Afroz stopping now and again to correct Jahanara's Arabic pronunciation. 'They've even started oiling and braiding each other's hair,' she told Sabrina, 'and taking siestas! When has Amma ever slept during the day, Sibby?' Unlike her son, who immersed himself in each of these activities – donning his mother's cardigan to tie around his head, or demanding they oil and braid his hair, and happily snuggling into one of their beds for a siesta – Nasrin, though frequently invited, found herself fleeing the scene in barely concealed embarrassment.

'Well,' Sabrina said, her voice stony, 'I did tell you to watch out for that one – she chummies up to the oldies, such a sypcophant.'

'No, I'm not blaming Afroz,' Nasrin said quickly, feeling ashamed, 'I mean it's weird that Mum seems fine with her, happy almost!'

'Well, she probably wishes she had a pious, respectable daughter like Afroz instead of us hussies!'

Despite herself, Nasrin laughed; but still something about it dragged at her.

15

Sabrina's phone buzzed, waking her. She had not intended to doze. It was an email from her sister. She noticed that it was 3 a.m. in London, and wondered why her sister was awake, writing emails to her at that hour.

'I found my hand fan, Sibby! You remember the one that was hanging in the Peacock? The one with the shapla in the middle? That graceful pond dancer, Budda's footprint, symbol of virtue? I read that somewhere and it's such a lovely description! Do you remember when the shital pati man came to Nirashapur and Abba bought all of his cane and then asked all the women in the village to come to the phorghor to weave baskets? Remember how happy Amma was, all those laughing, chattering women crouching over their bits of dyed shital weaving and weaving and talking and talking, sharing all the stories that Amma had missed while abroad? Whenever I see something made of shital, I think of those stories, I think of the weaving. Ironic isn't it – I wonder what the plant is that they get the cane from? I'm looking at this hand fan, and it's so amazing to think how this came from a plant – how this is in essence still that plant, sliced and dyed and woven into this.

This hand fan makes me miss Abba. He loved it so much. But now he is in darkness. There seems to be so much in the dark, Sib. I've been thinking a lot about it lately ...'

Sabrina put her phone down and blinked into the darkness outside the window. She thought about calling Nasrin, but what would she say? What was her sister even talking about? When Nasrin had called her from the Beacons a few days before, Sabrina had sensed that her sister was preoccupied. She read the email again, feeling discomfited by the tone of it. Her sister had always been someone easily troubled by questions of identity and of her place in the world and Sabrina sensed that being in the Beacons seemed to have intensified the fracture in Nasrin's psyche which Sabrina attributed to being of two places. Sabrina herself had sidestepped these afflictions by fiercely embracing one place, but she knew her sister had never succeeded in doing the same. In any case, over the last several weeks, Sabrina herself had seen how nostalgia for another place could become haunting; how the faintest trigger – the whiff of coriander from a kitchen window or the sound of Bollywood music in a passing yellow cab – could conjure up the Beacons in Wall Street.

She inched out from beneath the sheets and stood at the foot of the bed, staring down at Ashok. There were new lines around his eyes and mouth, and his full head of hair was now mostly grey. In the years since they had been together in this halfway between function and romance, when had she stopped to look at him? Fear, she realised, had made her avoid looking too closely, for he had deteriorated noticeably since she had first known him. The breeze coming through the window was a cool one, harsh against her skin. She wrapped her arms around herself but did not move, continuing to watch him and listening to his soft breathing. She thought of their walk through snowy Boston, five years back. They had been returning to their hotel after a last roadshow; she had been so young, and he an upwardly mobile VP, who had taken her under his wing. He had been warning her that her unwillingness to take risks would impact her career.

'But the risks sometimes seem so irrational!' she had protested, wrapping her scarf tighter around her neck. They were walking up the gentle incline of a cobbled street lined delicately with snow and brightened by the warm amber light thrown out by Beacon Hill's elegant brownstones.

'The right irrational acts are the ones that are going to reward you, Sabrina,' Ashok told her, putting on his best English accent to impersonate the firm's CEO. 'But you've gotta be brave enough to take them. That's what they pay us to do, the higher up the ladder we get.'

Sabrina nodded, accepting the gloves Ashok offered her. Flakes of wispy snow kissed his face before melting and she felt a sudden burst of happiness.

'It's beautiful,' she said, suddenly stopping. 'I can't believe you went to college here.'

He looked at her and smiled, visibly moved by her naivety. Then he bent forward and kissed her: their first kiss. The memory of it filled her with an exhuberant warmth.

Those first few years he had been a remarkably different Ashok and one of the prime reasons for her growing attachment to New York. It was the old Ashok who had fascinated her with the politics of high finance, who had helped her break free of her tourist's perspective and experience New York as as a local: jazz at Smalls, baseball at the Yankees, hiking up in Tarrytown and Shakespeare in Central Park. But this same Ashok had also spent his Sunday afternoons browsing old books at the Strand with her, had taken her for nihari at Jackson Heights, listened to Jagjit Singh in the privacy of his apartment in Koreatown and treated her to old Bollywood movies in the old Cineplex on Lexington. 'They don't make women like that anymore,' he'd whispered to her as Sharmila Tagore blinked out at them from the screen. He had once even taken her home for Diwali, to his parents' apartment in a rundown part of New Jersey, where his older brother sat and stared glumly from his wheelchair as their mother made sooji halwa. That had been an Ashok she would never hurt. But she didn't know if that Ashok existed anymore.

When he was sent on a secondment to their firm's London office, Sabrina and Ashok tacitly agreed to see other people. Yet, Sabrina was surprised at the distress she felt when, upon his return to New York, Ashok announced his engagement to Rachel.

'But Sab,' he had replied when she asked him to explain. 'People like you and me, we didn't come this far to marry each other. Did we?' He posed this last question with genuine curiosity, searching her face for her answer. She thought she glimpsed in his eyes some hope that she would contradict him. But, buried deep beneath her hurt, Sabrina knew that she agreed: Ashok had taken her off course, but Sabrina had always aspired to a marriage like her sister's – one that sought out a multicultural adventure rather than monocultural formality. So, she had swallowed her pain and kissed him to demonstrate that she understood, and that she would not let sentimentality spoil the immaculately-designed landscape of their future. And he had so wanted to be understood that he had continually sought her out, even after he married. They had become like addicts: unable to stop, but bitter with their objects of desire for making them insufferably, immorally weak.

Just this evening, he had attempted to fool her by reverting to the old Ashok, pulling up an old Jagjit Singh ghazal on his iTunes and treating her to takeaway from Pardes, their favourite old haunt on Lex. He had reassured her that she would be fine – and that now he was acting head, he would be better placed to look out for her. Not only would they work together again, but he would push for her MD promotion next quarter.

She knew all of it to be lies – the business did not require two MDs, so it was out of the question that she would be promoted while he was head. His eagerness to reassure her was too nervous, too fraught to be sincere. The last few years of being his mistress – she cringed at it, but yes, mistress – had at least taught her how to read him.

It would be so easy to de-throne him. She had gone through her old messages assiduously and unearthed a text he had sent her confirming that he had spoken with the clients and told them about the potential downgrade but that they had decided to proceed regardless. Now she had evidence demonstrating that he *had* known all along, and he had lied that he had told the client.

It would be so easy to send this to Compliance. But she knew she would not be able to do it. This was Ashok, *her* Ashok.

She bent over and kissed him softly on his head. Then she woke him with a soft nudge on his arm.

'Hey,' she said. 'Wake up. Rachel's expecting you, isn't she?'

Mention of his wife was always enough to rouse him.

He swung himself off the bed. She gazed at the soft flesh of his midriff and was suddenly reminded of her father and his smooth, hairless torso, damp after his bath, when he went in search of a clean kurtha for the jumma prayers.

'You're not still worrying about making MD, are you?' Ashok asked, smiling.

'No,' she said, feeling a tug at her chest.

He dressed in silence, eventually finding the box she had slipped into his trousers. He took it out.

'What's this?'

'A gift. Congratulations on making head.'

He opened it in short, sharp movements and then held the money clip up in the lamplight.

'What?' she asked. 'You don't like it?'

'Bulgari is a bit showy for me, but thanks.'

'Ash, it was a gift – you don't like it, throw the fucking thing out.'

'Well, what if I hadn't seen it and Rachel had found it? What then?'

'What,' she asked, her voice sharp with malice. 'Your wife doesn't do gifts?' She reached to switch the lamp off, letting the darkness swallow them.

Ashok extracted his shirt and socks from the mess of bedclothes.

'You,' he said as he laced up his shoes, 'are not, and will never be, on a par with my wife.'

'She's so exceptional,' Sabrina said coolly, lifting the duvet around her bare shoulders and hoping he could not hear the catch in her throat, 'that you creep into my apartment on a weekly basis.'

He glared at her. 'Like you're so faithful. What happened to Daniel?'

'Oh, please.'

'I don't see him around.'

'Fuck you.' She turned and lay on her side with her back to him.

'Sab,' Ashok whispered, and she heard him sigh when she did not answer. 'Why do we keep doing this to each other?'

Still she did not answer. Sabrina felt the darkness sink into her and waited for the click of the door to signal his departure.

She picked up her phone and called her sister.

Nasrin picked up almost immediately. 'Hey, I just emailed you.'

'I know. I read it. Did I wake you?'

She heard Nasrin yawn, painfully. 'I'm so tired, Sibby, but I'm having trouble sleeping. What about you? It must be bedtime there?'

'Yeh …'

'Are you okay?'

'You know, the usual, work hassles.'

'Is it that stuff with Compliance? Are you still worried about losing your job?'

'It makes me sick to even think about it, Dids. Forget me though. Your email – something's wrong. I can sense it.'

Nasrin was silent for a moment. 'Richard and I … we've been arguing a lot lately.'

'Oh,' Sabrina felt strangely relieved. 'Is that it? Is that why you're in the Beacons?'

Nasrin paused again and then in a small voice that Sabrina could barely hear, 'Partly.'

'What is it? I know there's something.'

'Sib, I'm pregnant.'

Sabrina sat up and fumbled to switch on the light. 'Say again?

You're pregnant? Didi, wow! That's amazing!' When Nasrin did not respond, Sabrina paused before saying: 'I mean, Dids, is it amazing?'

'I don't … don't know.'

'Okay. Don't cry. I mean it must be tough being a mum but look at what an amazing job you've done with Eli.'

Nasrin sniffled. 'It's not that.'

'So, what is it?'

Again Nasrin lapsed into silence. Sabrina shifted, feeling worry kneading her. 'Dids, listen, whatever it is, it's your decision. I mean whatever I think, or even Richard, we'd always support you. You just need to have the courage to decide, right? You can't be assertive until you know what *you* want.'

Nasrin sniffed. She said, 'I haven't told anyone yet, Sib, please don't say anything yet. To be honest, I just wanted to come here, be with Mum. I'm missing Abba so much.'

'Me too.'

'Remember when he made our hair?'

Sabrina laughed, for her father had been an expert at braiding their hair, well into their late teens.

'Like, you know, when he hugged you, you knew everything was going to be okay, no matter how messed up it all felt.'

'Yes.'

'Isn't it so sad that Afroz didn't get that side of him, Sib?'

Sabrina hesitated before asking, 'Has she said anything about the Peacock? Did Humayun talk to her about selling to me?'

'Sib,' Nasrin said firmly, 'you can't go pestering Humayun Bhai about this – it's not up to him.'

Sensing her sister was in a vulnerable state, Sabrina did not argue. After Nasrin said goodbye, Sabrina switched off the light, and lay in the darkness thinking about Nasrin's pregnancy and the surprising despondency she exhibited in respect of it. She wished she had asked about what Nasrin had been referring to in her email, about Abba being in the shadows: had she had a nightmare? Was her medication so strong that it was causing hallucinations? Her sister's voice had resounded with a deep and ingrained despondency – all the more potent because Nasrin had tried to hide it. Even in the midst of the BA disciplinary hearing Nasrin had not sounded this depressed. Sabrina shivered and reached for the duvet. She felt a cool hard object dig against her thigh. It was the Bulgari money clip lying next to Ashok's gloves. She gripped it in her hands and thought about how tense their recent meetings had become, fraught with suspicion and bitterness. She fell asleep in the abandoned silence of her apartment, anxious about her sister and grappling with thoughts of how she was going to wrench herself free of Ashok.

16

Every night, a little after midnight, Afroz heard the phone ring as she lay in bed. She heard the murmurs of her aunt, repeating the dozen words she spoke to her youngest daughter, on the other side of the Atlantic. *Are you well? Have you eaten? Are you on your way home? Call me tomorrow.* Afroz lay in the near darkness, straining to hear.

Since Nasrin had arrived, the calls were placed a little earlier in the evening, and the muttering often grew louder, into fully audible words that floated up to Afroz.

'Sib, they were talking about promoting you,' Nasrin said into the phone one night, her voice on edge, which could have been either with excitement or dismay, 'of course your job is safe, they're lucky to even have you!' Afroz had noticed a change in her sister, the short conversations in the mornings with Richard, and the rooftop excursions with Riaz. Her curiosity about what was happening on the flat roof each night had led her to sneak up the iron staircase one evening, an action she had regretted ever since. The two lay on a plank on top of the old tandoor ovens, talking.

'Go to bed, Riaz, you're yawning so badly!' Afroz heard her sister say.

'I'm not tired, Naz, just another smoke.' She heard Riaz yawn, and then Riaz and Nasrin both laughed.

'Not tired, yeh right.'

Afroz turned and had been about to descend the staircase when she heard Riaz ask Nasrin, 'Hey, do you ever feel like flying again?'

She stopped, listening into the silence, curious to hear her sister's answer.

'You always seemed so happy when you were flying,' Riaz said.

'That won't ever happen again,' Nasrin said in a voice so terse that it made Afroz squirm.

'Well, why did you like it so much?' Riaz asked, sitting up. 'If you can figure that out, then you can figure out what else you can do that'll make you that happy, right?'

'I don't know how to explain it,' Nasrin replied, 'it was just so … freeing … so liberating, you know?'

Afroz heard Riaz laugh. 'What!' She saw the flicker of his cigarette moving in the darkness as he rolled down his sleeve. 'You are free! Look at you, the life you have! What do you need freedom from?' and Afroz found herself nodding in the darkness to herself, sharing Riaz's incredulity. But then she heard Nasrin's answer and it stopped her cold.

'From … people … I mean, relationships, I suppose.'

Was Nasrin's marriage in trouble? Her aunt had led her to believe that Nasrin had come to stay in the Beacons because she wanted to spend time with Afroz. But Nasrin's strange behaviour, and the lack of visits from Richard now started to make more sense. Afroz was beginning to back down the staircase, when she heard Riaz say, 'You don't need to fly a plane to escape relationships, Naz,' and Afroz frowned, because the last thing Nasrin's troubled marriage needed was interference from Riaz.

As innocent as they proved to be, Afroz did not approve of these nightly exurcions, and had tried her best to counsel her sister against them, but her advice had been met with laughter and teasing. 'You sound like Amma!' Nasrin told her. 'Get with the times, Afi, men and women can be just friends, you know.'

'It's about appearances too,' she had tried to explain, 'about reputation and honour.'

'Oh my God,' Nasrin rolled her eyes, 'you are basically Amma.'

And Afroz had given up.

Now she heard the phone conversation in the hallway continuing.

'Sib, you're going to be just fine,' she heard Nasrin say in a reassuring way. 'When will you find out?'

Afroz lay in the darkness, feeling a pinch of envy that the two sisters' closeness remained unaffected by the distance between them. She turned away from Humayun, irritated by his snores, and wondered why it was that fortune favoured the already fortunate.

'Did someone call this morning?' Afroz asked her husband the next morning as she prepared breakfast. Humayun sat down at the dining table, crossing his ankles delicately, his shoulders hunched up against the morning chill.

'Can you use hot milk for the tea?' Humayun asked, hiding his yawn behind his hand.

She put bread into the toaster and poured milk into a milkpan to warm. Only when she began to butter the toast did she ask again.

'So, who called?'

'Hai?'

'This morning.'

'This morning, it was Ma that called,' he said with the correctitude of a man choosing his words very carefully. He stood up to fetch his sweater from the corner of the radiator where Afroz had hung it the night before.

'Is she okay?'

'Jamal took her to see Doctor Abul, I think her blood pressure has been high again. It's all this interfering in other people's business that's making her ill. And did all the interfering do any good? No, because they have found a groom and are setting a date for the wedding. Anyway, I told her,' his voice was muffled as he struggled to get his head through the wool fabric, 'that we would confirm our return tickets for next Friday.'

Afroz froze. She stabbed the knife into the slab of butter.

'Dorgagate's Sufia Khala is visiting, so we can see her before she heads home the week after.'

'Did you ask me?'

'What?' Humayun sat down.

'You didn't ask me.'

He turned at her raised tone, the surprise fanning out across his face.

'Afi,' Humayun said, his voice booming in the morning stillness. 'I have been very patient with you. We have our own shongshar – our own family!'

'What shongshar?' she snapped, turning to him. 'What shongshar and what family?'

He looked at her in stunned dismay. She had never uttered those words before. Even though she had felt them many times since they were told they would never have children.

'You should go,' she told him, her words swelling uncomfortably in her mouth. 'You should go, by yourself.'

'Kitha matho? What are you saying!'

'I can't go. Not yet. But I won't stop you.'

She finished buttering the toast with trembling fingers, and placed the plate in front of him, reaching behind her for the cup of tea. As she did so, he stood sharply, knocking her elbow so the cup slipped. Hot tea scalded her thigh and pieces of bone china were flung to the furthest reaches of the kitchen. They glared at each other, and it seemed to her that for the first time, in the midst of their anger and frustration, they actually saw each other.

'Did he hurt you?' her aunt asked as Afroz cleaned up the broken china.

'No.'

'Are you okay?' Nasrin asked, her eyes still bleary with sleep.

'Yes.'

'But everything is okay?' her Fufu asked again.

'It's fine!'

Afroz slipped the pieces of china into the bin, and slammed it shut. As she washed her hands, she could feel a splinter in her middle finger, but her anger prevented her from seeing it. She rubbed at the spot that hurt.

'But why hasn't Humayun eaten his breakfast?' her aunt asked. Afroz turned and saw the two of them staring blankly at his empty chair, the brittle toast sitting on a plate.

'I won't sell it,' Afroz said, sitting down heavily, 'and he won't stay.' And above her head, Nasrin and her mother looked at each other, and wondered about the choice Afroz would have to make.

Her aunt liked to spend the last half-hour before sunset in her back garden, tending to the vegetables she grew there. Afroz enjoyed sitting just inside the patio, reading her Ya Sin and watching her. There were potatoes, a vine of dhudhi that Humayun had helped Jahanara to tie to a weave of bamboo, there was coriander, and rows of spinach.

Her aunt, stooped but still sprightly, wore Shamsur's old green wellies and moved about the patch like she was walking on the moon. Her saree was hitched up to her knees and her achol folded into her hips. She crouched down and began to dig up the potatoes with a hand trowel.

This was the hour that Afroz loved the most, full of easy conversation and abundance of laughter – but that afternoon, she felt cut off from it, as though she were trapped in a world of black and white, gazing into a world of colour. Elias ran out with bare feet, calling to her as he picked up a garden fork, but she could barely muster a smile.

Nasrin followed him, carrying a pair of Crocs, which he refused to put on. He ran under the fig tree and stood scowling at his mother, and behind them, Jahanara tutted, 'Let him be, just let him be. It's only a bit of earth, at the end of the day; I mean, you used to eat it!'

Afroz watched. Until Humayun had forced her hand by setting a date for their return to Desh, she had not believed herself capable of admitting that she wanted to stay longer. But now that she had said it, she realised just how fiercely she wanted it. She asked Allah for his guidance, although she had already made up her mind. *Give me a sign if I am sinning*, she prayed. Upstairs, Humayun was packing his belongings.

Until the morning's betrayal, Afroz had observed, over the last fortnight, the quiet emergence of a different side to her husband. She was touched by the unexpected kindnesses he exhibited in his interactions with her aunt and surprised by the enthusiasm and curiosity with which he conversed with Nasrin and Elias. In Desh, she had seen glimpses of this side of him during Baba's temporary visits, and Afroz had asked herself whether it was possible that she had only been looking when her Baba was present.

But this morning, Humayun had reverted to form. He had returned to the role of sycophantic son to his hypochondriac mother. She should never have thought he had changed. All she had wanted was a little more time to be here, at the Peacock, living a tiny part of the life that should have been her birthright and had been denied her twice, first by Shamsur, now by him.

By the time the taxi arrived, she was prepared for the recriminations and the ultimatums she was sure would be hurled her way. So, as he packed his case into the boot of the taxi, his quiet glumness surprised her. They all stood around him – even Riaz, who put a tiffin of food into the car for the journey.

Humayun turned to her. 'Afi,' he said, checking his passport and sliding it into his pocket. 'Tell me now when you will come home.'

Afroz opened her mouth to say, 'Soon' but was immediately cut off by an outburst from Nasrin.

'You can't force her, Bhaiya!'

Afroz turned in surprise to Nasrin, who had stepped between them. Nasrin's cheeks were flushed pink and her eyes had a strange glint. Her voice shook with uncertainty. Afroz had never seen her sister like this.

Humayun's face was pale and perplexed. 'Force?' he sputtered.

'Don't you see that she isn't happy? That she has not ever been happy—'

'Naju!' Nasrin's mother stepped towards them, taking her daughter's hand, but Nasrin pushed her away.

'She doesn't want to go, Bhaiya. She never wanted to go, that's never been where she wants to be, do you see?'

Afroz felt a panic engulfing her, as though she were watching them all from behind a glass screen.

'Afi, tell him!' Nasrin pleaded.

'Na go boyn, you're wrong. I mean, you misunderstand,' Humayun said, addressing a handkerchief he had pulled out of his pocket. 'Our marriage was not forced.'

'Don't you see, Bhaiya?' Nasrin said with sudden gentleness. She reached out to touch Humayun's elbow. '*You* may not have been forced. But she was.'

Humayun looked at Afroz, who stared, wide-eyed, back at him.

His hands suddenly dropped by his sides, the handkerchief fluttering to the ground. 'What?' he said.

Then, after a few excruciating seconds, Humayun cleared his throat. 'Then is this something more? Are you saying you aren't coming home at all?'

Afroz, trapped inside herself, could not respond.

'No!' her aunt said, taking Humayun by the arm. 'No, baba, ignore Naju, she is sick, she is epileptic, and she doesn't know what she says. Afi *will* come home to you soon. Let her stay with us a little longer. I will send her home to you.'

'No!' Nasrin told him. 'She is not coming back to you.'

'Naju!' Afroz said, turning to face her. 'What are you doing? Stop it!'

'Aren't you sick of being good all the time?' Nasrin asked her. 'Goodness can be ugly too, Afi – I mean needing to please everyone, needing to be liked will always mean making these countless sacrifices. If you don't want to be in the marriage, leave it! Leave him and let him find happiness somewhere else! He's a good guy, Afi! And you don't need to be so self-sacrificial all the time. Who do you think will care? Stop being such a coward!'

'Naju! Don't you speak—' Afroz began, her heart pulsing with anger, but Humayun stopped her.

'Please, don't argue because of me.' He glanced at the cab driver who had sat through this exchange in stiff stillness, starting steadily at the road ahead. Then he turned to Afroz, gazing at her, his expression a mixture of confusion and shock. He opened his mouth to speak, and then closed it again. Then he whispered a faint 'Allah hafiz' and ducked into the cab. As the car drove away, he looked out at Afroz as though he was seeing her for the first time.

She had expected anger. Instead, as the car slipped away from them, she saw his dismay. He wasn't angry, she realised with a sudden sadness. He had simply never understood.

That evening, Jahanara stood in her kitchen. She had just put down the phone to Humayun. She had called him ostensibly to ensure he had checked in and there were no delays with the flight, but she had reminded him of the sanctity of marriage. 'Don't even think of divorce,' she had told him, her voice quivering with anxiety. 'My daughter is an epileptic; she has a disease of the mind. Sometimes she sees and says things that are not real. Afroz is your wife, and I will send her home to you very soon.' But Humayun had not responded, his silence reproaching her for making promises she could not keep.

Before her, several heart-shaped paan leaves floated in a sink of cold water. She scrubbed each one before wiping them dry on a dishcloth. Then she de-veined them, split them in half and placed them in a pile on a kuli which itself had been woven into the shape of a paan leaf. The kuli brought to mind the rainy afternoon it had been woven, the room ringing with the laughter caused by the vulgar jokes that Deshi women would only share in the company of other women.

Would her daughters, with their rigid, formal ways, ever know the joys of such crassness? Would they ever understand that the point of life wasn't ambition and striving, but acceptance and understanding? Her youngest had sounded increasingly stressed on their evening calls over the last week, and Jahanara complained to Naju that it was just a job, not worth such anxiety. 'Amma,' Naju had chided, 'it's not just a job to her, it's her life!' Jahanara, though comforted that her daughters were friends again, could not understand how a job could be a life. But the picture of Naju's face that afternoon as she confronted Humayun made Jahanara suddenly afraid. She could not work out what exactly frightened her, except how little she understood the daughters that Shamsur had left her with.

She finished preparing the paan, a time-consuming task of spreading the lime paste onto the betel leaf before twisting it into a cone, and folded it into a small, silver box for Mustafa. Now he was going back to Desh, this was the last paandan she would prepare for him. She finished the task with fond nostalgia, regretting that she had often mistaken his innocent concerns for her wellbeing as prying and judgemental – in those early days in the Beacons she had been unable to believe that the eyes of her community were not upon her, and she had latched on to the belief that Mustafa represented all the old forms of surveillance and judgement that she had been used to in Desh. She hoped she could make amends by the role she had procured for him in Nirashapur as caretaker of the old, neglected Islam estate. She cleaned the rim of the choona pot, slipped it in place next to the zarda and closed the latch on the paandan.

17

Despite having been born in the Beacons, Nasrin had never attempted the more challenging trails and was loyal to the rambler's paths Shamsur had preferred when she was a child. His most cherished had been the trail that led from the Glenllian barn along Offa's Dyke, the backdrop of the Black Mountains an endless source of consolation to him. The day after Humayun's departure, Nasrin parked on the dirt track and let Elias out of his car seat.

They walked hand in hand, their faces turneds up toward the meagre sunlight and the breeze ruffling through their hair, shaking through their jackets. Elias stooped to pick the pearliest pebbles. She watched him silently, breaking into a small smile each time he handed one to her. She stuffed them, grass and all, into the holey pocket of her jacket.

When they reached the abandoned building of the church of St Teilo, they stopped to eat the sandwiches made with panch poran fried mackerel that Afroz had packed for them. Afroz had seemed subdued since Nasrin's outburst and Humayun's departure and the thought made Nasrin ashamed.

'It's spicy!' Elias told his mother proudly. She opened his juice carton and passed it to him.

They sat on a patch of sunny grass in front of the long-since boarded-over priest's door, their gazes resting on the simple rectangular structure with its small bell turret. She had been here with Richard, five years ago, her belly swelling with a different pregnancy, and they had sat on that very same spot, her head laid contentedly on his lap.

She had been so happy for a time, had greedily counted her blessings as though they would soon run out– and perhaps by doing so, she had tempted fate. She had given nozor to herself, had attracted the evil eye, for suddenly that old life seemed far beyond her reach.

There had been no suggestion of reconciliation from Richard. The morning calls had mostly become a conversation between father and son, while she sat on the sofa and listened and grew anxious. The couple's rift was becoming apparent to everyone else too. Mrs Humphreys had called to ask why no one was home for the last few weeks and that despite her efforts, the window box looked thoroughly neglected. Her mother, who expected Richard to visit on the weekends, had begun interrogating. *Why hasn't he come to visit? Have you argued?* Nasrin sidled out of answering these questions any way that she could: by running off to help in the restaurant, or taking one of her long walks, as she was today. She was regressing, feeling again like a teenager who was anxious about her mother's disapproval. She would have to talk soon. The questions would not stop until she did. The trouble was that she didn't have any answers.

'Eli,' she called out, 'we should head back home soon.'

He skipped back from the church door where he had been fiddling with the lock. 'Back to London?'

'No,' she said, startled. 'Not London! Back to Nani's.'

She hadn't meant to confuse him, but in fact she surprised herself too, for she hadn't thought of the Beacons as her home for over a decade. But then, no other place had been home either. Why was it that she couldn't find her place? What was it about her that struggled to occupy and fully inhabit a place as others around her did?

Here, in the Beacons, in the old fabric of her childhood, she couldn't deny that she felt somewhat at peace. Beneath the trepidation about her future, and nostalgia about her past, Nasrin was aware of a deeper sense of calm. The familiarity of this place, and its people, and the slow, unharried pace of life, had begun to anchor her.

But her nightly terrors were becoming increasingly worse, and now seemed to follow her into the daylight hours too, taking the form of an uneasiness, the source of which she was unable to locate. This restlessness had even begun to accompany her into that place of refuge, the flat roof. The night before, she must have dozed off, for she had suddenly woken with a start and rushed to the edge of the roof.

'Oi!' Riaz had grabbed her arm. 'You could've fallen! Be careful.'

She pointed beneath them where, beside the fig tree, a spectre had appeared. It had her father's small nose, her father's eyes, her father's posture. But she knew it wasn't Abba.

'Do you see it?' she whispered.

Riaz peered into the gloom.

'Anyone there?' he called out. 'Junaid? Linds?'

'He stands so still,' Nasrin said, 'and so bright. Why don't you see him?'

She had not spoken to anyone before about the apparitions, and the look on Riaz's face made her wish she had not told him.

Riaz led her away from the edge and sat her down. He slipped his cigarette down a hole into the tandoor oven, and the ember glowed up at them from the bottom, like a glint of metal in a dark well. He wiped his face on the back of his wrist and knelt down in front of her.

'What's going on with you?'

It was the softness in his voice that undid her: the fact that he had cared – the fact that he had noticed when no one else had seemed to. She lay back down, and the tears slid down the side of her face and into her ears. Riaz lay back too, on the floor near her feet, and she was so thankful for his presence that she began to talk.

But she shouldn't have told him, she realised that now. Her pregnancy wouldn't have shown for another few months, she had plenty of time. Time for what? She wasn't sure, but now Riaz knew, and his knowledge sped time up, made the hours turn to minutes, and the passing of time harassed and bullied her about her indecision.

She even told him about Fabienne.

'Please don't tell anyone.'

'Didn't you once tell me that infidelity was the one thing you wouldn't do, the one thing you wouldn't take?'

'I have Eli to think about, Riaz,' she had told him. 'It's not that simple anymore.'

'Do you love him?' he asked.

'Yes. I do.' She silently considered her words after she uttered them. 'There are moments, you know, of difficulty.' The image of Fabienne appeared in her mind and she sat up to shake it away.

'Course there is,' Riaz said, 'in all relationships. Always.'

'But moments in mine, where I think, would this have been different if I had stuck to my own?'

Riaz did not reply to this, and she realised she had shocked him.

'I mean,' she said, her voice low and cautious, 'do you remember when the Manchester Arena bombing happened? All those terrible images on the TV and the shock of it all? You know, Richard came home that night, and we sat in front of the TV, stunned by the horror of it all, and I swear I heard him say, "Fucking Muslims, rot in hell."'

Riaz tutted. 'Yeh, but come on, Naz. He obviously meant the terrorists. He didn't mean you.'

'I know, and that's what he said too, but … it still felt strange, you know? Even though I hated the terrorists as much as he did, that comment just made me feel like I was immediately in a different camp. Just for being Muslim. And it would've been fine, but he's my husband. I want to be in the same camp.'

Riaz sat up to look at her. 'He's just human, Naz, aren't we all?'

She tore her eyes away from his, unable to bear the pity in them. 'Marriage, you know,' she said, wanting to change the subject, 'well, you don't know I suppose, but marriage, it's a sort of vision. It's like this journey you make together. Then something happens and one person doesn't want to go on that journey anymore ...'

'Does Richard not want to ... make the journey anymore?' Riaz asked gently.

Nasrin felt herself bristle.

'I love him. Always loved him, always will.' She made the statement staring down at him in the darkness, as though it would explain everything. 'You know, Riaz?'

'I know. Naz, look, call him and tell him this. Call him and tell him about the baby. He won't want to end things if he knows that.'

'But that's just it,' Nasrin said, hearing the edge of desperation that had entered her voice, because she wanted Riaz to understand her. 'Eli was conceived properly, by two people who loved each other, but this ...' Her voice trailed off; her fingers grazed her abdomen absently. 'This pregnancy is so different.'

Riaz had stood up then, feeling his pocket for his cigarettes. Below them, someone opened the wheelie bin and hauled a couple of rubbish bags in. They heard Lindsay calling out for Junaid to clean the pickle plates.

'I mean,' Nasrin said, sitting up, 'I mean I'm not sure that I should even keep—'

'Naz!'

'What? I'm just saying, if a child isn't conceived the proper way—'

'Naz, seriously! Don't finish that sentence! It's haram to abort—'

'Don't get all fundo on me, Riaz! Children should only ever be conceived in love.'

'Naz, seriously?' Riaz stood up. He took sharp, furious puffs on his cigarette and turned to glare at her. 'You think your folks understood some bullshit romantic notion of love before they had you? I know my parents didn't!'

'I didn't mean some bullshit romantic notion – it's not what I meant.'

The sky darkened as the moon slipped behind a cloud. Riaz was silent for a long time. Then he sat down slowly, brushing the dust off his work shirt and rolling down his sleeves against the night's chill.

'Tell him about the baby, Naz.'

'No!'

'You're driving yourself crazy. Tell him, and he'll leave that other woman and come back to you.'

'No!' She had sat up and grabbed his hands as he made to leave. 'And you can't tell him, do you understand?'

And she had seen that he didn't understand, and she wished she could take it all back.

'I'm worried about you, Naz,' Riaz said, reaching out to touch her face, but at the last moment, deciding against it.

She had watched him leave, unable to fathom his pain, steeped too deeply in her own. After he left, she peered down below the roof where she had seen her father.

'I miss you,' she had said softly into the empty space.

Throughout her hikes, Nasrin had searched the numinous domes in the horizon for an understanding of why her father had hidden Afroz. As they walked back to the car that afternoon, the sun already sinking into the horizon, it occurred to Nasrin that though she had not found an answer to that question, her pleas had not been ignored. She had learned for herself why Abba had been devoted to these soaring valleys, glowing amber with heather, with their gentle inclines that broke into towering peaks. She appreciated how the crunch of the gravel beneath the feet, the call of the birds mingling with the wind that whistled past the ears would have lulled him into a calmer state, just as it did her. She knew that the simple beauty of the panoramic views belied the treacherous turn in mood these mountains could take if the rain clouds skittered in and understood that it was possible for contradictory propositions to be true. Her father, who had feigned a simple morality, had also been complicated and out here, where nature's divinity humbled her, she could accept those contradictions. He had been her devoted father. He had also abandoned Afroz.

She reached the car, and leaned against the car door, waiting for Elias to catch up. 'Hurry up, boo!' she called to him.

Elias grinned mischievously, before diverting towards the barn where he began to pick through a mound of pebbles. Nasrin watched him, listening to his soft hums wafting out to her before recognition dawned on her.

'Not the Lalon, Eli!' she called and Elias giggled guiltily before running towards her. Nasrin picked up the tune and continue to sing it: 'Donno donno bole tare'. It delighted her that Elias had captured his grandfather by learning one of his beloved Lalongeet. As she settled Elias into his car seat, she smiled at the thought that Abba, like Lalon himself, had travelled far from his birthplace, ignoring cultural differences. Abba had navigated life with his feet on two boats – *duy naukar pa diye chole* – and it was no small feat, standing strong and steady in two cultures instead of one. Afroz seemed to have inherited this gift, embracing difference by focusing robustly on the singular power of shared moments. Nasrin had spent her life stressing about bicultural differences and yet Afroz's afternoon tea sessions each day showed just how simple it could be.

As she put the car into gear, she felt her phone vibrate.

It was a text from Richard: *'Why didn't you TELL me?'*

She closed her eyes, trying to contain the anger building inside her. Another text: *'Driving down after work, tonight.'*

She returned from her hike, bringing a storm of clouds with her. As she banged on Riaz's door, the rain smattered on the windowpanes and the distant thunder rolled in.

When he opened the door Nasrin couldn't prevent her voice from rising and rising almost to a shriek, and behind her, the lights in the other bedrooms were turned on, and floorboards creaked as people came to their doors to listen. But she didn't care. Her small son stared up at her with surprise and confusion, but she didn't care.

'How could you!' she demanded, and Riaz was unable to respond. He looked down at the floor, stood tall through it all until her last words, delivered after her anger was spent and in a sad, low whisper. 'I trusted you, Riaz.'

Elias saw the way Riaz's face collapsed. He saw that Riaz's knuckles, usually red and bruised from boxing, were now drained of colour as he clutched the doorframe. And as his mother led him away, her fury finally abated, Elias felt an inexplicable sadness and anxiety pour through him.

When her husband arrived some hours later, Nasrin was lying in bed. She heard the footsteps on the stairs followed by a perfunctory knock, before the door opened.

'You should have told me.'

'You shouldn't have come.'

'You should have told me, Naz!'

'I was going to!'

'If I'd known—'

'If you'd known? What? What if you'd known? Would you have made sure not to sleep with her? Would you turn back time somehow?'

'You had no right to keep it to yourself.'

'I had every right.'

Their voices were clipped, and the air in the room was stifling. Nasrin was not surprised when Richard left, banging the door behind him.

She heard voices downstairs; her mother and Afroz, then the footsteps coming up the stairs.

'Will you do this now?' her mother asked her from the door,

speaking in a loud and vicious whisper. 'Haven't I lost enough? Hasn't this family's honour already been attacked enough and now you will murder it? You will bring a child into the world without a father? What are you thinking, Naju? Where do you think sitting up there on the roof with Riaz will get you?'

Nasrin searched her mother's worried face. Just days ago, her mother had had the same expression as she called Humayun to entreat him not to view divorce as an option, had promised to send Afroz home.

'Amma,' Nasrin said, 'why are you always so afraid? Is marriage the only place you think women should be?'

Her mother retreated. Nasrin saw the wounded way she moved and felt the guilt slice her in half.

When Richard returned to the room, Nasrin had been lying in the darkness for some time. She shielded her eyes from the light flooding into the room.

'Naz.' He came to kneel by her bed. 'Look at me, please, sweetheart.'

Nasrin looked up at him, at the parts that made up the man Richard F. Wilson, the F of which had so long remained a secret in their relationship, until they had taken that trip to Monaco together and she had seen it printed on his passport. She looked at the brown freckle – mole, he always insisted – just to the left of the bridge of his nose, and she looked at the blue-green of his eyes, which reminded her of the colour of the ghat on a sunny day, and she asked herself: was she ready for a life without him? Was she ready for a life without a father to her children, a life without the home they had built together?

'We can't have a child like this,' he said, taking both her hands and pressing them to his chest.

'What?'

'Like this – like the way we are! We can't, it would be so cruel.'

'Do you mean … terminate the pregnancy?'

'Why the hell would you think that? No! I mean things have to change!'

'Where've you been for the last few weeks?'

'I've been at home.'

Nasrin watched his face, letting the silence grow long and stifling.

'What …' he said, looking uncertain.

'You're still lying.'

'Okay—'

'Okay, what?'

'Okay, I was … I was with her. Naz, I just …you and me … it just got tough, but I'm here now.'

She considered this in silence, letting the rage simmer around her temples. 'The thing is,' she said, her voice strangled, 'you were so ready to give one child up for her. And now what? Another child makes you come back?'

'It's not really about her, and I think you know that.'

'Of course it's about her! You left me for her!'

'*I* left *you*?'

'You gave me no choice!'

'You had a choice, but like with everything, you don't know what you want. You don't know how to commit to anything. We chose this life together – but you've spent the last several years moping like I forced you into it.'

Nasrin sat up. 'That's not true.'

'I don't know what's true. I know that things between us have been bad. You're moody and unresponsive – and ever since Eli, you've just, I don't know, stopped caring about me.'

'Moody!' she raged. 'You try being stuck in that house day in and day out!'

'But I've always encouraged you to go back to work!'

'It's not like I can just walk into a job!'

He shook his head. 'I just mean, things were bad. And yes, Fabienne came along during that bad time and I know that I screwed up, but what I'm saying is that it was never a choice between the two of you. It was always you.'

Nasrin was surprised by this last sentence. A sentence delivered with such clarity, such commitment. Did she believe him? She looked away from Richard's earnest face, dug her fingers into her palm.

'It was you. But … I just need to know that it's what you want too. You know? I want to know that you're in this relationship because you want to be in it.'

Nasrin blinked at him. She thought for a moment about Richard's face that evening she had donned a kurtha and prepared Bengali food for his clients. Then she suddenly thought of Riaz, the fear in his face as he told her that aborting was haram. Everyone, it seemed, only wanted a certain version of her. She squeezed her eyes shut.

Richard took her face and looked her in the eye. 'I can work on it, Naz. Let's work on it. Can we do that? Can we do that, honey? Let's not bring a child into the world without giving him or her …' His face lit up and he grabbed her hand and kissed it. 'Maybe a her, eh, Naz? But she has to have both her parents.'

'It's just that …' she faced him, 'you don't really know who I am, not really. You know?'

'Course I do, honey! I love you!'

'I mean *all* of me – you know like the brown bits of me as well as the—'

'Naz, not this again – I love your skin colour, you know that—'

'I mean the culture, the religion, all the bits of us that come from the other place …' She nodded, willing him to understand. 'You've got to understand, Rich, that living between cultures means always like, pining for home, because you know, the home I want, it doesn't really exist, see? And the only way to make it exist is to make the place I'm in and the place I long for, coexist … I don't … like my dad did … like Afroz – don't look at me like that!' Nasrin brushed her hair away from her face in frustration. 'What I mean is that I don't want to bring another child into the world pretending to be someone I'm not.'

'Okay … I get it, I'm sorry, okay?' Richard took her hands, but Nasrin wasn't sure he did understand. 'I'm sorry. Let's just try this again. Give us a chance – give us a chance, give the baby a chance. Right? We have to do that, don't we? For our kids?'

He leaned forward and embraced her, and in that embrace, Nasrin felt all the unease and mistrust that lay between them. Maybe love had brought them this far, Nasrin thought sadly, but it wasn't love that would keep them together. It was whatever love sometimes morphs into in middle age – a sense of duty, of responsibility and habit. Out in the soft darkness, the moon stilled the night, but Nasrin felt a flutter of panic. She felt suddenly trapped. She thought of what Eli would think, and what her as yet unborn child would want, and what her mother wanted, and what Afroz would disapprove of – and they all coalesced into a great ball of other people's needs and wants that threatened to overwhelm her. She felt strangled.

Then something Sabrina had said suddenly came back to her: *You can't be assertive until you know what* you *want.*

And in that tender moonlight, she saw it clearly.

'Rich,' she said, pushing him gently away, her voice quivering, 'I want a divorce.'

Hours later, after the recriminations became anger, and the anger became grief, and the tears led to embraces and an exhausted sleep, Nasrin woke up and gently extricated her fingers from Richard's. Leaving him softly snoring on her bed, she sought out Riaz. He was up on the flat roof, smoking, and she sat down next to him, pulling her knees up to her chin. Into his silence, she poured hers. The sky was alive with stars that blinked out at them but were too distant to offer any reassurance.

'There was a part of me that didn't want to,' he offered finally, 'but I just couldn't see you like that. It's like you're …' He shook his head. 'It's like you're unravelling.' He stood and began to walk away. He stopped at the top of the stairs and turned to face her.

She stared out at him, and in the moonlight, he seemed fragile: the skin on his face was gossamer and his sillouette seemed shrunken, absorbed by the darkness.

'I'm not angry at you,' she called out to him. 'It's just that now, I'll never know,' she said, 'if he'd ever have come back, just for me.' She stood up and joined him and together they descended the stairs. 'I'll never know if it was just for the baby. Now, I feel like it's always going to be a choice that *you* made.'

'I just wanted to help, Naz. I'm so sorry.'

Nasrin didn't respond to that.

At the bottom of the stairs, she stopped abruptly and stared out over the restaurant yard to her mother's rose bushes. Riaz followed her gaze.

'Naz,' he said softly, his voice pulling her away from what she saw in the garden. She turned to face him, searching his eyes.

'You don't see her, do you?' She looked back at the fig tree where her seven-year-old self stood. 'She's around a lot now.' She looked at Riaz. 'What do you think she wants?'

His eyes scanned the darkness beneath the fig tree, but she knew he saw nothing but the rake leaning against it.

'Do you mean,' he asked, falteringly, 'are you talking about the cat?'

She looked at him blankly, and let her hand drop over his for a moment before she walked back inside to her sleeping husband.

18

The last of Sabrina's compliance interviews was held in a more discreet location on the fiftieth floor. The fingers of her hand, clammy cold, gripped her knees beneath the tabletop. Across from her sat a fearsome panel of three senior directors, and though it was Sunil who led the interrogation, the men she cowered before were Monty and James.

'Why didn't you show this message to us before, Sabrina?' Sunil asked again, for what seemed to her to be the hundredth time.

After two weeks of experiencing the increasing aggressiveness of the compliance investigations and worrying about the likelihood that she would lose her job, Sabrina had met with Ashok to ask him for help. It had been a short meeting and Ashok had brushed her off with a 'just let the thing run its course, Sab, they'll get tired eventually', and for Sabrina, it had been the last straw. She had sent the old text message she had unearthed, showing that Ashok knew about the ratings downgrade, to Compliance and in doing so, she had unilaterally ended their relationship. There had been no word from Ashok since she had sent the email three days before, and with a heavy heart, she understood there was no turning back.

In respect of the ongoing investigation, she knew the only problematic issue was that she had not shown it to them before, and she had prepared for it. What she was not prepared for was this unrelenting dissection of her story so that it became confused in her own mind.

'I should have,' she said.

'Were you trying to protect him?'

'As I said, I didn't realise he was talking about that particular deal until much later when I went back over it in my mind.'

'Why was Mr Mistry using a personal cell phone to discuss business matters with you?'

'As I said before—'

'That tone will not be necessary. This is a very serious allegation of misconduct.'

'I wasn't – I'm trying to be helpful, he's a good friend, he's one of my best friends and this is very difficult.'

'This *relationship* of yours with Mr Mistry …' Sunil pursed his lips, and Sabrina realised with a pang that her secret was out. 'Is it the reason that you tried to protect him?'

'I did not try to protect him.' She sat up straighter in her seat. 'The moment I recognised my omission, I came to you.'

There was a silence in the room and the men glared at her. Sabrina's blood raced with panic, as she wondered if she had just made the most terrible mistake of her life. The interview was not going to plan.

She didn't hear anything for two days, days in which she slept little and had no appetite, floating about in deafening panic. It was Fanni who broke the news.

'Sabrina, did you hear the news? About Ashok?'

Sabrina looked over the rows of screens as her colleague stood to face her way. She tried to quieten the thrumming in her chest.

'Guy's been fired. Cold. Something about that Altieri deal!' Fanni threw a squidgy ball in the air and caught it.

Sabrina could not speak. But all around her, faces turned away from their screens, ready with questions.

'Am I hearing you correctly, Fan?'

'Oh shit! For real?'

'Wait, so, who is team head? Who are they making up?'

'Is Ralph back or something?'

Fanni walked through these questions and came to a halt behind Sabrina's chair.

Sabrina found her voice. 'When?'

Fanni eyed her before replying. 'This morning. They escorted him out. He called Jase.' She took a step back and shouted, 'Hey, Jase, come over, would you?'

'If you're asking about Ashok,' Jason said, breathless with the excitement of knowing. 'He's a goner. They're announcing the acting head in a couple of days.'

After that, it all happened very quickly. A meeting invitation from Monty and James slipped into her calendar that afternoon. The call from up on high came shortly thereafter. Then Mercedes arrived with the paperwork, a glimmer in her eye as she smiled at her newly promoted boss.

That night, Sabrina leaned over her balcony as she waited for her mother or sister to pick up the phone. Nine floors below her, Broadway was at a standstill. An accident of some sort. She saw a delivery man outside the Food Emporium, exchanging curses with a cabbie, and the blare of the horns made its way up to her. She considered going inside to get away from the noise, but the apartment felt darker than usual. It felt safer on the balcony.

'Hello?'

'Didi, it's me.' Sabrina felt anxious. 'Sorry for ringing so late.'

'It's okay, I wasn't sleeping. What's wrong? How did the compliance stuff go?'

'Fine. They called me in this afternoon,' Sabrina swallowed, 'about the MD thing.'

'Okay?' Nasrin said. Her sister's voice was measured, holding so much at bay. Sabrina was overwhelmed by this simple act of control.

'Well.' Her voice struggled against the din of the street sounds. 'Ashok got fired. I'm acting head. They promoted me. They made me MD.' Sabrina waited for the euphoria to descend on her. She had thought that sharing the news with her sister would release the pent-up excitement and joy, but she found the only delight expressed was coming at her through the receiver.

'Ohmygod, oh God, Amma!' She heard her sister running. 'Wake up! Amma, Sabrina's been promoted to director!'

'Hey, are you running?' Sabrina laughed. 'Calm down, fool! You're going to fall!'

'I can't believe it!' Her sister laughed too, and Sabrina heard her mother's voice, alarmed, then confused. She heard Nasrin explain to her mother, and then her mother came on the line.

'Sibby?'

'Ji, Amma?' Sabrina felt the earlier anxiety return. She had only ever, she suddenly realised, shared good news with her father. Her broker. Her distributor of good as well as bad news.

Her mother felt this too, for she said: 'If he was here, he would have been so proud.'

And you, Amma, are you proud? Sabrina thought, but instead she said, 'Yes.' For a moment the din outside muted, and an incredible sadness flooded her. She shook it away.

'Sib!' Nasrin laughed. 'Finally some good news! It's wonderful! But wait. Poor Ashok! That's your old manager, right? The one who married the boss's daughter? Did he do something wrong?'

'Yes,' Sabrina said, trying to control her voice. Pistons of rage and pity pumped inside her and for a moment she couldn't see a thing. 'Yes.'

'Well,' Nasrin said, 'not your fault. Just, I can't believe my sister is an MD? I just have this feeling, Sib, like this family deserves some good luck. I just have this feeling like the tide's turning now, you know?'

'Didi, how are you feeling?' Sabrina asked, taking care to keep her voice low in case their mother was near the phone. 'Have you thought any more about the pregnancy? What does Richard say?'

'I will,' Nasrin in a barely audible whisper, 'when I'm ready. Can't really talk as Amma's following me down to the kitchen. We're celebrating your win with a cup of tea!'

When she hung up, Sabrina remained outside. Something about Nasrin's voice nagged at her. Even when excited, her sister's voice had never seemed as manic as it had just now. Then an email pinged into her inbox, from Nasrin:

'I'm so sorry, I must have sounded so demented just now!' Sabrina smiled with relief. *'I'm just so proud of you. So proud of you. Mum is too, though she's no good at saying that sort of thing. She's doing some special nafal namaz for you tonight. She says that you should pay a sadka out of your new salary, gratitude to God. Never forgets God, our mother.'*

Sabrina switched off her phone and stared down at the Broadway traffic snaking through Midtown and wished suddenly that she could sense some divine presence in the City's throbbing, moving body, to help her escape the feeling that she was utterly alone.

The days were now crowded with meetings and paperwork and celebratory lunches and drinks, but amid it all, Sabrina's feelings of isolation persisted, exacerbated by the new reporting lines which meant that her hitherto peers were required suddenly to report up to her. Fanni in particular was resistant and having to deal with her daily petulance was emotionally and physically exhausting. When Fanni's sulking led to the team losing out on a new transaction, Sabrina made the rookie mistake of restructuring the team so she would not need to work so closely with Fanni. This effective demotion of Fanni only served to attract the sympathies of the rest of the team, leaving Sabrina feeling all the more alienated.

One night, Sabrina was awoken a couple of hours before dawn by a text message from Humayun.

'Sabrina, I am very sorry, but I could not convince Afroz to sell the restaurant. I regretfully decline your offer. I hope you understand. Stay well, Allah hafiz.'

Sabrina frowned. Her particularly troublesome week with morale at work meant that for the first time since the will reading, she found that even the thought of Afroz's victory over her could not move her to rage. She simply did not have the energy. She threw the phone on the bed beside her. Then she picked it up and read the formally worded message again for an indication of what had happened between Humayun and Afroz. Her mother had mentioned that Humayun had left, and it did not surprise her that Afroz was reluctant to sell, especially to Sabrina. But had something more happened?

Fully awake now, Sabrina sat up and opened her inbox to see if she had any confirmations yet from the firm's Hong Kong's office on a deal she needed to close in the morning. There were no messages apart from an email from Nasrin.

'Riaz and I went to say goodbye to Mustafa today, Sib. Amma's told him to live in our bari, like a sort of caretaker, I suppose, so she will give him a monthly stipend. He seemed so relieved and I feel so proud of our parents! They've always looked out for others.

So, there is something I have been keeping from you … The reason I'm so conflicted about the pregnancy is because my marriage has been falling apart. I'm sorry I kept it to myself for so long but I needed space to get my head around it … Richard and I, we had some issues to work through, and I just wanted to be sure, you know? My life feels a bit like a series of decisions that were sort of made for me, by circumstances or the actions or inactions of others … I just wanted to be sure.

And I am sure. Sibby, I've decided to get a divorce.'

Sabrina stumbled out of bed and switched the light on. She read the line again.

'I know you're shocked. Don't call me and ask for explanations. Everyone's already made up their mind that it has something to do with

my sitting up on the flat roof with Riaz … but I'm not the one that cheated. Sometimes I feel that that rooftop is the only place in the world where I feel I belong and that Riaz is the only one who truly listens. I don't mean that you don't – but you have your own life, and you're so far away. Riaz is always here, and it's so powerful, you know, to be listened to that intensely – to be noticed in that way. Especially now, when things feel so perilous.'

Sabrina stopped reading and went to the window to let in some air. She couldn't believe it. Richard had cheated? How could Richard have cheated? Why would he have cheated? Then, without warning, Sabrina thought of Ashok and squeezed her eyes shut, felt prickles of shame, rage and pity run through her. She too had had an affair with a married man. A married man that she had then betrayed. She had not heard a word from him since he had been fired. His silence had suddenly demonstrated to her how much of her work life had been invisibly mentored by him. The daily challenges she faced in her new role were rife with pitfalls and more than once she had reached for her phone to ask his advice, for he had been so good at it. Once when they had been much younger, he had observed a presentation she had given and reprimanded her on it. 'Don't play the female in a room full of men,' he had told her. 'That's not very feminist of you!' she had retorted, hurt by his criticism. He had nodded. 'No, Sab. It's not about being a feminist. Be an individualist. Don't fall into this role of placater to the male ego and don't be afraid of being impressive. You are impressive. Understand?' The memory made a lump rise to her throat.

She opened her eyes and picked up her phone again.

'You always had Abba. And he always had you. Your little bubble made you complete, and neither of you ever really understood how lonely Amma and I were outside it. I know you'll say we had each other but that's never been very true. I tried to have Amma – but it's odd – how even in your mischief, Abba adored you. And yet in my goody-two-shoes ways, Amma never saw anything she particularly warmed to. And now,

she has Afroz. The two of them are so happy in each other's company.
They're so damn alike! Afroz was talking about how spending time with
Riaz was bad for my reputation and I swear I felt like it was Amma I was
talking to!

I don't know why, Sib, but I feel constantly afraid. I should be happy
– the baby – your job – and can you believe, I'm finally enjoying being
in the Beacons – but I'm afraid. And it's not the prospect of getting
a divorce – somewhere along the way, Richard and I just stopped being
good to each other. Deciding it has been a relief, Sibby. I feel like I can
breathe again. But still. I feel afraid. The real reason I'm up on that flat
roof with Riaz is because there's something in my room. Do you remember
that time that Abba took you to the dentist and Amma popped next door
to the Peacock to get something, and I was so scared – I was convinced
there was something in the house? I have that same feeling. But every
single night.'

Sabrina sat up. She had a vivid memory of her sister as a seven-year-old, climbing out of their parents' bedroom window on the third floor to escape something that only she could see, and which she later would not be able to explain to her family. Sabrina remembered Abba scrambling out of the car and Amma and the staff running out of the Peacock. But most of all, she saw the terror in her sister's face and in the way her body curled in on itself as she let go of the windowsill, and fell, and seemed to fall for a long time before her body hit the mattress that Mustafa had managed to drag out onto the street beneath her just in time.

'Like everything is covered in shadows, have you noticed? The way these
shadows play with form, they play with length, they get more cunning
as the world darkens? Movement is what they are, always flickering and
moving in their mischievous way. They're coming out of their world and
into ours.'

Sabrina switched on her light and called the house. It rang and rang, and when it was picked up, it was Afroz.

'Hello?'

Sabrina hesitated. 'It's me.'

'Sibby?'

Sabrina softened for a moment at the hope and fear in Afroz's voice.

'Is something wrong?'

'It's Didi,' Sabrina said, hating the panic in her voice. 'What's wrong with her? Something's wrong!'

'Did Naju tell you?' Afroz asked, her voice hesitant.

'She just emailed me.'

'Yes, divorce … it all must be stressful. But also …' Afroz paused momentarily. 'She is not herself.'

'What the fuck does that mean?'

'Sibby, I don't know what it means.'

'It's like … it's like when she was young, remember, she was so afraid of the darkness?'

'Yes, it is exactly that. But, she's not afraid of it – I mean the darkness – anymore, but she … she is … she stares into it like there's something there.'

They were quiet.

'What's happening to her?' Sabrina asked again, unable to keep the terror from her voice.

'Sibby, don't worry. You focus on your work. We are all here, and we are keeping an eye on her. Always.'

Sabrina considered this, the sincerity of it.

'I just need you to make sure she's okay,' Sabrina said, swallowing her pride, her voice an almost-whisper. 'I'll take some time off from work, before Christmas, as soon as I can. Things here are just a bit precarious.'

'I heard about your promotion,' Afroz said. 'Congratulations. Naju said you worked so hard for it.'

'Okay. Thanks.' Sabrina winced at the sarcasm in her voice.

'So, come when you are ready,' Afroz said, seeming not to have noticed. 'And don't worry, Sibby … but are you alone there? Do you have anyone? Some good friends? I don't want to think you are worrying all alone.'

Sabrina considered this in silence. Some part of her was surprised, and yet another part of her scorned the idea that Afroz might care about her.

'Don't worry at all,' Afroz said when Sabrina did not reply. 'We are here, it is probably the baby, you know? They return to London next week and—'

'No! She's all alone in London with Eli – don't let her do that!'

'Okay, Sibby, I won't. Nothing to worry – just do your work and come. I will look after her.'

'Promise?'

'Promise.'

After the call ended, Sabrina lay in bed awake, until the dawn seeped in through the curtain edges and it was time to get up.

19

They had not run together since they were children, but Afroz discovered a surprising familiarity to the rhythm. Beside her, Nasrin's breaths erupted as small mists covering her mouth before disappearing, her shoulder occasionally brushing against Afroz. A warm nostalgia filtered through Afroz, easing the anxiety that had been hounding her ever since Riaz had found Nasrin days ago, barefoot and shivering on the driveway. He had tugged her back to the house, calling out to Afroz, the alarm in his voice a rude awakening. They had sat at the kitchen table and listened as Nasrin told them she had decided to end the marriage. She had said it again and again: 'It's over.' Afroz had searched these words for all manner of other explanations that might be hidden in them, but it was only her Fufu, standing in the doorway, for how long Afroz did not know, who broke the silence and uttered one word into the morning gloom, 'Why?'

But Fufu's question had remained unanswered. The certainty with which Nasrin answered again, 'It's over' made the question seem irrelevant. And in any case, they became, all of them, more concerned about the physical state of Nasrin. She seemed trapped in a quagmire of inaction – a stillness so complete, that if she had not blinked, Afroz would have checked to see if she had stopped breathing. Even Elias backed out of a room when he saw his mother, so still that even the air around her seemed to stop circulating, so still that even the silence seemed a state of paralysis rather than an absence of sound. He ran to his grandmother or Afroz in such fear that Afroz wanted to shake her sister.

'It's only been a few days,' Lindsay had tried to soothe Afroz, 'give her a bit of time, poor thing.' Along with Riaz and Lindsay, Afroz had tried to draw Nasrin out, but her sister seemed marooned far, far away from them, and their entreaties and reassurances didn't seem to reach her. What did seem to reach her, though, were her mother's silent rebukes: for when Fufu entered the room, only then did Nasrin look up, her eyes urgently following her mother's movements, seeking understanding or forgiveness, Afroz did not know.

So, it was a surprise when Nasrin asked to join Afroz for her run that afternoon. The sky was crisp and white, and it seemed to Afroz that its singular clarity was echoed in the solid, rhythmic thump of her sister's steps beside her. Afroz felt a swell of pity for her sister – for her aunt too – but mostly for Nasrin. 'The funny thing, Afi,' Nasrin had said to her the night before when Afroz had returned from the Peacock to find her sister sitting in the kitchen in complete darkness, 'the funny thing is that I'm so relieved … I know that I'm so relieved, but I can't feel it. I can't feel anything.' And Afroz had switched the light on and warmed a cup of milk, adding a touch of turmeric before handed it to her, saying, 'Drink it, Naju: it has holud – holud heals.'

'Yes?' Nasrin had asked, staring into the golden liquid. 'And what will it heal? Where would it start? Would it start with them?' and she had nodded towards the patio. Afroz took a torch out onto the patio and flashed it beneath the fig tree and in the corner where the shed stood. She had found nothing out of the ordinary.

The high street was unusually empty, and the two sisters ran in silence until they turned into Calbot Square and the Peacock came into view. Then, suddenly seized by a bout of energy, Nasrin picked up the pace and sprinted ahead of Afroz, and Afroz, laughing, called out to her: 'Ey Naju! Not so fast, remember your condition!'

'Come on, Afroz!' Nasrin called, turning fleetingly. 'Catch up!'

By the time Afroz had caught up to her sister, Nasrin was sitting on the pavement, looking up at the Peacock.

'Ish!' Afroz said, sitting down beside her. 'You're not supposed to be sprinting in your condition!'

Nasrin pointed up to the corner of one of the Peacock's awnings. 'How long has that been broken?'

Afroz squinted at the broken awning and shrugged.

'And the C in the sign,' Nasrin said, still pointing, 'it's crooked.'

'We can fix it,' Afroz said, her voice gentle.

'Abba used to look after it, you know. Every few years he would refurbish. And now he's been gone a few months and look at it.'

Afroz tensed for a moment. 'Riaz says business is slow. There is no money to refurbish.' The look on her sister's face made Afroz take her arm. 'Don't worry, Naju, in your condition, you should not worry about these things. We will fix it. We will see what we can do. There's a ladder in the garage, you hold it, I will go up and fix that. Easy, no problem.'

Nasrin's face creased open in the first smile in days. 'You up on a ladder? Afi, when have you done any DIY?'

'What is DIY? I'm just saying we won't have to pay if I do it myself.'

Nasrin laughed. She squeezed Afroz's arm and leaned into her shoulder. Afroz opened a bottle of water and passed it to her.

'Sometimes,' Nasrin said, ignoring the bottle, 'I find myself reaching for the phone to call Richard. To remind him to do something, I don't know, call the marble repair man before it's too late, or to water the window box before Mrs Humphreys has a heart attack about it. Or, I don't know, fill up the salt in the water softener. It's not—' Nasrin stopped and sighed. 'It's not that I regret my decision. I don't regret it, Afi, it's over. But it's just that sometimes, I just want to speak to him.'

'Why can't you speak to him?' Afroz asked. 'Why can't you call him?'

'That's it,' Nasrin said, her face wet now. 'That's the hardest part, to think I can't call him anymore.'

'But you can call him,' Afroz said. 'When we get home, you should call him.'

Nasrin wiped her face and looked at her. 'Do you miss Humayun Bhaiya like that?'

Afroz frowned. 'It's not the same, Naju re. Richard and you are different. He was your best friend.'

Nasrin turned back to stare at the Peacock. Almost imperceptibly, she whispered, 'I'm sorry, Afi, I'm sorry for interfering.'

Afroz did not reply to this, for an apology was an expression of regret for causing an injury, and Afroz could not yet see what, if any, injury had been caused. Humayun had left. He had not called. Until becoming preoccupied with Nasrin's condition, Afroz had languished in a state of abject anxiety into which she had been pummelled by her aunt's worry that Humayun would end their marriage. A divorced woman was stateless. A divorced woman was devoid of both presence and destination. It was true she had not entered the marriage by her own volition, but she was also reluctant to relinquish control over how or if she exited it. So, it was true she had been angry with Nasrin for her outburst. But then over the last few days, Nasrin's problems had somewhat displaced her own. And yet, she realised with a sudden clarity, they each dealt with marriages that were moribund – very different marriages, and very different people, but the pain and the uncertainty were surely of the same ilk.

'Afi,' Nasrin said, cutting through her reverie. 'Let me renovate it.'

'What?' Afroz asked, puzzled.

'The Peacock. I've got some savings.' Nasrin grabbed Afroz's hands to prevent her protestations. 'Listen to me, I've been … it's like I'm lost and everything's misty and I can't see where I'm going, you know? I feel so, so stuck, Afi. Like I'm paralysed, I can't move. But this run … it reminded me of how I felt when I used to fly … that feeling of soaring, that rush of adrenaline … Riaz told me to remember what I loved about it, and actually it's so true! What I loved about it was the movement. That sense that you're leaving difficult things behind and heading somewhere. Please, Afi, let me do this. It'll give me something to do! Even for just a few weeks! We can shut up shop—'

'Close the restaurant?'

'Just for a few weeks—'

'But, Naju, we are already struggling to pay our bills!'

'No, that's why I'm saying, I have savings. I saved a lot during the BA years, and Sibby has been sending money to me every year. Let me do this. Please.'

In the end, it was overhearing Nasrin speaking with Richard on the phone that made Afroz decide to let her sister have her way.

'It *is* final, Rich.' She heard her sister's voice break as she said it. 'It's final, and you know it's the right thing. But I still … I still want to speak to you. I want to see you. I know it doesn't make sense, but there it is. Does it have to be like this?'

There was a silence and then Afroz heard her sister say, 'Yes, I'm going to have this child. But even then, you know it's the right thing. I'm not saying we can't do it together. Just not as a married couple.'

As she passed her aunt's room, Afroz saw through the open door that Elias was lying asleep on his grandmother's janamaz, as she rocked gently back and forth beside him, praying on her thasbih beads. Jahanara moved her hands over her grandson's face as though swatting away mosquitos and let out a sigh laden with such sadness that Afroz felt oppressed by it. She fled the house as quietly as she could and made for the Peacock. Night was descending and beyond the main road, amber lights lit up the village like the reflection of stars on a dark blue sea. Inside the Peacock, Riaz was already at the bar, setting out the Bombay mix.

'How is she?' he asked, looking up.

Afroz came to stand beside him. 'We need to close the restaurant, Riaz.'

He frowned.

'Just for a few weeks. It needs work. Renovations.'

'We can't afford it, Afa.'

'Nasrin insists. She says she will pay.'

'But the staff …' Riaz's face was ashen. 'How are you going to pay the staff for those weeks?'

Afroz realised with a pang of guilt that she had not thought of this. She watched as a visibly upset Riaz moved about the restaurant to light the candles, his shadow long and thin behind him. She had noticed how Riaz watched the pennies, both his own and the Peacock's.

She fetched her chef's cap and adjusted her headscarf under it. Out of the window, she saw Nasrin's silhouette sitting still as a statue on the wall dividing the house and the Peacock, staring out at a fixed spot near the disabled parking space at something or someone only she could see. In the moonlight, she seemed to Afroz like one of the apparitions she spoke of: pale and phantasmal. She felt Riaz come and stand beside her, heard him sigh.

'What do you think she sees?' Afroz asked him, hoping he would chastise her for her superstitions.

He shook his head. 'Something we don't.'

She shuddered. 'My Baba used to say there are no such things as ghosts. Jinns and angels, yes, but no ghosts.'

'What's a ghost though?' Riaz asked, touching the windowpane with his fingers. 'I mean, she doesn't look scared, does she?' They both peered at her through the window.

'I'm scared though, I'm scared for her.'

'Well, don't be, Afa,' Riaz said, not sounding very certain himself. 'You know, I read somewhere that we're all haunted by ghosts – versions of people we once knew, people we once were. It's like a longing rather than … a supernatural scary thing.'

They watched a car turn into the car park, the headlights lighting up Nasrin's face for an instant. It was true that Nasrin did not seem afraid, but this frightened Afroz more.

'You're right, though,' Riaz said. 'Course we'll shut up shop for a bit. It'll be good for her. We'll manage.'

Afroz turned to thank him, but he had already begun to walk away. She watched him flip the sign to *Open* and she sighed and headed for the kitchen.

20

After sending Richard away, Nasrin discovered that the price of freedom was a numb disequilibrium. Her apparitions stood sentinel over her as her days and nights merged and she waited to be rescued. But try as they did, Afroz, Riaz and Elias could not reach her: she heard their voices as though from the bottom of a deep well, unable to respond for the weight of the remorse and indecision that buried her. Only her mother's sharp glare of reproach managed to penetrate her torpor.

'Amma,' she croaked one morning when she could bear the silence no longer.

'Why will you call me Amma now?' her mother asked, slicing a loaf of bread for breakfast. 'In my world, our parents' words were the words of God.' She put the knife down. 'Did you even tell me you are pregnant? That you are unhappy? You told me nothing, re Naju. Now you call me, for what?'

'But Amma, I—'

'You did not think about your family and the shame? You did not think about your children?'

Her mother left the kitchen and the apparitions inched closer to Nasrin as her skin crawled with dread. What if her mother was right? How would she do it alone? No career, no future, and now another child? She picked up her phone and dialled Richard. The phone rang twice before the call was rejected.

She placed the phone carefully on the table and tried to calm herself. But rather than abating, the cold dread seemed only to penetrate deeper, and frustrated at her own cowardice and indecision, she shoved the kitchen table and was startled when the bread knife hurtled to the ground. She bent to retrieve it and as her father and her seven-year-old self watched expressionless, she pressed the blade flat against her palm, first one side and then the other, noting the cool relief of the metal, angling the sharper edge so it pressed decisively into her skin. There was a delicious clarity in focusing pain to a single place. When she heard Afroz's key in the lock and Elias's chirpy voice calling out to her, she shoved the knife across the table, and it fell with a clatter to the floor.

A worried Afroz called her from the hallway. 'Naju? Are you okay?'

Unable to reply, Nasrin stared down at the small cut in her palm. When Elias came into the kitchen, she picked up the knife and stood to place it into the dishwasher, away from her young son and away from herself.

The week that followed Afroz's agreement to renovate the Peacock was one of unseasonable warmth, causing a bustle that was unnatural for November. 'Look at all the business we're missing!' she heard Lindsay complain to Riaz, referring to the last-minute visitors who arrived in droves to hike the nearby mountains. But Afroz kept to her word and the Peacock was closed.

Nasrin seized upon the project with an enthusiastic zeal. Concentrating on it helped shake her free from her anxiety, and thankful for this reprieve, she demonstrated her gratefulness by being extravagant and overindulgent in her design choices and purchases. Money could do unfathomable things, could reach inside you where there was darkness and discomfort and make it brighter and easier to bear. Though the apparitions and the shadows of their foreboding were ever-present, she was able to ignore them for hours by focusing on the tangible world of colour and texture and pile that folded out before her in rolls of fabric and binders of samples.

One afternoon, Riaz drove her up the A5 to Abergavenny so that Nasrin could buy paint. He was trying to persuade her to buy a cheaper alternative to the expensive brand she wanted to order. 'It's the exact same colour as the one you liked at that Farrah place!' he told her.

'It is not!' she insisted. 'Mole's Breath is … it's deeper.'

'Mole's Breath!' Riaz exclaimed, his voice tight with exasperation. 'It's the same, Naz! We can just get it mixed by these guys I know, and it'll be the same colour and be cheaper than that Farrah place!'

'But I want it to be perfect, Riaz! I know it's more expensive but it's just money.'

'Just money?'

She flinched at Riaz's tone, but just as quickly he recovered himself, smiling and shaking his head. Nasrin knew he was going to be late for work – Riaz was delivering meals which Afroz cooked in her aunt's kitchen while the Peacock was closed – but even so, he hummed along to every song that played on Heart South Wales. Autumn colours spread before them as they dipped and twisted through the roads past rusty brown fields and a misty sky sprayed orange by the setting sun.

'What would I do without you?' she asked him. Riaz glanced at her, a small smile playing on his lips.

'You're going to be okay, Naz.'

'Amma's never going to forgive me.'

'She's just worried about you, that's all, but you know she'll come round. She always does. Anything from Richard?'

Nasrin shook her head. Ahead of them, cars slowed down to a standstill as rush hour in Abergavenny began. After a promising start, her attempts to contact Richard, to entreat him into some form of amicability was overturned by his law firm's rejection of his bid for partnership – a failure which he laid squarely at her feet. 'These last few months have been so difficult, that I just let the side down.' When she had tried to call him the week before to tell him about the renovations, he had refused to answer the phone. He called the house phone every few days to speak to Elias but had not asked after her or the pregnancy.

'I hoped,' she said uncertainly, 'I thought that Richard and I would still bring up the children together, you know? Sort of a modern family style, still be friends, still care for each other. But …'

Riaz patted her arm. 'Give the guy time, Naz. Give it some time.'

When his phone rang, he picked it up quickly.

'Hey, Thanni,' he said, 'what's wrong?'

He switched the radio off to listen to his sister. When the call ended, Nasrin turned to him.

'What's wrong?'

Riaz was silent.

'Riaz,' Nasrin said, more forcefully this time, brushing aside Riaz's usual reticence about his family. 'What's wrong?'

'My dad …'

'Yes?'

'He's been gambling.' Once he said it, the darkness seemed to collapse in all around him. Nasrin turned in her seat to face him. 'All our life, the fucking horses, and now. That was my sister. They've been evicted.'

She let this sink in. 'You never said … Oh, Riaz …'

Riaz was silent. She stared out at the darkening road, remembering the photo he used to have pinned to his mirror, of him and his sister standing shoulder to shoulder on their front gate as it swung back and forth, giggling as the snow fell about them. She imagined the two of them standing on the gate, turning their faces heavenwards and feeling the landing of each flake of ice on their tongue. Such a simple, beautiful thing; not denied them, even in the darkest, poorest reaches of Lozells.

'Let me lend you some money, Riaz.'

'No.'

'This isn't about your pride!' she scolded. 'This is about your family!'

'I don't want your money!'

'It's just money.'

The look Riaz gave her when she said this made her recoil.

She went out to the roof that night, the first time since Richard had left, hoping Riaz would see her there and come out. She waited for over an hour, full of self-reproach at offering him money when she knew it would sting. What had her father told her once? *When you want to give a proud Bengali man money, offer advice.* Later, when she was back in her room, she saw him out on the square, holding a lit cigarette as the inky night spread around him.

Painting the walls was the last task to be completed before the new furniture was delivered. The decorators applied three layers of Mole's Breath, only for Nasrin to change her mind and ask Riaz to drive her to Abergavenny to buy twelve tins of Purbeck Stone instead. But he did not ask her to accompany him and when he returned, he placed the tins at her feet and handed her the receipt, turning away before she could pluck up the courage to ask about his family. The next two days were abuzz with activity: the coming and going of deliveries and decorators and the positioning of the furniture, until finally, the Peacock was ready.

Nasrin glowed with pleasure as she showed Lindsay the bespoke chairs she had positioned beside the fireplace and on which much of the furniture budget had been spent.

'What do you think?' she asked, running her hand over one of them.

'Oh Naz, you've transformed this place,' Lindsay said.

Nasrin began folding napkins into peacocks just as her father had taught her, and Lindsay sat down beside her to help. Nasrin searched her friend's face, surprised by the reluctance in her tone.

'Riaz would have me go to Ikea if he had had his way!'

'Not my way,' Riaz said, his voice sulky, his eyes darting away. 'Afroz. She was worried about the cost of things. But you did good.'

'We did good,' she said lightly, creasing the line in her peacock. 'She stresses too much, but I told her that I would pay for it all.'

'Well, she probably didn't want you to spend all your savings,' Lindsay reasoned.

From the corner of her eye, Nasrin caught Riaz watching her. She turned towards him, wanting to explain, when her phone rang.

'Richard?'

'Your Amex bill arrived,' Richard spluttered, his voice raised. 'And seriously, Naz, you want a fucking divorce, but you're going to expect me to pay your Amex bill?'

'No!' Nasrin protested, leaving the restaurant to find privacy. 'Rich, that's why I was calling you last week – I'm paying for the renovations to the Peacock, from my savings.'

'The Peacock needed Malerba dining tables?' he asked, but there was no sarcasm to his voice, only tiredness.

'They were floor samples,' Nasrin explained. 'Massive discount on the price. It's good to hear your voice, Rich,' she said softly.

She heard Richard sigh. 'Is the baby all right?'

'I have a scan coming up, I think it's in two weeks. I'll come up to London for it.'

'Shall I come with you?'

Nasrin caught the tremor in his voice and cried out, 'Please come, Rich. Please be a part of this. I don't want to take this away from you.'

She heard a snuffle and Richard croaked, 'Well, you did.'

Nasrin ignored this. 'You know we're having a big opening party here next weekend? Won't you come and see what those Malerba tables look like?'

She heard him groan. 'Heck, Naz, you sure know how to spend it.'

'Will you come?'

'Only if we can talk about … all of this …'

'Nothing will change, Rich.'

'Naz, all I'm asking for is a chance to talk.'

After he hung up, she headed back into the Peacock, rankled by the conversation. She saw Riaz switching out the lights and called out to him.

'Why are you still so angry at me?' she asked. 'I'm sorry. I just wanted to help.'

Riaz turned to look at her.

'Riaz, please? I can't stand your silence.'

Riaz shook his head. 'I'm not angry, Naz. I'm just stressed out. And I can't talk to you about it because then you're going to try and force me to take your money. And I'm not taking your money.'

He held up his hands and turned to leave. Nasrin stepped forward to prevent him and then from the corner of her eye, she saw them both, waiting in the shadows of the bar, her father and her seven-year-old self. She tried to call out to Riaz, but found she had no voice, as though she were trapped in a dream. She watched helplessly as he walked away.

21

Seated beside Elias at her aunt's kitchen table, Afroz was trying to concentrate on the menu for the restaurant's opening party, but she was distracted by her aunt, who could be heard upstairs, moving about her room. For days now, Fufu's anger towards Nasrin sapped the energy in the house. 'Fufu,' Afroz had tried to reassure her, 'please don't worry so much, Naju will be okay.' But these words only served to turn her aunt's attention to her own plight: 'What about you, Afi? Have you spoken to your husband yet? Or have my daughters fooled you into thinking you don't need one?'

But Afroz had not called Humayun, because she knew she could not respond to the one question he would inevitably ask – when was she returning to Desh? Humayun would not understand the joyful surprise of Elias's small hand slipping into hers frequently throughout the day, needing her to navigate every meal, activity, bath and bedtime. He would not appreciate how alive it made her to feel needed by her aunt and her sister, how the Peacock had not only given her a sense of purpose but had also surprised her with the discovery of her own capability.

Each day she took Elias to Mr Ruane's newsagent to treat him to a Milkybar and she found herself daydreaming about taking this walk with him when he was older – picturing him as a young man with strides vigorous and impatient – and each day she chided herself on daring to envisage such a future.

'What are you writing?' Elias asked.

Sighing, Afroz looked down at her notepad, willing herself to concentrate.

'Do you think,' she asked Elias, 'the guests would like daler boras – you know those lentil pakuras I make, Baba?'

'I like them,' he responded, looking up. 'Can I have some? Now?'

She laughed, moving his hair out of his face. 'But you just had lunch!'

'I miss the yummy afternoon tea, with daler boras and samosas,' Elias pouted, 'why don't we do that anymore? When can we have some again?'

It was true that she had cancelled the afternoon teas, wanting to give Nasrin space to grieve, but perhaps Elias was right. She should call Dorothy and the others – perhaps their company would coax Nasrin out of herself and divert her aunt's attention. Heartened by this plan, she returned to the list with enthusiasm. She wondered if the gual tomato stew was a little too bland for vindaloo-assaulted taste buds and whether the mishti dhoi yoghurts would be too delicate a flavour. When the phone rang, she answered it without checking the caller ID.

'Afroz, are you there?'

Heart in her throat, Afroz managed only to croak, 'Ji.'

'Accha,' Humayun said, also fumbling for his words. 'Is everything … are you well?'

'Yes,' Afroz said, closing her eyes.

'Who is it?' Elias whispered.

Afroz shushed him. 'How are you?' she asked Humayun. 'And Ma?'

'Ha, everyone is fine.' Humayun cleared his throat.

'You haven't called since you left,' she said, her voice so low that she could barely hear it herself over the clamouring in her chest. 'I know you must be angry after …' She was unable to finish her sentence.

'Why do you want to stay there, Afi?' Humayun asked after

a short pause. 'Is it because you like the Beacons or because you're trying to get away from Desh … from me?'

'No,' she cried in dismay. Beside her, Elias looked up in alarm. 'I love Desh … But you know Naju is sick, she needs help with Eli.' She paused, realising that these sounded like mere excuses. She tried again, her voice softening in earnestness: 'This place, it just lets me be. In Desh, everything else is so overbearing – the heat, the rain, the dust, the poverty all around us, all of it. Don't you find that, Humayun? Just every day feels like a struggle? I'm so busy being a wife and a daughter-in-law, I'm so busy making sure I don't do anything to hurt our reputation, that I … It doesn't mean I don't love Desh – I do! It's just that Desh asks so much of me! It's *easier* to love this place.'

There was silence on the line.

'Are you still there?' she asked.

'Is it supposed to be easy?' Humayun asked.

When she did not answer, he sighed. 'Dekho, I called because I thought you would worry … about Munni, I mean. The thing is that the family finally saw sense. There is no wedding for now. She's going to stay with us for a few weeks while her foolish brother calms down.'

Afroz, growing increasingly bewildered by the lack of recrimination and reproach, barely registered what he told her about Munni. Then she grew fearful that he would ask her the dreaded question and force her to seal their future. But Humayun talked for some minutes, in a voice that seemed deliberately humorous, about the new house guest; at his surprise that Munni was a vegetarian, 'Did you know this, Afi?', and the great friendship budding between Munni and his mother, and then when he ended the call without asking the dreaded question, Afroz found herself assailed by a different sort of anxiety. Every interaction since she had arrived at the Beacons had ended with an insistence from Humayun that she return, except this one. What did this mean?

'Mumma,' Elias said, the catch in his voice interrupting her thoughts. She turned to see Nasrin sat out on the patio, her lips moving in conversation.

'Finish your colouring,' she told Elias as she walked to the kitchen door.

'Naju?' she called.

Nasrin turned to her with an unreadable expression, appearing for a moment not to recognise Afroz.

'Naju, come inside.'

Nasrin frowned. 'In a second.'

Afroz hesitated before closing the door.

'Come, Baba,' she pulled Elias off his chair, 'it's time for Asr.'

'Who is Mumma talking too?'

She picked him up. 'Remember I told you about the faristha that come? Throughout the day? Maybe she is talking to hers. Now we will go and talk to ours. Who should we make dua for today, amar shunar Baba?'

'Mummy,' he replied without a moment's hesitation.

Afroz tightened her grip around him, picturing her sister's expression out on the patio. *Y'Allah,* she prayed, *Rokko khoro rebo.*

When the builders who had been called in to fit new toilets in the customer restrooms found a drainage problem that needed to be fixed immediately and at great expense, Afroz began to worry about the cost of the renovations. 'I was thinking just some paint, Naju!' she had said, shaking her head. 'Not this scale of renovation – we can't afford it. And I don't want you to spend this sort of money!' But Nasrin's exuberance and excitement were hard to contain.

'Afi, don't worry,' Nasrin had said every time Afroz vetoed a purchase, such as the ridiculous bespoke chairs. But Afroz did worry. She couldn't stomach Nasrin's extravagance and the amount of money she spent on paint, on chairs, even new uniforms for the waiters, and now the clogged gutters and drainpipes. Afroz found herself constantly comparing the pounds spent to Bangladeshi takas – the fact that one of the tables Nasrin had bought was equal to the annual salary of Jamal, their house help in Desh, appalled Afroz.

After Riaz had paid the staff salaries last month, he had shown her the remaining balance, suggesting that they buy the following week's poultry supplies from a local farmer who he knew would give them a good discount. The farmer's chickens were scrawny, underweight and malnourished, but she had not complained because what else could they do? The twenty-thousand-pound penalty from the local authorities for knowingly employing an illegal worker, due to be paid in a few weeks, would wipe their balance sheet clean. To make matters worse, Richard had made such a fuss over the latest of Nasrin's Amex bills that Afroz had put Nasrin on the Peacock's business account as a signatory, so she could use it to pay for the renovations. 'It'll be easier this way, Naju,' Afroz had told her, 'you can just transfer a lump sum from your savings account when it's all done.' But it was a decision she was beginning to regret, especially when Nasrin decided unilaterally to use the drainage issue as an excuse to do a full structural renovation of the restrooms.

But in Nasrin's increasingly hyper, unpredictable moods, Afroz sensed the more sinister causes to her sister's profligacy.

'I don't think she is coping, Fufu,' Afroz told her aunt later that evening. 'Don't you think she should see her doctor? Should we have her see someone here?'

'I have asked your father to send her a Taweez, Afi,' her aunt said, handing a needle to Afroz for her to thread because her eyesight was failing her, 'and we really need to persuade her to see the doctor again. I am so worried about her – of course she is not coping!' and here, Fufu took Afroz's arm, 'but also Afi, how she will cope in the future? Y'Allah! Two daughters' marriages shobbonash at the same time. Gordish gordish.'

In the mornings Nasrin could be heard chattering away to whoever was at hand, but at night, when Afroz stood outside the Peacock's kitchen keeping Lindsay company while she smoked, she would see Nasrin up on the roof, staring into her mother's garden.

One night, Afroz climbed up to the flat roof. 'Naju?' she called.

Nasrin turned to her, with a look of surprise on her face.

'What are you doing up here, alone? Where is Riaz?' Afroz asked her. When her sister didn't answer, Afroz sat down beside her.

'Naju?'

'He's angry,' Narin said, her voice soft. 'Because I offered him money … for a problem he had, and I just wanted to help.'

Afroz nodded. 'Just be his friend instead. Give him support. Nobody likes to be offered money.'

Nasrin smiled. 'Abba used to say the same thing!'

'Naju, I'm worried about you. If you don't want to divorce—'

'But I do, Afi! I do! It's just this … feeling … Something feels off. You know? What if it's the wrong decision?'

'Have faith, Naju re, trust in Allah.'

'I wish I could. But when you make your own decisions, you can't very well blame God when they go wrong.'

'Which decisions have gone wrong? That's not how faith works, Naju. You have to open your heart to him, trust him.'

'I trust you. You … don't think I don't notice how you look after Eli, Afi.'

'Oh Naju,'

'No – I mean I'm grateful. I feel like there's this shadow around me … this darkness … I don't want it to hurt him.'

'You could never hurt him, Naju, you are his mother.'

'Mothers can hurt their children, Afi.'

Afroz turned to look at her sister's face, wanting to defend her aunt, but the words eluded her.

'And Sibby, poor thing, I can tell she's so worried. I tell her everything, but not about the darkness … she's got so much going on, and she's so far from here, I don't want to worry her with it. Then there's Riaz,' Nasrin continued, 'all this time he's been so strong for me, and I've never appreciated all the worries he has of his own.'

'Naju,' Afroz said, 'is it Riaz you want? I just wanted to – I – You know, Allah is most displeased by adultery.' The words spilled out of her mouth, clumsy and awkward.

'What?'

'I just mean that – with Riaz, if you want Riaz, then, please, do it properly, cleanly, so there is no shame. I mean do it after the divorce is finalised.'

Nasrin stared at her sister and then let out a laugh. Afroz wondered what sadness was hidden there.

'It's not like that,' said Nasrin, putting her head on Afroz's shoulder.

That night as she prepared for her Isha namaz, Afroz thought of her conversation with Humayun and was suddenly wistful to hear the adhan, to hear the clatter of Jamal in the kitchen cleaning the dinner dishes. Nasrin had seemed so disorientated and helpless in the face of all her options – Richard, Riaz or neither – that Afroz felt some nostalgia for the disciplined order of her husband's home, for a society where religious rules and community values were so absolute that there was little room to be paralysed by too many choices. As she contemplated the fine balance between freedom and restraint, it occurred to Afroz that she could not possibly leave Nasrin in this state, nor Elias. They needed her – and they needed Sabrina too. She would urge Sabrina to return as early as possible. She would also need to communicate her decision to remain indefinitely to Humayun. With a sinking heart, Afroz realised that she would have to offer her husband his freedom in exchange for her own. The thought of this filled her with dread, and she lay awake, insomniac, until late into the night.

On the morning of the restaurant's opening party, Afroz rose just before dawn. The alarm clock on her bedside table bleated the Fajr adhan, and she whispered *bismillahirahmanirahim* as she slipped out of bed. She shivered as she walked out into the hallway, agitated and tired having woken several times during the night, worrying about the menu she had chosen.

Her anxiety clung to her as she washed her face and looked out of the window at the light spreading over the horizon, revealing the huge clouds rolling in. She pushed open the window and inhaled deeply as the cold air hit her. She crept downstairs slowly, hoping not to wake anyone but found her aunt already praying. In the anaemic light of the dawn, the elderly woman looked more frail than usual as Afroz placed her janamaz next to her Fufu's.

The next few hours spent in preparations at the Peacock kitchen rushed by swiftly, and when Afroz returned for a brief lunch at her aunt's, she felt her limbs already heavy and weary and wondered how she would get through the evening. At five o' clock, she made her way downstairs carrying her prayerbook with the intention to read a prayer in the restaurant before the staff began to arrive. She heard her aunt in the kitchen, murmuring into the telephone.

'Masoom, no more of this talk!'

Realising Fufu was talking to Baba, Afroz made for the kitchen, wanting to speak with him and receive his blessings. He was angry with her, she knew this, because she had let Humayun leave England alone, but he couldn't be angry at her forever.

The tone of Jahanara's voice stopped her.

'Don't you think I wish I could?' her aunt shrieked. 'Don't you think it's all I've ever wished since she was born?'

Afroz froze before realising they were discussing the news of Nasrin's divorce. She retreated to the living room where Nasrin and Elias were fast asleep on the armchair. When had her sister's face turned so pale, so thin? She reminded herself to call Sabrina as she placed a blanket on them, before letting herself out of the house.

In the Peacock's kitchen, she read Surah Ya-Sin, blowing into the corners of the room and praying for success. She walked into the main restaurant, feeling the shock of the new all over again. The restaurant's plush blue carpet and polished tabletops made it unrecognisable from the place she had bonded with on her arrival in the Beacons. She mourned the humble, faded pink tablecloths and the worn diamond-patterned carpet. And now here they were, a restaurant full of gleaming new furniture and an account maxed to the hilt. She would need to remind Nasrin to make a transfer in the next few days to ensure there was enough money in the account for all the renovation bills to be paid.

Back in the kitchen, she read Surah Al-Fatiha, the print now blurring in her vision. *Guide us into taking the righteous and just path*, she prayed, for herself, for her sister and her aunt. *The path of those upon whom You have bestowed Your favours, who have not incurred Your anger and who have not gone astray.* The changes were coming at her too fast and strong and Afroz held on to Allah as her only buoy.

22

That same morning, Nasrin awoke into a world of darkness. This was a darkness she had never experienced before: a darkness which seemed to be pouring out from deep within her, teeming with life. It pulsed against her ribs like a baby carried to term, squirming to be let out; she felt it squeeze into the hollow of her bones, cling to the rasp in her throat and then she felt it reaching for her throat and she cried out.

'Mummy.'

She opened her eyes to see that it was only her son's hands around her neck, the warmth of him burrowing into her chest and making the cold terror dissipate.

'You're squashing me,' he protested, but she only tightened her embrace. 'Mumma?' he said, alarmed at the need in her.

'I love you.' She told him, turning his face to her and kissing his nose. 'You are the only perfection in my life. You know that, don't you?'

'I know that,' Elias said, noting the rusty catch in her throat.

They heard Jahanara humming a zikr downstairs, and they rushed down to her. Nasrin noticed that all ordinary household objects, trapped in the morning gloom, had become animated. *Notice me*, said the money plant they passed in the hallway; *notice me*, said the porcelain figurines on the table at the foot of the stairs; *notice me*, said the umbrella stand where her father's black Fulton still waited.

Elias joined his grandmother in the living room where she was dusting the side tables, while Nasrin went to the kitchen and accepted the cup of tea Afroz poured for her.

From the corner of her eye, she saw it: her seven-year-old self hovering near the kitchen door. Nasrin looked away, a sudden terror within her. She closed her eyes and tried to escape the darkness.

'I love the way you make your tea, Afa,' she told Afroz, and even as she said it, she heard the shakiness in her voice. 'You don't cut corners with it, you do it properly. Loose tea, and you give it time to brew. It's like everything you do, you don't do it half-heartedly, like I do. You wear your kameezes, and you do your namaz and make your curries, and the Beacons still loves you. You don't compromise on who you are, and I like that, Afa.'

Afroz frowned.

'What?' Nasrin asked.

'I don't … You haven't called me *Afa* in a long time.'

'I haven't? In my head you're always that, though. Big sister.' She wanted it to come out more genuinely than it did, but the thing by the kitchen door unsettled her, and her words were slippery and careless. Why was she suddenly afraid of it? She blinked to rid herself both of her terror and the vision.

'Have you taken your medicine this morning?' Afroz asked, following Nasrin's glances. 'Shall I get them for you?' Afroz pulled out the box of yellow epilepsy pills from the medicine cupboard.

'Can't have any mishaps today!' Nasrin said, taking them from her.

Afroz passed her a glass of water.

'Are you angry with me?' Nasrin asked. 'Because I've spent so much money?'

Afroz shook her head. 'No.'

'Think of it as all the birthday gifts I should have given my sister over the years, all those years I didn't know that you were my sister.'

'You treated me like your sister, even back then.'

'No,' Nasrin said. 'I didn't. I treated you like you were a cousin,

342

Afi – a cousin is only half a sister – I treated you like a poor relative that I felt guilty for.'

Afroz frowned, but Nasrin was undeterred. 'I treated you like everything I gave you, the gifts, the attention, was like a sort of zakat, a sort of charity to a poorer relative. Not how I treat Sabrina.' Nasrin looked up at her sister. In the next room, they heard Jahanara's zikr drumming a rhythm into the air. 'I'm sorry,' she whispered, torn.

'You don't need to tell me this,' Afroz said, her face folding in on itself with dismay.

'I do. I do, because from now, it will all be different. You are my sister. As important and as equal to me as Sabrina.'

The mention of Sabrina silenced them both for a moment.

Then Nasrin said, 'She's taking longer to come round because she was so close to Abba. It's not you, it's him that she's angry with. She idolised him.'

Jahanara came into the kitchen.

'What is this? Why are you eating Rice Krispies when I made a special breakfast porotha?' She took a foiled package out of the fridge. For once Nasrin didn't feel nauseous. As her mother warmed the bread, she stood at her side and pinched off the corners.

'Wait for it to heat properly, bebat!' her mother admonished.

Nasrin took the porotha off the pan, and stuffed it whole into her mouth, blinking at Jahanara as she chewed, daring her mother to challenge her. Her mother's eyes widened in surprise. Then a reluctant smile turned up the corners of her mouth and beside her, Elias giggled, 'Mummy, you greedy greedy!'

Nasrin finished her tea and handed the cup to Afroz for a refill.

'Morning sickness is over, then?' her mother asked, and Afroz laughed.

New beginnings, Nasrin thought, trying to smile at her sister. That was what these nerves were about. New beginnings. As Afroz handed her another cup of tea, Nasrin watched her mother taking out more porothas from the freezer, and she felt a queer sinking feeling in her stomach.

Later that afternoon, the morning's gloom still lingered, along with Nasrin's sense of unease. She lay on the sofa with Elias, drifting in and out of sleep, before finally dragging herself upstairs to get ready. She tucked the end of her saree into her petticoat's waistband, and as she began to wrap it around her, she heard her mother in the bathroom. She stopped to listen, for all of a sudden, a great many noises could be heard: the shower was running, the taps were gushing, and then she heard the flush being pulled twice.

'Shhh, Eli, just be quiet a moment.'

Elias looked at her and paused the battle between his two Lego soldiers. He watched her tread quietly out of the room and approach the bathroom. She held the bangles on her wrists to stop them tinkling.

She blanched and quickly returned to her room. She flopped down on the bed and let Elias clamber onto her, creasing the folds of the purple silk she had so painstakingly spent the afternoon ironing.

'When is Daddy coming?' he asked her.

'He's almost here, sweetheart. A couple of miles away.'

'How long will he be? Will he give me a bath?'

'If he gets back in time.'

'I want you to give me a bath, Mumma.'

But Nasrin was too preoccupied to mollify her son, for she was thinking about the sobs she had heard from her mother in the bathroom. She wondered if it had anything to do with the conversation she had overheard just an hour before, when she and Elias were curled on the sofa.

'Don't you think it's all I've ever wished since she was born?' she had heard her mother cry down the phone.

And now her mother wept in the bathroom while attempting to camouflage the sounds by turning on all the taps.

It was she, Nasrin, who caused her such pain.

She was such a problem to her mother that Jahanara had sought out her brother in Bangladesh to complain. Not only had Nasrin married a foreigner, but she had then decided to leave him, and to top things off, she was pregnant. She was an abysmal mess. No wonder then that her mother had become so close to Afroz, the obedient stepdaughter who gave her so much. Nasrin had seen how fond her mother was of Humayun during his stay – how easily and confidently she had conversed with him. She had never done this with Richard – had always held a wall of misunderstanding and miscommunication between them, giving in easily to the idea that their differences were insurmountable.

And then the turquoise saree.

Nasrin and Sabrina had fought over their mother's wedding saree as children.

'It's mine!'

'No, I said it's mine first!'

'No,' their mother had said, carefully placing the tissue into the folds to protect it, the scent of the mothballs she had inserted lingering in the air. 'This is mine, I won't give it away.' And Sabrina and Nasrin had watched their mother's teasing smile, knowing this meant she had yet to decide who it would go to.

But today her mother had given it to Afroz.

'I can't wear this,' Afroz had protested, staring at the turquoise silk and its beautiful pink border.

'That's your nikkah saree,' Nasrin had reminded her mother, her voice strained.

'Yes,' said Jahanara, stroking the silk and pulling out the tissue paper from its folds. 'I think Afroz should wear this tonight.'

'Fufu,' Afroz had cried, 'it will get ruined in the kitchen! Let me wear a shalwar—'

'When you are done in the kitchen, just come here and put it on,' Jahanara had interrupted. 'It will take five minutes. You are the owner of the Peacock, and so many eyes will be on you. I want you to have it.'

Thinking back to this conversation, Nasrin suddenly felt chilled to the bone.

'It doesn't make sense to me,' she murmured.

'What?' Elias slipped off her lap and looked at her.

'Nani and Afroz,' she replied, more to herself than her son. 'None of it makes sense to me.'

She stood and walked slowly into her mother's room, Elias following her. She stood in front of her mother's dresser, still deep in thought.

'Why would she give that saree to Afroz?'

She began to open drawers, and then the cupboard, forgetting to close one before opening another.

'Mumma,' Elias said, 'Mumma, what are you looking for?'

He watched her pace, back and forth. It went on for some minutes, before she suddenly stopped in the far corner of the room and stood staring at the empty wall.

'Are you here to tell me something?' her voice trembled. 'What do you want?'

'Mumma?'

'Just say something!'

Elias dropped his Lego and ran out of the room in terror. By the time he returned with his grandmother in tow, Nasrin was on the floor.

'God is testing me today,' her mother said as Nasrin opened her eyes. She was still in her mother's room, the purple silk spread out around her, damp and creased.

'Amma!' Nasrin said, the remnants of the seizure loosening her emotions.

'Shhh, be still.' Her mother brushed back strands of her hair. 'Maybe Afroz was right. You should go back with Richard today and see your doctor. I have asked Masoom to send another Taweez.'

'I'm fine.' Nasrin didn't want to return to London, nor tell her mother, once and for all, that she didn't believe in amulets. 'Amma, you know we are not getting back together? Richard is coming because we are trying to be friends, for the children's sake. Do you see?'

Her mother stiffened. 'If you can be friends, then why can't you be married? If you will be friends for the children's sake, then why can't you stay married for the children's sake?'

'Amma please!' Nasrin cried.

'Do you know what I have done for my children's sake?' her mother asked her, a pleading in her voice that only deepened Nasrin's wretchedness. 'It's what mothers do, Naju re, mothers sacrifice, for the sake of their children, for the sake of their families.'

'I know it's hard, Amma,' Nasrin said, a catch in her voice. 'I know it, but you have to understand, it's my decision. I can't stay married to Richard.'

Her mother stood up.

'I'm sorry. I know you're disappointed in me. I heard you crying in the bathroom. I heard you speaking to Mamu today.'

Her mother stared at her. She seemed confused. 'What?'

'I heard you talking—'

'You were sleeping.'

'No, I heard.'

'What did you hear?'

Nasrin sat up slowly, nursing her hipbone. It throbbed with pain. She must have caught it on the radiator when she fell.

She looked at her mother. 'I heard you talking about me. And I'm sorry I disappointed you, Amma.'

Her mother did not respond and began instead to unravel the saree from around Nasrin's waist.

Nasrin watched her mother's face. 'Amma, is there something wrong? I mean something else?'

'What can be wrong?' snapped her mother. 'Two daughters of this family have made a mess of their marriages, and the other doesn't even want to discuss marriage at all – what more needs to be wrong? A woman can't speak to her brother about it?'

'Of course you can.' Nasrin shook her head, uncertain. 'I don't mean that.' She tugged at the sleeve of her blouse which suddenly seemed too tight. It occurred to her that this was the longest conversation she had had with her mother since Richard had left. 'Is he angry with Afroz,' she asked, 'because she let Humayun leave alone?'

'You children think you know best,' Jahanara said with a shake of her head. 'That is what this country's education has given you – it has taken away respect for your elders and replaced it with this ohonkar, this arrogance, that you know better. At least Afroz still has some sense left in her. At least she still understands that a woman is nothing without her husband, without her family honour. I would have done better to have left you in Desh, at least then you wouldn't have all these Western notions.'

'Well,' Nasrin said tightly, letting her mother untangle the purple saree from her body. 'I'm sorry I'm not Afroz.'

Jahanara gathered the saree and stood up.

'Where are you going?' Nasrin asked.

'I need to iron this. Look at it.'

'Aren't you going to be late, Amma? You're not ready either.'

'I will be late – Mustafa is coming to pick up the keys, so I should wait for him before I come.' Nasrin remembered that Mustafa's flight was scheduled for that evening, and that he would be stopping en route to the airport to pick up the keys of the Nirashapur villa from her mother. Jahanara glanced back from the hallway momentarily with a pinched expression before disappearing from the room.

Half an hour later, steadier on her feet and dressed in the freshly ironed saree, Nasrin went out to look for Riaz. The sky was even darker now, still an hour before sunset, and the horizon was curling into the mist. The Peacock was empty and in total darkness, so she walked over to the staff cottage instead. The ramshackle bungalow hidden behind the back yard of the Peacock was where her family had first lived before her parents had upsized to the house next door. Here, amid the memories of their old life together, Nasrin suddenly missed Sabrina and Abba.

Finding Riaz's bedroom door open, she stepped lightly in, opening the window to alleviate the stench of stale tobacco. She looked out over the hills, unchanging amid all that had become unfamiliar, and wondered about her conversation with her mother. What was it that was different about Amma? When Riaz had announced to the family that her father had left the Peacock to Afroz, her mother had reacted in the way Nasrin would expect her to – locking herself in her room for days. What puzzled Nasrin was the way she behaved since she had emerged from that room – she harboured no resentment towards Afroz and uttered no complaint of her husband's misdeed. And yet, she was quite capable of showing her disapproval of Nasrin's decision to end her marriage and openly suspected Nasrin's relationship with Riaz. This made her lack of disapproval towards Abba and Afroz bewildering.

She heard laughter outside and, looking out of the window, saw that Richard had arrived. He was carrying Elias on his shoulders with a ball under one arm and was walking towards the small patch of grass that served as the village green. He seemed smaller and his face had the shadow of a beard. She felt an ache in her gut and turned away from the window. She looked around at the greyness of Riaz's room. The walls were scratched, and the bed was unmade. An ugly metal hook dangled in the corner without the punching bag that usually hung from it. She picked up Riaz's well-thumbed edition of *Great Expectations* from the stack of books beside his bed and flipped the pages, absent-mindedly.

In the half-open wardrobe hung his pristinely ironed work shirts. She pulled the door open all the way and smiled when she saw his can of starch and the laundry whiteners that stood on the shelf. On the inside of the door were two photos: the first of Riaz and his sister as children, the two of them standing on the gate outside their parents' home, the snow falling about them. The second was of the three of them: Sabrina slipping off the banks of the river Usk and Nasrin pulling her back, Riaz standing slightly away from them and calling out. She remembered this photo – they had been home from university one summer and Riaz's sister had been visiting. She remembered Thanni's cheeky smile, the shy, adoring way she watched her brother. It was Thanni who had taken the photo – and stepping back to get a better shot, she had fallen into the river. Nasrin reached up and touched the photo, remembering Riaz's joy when she and Sabrina had taken an instant liking to his younger sister. She touched his smiling face, recalling the feel of his beard when she had stroked it over six weeks ago.

She left the cottage and made her way to the Peacock. Inside, she found Riaz standing in the dark and holding his phone to his ear.

'Riaz?' she called out to him. 'Why haven't you put the lights on?'

Riaz turned to her and put his phone away. He fiddled with his wine-coloured cummerbund, which Nasrin had bought for all the waitstaff. He seemed agitated as he walked around the restaurant, lighting the candles.

'Please talk to me, Riaz! Have your parents found somewhere?'

'They need money to find somewhere, Naz. I need a couple of weeks.'

'So where are they staying?'

'At an uncle's.'

He pushed past her, walking briskly down the corridor and through the kitchen doorway, Nasrin rushing to keep up.

They almost walked straight into a surprised Afroz, who was standing in the kitchen holding a tiny prayerbook.

'What are you doing?' Riaz asked her.

'A quick dua.' She looked down at her hands. 'We do it in Desh, when we embark on new beginnings. For blessing.' She said this quickly and with a frown, as though sure it would elicit their disapproval or humour.

It did neither, though Nasrin stifled a smile before following Riaz back out into the corridor.

'Wait, Riaz!'

She reached out and grabbed his wrist. He twisted out of her grip, turning away, but she pressed both her arms around his chest, and held him close. Riaz struggled to unclasp her hands but she held firm. He let his hands rest on top of hers, his breathing quiet but erratic. She closed her eyes and rested her head against his back.

If someone were to happen upon them at that moment, they looked to be in the position of joint salah, praying with hands held to the chest, faces directed to the ground, lips parted, possibly in prayer. There was a strange and mysterious beauty in feeling his heart race somewhere midway between where her hands pressed against his ribs and where her face pressed into his spine: as though she were protecting a hurt bird that might attempt to fly away and cause itself more damage. It occurred to her gradually, as they stood in the dim corridor, as still as the painting of a Mughal court hanging on the wall beside them, that perhaps she should not have barged through the platonic bounds of their friendship into this strange hinterland whose intensity she had no bandwidth to navigate. But still, the thought did not prevent her pressing him closer, did not prevent her inhaling the familiar smell of Peacock, cologne and Marlboro Lights. It was a smell she had missed over these last few days; a smell that not only reminded her of his friendship, but one that held now notes of other possibilities.

'Naz,' Riaz whispered, and the uncertainties in his voice made her open her eyes.

'I won't ask you to take my money,' she said, 'I just want you to stop being angry.'

His hands circled her wrists and pulled them apart before he slowly turned to face her.

'I'm not mad.' He smiled.

'You are.'

'I'm not!'

'Then why have you been avoiding me?'

He shrugged sheepishly. 'I suppose it did feel awkward. But I could never be mad at you, Naz.' He looked at her and then glanced away, the shyest of smiles playing on his lips. She nodded.

'Rich is here,' Riaz said.

She nodded again, mute, reminded suddenly of the baby, of Elias and Richard, and the tangled relationships that already crowded her. What was she thinking, adding yet another layer to her mess?

She blinked at him.

'Are you guys … are you getting back together?' he asked. His voice was so low that it took Nasrin a few seconds before she understood. She recoiled from the exposure of this tender underbelly of his vulnerability. A shock of remorse shot through her. Why had she done this?

'No,' she said finally. 'But it *is* complicated, Riaz, you know? It's so complicated at the moment.'

His face fell for a split second before he bravely righted it by smiling.

'It'll be okay, Naz.'

Nasrin stepped back if only to prevent herself from reaching out to hug him again.

'How will you help your family?' she asked. 'How will you find the money you need?'

'Don't worry about me, I'll figure it out,' Riaz said, unrolling the sleeves of his shirt. 'Maybe I'll ask Afi for an advance.'

Nasrin watched him shake his sleeve out to smooth it before rolling it back up more neatly. 'Abba used to do that.'

Riaz looked surprised. They stood in the dimness smiling foolishly at each other before Riaz stepped back towards the swinging door and then disappeared into the restaurant. Nasrin remained in the corridor, the smile stuck on her face. A few minutes later, she too walked out into the restaurant and over to the bar where her phone lay behind the till. She logged into the Peacock's account and, with trembling fingers and her heart thudding anxiously in her chest, she transferred the twenty thousand pounds she knew was allocated for paying the fine to the local authority, into Riaz's account.

'All okay, Naz?' Riaz called from the front door. She looked up at him, his face lit up in earnest in the candlelight, her truest friend in the world. If he wouldn't take money from her, he would take it from the Peacock in the form of an advance. His pride would allow such a transaction. This was sizeable enough to give his family a new start and reduce his stress for a while. And she would make a transfer from her personal account straight after the party before Afroz had any time to worry about paying the fine. She would also need to ask Sabrina to help her pay for some of the renovations, as after this transfer she would be about five grand short.

'Naz?' Riaz said. 'Can you bring in the chutney dishes?'

She nodded and walked into the kitchen where Afroz was pouring raita from a large jug into smaller serving dishes.

'Afi!' Nasrin said, pushing back her saree achol with one hand. 'I gave Riaz an advance on his wages, I transferred it from the Peacock account, because you know he won't take it from me!'

Afroz frowned. 'But why? How much?'

'Afi, you stress so much about money – Riaz is family! I promise, I'll make a transfer as soon as the party's over.'

Afroz looked like she was about to object but something in her sister's expression made her stop stirring and looked closely at Nasrin. 'Naju, you look so red. So feverish.' She put the jug down. 'Come here, let me check if you have a temperature.'

Nasrin shook Afroz's hand away. 'Forget all that!' she said. 'Are the chutney dishes ready? I'll take them out, people will start arriving soon!'

23

Sabrina was in Monty's room with Fanni when she saw her phone flashing. Her immediate impulse was to answer it and make sure Afroz wasn't calling with any concerning news from the Beacons, but Monty forced her attention back to the matter at hand.

'It's just not on!' Monty raged. He was berating them for lowering team morale by the constant strain in their relationship. Sabrina wondered vaguely if this was how parents told off young children for quarrelling and it occurred to her that she and Nasrin had not really argued when they were young. The thought made her want to smile, though immediately, a pang of anxiety whipped through her as she wondered again why Afroz had called.

Beside her, Fanni sat rigidly, keeping her gaze directed at Monty, but Sabrina could feel the anger and resentment emanating towards her. She herself felt too preoccupied to feel angry – though she would have been justified, given that Fanni had not only begun to sabotage her relationships with her clients but was also making personal attacks on Sabrina's credibility as a manager. 'You're nothing but a fucking homewrecker,' she'd hissed into Sabrina's ear the night before at the firm's annual client reception at the Met. The words had paralysed Sabrina, and she had stared at the Modigliani painting before her, feeling her heart stretch in her chest like the elongated face in the painting. Following this incident she had enlisted Monty's help. Though now she wished she had chosen a different slot in his calendar, as Afroz was surely calling for something urgent.

'This bickering has to stop!' Monty continued, jabbing the desk with his index finger, and Sabrina wondered at his choice of words, how belittling it seemed. Would he use 'bickering' if this was Ashok complaining of Fanni's insubordination instead of Sabrina?

'I agree, and I just want to be clear – Fanni is an important member of my team, and I fully trust her and rely on her to run these projects, but,' and here Sabrina turned to Fanni, twisting in her chair so she could face her collegue square on, 'what I need from you, is to keep me in the loop.'

'That's obviously bullshit,' scoffed Fanni. 'You don't trust me if you need me to come to you with every single thing!'

Realising suddenly that she could not put calling Afroz back for a moment more, Sabrina stood. She turned to Monty. 'Sorry, Monty, I have an important meeting, which I'm already late for; but bottom line for me – these are clients that I've spent years building relationships with. Put it this way: I know how much you value your business relationships – would you want someone contacting them behind your back?'

As she left his office, Sabrina felt relieved at hearing Monty reprimanding Fanni, commanding her to report all further communication with Sabrina's clients back to Sabrina. As she walked towards the lobby, Sabrina caught, through the darkening window, a glimpse of the Christmas lights outside on the street. When had they gone up? How had she missed it? Had it only been three years since her family's visit to New York, their faces flushed by the lights of the Rockefeller tree as she took their photo in front of it? Her mother had loved the roasted chestnuts, insisting on stopping at the roadside stalls as they crawled slowly through Midtown, sidestepping the grey mounds of snow. Nasrin had bought their father a grey wool felt fedora, but he had been so cold, he had insisted on wearing his old beanie beneath it. And Eli, tiny and pink from the chill, reaching up from his pushchair wanting to be held … Sabrina closed her eyes, willing away the images of them, feeling her chest swelling. Then she opened them and dialled Afroz's number.

'Hi,' she said when Afroz answered, 'I was in a meeting when you called – is something wrong?'

'Sibby, sorry, I …' Afroz sounded unsure.

'Where are you? Isn't it the opening party today?' Sabrina asked.

'Yes, it's starting in about an hour. I'm in the Peacock kitchen, doing a quick dua.' Afroz paused. 'She's not doing too well, Sibby. I think you should come. I think it will help her if you come.'

Sabrina swallowed. 'Has something happened?'

'No. But she is not sleeping, and her … her imagination is … I think it would be good for her if you came sooner.'

'Okay.' Sabrina nodded slowly, wondering how she would manage. 'I'll rearrange my work meetings and look at some flights first thing tomorrow.'

'I think that would be good, Sibby. Maybe it will be good for you too? Fufu says you have seemed stressed lately?'

Sabrina did not respond to this, but the image of Ashok's face suddenly came to her. She closed her eyes.

'What about Eli?' she asked. 'Is he okay?'

Afroz laughed gently. 'That little baba is the life of this household.'

'Has Didi told him yet?'

'I think he has guessed something is wrong. Children know more than we give them credit for.'

'I wish he had a sibling … someone to share it with, a brother or sister.'

'InshAllah, he will have one soon!' Afroz said, giving a gentle laugh. 'I think being with his Nani gives him a sense of stability. I think it is good for Fufu too. She's been finding it all very difficult.'

'Oh, don't tell me,' Sabrina retorted, 'Amma's giving Didi a hard time, isn't she?' Afroz sighed in reply and Sabrina paused before asking, 'She's giving you a hard time too, I suppose? About Humayun Bhai, I mean?'

'It's to be expected, Sibby. Fufu has had to deal with so many changes, maybe it's just getting too much.'

'Amma,' said Sabrina hotly, 'just clings to the past like it's a fucking life-jacket. Sometimes I want to shake her.'

'She will come round. She's worried about Naju too, just like we are.'

'Can you promise me something?'

'Yes?'

'Just keep her safe till I get there, okay?'

'I will, Sibby. Just come as soon as you can.'

'I will. I've got to run now – so late for a client meeting!'

'Go, go – Allah hafiz.'

'Bye.'

Sabrina took the lift down to the lobby to meet her client, apologising profusely for being late. As she took them through her meticulously prepared deck, Sabrina was preoccupied, her thoughts returning over and over to her sister. When she had spoken to her the night before, Nasrin had sounded low and Sabrina, who found that the pain increasingly contained in Nasrin's voice felt like whiplash to her, had not tried hard enough to find out the root of it, allowing her fears to be easily assuaged by her sister's reassurances that everything was fine.

'Sabrina?'

She looked up, apologetic for her inability to focus. 'I'm sorry, would you mind repeating what you just said?'

She chided herself for not concentrating, and promised herself she would be on a plane very soon and would not leave her sister's side until she was better.

24

At a quarter to six, cars jostled for space outside the Peacock. Across the road, Tom stood in the bar at Chez Jones, waiting for his last customers to leave. At the crossroads, Mr Ruane stood and watched the parking frenzy unfold, thinking how a lavishly done-up restaurant was not an appropriate eulogy to a man known for his frugality.

Inside, Nasrin left the main restaurant area and headed to the kitchen, buzzing with anticipation. She burst through the kitchen doors and stood for a moment, awed by the frenetic energy. She could hear the hiss of seafood sizzling on a pan and the deep hum of the fryer where Lindsay was frying the puris; the rest of the kitchen staff were rushing to and fro preparing the salads on the appetiser plates and wiping the sides of the revolving chutney dishes, their voices like swarms of bees.

'Oh ba! Ek ta phiyaiz khatya diyo sain!'

'Khene ba salado phiyaiz nai ni?'

'Don't you dare put more onions in that salad, Hannan, I'm telling you now!'

Nasrin slid behind the counter and held a container still as Afroz deposited fried calamari, prawns and sea bass into it, still dripping with oil.

'It's like there are more people in this kitchen than usual,' she whispered.

'There are, Naju,' Afroz told her, a frown appearing on her fore-head. 'Remember? Lindsay brought in three temps for tonight.'

Nasrin nodded, though she could not recall why she was supposed to know this. 'Are you okay?' she asked.

Afroz nodded, without lifting her eyes from the frying pan. Her face was flushed red, her mouth open in concentration. While Nasrin had been out in the foyer rearranging the flowers and instructing the waiters to tie their cummerbunds higher, her sister had been in here doing the hard work. Riaz had disappeared to answer a phone call, and she saw him now enter the kitchen from the back entrance, a glum look on his face. Even so, when he passed her, he threw her a smile. Afroz finished the seafood appetisers and then handed them to Lindsay. The two sisters watched her dish them out.

'Are you done now?' she asked Afroz. 'Then come out with me and greet the guests.'

Afroz shook her head. 'They might still need me here; besides, I have to start on the mains soon.'

'Mum's cousins from Birmingham are here – they've been wanting to meet you. Did you know that Riaz is also related to them?'

'Naju,' pleaded Afroz, 'I'm too busy. Not right now.'

Nasrin nodded. 'Are you angry at me, Afi?'

Afroz shook her head. 'No.'

'Are you worried about the money?'

Afroz's silence was telling.

'Afi, I promise,' Nasrin said, 'I will transfer the money as soon as the party is over.'

An hour and a half later, the restaurant was full to the rafters. Nasrin pictured her father smiling his gap-toothed smile and saying, 'Houseful!' with satisfaction. He would have walked from group to group, each a clique unto their own, but it would not have both-ered him. She did not attempt to imitate her gregarious father, but instead squeezed wordlessly through the bodies, an awkward smile plastered on her face. The unease from the morning was beginning to metastasize into a feverish lightheadedness.

She stepped behind the bar, placed her hands on either side of the beer taps, and leaned forward. Watching from this vantage point, above the hum of conversation, and the gentle clatter of cutlery and glasses, it dawned on Nasrin how unrecognisable her father's restaurant had become. She felt suddenly overwhelmed by remorse.

What had she done? Why had she scrubbed every vestige of her father from this place? Why had she camouflaged his life's work with this veneer of modernity and gloss?

Blinking back tears, she looked about her at the peacock-shaped napkins that were already crumpled and discarded on the starter plates. In the magnificence of the clementine chairs, the polished sheesham, and the lush sapphire carpet, what Nasrin saw clearly was a destruction of the very qualities that she had set out only to improve.

She felt suddenly sick.

All about her, the newly-hung frames and ceiling lights began to undulate. She leaned over the bar and took a slice of lemon from the canister. The tart bitterness of the zest brought tears to her eyes. She spotted her mother by the entrance, introducing Afroz to a group of women in sarees and headscarves. In front of the fireplace, Richard was deep in conversation with the local police commissioner, Elias curled up on his lap and two wine glasses, already empty, on the table before him. Then she spotted Riaz, snaking his way through the crowds towards the bar, depositing bottles of beer on a table full of local youths. His face was pale and drawn. He glanced over at Nasrin, and she saw that something was wrong. He leaned forward.

'What is it?' she asked.

'My mum called, Naz, I need to drive down to Lozells tonight,' he said. 'I don't want to leave you in the middle of this … but—'

Nasrin moved to the front of the bar so she could hear him better but missed the last part of this sentence. She shook her head. 'I didn't hear you, what?'

'My dad – he's in hospital – got into a fight at the bookies. Will you guys be all right?'

She nodded. 'Oh gosh, Riaz! We'll manage – you have to go, Riaz, of course you do!'

She watched him walk away and then ran after him and grabbed his hand.

'Afi gave you that advance you needed,' she whispered into his ear. 'It's in your account.'

'Naz …'

'I swear I didn't do anything!' she protested. He gazed at her with an expression she could not read. Then he smiled and reached up to touch her cheek.

'You swear, huh?'

She nodded but did not return his smile. She felt an inexplicable fear tighten around her chest. He squeezed her hand and took his car keys from his pocket. 'I'll be back later tonight,' he said. 'See you up on the flat roof for a smoke?'

She said, 'You need to stop that smoking, Riaz.'

He laughed and she watched him navigate the crowds, watched him open the door and leave.

Then she too turned and walked over to Richard. She sat down next to him and let Elias climb onto her lap. Richard smiled at her. He needed a haircut as well as a shave and his shirt hung from him, making his shoulders look disproportionately large. The fear that squeezed her chest tightened its grip.

'It's good to see you,' he told her, but there was no tenderness in his voice, only a strange briskness, as though he had rehearsed these words and wanted them out. She nodded, unable to speak. 'I guess we should discuss things?' he said, leaning forward so that she could hear him in the din. 'Eli's school – they called – about when he'd start. We need to start thinking about these things. That is …' his eyes scurried over her face, 'that is if you're still sure.'

Nasrin nodded again, but still found she could not find her voice. Instead, she turned away from him and Richard sighed loud enough for her to hear before turning back to the commissioner. Nasrin inhaled the scent of her son's hair, letting it warm and settle her.

The arrival of Mustafa made Nasrin stand up: Mustafa, dressed awkwardly in a Western suit, the lapels flapping untidily around his chest and his sleeves so long they slipped over his knuckles. In the crowded restaurant, she seemed to be the only one to have noticed him. He stood staring about, and she could see, even from this distance, the alarm in his eyes, and in the stoop of his shoulders. She stepped forward, to save him from what she had done.

'Naz! Naz!'

She turned to find Tom, his face pink and glossy with laughter, reaching out to her. 'Come and have a drink with us!' he said.

She smiled at him and at the girl at his elbow – the disarming green of her eyes, the cascading fall of strawberry blonde about her shoulders. Nasrin's smile froze on her lips.

'Hi, Naz,' the girl said, leaning forward and embracing her. 'Haven't seen you in aeons!'

'Naz,' Tom said, 'Vicky says you two were at school together? Same class, even?'

Nasrin stared at the still recognisable face and felt herself turn slowly numb. Suddenly she was seven and back in the gym hall, retreating into the darkness of the trampoline cupboard. Those green eyes, the last things she saw as the doors closed in her face and the darkness swallowed her screams. She felt the pins and needles crawling up her arms. Inhaling sharply, she backed away.

'Mumma.' Elias's hands had slipped into hers and was tugging her away from the darkness. 'I'm hungry, Mummy!'

'Are you okay?' The green eyes came towards her. Nasrin picked up Elias and rushed for the door.

She ran down the path to her parents' house, clutching Elias to her, willing the agitation simmering up her arms to retreat. Her head was beginning to feel congested again, as it had that morning, with its shadows and the incipient folds of darkness lapping like a sea at high tide, blurring her vision.

She let herself into the house and heard her mother and Mustafa in the kitchen.

'Here, this key is for the main house, and these are for the guest house.' Her mother's voice was measured. She had never been easy with Mustafa. 'Is someone there?' her mother called from the kitchen.

'Just me, Amma,' Nasrin replied.

'Are you okay?' Her mother's worried face peered out of the kitchen door.

'Fine. I just need to lie down for a few minutes.'

'Accha, jao. I'll come and check on you in a minute.'

Nasrin made her way up the stairs, Elias heavy in her arms.

'How will I remember all these keys, Bhabhi!' she heard Mustafa ask.

'Here, I've written it down, see?'

'You are good to me, Bhabhi.'

'The tamarind tree by the guest house, it will need some attention, Bhaisab. Speak to the tree doctor from Gulapgoynj, Masoom tells me he is very good.'

'All in good time, Bhabhi. You have all been so good to me. Always, you have been so good to me.'

Nasrin lay on her bed and stared up at the ceiling. Elias sat on the floor beside her and made roaring sounds as he collided the wooden lion that Afroz had given him against the divan. Outside, there was a burst of raucous laughter from the smokers congregated on the square, but Nasrin barely registered. She was inside the dark trampoline cupboard again, clinging to the image of those large green eyes. 'Vicky!' she called. 'Open the door!'

'Mumma?' she heard Elias calling her from outside the trampoline cupboard. His voice was faint as though he called her from a great distance.

'Vicky,' Nasrin said, fear in her throat, in her eyes, fear crawling all along her goosebumped arms. 'It's not funny, Vicky! Open the door!'

'Mumma!' Elias said, and his voice was even fainter than before, but her fear had become a tornado that ravaged her senses, cutting her off, tossing her body about in ways she could not imagine would be possible. She curled into a ball and squeezed her eyes to prevent herself reliving that very first seizure. But the pain came anyway, fresh and angry, hardly a memory from decades ago.

Slowly it subsided. Nasrin blinked her way out of the trampoline cupboard and back into her bedroom. She opened her eyes to find her seven-year-old self lying curled beside her. 'You never really left that cupboard, did you?' she asked her, pity catching fire to her throat, making her eyes burn.

And yet, she *had* left the cupboard all those years ago. She had awoken in the nurse's room, her mother sobbing uncontrollably beside her. She had been unconscious for almost half an hour. 'What did they do to my child? Where were you when they did this to my child? Oh, amar bacha!' her mother had cried. 'Oh, amar futh! They are sending an ambulance!' She had smoothed Nasrin's hair away from her face, and Nasrin too had reached out to smooth the tears from her mother's face. 'I am fine, Amma, don't cry.' But her mother had only cried harder. 'It is my lot to cry, re futh! You had a seizure. A seizure! If only I can be in more places than one! As if *she* is not worry enough for me, that Allah sends me this too.'

Nasrin now gazed at her seven-year-old self lying beside her. She reached out to touch her but stopped in mid-air because a sudden thought came to her. What had her mother meant by those words? *As if she is not worry enough for me.* Who was *she*? Nasrin had thought her mother had meant Sabrina, but her mother had never before or after professed concern about Sabrina, perhaps because Abba and

Sabrina's closeness was a reassurance that Sabrina was under Abba's care. Now Nasrin sat up. She was sure that her mother had not meant Sabrina. She could not have meant Nasrin either. So who had she been talking about? Nasrin thought again of the day Riaz had announced the will. She remembered again the pale face of her mother as Riaz handed her the letter. The letter her father had written her. Her mother had not been angry – what was it she had said? '*She came because she has as much right as any of you to be here.*'

Nasrin jumped off the bed.

She left her room, barely noticing Elias following her out. She switched the light on in her mother's room. *I think you know*, she whispered to her seven-year-old self standing now by her mother's window. She opened her mother's wardrobe and gazed into the gloom. *There must be something in this room that confirms it.*

Elias wondered what it was that made his mother, muttering and whimpering, go into his Nani's room. He watched from Nani's bed as she stood mutely, biting her lip, her eyes combing familiar objects, searching for a clue. She began rummaging through bedside drawers and then the dresser, her searching becoming more frantic.

'What is it, Mummy?' he asked her. 'What are you looking for?'

She paused and sank heavily down on the floor as though in surrender. Then rousing herself, she ducked to look beneath her mother's bed. Heart in his throat, Elias laid his head gently beside hers and stared at the boxes that gathered dust under the bed. But his mother changed her mind again and sat up, staring listlessly at the bed before picking up her phone and leaving Sabrina a long, meandering message.

'Sibby – that Vicky from the gym hall? She's here – can you believe it, she's here! Or is she here? Maybe she's not here? I don't know … I don't know anymore, Sib. I've completely messed everything up – I've completely destroyed the Peacock – I didn't mean to do it! I wanted to do something nice for Afroz, you know, because poor Afroz, I feel like we've all let her down, all her life. And then Amma and I are arguing, I feel like she's so disappointed, and there's something not quite right. Will you call me, Sib? Will you come? I need you, right now, I need my sister.' She began to cry then, softly, her tears distorting her vision. 'Everything's got so dark, Sib, everything is so dark!' She paused momentarily as if to reflect, then she put the phone down and, still crying, began to pull boxes out from under the bed.

Elias sat beside her and watched, emitting small whimpers of distress as she flung papers out of the boxes with an impatience that he found frightening. Then when he felt tired and lay down on the carpet, he would remember the way that a single sheet of folded paper, cast aside by Nasrin, settled beside him, like an act of God. He would remember how he picked it up, this one cataclysmic act of his that would undo everything.

He studied the foreign scrawls – the beautiful, firm lines and characters curling over and below words like the tails of exquisite creatures – until, finally, she noticed him.

She took it from him, her hands shaking. She stared at the page in dismay. She looked up at a spot beside the open window where the curtain shook with the wind and said, 'Abba's letter! But in Bengali!'

A moment passed and then she nodded, as though she were in conversation, except there was only Elias in the room.

'Naju!'

Elias looked up in relief as his Nani came into the room.

Nasrin blinked, ashamed to be caught red-handed intruding on her mother's privacy. But she felt the seven-year-old watching her from beside the dancing curtains. Her mother's face was grey with fear and Nasrin followed her gaze to the letter in her hand. So, there must be something in her father's last words to her mother, some explanation for her mother's lack of anger, some reassurance for the conviction with which she had accepted Afroz as her own. But it was in a language she could not read: characters that were so familiar to her and yet so illegible. Just like her parents, just like the Desh she was bound to and yet unable to comprehend. She frowned. Why was her mother so afraid?

'What does it say?' she asked her mother, holding the letter towards her.

'What are you doing? Why are you crying?'

'Sorry, Amma.' Nasrin bought the letter down and stared at it. 'Eli found it, here under the bed …'

'Naju, give that to me!'

Nasrin stared at her mother. Why was her mother's voice so shaky? Why was her face so pale? 'Amma,' she said, 'why are you so afraid? What's in here?'

Her mother said nothing.

'Naju? Bhabhi?' It was Mustafa's voice calling from downstairs. 'Ami zai gi – I had better go, the car is waiting.'

Nasrin stared at her mother, then she turned to look at the seven-year-old still watching her from beside the curtains. Within seconds, she was running out of the room and down the stairs and was at Mustafa's side in a flash. Not waiting to think, she pressed the letter to his chest. A buzzing sound hovered ominously at her temples.

'What does it say,' she said to Mustafa. It was not a question but a command. Mustafa frowned. Behind them, Jahanara slowly descended the stairs.

'Read it, Sasa, what does it say?'

Mustafa read the letter. Then he read it again. Moments passed, and in torturous slow motion, the frown on his face dissolved, only to be replaced by an expression she could not read.

'What is it? What does it say?' Nasrin pleaded. It felt now imperative that she know the contents of this letter. As though, and she knew this was bizarre, but as though it held the secrets to all of her unhappiness

– not just hers but also all the unhappinesses of her family. At the top of the stairs, her seven-year-old self stared glumly down at her through the banisters. Elias too stood there at the top of the stairs, watching the scene unfold. 'Sasa,' Nasrin said, turning to him, 'please?'

Mustafa glanced at her, and then at her mother.

'Futh,' Mustafa said in a voice that was so low that it was only just audible to Nasrin, standing close beside him. 'Don't do this. Don't torture your mother – she has suffered more than you know.'

'What?' Nasrin whispered, but Mustafa said no more. The horn of the car seemed to rouse him. He reached up and placed his hands on Nasrin's head. 'You don't seem well, re futh. Go on and get some rest. Leave this be.' He placed the letter on the desk, beside the orchid, as neatly as his trembling fingers allowed.

'Allah hafiz,' he croaked and then he turned and opened the door.

'What does it say, Sasa?' Nasrin said, reaching for him, but her mother was already at her side, slamming the door behind him.

They stared at each other. Her mother picked up the letter that Mustafa had left and stared at it. Then she took Nasrin by the shoulders and shook her, crying, with a high shrill voice Nasrin had never heard before. 'Why? Why did you do this?' The letter slipped from her fingers and sank lightly down to the floor.

Their raised voices, more shrieks than conversation, drifted up to Elias where he stood and watched from the top of the stairs. The shaking outraged and frightened him. He ran down the stairs and clung to his mother's leg, as much to protect her as for protection.

He had never seen his grandmother this way. Her face was contorted in rage, such an unfamiliar and ugly expression. Elias hid his face in the folds of his mother's saree.

'Amma, I'm sorry, I'm sorry, stop crying please!'

'It wasn't meant for you! Amar siti thuy phorle kila! It wasn't meant for anyone but me – and now you let a stranger read it—'

'Mustafa Sasa is no stranger! He will keep quiet—'

'Quiet!' Nani shouted. 'What do you know of quiet? Have you ever had your screams muffled or bitten your knuckles to keep your tears away! Quiet, keep quiet, that's what they told me every day. Chup kor! All that pain they locked inside me with that Chup kor! Hai re Naju – you've had it all, you've never known how *we* had to live, all the choices denied us, all the duties that bound us and through it all, the damnation of quiet! To keep all that rage, all those tears, those heartaches, behind a wall of silence!'

'Amma, please!'

'And yet, it's not enough for you! You need to know all the dirty details of my suffering?'

'What suffering, Amma? Tell me, what happened to you? What do you mean?'

'And now Mustafa knows, and what will stop him from telling everyone? He'll tell the world, all the things they'll say about me, Naju, how could you do this to me? You were the only one – you were my amulet, my protection – you who have always saved me! How could you do this?'

'Amma, please, please calm down – everyone already knows about Afroz – they know he kept her a secret.'

But Jahanara's voice rose higher, her words flew out of her mouth like a waterfall whose force she could not control. 'What do you know?' she raged at her daughter, who stared at her in open-mouthed dismay. 'You who are spoilt with choice, greedy for more! You chose your husband and now you don't know if it's him you want, or if it's the man you left behind.'

'Amma! Please! I said, I'm sorry, I am. But Abba—'

'What Abba? What Abba? You think your father is such a saint?'

'I don't. Of course, I don't, Amma – he fathered a child, he possibly cheated on you, of course he's no saint. You're the saint, Amma – for forgiving him so easily – for being so good to Afroz when she must remind you every day of what he's done.' Nasrin took her mother's hand, put it to her damp face, her eyes pleading for forgiveness. 'Not him, Amma – but you – I think you are the saint.'

Jahanara became very still. The suddenly distant expression on her face terrified Nasrin more than her rage had. She shook her mother's hand. 'I'm so sorry, Amma – please, I shouldn't have gone through your things. Please, Amma, don't look at me like that.'

Her mother withdrew her hand and took a step back.

She stared at her daughter, reached out to touch her pink cheeks but then snatched her fingers back and held them to her chest as though scalded.

'But he *was* a saint,' she whimpered, 'and I … I'm so sick of being punished, I'm sick of suffering like this.'

As her mother spoke, Nasrin noticed from the periphery of her vision that her father was standing beside her seven-year-old self. She looked up at him, feeling a surge of reassurance at his presence, and then it came to her with a sudden flash of clarity.

She took her mother's hand, a choked sound escaping her.

'Amma, is Afroz your daughter?'

Shock exploded across her mother's face.

For a moment neither of them moved.

Then, Jahanara opened her mouth to speak, but she turned around instead, opened the front door and was gone.

'Amma!' Nasrin shouted, moving towards the door, but Elias clung to her legs.

'Don't go, Mumma!' he shrieked. 'Don't go!'

The door closed with a click.

'Amma,' Nasrin whispered into the silence.

They sat on the bottom of the staircase, Elias and his mother, as the silence coiled about them like a mist over a cold lake. Elias picked up the letter and looked at the scrawl, wondering what it was that had unleashed such hurt and anger. Nasrin muttered under her breath, and occasionally began to cry before lapsing into silence. Elias held fast to her arm, afraid of the silence, and the darkness, and all the things he could not see but were alive to his mother.

Finally the door opened, and Richard stood before them.

'Rich,' Nasrin wriggled away from her son's clutches, 'my mum, I think it's all been a lie – I think Afroz is not Abba's daughter, I think she is my mum's!'

'Naz, slow down, I don't—'

'I confronted her with it, and she was so shocked, she's run away! She's so distraught! What if she gets lost? It's so dark outside!'

'Naz? What – where has she gone?'

'Ohmygod, Oh God, I pushed her to the brink – it's my fault she left! I need to go and find her, Rich.'

'Honey, look, she's probably just gone next door—'

'They said she went that way – up towards the hills!'

'Who said? Who!'

'*They* … I just know it, why do you do that? Make out that I'm stupid?'

'Naz, can you calm down? Eli is right there, he's listening!'

'Eli?' She turned and looked at her son. Her lips quivered.

Richard took her shoulders. 'Naz, honey, what's happening? You're shaking!'

'And my poor mum, all the horrible things she must have suffered … do you think I'm right? Is Afroz hers?'

'I think we need to get you to a doctor!'

'She's lost out there, Rich. I'm going to lose my mum too, and I can't do that, I can't lose everyone!'

'Stop, Naz, you're in such a state!' He took her arm, stroked her face. 'I'll go and find her, okay? You stay here with Eli!'

Then the front door opened again. Afroz stood there, taking everything in, her words frozen on her lips.

'Afi!' Nasrin clutched her sister's arm and drew her close. 'Afi … It's all going to be okay!'

Afroz pulled back. 'What's going to be okay? What's happening here?'

Nasrin shook her head. 'Stay here with Eli!'

With those last instructions, Elias's mother ran out of the house, Richard following at her heels.

Once a Teacher's Pet

Jahanara is sitting outside on the veranda crouched on a low stool. The folds of her elbows and knees are slippery with sweat because her mother's cotton saree has stuck itself to every bare inch of her and it is unrelentingly, stiflingly hot. She is holding five smooth pebbles which she carries around with her everywhere. She fidgets with them as her mother runs a comb through her knotted hair. But the stones fail to divert her from the demented heat of the afternoon sun and her mother's mirthless, discordant humming. Jahanara wriggles and sighs, and after a few sharp smacks from her mother, gives up her resistance.

She stares up at the sky, where the approaching swollen clouds only compound her anxiety. She would like nothing more than for those clouds to drift towards her and drench her free of this hellish heat. But rain will make Jahanara late or worse still, might cancel her plans altogether. She does not want it to rain after all.

'Kuthar bacha!' swears the myna in her cage. Chinthamoni hates rain.

'Sit still!' her mother shrieks, whether to Chinthamoni or to Jahanara, who knew? She taps the top of Jahanara's head with the sharp end of the comb.

Jahanara sullenly continues to watch the sky. Her mother thumps the last few drops of coconut oil from the bottle into her hand before rubbing it the length of Jahanara's hair. The comb begins its descent again. She feels her mother's breath on the back of her neck, heavy and laboured in the heat. The comb finds another enemy knot to vanquish.

'Ouch, Amma!'

'Didn't I say, sit still? You move, that's when it hurts!'

'It hurts even when I'm still! Eeesh, you're hurting me!'

Her mother turns Jahanara's head around with one hand and twists her cheek with the other.

'Speak like that to me again, and I'll show you what hurts!'

'Malyar fal!' swears Chinthamoni in her cage.

'If you don't stop that swearing,' her mother threatens the myna, 'I'll boil you for supper tonight.'

Chinthamoni cocks her head and considers this ultimatum. 'Malyar fal!' she says.

'Jalo!' Jahanara's mother calls out to the maid. 'Prepare the kodu. Slice it lengthways, it'll go nice with myna meat.'

'Jalo!' imitates Chinthamoni. 'Malyar fal!'

A giggle rises in Jahanara's chest, but her anxiety is too strong, and it dies before it reaches her lips. She squeezes hard and the pebbles roll over one another in her damp palm. After several minutes, her mother is done, and two long plaits drape over Jahanara's chest. She extricates herself carefully from the folds of her mother's saree, and heads towards her room.

'Where are you going?' her mother calls out after her. 'Come and oil my hair! Allah re, this heat, it's going to kill us!'

'Amma, I told you this morning! I'm going for class!'

'What?'

'Sir is giving an extra class on English.' She pauses and then adds, 'For the finals. Revision class.'

Her mother grunts, and Jahanara wraps her scarf hurriedly around her head. She takes a ten-taka note and folds it neatly into the folds of her shalwar. She presses her fingers against Chinthamoni's cage, and then presses her finger against her lips, shhhh! The myna cocks her head and remains silent. Just as she steps off the veranda, her mother calls out.

'Take Masoom with you!'

Jahanara wants to scream. Her plaits feel tight, tearing at her scalp.

'He's not here! I'm late!'

But he is here. Her twin, younger by three minutes, is always here.

Masoom appears out of the study room, buttoning a short-sleeved shirt over his vest, and he takes a running jump off the veranda, landing neatly at his sister's sandalled feet.

She glares at him, mouthing *idiot*, and scowls when he returns this with one of his grins.

They walk slowly in the direction of the clouds, passing the tube well where a lethargic line of villagers dangle empty water jugs at their sides. Najma Apa is taking her time at the well, oblivious to the impatience of the queue. She lets her jug overfill so that the cool water splashes out over her forearms and her ankles. Najma Apa is their next-door neighbour, a distant relative of Jahanara's father, and a childless widow. Behind her back, she is known as silan, a term whose meaning Jahanara was unsure of, except that it is reserved for the most dishonourable of women. There are rumours that but for the intervention from Jahanara's father, Najma Apa would have received a sentence of lashings from the local panchayat.

Something about Najma Apa repulses Jahanara. Perhaps it is the woman's indifference to the way others perceive her. Jahanara can't understand such a callous disregard for the rules of society. One's reputation is paramount, as her mother and father have told her over and over again whenever she wants to wear churidars, or attend the village mela unchaperoned. As Jahanara and Masoom pass by the tube well, Najma looks up and splashes water at them, laughing as Masoom comically lunges out of the way. Jahanara frowns and looks away. The woman has no shame.

They reach the edge of the village, where the air is less still, and a tender breeze licks at their bare heels. Jahanara begins to bounce sideways into her brother, shoving him playfully towards the almost-dry creek as they pass it, and he giggles and dodges her, grabbing her when she almost falls in. They walk the long way around the jackfruit tree so as not to offend it by stepping on its shadow. Then they wander off the path into the shade of the bamboo; sometimes Masoom runs ahead, and sometimes Jahanara runs with him. They push a cow gently out of the way, swatting her clean of the mosquitos that have gathered around a wound at her tail, and the cow walks with them for a while until it finds a patch of grass.

The clouds shield them from the sun until a clap of thunder rips out over the horizon just before they arrive at the bazaar. They run, delighting in the cool fat drops that fall on them, Jahanara's shalwar soon sticking around her calves, and Masoom's shirt plastered against his chest. She leads them into Shubhon's teahouse.

'Aren't you going to be late for your lesson?' Masoom asks, as Jahanara leads him to the table at the back of the tiny shack. It is dark inside, with only a single shaft of daylight that shoots through a hole in the clay and bamboo wall, revealing dust particles that float down from the low ceiling.

'Chup baba! Always such interrogation with you! Did I tell you to come?'

She regrets her sharpness.

She is quick to spit caustic words, quick to feel the instant remorse that explodes within her. Like a honeybee, she stings those close to her and is unable to pull the barbed stinger back out, leaving behind a part of herself, her regret and her guilt. Her sharp tongue is a wall between her and every one of her family and friends.

Except for her brother, who usually just gives a simple shrug or a light sarcastic retort. But today he merely smiles and sits down across from her, and then proceeds to exchange cricket updates with the tea boy.

They sit for some time, as the rain thrashes the fragile tin roof. Jahanara watches her brother fidget with her five round stones for some minutes before she grabs them from him. Again, she is awash with regret, and again Masoom allows her to make amends. She orders a roshogolla for him, a bite of which he offers to her, but she can barely stomach the saliva in her mouth.

She waits. Every few minutes she turns to look out at the door.

Every cyclist that whizzes past could be him.

Every man that takes refuge in the doorway could be him.

Masoom finishes the roshogolla and reaches for her pebbles. She lets him, and watches as he flicks them off the table one by one, bending down to retrieve them.

They wait.

'Maybe he forgot?' Masoom says, after some time. He shakes the pebbles in his hands like castanets.

Jahanara looks up at him, her tongue ready with a swear word. But her brother looks back at her with an expression full of compassion, and instead her eyes fill with tears.

Only later will she wonder how Masoom knew. Had he seen them together, after class, in the disused staffroom with its door that wouldn't lock, her against the back wall, with Sir pressing into her, his one sandalled foot jamming the door shut, the smell of his rose-scented attar filling the small space? Or had he noticed that when she got her homework arithmetic wrong, Sir would only tap the top of her knuckles rather than smack hard enough to bruise the bone like he did with Mala or Boshir? Or had he noticed, as she had, how Sir looked at her across the classroom, his stare penetrating her clothes, even her skin, to somewhere deep inside her where her terror of him lay under layers and layers of duty?

'I'll run across to the school,' Masoom says, as he stands up from the bench. She turns to watch him run through the rain, surprised at the outline of his shoulder muscles that strain against his wet shirt. When has he become a man? She has taunted him so about his lack of facial hair, but it is the only thing left to come, to herald his manhood. She has been too busy with her fears of dishonour to notice that her little brother was growing up.

'Apa,' the tea boy says, 'do you want my gamcha?'

She realises she is shivering. She shakes her head at the tea boy and puts her head down on her arms. The significance of the weeks that have passed since school broke up for the Eid holidays dawns on her. How long it has been. How unlike Sir not to come looking for her. He has always sought her out during past holidays, found reasons to come to her home, to drop a book for her or Masoom, or chat with her father. During each visit he found a moment to brush past her or to hold her gaze. Or he would send word through Mala about an extra class at school, during which he would ask her to clean out the equipment cupboard, finding some pretext to join her there.

The last time they met, they walked behind the school compound and she slipped her foot out of her sandal and drew circles in the dust with her toe. She asked him, with a tug in her chest, when he would speak to her father. It was after all, a matter of her honour. They should be married before tongues began to wag. She noticed how the postman stared when she passed the small post house on her way to school. She was not a dishonourable girl. She was not Najma Apa. But Sir laughed. The postman was a madman, he retorted. Who would take his word for anything? Some people's words, he reminded her pointedly, had more value than others. She ran home, fat tears raging down her cheeks. But the weeks passed, and she knew she had to try again; had to convince him that what he had done – what they had done – required action. She begged Mala to pass on a message to him to meet her at the teashop, and Mala had promised that she had delivered it. So, why hasn't he come?

When Masoom returns, water dripping off his nose no matter how many times he wipes it, he speaks so fast that she barely understands. Certain words drip slowly into her consciousness. *Married. Resigned. Back to Kulna. New teacher.*

They walk in the direction of home. They pass the cow that

hovers beneath the bamboo, blinking into the dying light. The rain has slowed to a drizzle and the earth seems to give off a steam.

'Don't cry!' Masoom says more than once, pushing back his wet hair in agitation. 'That bastard!'

But she does cry.

'You're a good girl. Not girl, woman. You're a beautiful woman – the most beautiful I've ever set eyes on,' Sir had said to her, in English. 'How am I supposed to resist you?' She had allowed herself to seek refuge in the fact that all teachers were honourable souls. He had done this to her, but he would marry her now. She would marry a teacher. She would become a teacher's wife.

As she cries and walks, she finds she still has faith in those words of his. He will come for her. Surely, he will come for her.

25

The cold air cuts through their clothes, making them shiver. Around them, the black shadows of the Beacons are merging into one another. They realise with heavy hearts how quick the transition between twilight and dusk is. How swiftly the light is knocked out of the horizon, astonishingly indifferent to their panic.

They stand for a moment and turn around, fast and then slow. They try to recognise something, anything, that might show them a way home, and if not home, then to safety. But all they see are different shades of darkness.

Richard takes Nasrin's hands and he blows on them. He means to warm her fingers and reassure her, but she sees the panic on his face.

'Oh my God, oh my God,' she whispers over and over.

'We'll find her,' he says. 'You're sure you saw her come up here, so she must be here somewhere.' He begins to walk, pulling her along.

She can feel herself falling headlong into inconsolable despair. There is the familiar tingling at her elbow, and her panic increases.

'Naz! Naz?'

She cannot let the seizure come now.

Because she must think about Amma. Out there somewhere, because of her.

And Richard. Loaded with dread, walking next to her. Dear, darling, beloved Richard! Was it just minutes ago that she had questioned him? Had questioned his affections for her? In the darkness she can just make out the way he rubs the back of his head – as he does when he is agitated – and she feels a tenderness swallow her panic. She reaches out to smooth his hair, and instead grabs his neck and pulls him towards her.

'How the fuck are we here?' she asks. 'Rich, how did we get here?'

And she begins to cry, because she doesn't mean just *here* – in the middle of what she thinks is Pen y Fan but could just as well be a mountain in Africa it is so foreign to her, camouflaged by the descending night. How is it that they have arrived at this bleak moment in their marriage, with each of them seeking solace in another's arms but a baby in her womb that would still have them draw out some semblance of a family? A messy togetherness, a complicated, convoluted togetherness: a future that seemed as frightening as the thick foggy darkness of this mountain at this moment.

He seems to sense her many meanings. He kisses her nose, then firmly on the lips. He holds her tight and, feeling the quake in her small body, is reminded of the child she carries.

'Naz, listen to me.' The panic engulfs them again and they breathe hard, both of them. 'Do you think your mum might have gone home already?'

Nasrin doesn't know.

Her father and seven-year-old self pointed her this way. She had been glad that they were finally communicating. She had thought that she finally understood why they were here: they were here to tell her the way – the way to her mother.

But her mother is not here and the darkness she had woken up with that morning now spills out of her, adding to the thick fog that curls around them, hiding their way back home. She and Richard were lost, high up on a precipitous hillside with the darkness tumbling in and the chill penetrating their flimsy clothes.

'Naz, you know the way back?' Richard asks.

On the left of them, at the turn in the path, she sees two shadows lengthen over a large rock. She knows that rock: it was the old Tommy Jones obelisk. Why are they here, so far from where she thought they were? She looks at Richard and feels her heart begin to race again in a blind panic. But she breathes deeply to control it. She has bought him here, and she will get him back to safety.

'Yes,' she says, being careful to keep her voice steady. She takes Richard's cold hands in hers. 'Follow me.'

As he walks beside her, Richard momentarily doubts her certainty – but he is too cold and exhausted to challenge it, and so he follows her lead in silence.

Lost in Low Cloud

His Aunt Afroz always told him that a premonition of one's death is the last full blessing in life, and it comes without warning. In those final days, a person's subconscious is torn in half: one half is cursed with foresight and the other half blessed without. The prescient part of the soul can sense the angel of death's approach, and so begins to grieve and to prepare. It tries to reach out to warn its ignorant counterpart, tries to hint that the end is near, and often the message from subconscious to conscious successfully transmits, and loved ones will recall inexplicable acts of affection and kindness that the soon to be deceased had indulged on them. These last gestures of leave-taking, mired in the pathos of hindsight and finality, are memories that would help family members through their bereavement when their beloved finally departs.

But his mother, blindsided by Azrael, did not heed the warnings from the wise part of her subconscious, and she did not bequeath her loved ones with any last moment they could cherish. She departed in a state of bewilderment, leaving those she loved only a handful of speculations about her last moments. She ran up into the mountains and she died, with Richard, on Corn Du, the twin summit of Pen y Fan, lost in the descending cloud.

The postmortem found many things. His father's broken ankle and his mother's overdose of her seizure medication, a fact that drove his Aunt Afroz to the brink of despair as she had encouraged her to take that morning's dosage. The fact that his mother was just over twenty-four weeks pregnant. Possibly, the coroner muttered, possibly they might have saved the foetus if only the couple had been found an hour or so earlier.

Those they left behind did not want to think about why they were found on Corn Du when they had set off for Pen y Fan, or of their shivering bodies, and their interlaced fingers, fastened together when Brecon Mountain Rescue found them almost two days later. They did not want to think any of these things, but how could they not, when imagining death is, at these moments, the only thing left for the living?

Elias, when he is old enough to speculate, likes to think that at some point, they would have surrendered their panic and anxiety, up there with nothing but the thin air, and the morning sun filtering through the clouds in a haze, hoping that they would be found soon, that they would spend their days laughing about this expedition, and how terrified they had been. They would have been happy knowing that inside Nasrin was another child, a child that would tie them together, mend them, and make them a family again. It would have imbued them with such optimism and gratitude, and they would have thought of their Elias, and wondered if he had eaten, had he slept, was he anxious as to where his parents had disappeared. They might have sat, as they sometimes liked to, by Giant's Elbow, gazing out at the beautiful curves tossed out by the landscape. They might have watched the funfair's caravans leaving the village, and if they had, they would have been pleased by the splashes of colours that lit up the valley, because those were the sorts of things that delighted her, and in delighting her, delighted him. Elias likes to imagine that as they took their last breaths, too weak and sleepy and hypothermic to fully appreciate that there would be no rescue, they watched a swallow swoop beside them and cock its head at them.

Perhaps in the end, Richard too saw Nasrin's apparitions. Her father and her seven-year-old self. Sitting on a rock beside them. Ready to catch her when she fell.

PART III

1

Sabrina woke with a sensation of being pinned down. Her body, carrying with it the memory of the previous day's cramped flight, sought refuge and curved towards the ball of warmth at her side. Spiky hair prickled her chin, and she swiped it away before the unfamiliarity of it startled her. Suddenly she was awake and wide-eyed, staring at Elias lying beside her, still fast asleep.

She had left the window ajar during the night, but aside from the faint murmur of morning traffic, there was silence. It was remarkable, the difference between one morning and the next. Disconcerting to have, only yesterday, woken to the melodic call to prayer from her mother's adhan receiver and the mournful Quran readings by their relatives and friends interrupted now and again by a fresh bout of her mother's wailing in the background.

'Why would you take Elias away too?' her mother had asked her as she packed his belongings into a suitcase. 'How much more will I need to lose before Allah has mercy on me?'

Sabrina had sat down beside her, deflated. She had had to deal with the same questions from Afroz, and she was exhausted from trying to explain. Her mother's forlornness tore at her and she closed her eyes to stem the guilt pouring through her. 'This is the right thing for Eli, Amma.' She took her mother's cold hands and rubbed them. 'Think about it – what did Didi have him call me? He calls me Khala-Amma: there's an Amma in that word, and I have to … I have to step in because she would have wanted me to. I really believe that. I'm not doing it to hurt you, Amma, it's not to punish you. Why would I do that?'

And her mother had sat silently as though she had not heard, and they had sat like that for a long time, listening to the Quran readings until Afroz came to call them for the final prayer.

Today Sabrina awoke only to this moody, recalcitrant dawn.

Elias began to stir but then he fell back to sleeping. Sabrina's head felt leaden with jetlag, but she eased herself out of the bed and made her way to the bathroom, trying to avoid stepping on the creakiest of the floorboards. She heard a small whimper behind her, and then a return to the rhythmic breathing of someone still very much asleep.

She surveyed the kitchen for breakfast. She had little idea what he might want to eat. She opened her fridge and stared into it, half-heartedly stabbing a slab of cheese with her finger. No milk. No eggs. Perhaps they could have breakfast out? She felt strangely relieved by the idea.

She stepped back into the bedroom and was startled to find Elias sitting up in her bed, watching her from behind his heavy eyelashes. She found them almost offensive – they were her sister's lashes, thick and luxurious, but framing someone else's eyes.

They surveyed each other for a moment, their awkwardness almost miscommunicating hostility. She broke the spell. 'Are you hungry?'

He shook his head in that way that could mean yes or no, but basically agreed with the questioner. This Bangladeshi headshake infuriated her. Something he had picked up from Afroz? How had Sabrina not noticed it before?

'Up then! Let's get your face washed and some clothes on you. We can grab something outside.'

A cold December wind swirled around them and the air was icy against their cheeks. She could hear his teeth chattering so she zipped his jacket up to his chin, but she could see that it was too thin to get him through the Manhattan winter. Even though he was

390

wearing wool trousers and lots of layers, the wind seemed to snap right through him.

She remembered reading once that when a child loses someone, it was the physical reality that they miss the most. He had constantly been with his mother – clinging to her arm, to her leg or on her hip. It was no wonder that he felt so cold. The thought brought a lump to her throat. No, these clothes wouldn't do here, not when the snow came.

They ducked into Zabar's and perched on the high stools, her legs crossed, and his swinging just short of the lower rung. They blew on hot porridge laced with honey before slurping it down, too hungry to avoid scalding their tongues. When they finished, she poured a quarter of her tea into a small plastic cup and handed it to him, hoping people wouldn't notice that a four-year-old was being allowed a caffeinated drink.

They sat there in silence while she made notes on her phone of the errands she needed to do before her compassionate leave ended in a few days: find a good pre-school, the shopping, flat-hunting for a larger place; and he, warming his palms against the cup, blew ripples into his tea.

She glanced at him. He was staring out into the street, his mouth pushed out in an unconscious pout. His eyelashes glistened and were unnaturally still. She felt a sudden desperation looking at him – desperate with his grief and hers, and she was frightened. What had she done? How would she cope?

They caught a cab to Fifth Avenue so they could buy him warmer clothes. The cab driver was holding his phone close to his mouth and was quarrelling with someone in her fricative Sylheti mother tongue. Bangladeshi cab drivers never guessed her heritage, and simply mistook her as Indian. Now she listened to this one, she felt a tug in her chest. She wanted to butt in, to declare herself a fellow countryman and enlist his help. Instead she watched Elias stare glumly out of the window at the Fifth Avenue shoppers.

She took him up to the children's section in Saks and picked out a few pairs of brightly coloured cashmere sweaters, some navy dungarees, long-sleeved thermals and a pair of snow boots. The two of them walked into the changing room and stared at each other. She wondered if she should let him undress or if he would need her help. She wished she knew more about children his age. She drew the curtain around them. He stared at her blankly. She put down the clothes and knelt on the floor in front of him. She reached out and began to unzip his coat, then unbuttoned his shirt. Tears fell on her fingers, tears that had silently slipped down his cheeks. She froze, and watched as his chest hiccupped, little eruptions from the ball of sadness he held in there.

Suddenly she was angry – just for a moment – she was enraged, and she wanted to push him away, turn around and run back to the elevator, to her studio apartment, and to work and her friends. He was just a boy. He was not her nephew. Because if he was her nephew, what did that mean? What did that mean, except that her sister was gone? Gone. Then she too succumbed, her tears streaming into her open mouth. She was so afraid. They both cried, he standing facing her, and she on her knees staring at his quaking chest. She took his hand and he sat down on the floor next to her and cried into her neck.

They sat for some time, surrounded by the beige curtain, and their tears seemed to shift their grief, as though it were a burden transferred from one hip to the other. It made it slightly easier to bear for the next short while. They had exchanged their condolences. They had acknowledged their loss. Sister and mother. Left behind, laid out beside her father and Richard, swallowed by a few yards of Beacons soil.

They regarded each other with red eyes and flushed cheeks. She held up the clothes and asked if he wanted to try them. He undressed himself and then asked for her help in putting the clothes on. Barely-there giggles passed between them as they extricated his arms from the shirt he wore, and the dungarees slid back down his waist and legs. They walked back up to the cashiers' desk, their limbs moving more freely, lubricated by the shedding of those tears, and sharing the weight of their bereavement and the shopping basket they carried between them.

Upon receiving news from Afroz that her mother was in hospital, Sabrina briefly considered returning to the Beacons. But the doctor reassured her that her mother had collapsed from shock and that he would be keeping her in hospital a few days for monitoring. 'Amma, shall I come?' she had asked her mother as Afroz held up the phone, but her mother's silence had cut through her. She knew that her return would make no difference – Amma was inconsolable for now, whereas Elias was just a child. Staying in Manhattan and making plans for a future was important in reassuring him that she would not abandon him. So, over the next few days, Sabrina made appointments with several real-estate agents to look at larger apartments.

They woke early for their first viewing, walked up Broadway towards Amsterdam, their breath rising like a mist before them. The avenue was inhabited by delivery vans, early risers and dog walkers. The smell of roast coffee made Sabrina stop at a local deli, and as she ordered, Elias stared at the aisles lined with unfamiliar items.

'That's a knish,' she whispered, following his gaze. He did not respond. He had been silent since his mother's death, but she was not one to force him to talk. Talking, she knew, would not help. Talking would not stem the despair.

They reached the apartment just as the estate agent did. The agent remained standing near the alcove that separated the kitchen from the reception as they looked around. Inane sales banter poured forth from her lips, but Sabrina paid hardly any attention. There were two good double rooms, two bathrooms and a kitchen that was so state of the art, she had to ask which appliance was the microwave. She took Elias and stepped onto the little balcony. Even fifteen floors up, the midday Broadway traffic loudly proclaimed itself. Downtown, in the distance, she could see the Lincoln Center, a vestige of her old life, and then uptown, the brand-new Apple Store. This was to be their first home together. A place to separate them from their grief. It was the promise of relief that they needed.

They moved in a few days later, and the following week was a blur of nanny interviews, school visits, window shopping at furniture stores, then a second round of nanny interviews, and a final enrolment visit at the chosen pre-school where Elias would start in a few weeks. They didn't mind how bone tired they were, for it was a relief to eat out, breakfasting on pastries as they walked to their next appointment, or munching on sandwiches in a cab, and it was a relief to sink into bed, too exhausted to do anything but say goodnight. Those first few nights, their first in separate bedrooms since they had arrived in the City, were difficult for both of them. Sabrina's room was bare and anonymous in the way that rented accommodation is and it made her feel unsettled. Elias's nights were frequented by the demons he managed to suppress during the day. She spent the nights running between her room and his, growing increasingly desperate and tired; but she couldn't ignore his shrieks or moans. She usually woke each morning, curled up at the foot of his bed, her back aching from the awkward position she had slept in.

On the morning she was due back at work, Sabrina ran up and down the unfamiliar hallway in her stockinged feet making sure Elias was eating his breakfast as she prepared for work. She was anxious at the thought of being separated from him for the first time in three weeks.

When the doorbell rang, she opened the door. The new nanny was a tall, blonde woman with huge doll-like eyes.

'Elias! Wow! So nice to see you again! You can call me Mel,' she said, stretching out a finger to stroke his cheek. 'Are we going to have fun today? I think we are!'

As Sabrina left the apartment, she took with her the memory of her nephew's contorted face, a fearful face that said, *Please don't go*! Her stomach felt too unsettled for her morning espresso, and she bought a bottle of water instead, sipping it slowly.

She exited the subway station and joined the hordes walking to Wall Street. When she walked across the road without waiting for the pedestrian lights, she was beeped by a yellow Hummer, the driver shouting, 'No fucking jaywalking, man!' out of the open window. Someone pushed past her, the corner of their handbag jabbing Sabrina in the arm. It all seemed too fast for her this morning – this city, this crowd, this traffic.

When she reached the office, Monty was in the elevator, and Sabrina nodded to him as she stepped in. They listened to someone's fingers tapping loudly on their phone, *click click click*.

'Your sister, Sabrina,' he whispered, leaning into her, 'I'm so sorry. Such a tragedy.'

Sabrina nodded. She readjusted the strap of her handbag on her shoulder.

'Sabrina?'

She looked up at him and wondered how he was so calm and polished, his jacket so pristine, and his shirt collar painfully bright when she was in such turmoil, like a capsizing boat. What was her nephew, with his tiny frightened face, and his small hands tugging at hers ... what was he doing now?

Monty shifted. 'Sabrina? If you need a bit more time ...'

She shook her head. 'No. What I need is this.'

Relief spread across his face, and he nodded vigorously. 'Work, exactly.' He cleared his throat. 'Hey, listen, did you hear about the French transaction tax?'

'Yes ...' she said.

'When you're settled in, let's have a quick chat about it. Fanni mentioned some concern now about the Geever deal, so you guys will probably need to run the numbers again, make sure they work. Listen, Sabrina ...' They exited the elevator together.

'I know it's tough right now, but you're going to get through this. And me? I'm so glad you're back. The desk is going through hell and it needs you right now. I'll see you at the MD initiation this weekend, okay?'

She nodded as he walked away. The MD initiation … a weekend in Las Vegas, far away from Elias, forced into a charade of networking and drinking and brainstorming. And even after that, there would be late nights, early mornings, entire weekends – where would Elias fit into all of this? She stood beside the elevators, gazing through the glass doors beyond, where a familiar world of Bloomberg screens and number-crunchers and the dizzying, all-consuming financial markets pulled at her.

How hard she had worked for it all.

And yet, all it took was a split second to turn away and press the elevator button.

As she made her way home, Sabrina held the phone in her hand, willing for it to ring. Her mother. Ashok. Even Afroz. She didn't care. She felt an urgent need to speak to someone, anyone, who would reassure her. She boarded the 1 train and sat down, the clammy metal of the seat sticking to her calves. She moved over as a woman slid in next to her.

'Jesus, it's freezing out there and then hot enough to burn a polar bear's butt in here!' the woman said.

Sabrina smiled gratefully – someone had seen her and had spoken to her. She turned back to the window, and when she saw her smile in the reflection of the window, something inside of her came undone. She began to cry, hiccupping silently into her chest. She accepted the brown paper napkin the woman handed to her, still smelling of fast food.

'Thank you,' she said after a few moments.

'Ah, nothing. It came free with this coffee.'

'I resigned from my job today.'

'Well, congratulations to you!'

Sabrina nodded. When the train stopped at her subway station, Sabrina did not get off. She rode the metro all the way to the end of the line. Then she crossed the platform at Norwood and boarded the train back to 81st Street.

2

Towards the end of her stay in hospital, Jahanara begged her brother to take her home to Desh. The yearning came with a sudden intensity – she needed to smell the air of Desh, to let her eyes roam over the flat, green fields, and to feel that warm red soil beneath her feet. She clung to the idea with childish delusion.

'Imagine re Masoom,' she told her brother on one of their daily phone calls. 'I will make those gur muri balls that you love so much, remember? We will eat those sweet rice balls together again, have the treacle stick to our teeth.'

And her brother sighed sadly. 'Oh, re Afa.'

'You make sure there are a good few jars of the date palm jaggery in the kitchen,' she continued, for it was soothing to plan as though they were children again, as though the tragedy of her loss could be averted that way.

'Afa,' Masoom said. 'Why do you insist on this, ha? Let Afroz stay and look after you there. You will have better healthcare, you will be better there.'

'Afroz?' Jahanara shrank back into herself. 'Oh, no no no.'

The day she returned from the hospital, Jahanara sat slumped on a chair in the kitchen. It was her own kitchen, but it no longer resembled it. There was dust on everything she touched, even beneath her feet as she walked about the house. She sat there for a long time, afraid of the dirt and this place that had once been her home. She waited for Afroz to finish her Zuhr prayers and come downstairs. Jahanara herself had not prayed since the day they found Nasrin.

She looked out onto the patio, where the day disregarded her mourning with its cascading sunshine. The blue sky knew no sorrow. But at least if she looked outside, she could avoid the shock of all that waited for her in the house: Naju's phone on the mantelpiece, the books on the shelves that Naju had spent her girlhood reading, the carpet beneath her feet which Naju had christened thirty-three years ago, defecating on it a week after its fitting. All these things remained, but her baby was lying up on those hills buried beside her husband and her father.

It occurred to Jahanara that those hills resounded with her life's complaints. It also occurred to her that her yearnings had always been misplaced. Where she had once been rooted with sorrow on this foreign soil, and yearned for one daughter, who was shaath shomudhro paare, living seven seas away, she now wept for another. Oh, her Naju. Her sweet, kind, always unselfish Naju. This land no longer gave solace to Jahanara – indeed it was sick of her mourning; the limits of its patience had been reached, and it refused to reclaim her. She understood that she had to move on. She understood that the punishment for her sins was to feel perpetually displaced.

To think that the last time she had seen her daughter, Jahanara had been afraid: terror had made her a monster, had pushed her love out of reach. What had she been so frightened of? What was it that she still feared? She thought of how her daughter had looked that night; her hair had come free of its clasp and fallen around her face in wild disarray; the edge of her saree had fallen from her shoulder, trailed about her feet, making her trip, her gait unbalanced as she paced about. But it had been the wild expression in her eyes, the high-pitched tilt of her voice which had frightened Jahanara.

Her darling, sweet daughter, who had hidden in the folds of her saree when shyness overcame her, who had cried out, 'Amma' in the early hours when she woke from a nightmare, how beautiful she had always been, so beautiful that Jahanara had drawn a black dot of kajal on her temple to protect her even from her mother's nozor! But something had become dislodged in Naju that evening – there had been a manic intensity in the way she had rummaged through her mother's possessions and found the secret that Jahanara had guarded with her life – the secret her husband had guarded even in death. And the fear of being discovered had made Jahanara run out of the house. Run, run, run, as she should have done when her father made her board a train to Rangamati all those decades ago to a house so lonely, so bleak, that without the random chatter of her myna bird, she would surely have gone mad; run, as she should have run when her brother, Masoom, arrived in Rangamati with his new bride to adopt her newborn child; run, as she should have run when her marriage was arranged to a man who wanted to travel the seven seas, far away from the people and the land she had been born to. She had run out of that house, away from her shame: *Haven't I suffered enough?* she had asked the street lamps, her saree tripping her sandalled feet – *haven't I suffered enough watching my child be raised by that vicious sister-in-law?* She had muttered these questions as she ran. Her motherhood had been reduced to a few embraces stolen in the cover of night, a friendship in the guise of an aunt and niece destined only to meet on summer holidays. And then to stand by as her daughter was forced into a marriage she did not want.

That was how Dorothy had found her, chattering to herself as she walked beneath the lengthening shadows of the beech trees, her saree wrapped around her against the chilly Beacons air. Dorothy had had enough of the noisy crowd at the party and was hobbling home with the aid of her stick when she saw Jahanara's lonely figure out on the path that led to Pen y Fan. She called out to her friend, who turned and walked slowly back to her.

'I don't understand his justice,' Jahanara said to Dorothy, when she reached her. Dorothy coaxed her into her home with the promise of tea. 'He is not just, He is not all-forgiving,' Jahanara told her, as Dorothy gently pushed her into a chair near the radiator.

'Afroz coming, Afroz staying, it made me so happy,' she said as Dorothy tried to call the Peacock.

'She's a lovely woman, your Afroz,' Dorothy agreed as she put the phone down. 'There's no one answering the phone.'

'I thought maybe Allah had finally forgiven me, I thought He was finally giving me my chance, at last. All those moments lost, when she was young. I thought now's my chance. I thought it was justice, you know? Nyay?'

Dorothy frowned at the unfamiliar word before saying, 'It's awful when your children go off. I know it.' She groaned as she sat down beside Jahanara. 'They have lives of their own, but our lives are never coming back, are they? They don't realise how much of ours they take with them – they split us open when they're born and then halve us again when they leave. Don't leave us with much, do they? Mothers without their children, we're forever incomplete, aren't we?' She smiled ruefully. 'Afroz staying has been good for you, I know. Is she going back? Is that why you're upset?'

Jahanara wished she could share her turmoil with Dorothy, wished she did not need to hide behind cryptic sentences. But the covenant she had made with her parents and God was to keep the secret bolted within her in exchange for avoiding social disgrace and exile. She had abided by this pact for so many years that she no longer knew how to speak of it. But God had not kept his side, for the secret was out anyway – Mustafa knew and now her honour, Sham's honour, her family honour was ruined. The sacrifices of the last four decades had all been for nothing, for there was no divine justice behind her suffering after all: justice had been an illusion.

But of course, God had other plans. By the time Dorothy got through to the Peacock, Nasrin and Richard had been missing for over an hour.

Exposing her had not been enough. Jahanara's punishment was

not over. God may have returned one first-born to her, but now reached out to snatch the other away. Soker bodla soke, an eye for an eye, a daughter for a daughter.

Jahanara heard Afroz coming down the stairs. Instinctively, her frail shoulders drew inwards and her chin squeezed into her chest. Afroz frightened Jahanara now, caught up as she was in her tangled web of maternal yearning, regret and fear.

She watched Afroz walk to the kitchen sink, look out of the window. 'Fufu, your plants, I haven't looked after them well.' Afroz's voice quivered with trepidation.

'I want to go back to Desh, Afi,' Jahanara said.

Afroz walked slowly to the mantelpiece, considering this. 'I know. Fufu,' she said, 'I'm a curse to this family, ekta bodhwa.'

Jahanara peered out at the grown woman leaning against the mantelpiece in distraught submission but saw only the little girl the woman had been; a little girl with eyes that hungrily sought out a smile. She struggled out of her chair and reached up to Afroz, took her face in her hands, looked into the eyes that were reflections of her own.

'When your mother was pregnant with you,' she whispered to her, rubbing her nose against Afroz's, 'the moths, they went crazy.'

Afroz frowned. 'You knew my mother?'

'They fluttered all over her swollen belly.'

'Fufu?'

'And the moths loved you – do you know why?'

'Darao, Fufu, are you saying you knew my mother?'

'Because you are dear to Allah.'

'But Fufu!'

Jahanara looked into these eyes that she loved so well. She wished she had learned the language of truth – but all those years ago, they had done jadootona on her, bewitched her tongue with black magic so it would never again be able to speak the words to tell this particular truth – to call a niece, a daughter, to call the act of zina – of fornication outside of marriage – the preying on a mere child by a middle-aged man in a position of power. She tried: she opened her mouth and uttered a sound. But the black jadootona held firm and reminded her that she would never again utter those first and last words she had said to the baby moments after she delivered her, *ami thumar ma, I am your mother*. So, instead she hugged Afroz tight and said, 'You will never think of yourself in that horrible way, bucchos? You are no curse. You are beloved to the moths. You are Allah's dear one.'

'You know—'

'Those moths, they loved you.'

Jahanara dropped her hands to her side and hobbled up the stairs. It was time to take her place on her prayer mat. Even if she did not understand his ways, she was a woman of faith. *Give in to Allah's plans*, she told herself. *Submit.*

3

The day after Sabrina took Elias away, only three days after his parents' death, Afroz walked silently down the stairs and stood in front of the mantelpiece. It was an altar to those that had left – Shamsur's glasses, his pint glass with the picture of the cobra; a set of knotted Apple earphones Sabrina had left behind; her aunt's green jade thasbih, which she kept forgetting to take with her to the hospital; and Nasrin's phone, long drained of battery. She picked up a block of yellow Lego belonging to Elias and clutched it to her chest, recalling their time spent together in this house – the afternoon chai, the companionable prayers, the siestas, the massages, and the adda.

When the phone began to trill, Afroz jumped. She blinked, as though unable to recognise the sound. Finally, she picked it up.

'Hello?'

'Humayun?' she asked, surprised. She had not heard from him since he had called to update her on Munni.

'Yes. We just heard the news about Naju!' She had never heard this urgency in his voice.

'I meant to call – but everything … there was so much to do.'

'Ish, Afi … How? How has this happened?'

The sincerity in his voice made Afroz want to weep. 'I don't know,' she croaked.

'Inna lillahi wa inna ilayhi raji'un,' Humayun said, and the familiar prayer sent the kitchen in a spin. We belong to God and to Him we shall return. Afroz's knees gave way, and she sat down on the cold floor. 'Afi? Afroz, please say something? Please? You – all of you, are in our prayers.' She began to cry then, all the tears she had not allowed herself before now, spilled out of her. 'Afi, you of all people you will trust in Allah. You will be brave?'

For some minutes, Humayun reminded her in a voice uncharacteristically gentle that life is a test for what comes after, and gradually Afroz's tears abated. She was conscious of the terror lurking behind his voice and now tried to give the conversation some semblance of normality. 'How is Ammi?' she asked through force of habit.

'Fine. Afi, how is your little nephew? Elias?'

Afroz was silent for a moment.

'Afi?'

'She took him.'

'She? Who?'

Afroz remembered how Sabrina had thrown her nephew's clothes into a small suitcase that lay open on the bed as Afroz followed her round the room, grey-faced with shock, entreating her, 'Don't take him away, let him be here, he needs to be here.'

'This is exactly where he does NOT need to be,' Sabrina had said, 'he needs to be with me.'

Afroz had watched her nephew napping on the bed next to his suitcase. He had been sleeping a lot over the last three days – a consequence of his shock, the doctor had reassured them. Afroz stared at his button nose and at his curly hair. She blinked rapidly and took a step into the room.

'Let him stay, Sabrina.' She was aware of the pleading in her voice.

Sabrina turned to her. 'You were supposed to look after her,' she had said and there was not the usual hatred and rage, but a look of dismay. Afroz had been unable to respond.

'Afi? Are you there?' Humayun asked now. 'Who took him?'

'Sibby took him,' she cried.

'Why would she do that?'

'Because it was my fault – because I promised that I would look after Naju, and I didn't.'

'Afi, how can it be your fault?' Humayun said, sounding flustered. 'Where is your Fufu? Afi?'

'Fufu's in hospital. She collapsed yesterday, after Sabrina and Elias left.'

'Ish re. Gordish ta bujo!'

Afroz had sat in the hospital beside her sedated aunt and stared at the spotless floor, letting Sabrina's words spread through her like ink on blotting paper.

'You promised,' Sabrina had said. 'You promised she'd be okay.'

Now, Humayun asked her: 'Afi, do you want me to come?'

'She is okay – they are keeping her in for observation.'

'Na – I mean for you.'

'I'm fine,' she whispered. 'Tik asi, I'm fine.'

Each morning, after Fajr namaz, Afroz made herself tea which sat untouched in front of her as she stared vacantly out into the garden where rows of carrots and kale waited to be picked. By the shed, her father's green wellies stood on a cracked slab, the sunlight catching the silver of a spider web that dangled between them. As the hours wore on, the silence grew louder, holding her more captive inside her grief. She knew she should dust and hoover so that Fufu could return to a clean house, but Afroz did nothing because houses, like humans, could be demolished by death, becoming nothing more than a carcass after the soul has left. And the soul of this home, decimated by two deaths so shortly after one another, had departed.

Sometimes a phone call or the chime of the doorbell alarmed her out of her reveries. The visits were usually from Lindsay or Dorothy, checking to see she was all right. The calls were usually from Humayun, or his mother, who now called her every day. One afternoon, at five o'clock, the doorbell chimed. It was Dorothy, holding a plate of scones.

'I don't have any cream,' Dorothy said as she stepped in, her slippers making a soft flapping sound as she hobbled down the corridor. 'But I do have a bit of mulberry jam.'

Each morning, Afroz sat and waited for the clock hands to move around to nine o'clock before she got into her father's Volvo and drove the seventeen miles to the hospital, where Jahanara was being kept under observation. At the hospital, there were times that Afroz found a person or two standing at the foot of her aunt's bed, entreating Jahanara to be strong. Afroz recognised these visitors from the funeral, the women wiping away tears as they held Fufu's hand and the men looking awkward in the face of this excessive display of emotion.

Afroz remembered the looks of horror on the faces of Richard's family at the funeral. They had sat frozen in their grief like porcelain statues, affronted by the hysterical grief of the Bangladeshis.

Afroz herself had been unable to cry. She was still unable to cry, at least for Nasrin. She had cried for the others: for Elias, for Jahanara, even for Richard whom she barely knew. But when she thought of Nasrin, she thought of that last morning in the kitchen when she had unknowingly given her sister the extra dosage of medication, and she felt an icy dread paralyse her, and she feared her heart would stop beating if she didn't think of something else.

Mostly though, Afroz was alone in the hospital with her aunt. She sat on the chair next to the bed, remaining there for the full three hours of visiting time before lunch, and bravely ignoring the fear on Jahanara's face and the determined way she kept her face averted from Afroz.

'Fufu,' Afroz had said one afternoon. She had timidly made attempts at conversation each time she visited, but she was unused to the realm of monstrous grief which Jahanara inhabited, and to the older woman's frostiness. 'Fufu, Baba wanted to speak with you.'

She saw her aunt's head move slightly. 'Should I call him? Will you speak to your brother?'

Her aunt's eyes had flickered to Afroz's hands holding the phone. Afroz dialled Baba's number and handed the receiver over to her aunt.

She heard Baba say 'Afa?' repeatedly.

But her Fufu simply held the phone to her ear. Afroz watched Jahanara's breaths gather in her chest, and then with a ferocious clarity she called out to her brother, 'Bhai!' and began to cry. But these tears were quiet and different to the hysteria of before. 'I want to come home, Bhai.'

Afroz, misunderstanding Jahanara's request, felt a certain relief settle over her. Things would slowly return to normal when her aunt was back in the house. They would gradually adapt and maybe convince Sabrina to let Elias return. Afroz slipped into the car and drove back comforted by these thoughts.

The Peacock wore the cloak of mourning, its beautiful new sign and gleaming interior a memorial to Nasrin. A memorial that Nasrin had constructed for herself just before running up into those mountains, almost as though she had a premonition of her own death. Every piece of furniture and accessory came with a story of Nasrin. Nasrin holding up strips of curtain fabric, all shades of ivory which were indistinguishable to Afroz. The cost had been all that Afroz had been able to think about at the time. She wished that she had not. She wished that she had enjoyed it instead.

Nonetheless that Sunday, as Afroz did the books with Lindsay, she felt a certain trepidation. She wished Riaz was still with them, to help her as he always had.

'At least the fine's been paid,' Lindsay said as she scrolled through the business account balance depleted by a recent twenty-thousand-pound payment. 'How much did you say we owe for all the work?'

'Thirty-four thousand, four hundred and ninety, including the credit card bill,' Afroz said.

'Yeh.' Lindsay was silent a moment, contemplating the numbers in front of her. She looked up at Afroz. 'We can just ask the estate solicitors, you know, make them aware that Nasrin was going to pay for it—'

'No!' Afroz exclaimed. She would not take money from her orphaned nephew.

'Then I guess we have to ask if we can pay for it in instalments.'

'I don't even know who all the contractors are – Riaz dealt with the builders and the furniture companies.'

'Look,' Lindsay said, snapping shut the laptop. 'Don't worry about that, if the money's important to them, and it always is, they'll come looking for you.' She smiled at her friend. 'We'll manage, Afroz. You can pay me at the end of the month instead of weekly. Where the hell do you think Riaz has gone? He's still not answering my calls.'

'I haven't spoken to him since they found …'

'He didn't even come for the funeral.'

'You know, I thought I saw him? I thought I saw him, but when I looked for him later, he was gone.'

The other staff members, stunned by the news of Nasrin's death and Riaz's sudden disappearance, had become distressed and unco-operative. Over the next fortnight, Afroz felt the Peacock begin to overwhelm her. On Saturday evening, she entered the staff house, looking for Junaid, only to overhear him discussing a new job on his phone. She retreated. How could she blame him? She was in a condemned building, trying to hold it together.

'Afroz,' Lindsay said, holding up the frying pan Afroz had been stirring. 'Did I see you just put ground almond in this? The customer said she had a nut allergy, remember? Jesus! You could have killed her!' Afroz watched her friend throw the contents of the frying pan into the bin and begin the curry again. 'Why don't you go and take your break? I've got it covered.'

Afroz walked back to the house, feeling shame burn through her. What had made her think she could run a restaurant? She was just a naive, unworldly housewife with no business acumen whatsoever. She had been lulled into false reassurance by the kindness of others.

So, when she opened the letter from the bank a few days later, she already had a sense of foreboding.

There it was in black print, the evidence that there was still further misfortune to be found in her life. It was a final notice demanding that the fine for the Peacock's employment of an illegal immigrant be paid immediately.

Which meant that the twenty-thousand-pound fine, which she thought Riaz had paid, had in fact not been transferred. That twenty thousand pounds had gone into Riaz's account.

The money had gone wherever Riaz had. Afroz had forgotten that Nasrin had transferred money to Riaz on the night of the party, but in any case, it had never occurred to Afroz that it would be such a hefty sum. At most, she believed, it would be a few weeks' wages.

She sat down on the floor and leaned against the cushioned leather wall of the bar and read the letter again, but her mind remained blank.

Never mind, she thought to herself, standing up. For it was almost time for Maghrib namaz. Fufu would be home soon, and they would start over. There would be a way.

When she first told Lindsay about her plan, Lindsay had been unenthused. 'I think it's a bad idea. What are you going to do? Confront him? Better to get the police involved.'

'Police?' Afroz asked, bristling. 'Why? He is not a thief!'

Her friend shrugged, sadly. 'I know.' Since the reminder bills had started arriving Lindsay had been resigned to their fate. She had given up before the fight had even started. 'It's like this place is cursed,' she'd told Afroz after they'd done the numbers together and realised that the Peacock was on the verge of bankruptcy.

But Afroz was determined and set off to navigate the great spaghetti junction of Birmingham by herself. 'Keep left,' the man on her GPS told her, and she took the left turn, before remembering that keeping left and turning left meant two different things. The GPS rerouted and added an extra seven miles and twenty-five minutes to her journey. 'Ya Allah!' she cried over the crackle of the West Midlands radio station. But she couldn't watch any more final warning bills burn a hole on the doormat without trying something. This was her something. She had phoned nearly a dozen of her Fufu's relatives and friends in the Birmingham area before finding the new address where Riaz's parents had moved into.

Seated at Riaz's parents' house, Afroz noticed the black lines on his mother's fingers as she handed her a cup of tea. She noticed the grime on the windowsill, the clattering sound that Riaz's father's rickety chair made each time the old man coughed, a cough that was dangerously deep and phlegmy. She sat and she noticed, and as she drank the tea, she swallowed mouthfuls of her own disappointment. There was no money to be found here.

When Riaz returned home, armed with a blue carrier bag of groceries, he simply nodded at her. As though he had expected her. They walked together towards the main road, passing a compound with a petrol station that had been turned into a Bengali fish bazaar.

'No coffee shops around here,' Riaz said. 'Do you mind if we go into a pub?' He saw her hesitate. 'They do coffee in there, too.'

She followed him inside. Immediately the sour stench of beer assaulted her, and she took a few moments to adjust to the darkness, sliding into a booth as Riaz went to the bar.

She ignored the pint of beer he placed in front of himself and concentrated on stirring sugar into the cup of lukewarm coffee he placed in front of her.

'I'm sorry,' Riaz said.

His voice was clear, his words focused, but in them there was little apology that she could detect. She looked at the red at the edges of his eyes. He had lost so much weight that he looked like a teenage boy. She realised, with a pang, that a man couldn't apologise when he was this lost in his grief and wretchedness. Nasrin's death had plunged him far, far away.

Most of the money had gone to his father's creditors, he told Afroz, in the same clear voice, stripped of emotion. The night he had driven away, his father had been hospitalised. Beaten within an inch of his life outside the bookies. Riaz had used much of the remainder to pay a year's rent in advance on this new place to ensure his father would not gamble it away.

'I still have four grand left, which I'll wire back to you. The Peacock was everything to me, you know?' Riaz said, staring at his empty pint glass. 'It's the only place I've ever wanted to be. The only place. And now, look what I've done. I've destroyed it, right, Afa?' He didn't wait for her to answer. 'She said you'd transferred it, like as an advance,' he said. He saw the look on Afroz's face and shook his head. 'I was so fucking stupid; I didn't stop to think. I'll pay it back, every fucking penny. With interest.'

She looked at him, feeling discomfort at the base of her throat. 'When will you come back?' she asked him, for suddenly Afroz would do anything for Riaz to return to the Peacock. With him and Lindsay by her side, she was sure she could make it work.

He shook his head, staring at her as though she had said a devil thing. 'No way. Fuck, no way.' He looked down at his hands. 'She'd be everywhere.' He looked up and she wondered if he saw her everywhere here. He seemed to have read her mind. 'No,' he said shaking his head, 'she's nowhere in this scum of a place.'

They sat for some time in silence. Then he looked up. 'I have to stay here, in this fucked-up place, at least for now.' He took a long gulp of his beer. 'My dad, he'd be back at the bookies first chance he got, see? So I've got to stay, to keep him away from there. My family, they need me around.'

She looked up at him, trying her best to suppress the wave of pity bursting out of her. She nodded.

'Sorry, Afa,' he said, real emotion suddenly filling his voice. 'I promise I'll pay it back.'

She didn't tell him that it would be too late.

After her aunt announced she would be returning to Desh, the house was put up for sale, and Afroz decided she would move into Riaz's old room in the staff cottage. Aside from Lindsay and Junaid, the remainder of the staff had all left, and Afroz would have the place to herself. She began to clear it out but left the living room as a homage to the recent past: the carom board, its pieces still powdered from the last game, remained in the centre of the room; the poster of Michael Jackson and his zombies from the 'Thriller' video still took up the bulk of the main wall; and Riaz's punchbag and gloves hung from the corner by the window. She walked around these as though walking through a graveyard, picking her way among tombstones.

Since she had closed the restaurant a few weeks ago, she had been busy packing. She had spent days in her aunt's house boxing up her things for shipping to Sylhet with her. Then Lindsay had driven with her to Islington, where the two of them packed up Nasrin and Richard's things, some for shipping to Elias and others for storage. She walked through Nasrin's home, not recognising her in the minimalist furnishing – the pristine white modular sofa and the tiny metal coffee tables – until she opened her sister's cupboards and found her lavish silk sarees and kurthas, still smelling of Nasrin's perfume mixed with mothballs. She stepped into it, pressed the fabric to her face, and sat there until she heard Lindsay calling. She crawled out, smoothed her kameez and began to pack the silks into a box. She put paper between the folds, and vacuum packed each bag. She would make sure they stayed pristine, for the future generations. Elias would one day marry. Elias would one day have daughters. Until then, Afroz would play her role of steward and custodian – not only of these tussar silks, but also of the memory of the woman who had worn them.

The next day she walked towards the path that led up to Pen y Fan. She no longer ran; she found she did not possess the energy nor the inclination. She had seen Tom, once or twice, running past her. Nasrin and Richard's deaths seemed to have made her easy relationships – with Tom, with Mr Ruane, even Dorothy – tremendously difficult. Reflected in the pity on their faces she saw only the image of her own fragility.

She passed her aunt's house, dark and abandoned except for the one light in her bedroom. It was no surprise that Fufu was absconding, escaping this place that was responsible for snatching away her first-born, to find refuge in a place where the memories were easier to bear.

Afroz called Sylhet every evening and Baba gave her updates on his preparations for his sister's return. Nirashapur was excited at the prospect of her arrival: she was the absentee daughter-in-law, the wife of their once beloved Sham Bhai. There were many there who had lost children or spouses, and Afroz was sure that in their company, Fufu would find some consolation. Mustafa had already taken up residence at the guesthouse across the courtyard from the main house, and was busy with the workmen, ensuring the house's smooth running for her return. One afternoon, Baba reported to her that Humayun and his mother had also made the trip to Nirashapur, bearing all manner of rice and spices to replenish the larder. Humayun, who continued to call Afroz every day, seemed to have struggled out of the old shell of their marriage, emerging resplendent, a white knight showing a different sort of promise.

As she walked up the uneven path, Afroz tried to imagine her aunt in Sylhet. Would it still feel like home or would she be disappointed that the old Desh had lost its childlike innocence and matured in a way that did not accord with her expectations?

Afroz was disappointed at being abandoned – disappointed too that Fufu was giving up on the Beacons after decades of learning to love its gentle hills and drizzle, of assimilating with the ways of its people, even bringing up her children in their ways. But she understood that Fufu had always perceived this as an exile and that creating new bonds with her adopted country had always been a struggle. She prayed Desh gave Fufu the consolation she needed at this moment.

She reached the summit and halted beside the obelisk of Tommy Jones. Her aunt had never liked them to be near it – superstitious about attracting the intense grief sure to be rife in a memorial erected for the loss of a child. Afroz, reaching out to touch it, felt a numinous energy in the rough stone edges. She closed her eyes and pressed her cheek against it, the eerie parallel between her sister's death and this ancient tragedy made her heart swell with a renewed sense of grief.

Retracing her steps back into town, she considered the only offer she had received on the Peacock. Accepting it would mean she could settle the debts, pay Lindsay her last few weeks of salary and take away a sizeable amount of money. She could return to Desh with Fufu and set up a business in Sylhet with Baba's help. Perhaps even with Humayun's support. Humayun, rather than uttering talaq three times and ridding himself of her, seemed instead compellingly committed to their marriage. During their call the night before, when she had confessed that she had no appetite for dinner, Humayun had responded with simple words that touched her more than any he had spoken before: 'If you go hungry, then I will too. Your decision.'

The Peacock came into view as she turned into the village square. It saddened her that Elias would not grow up loving the sight of this property exuding its own peculiar brand of dignity, like a weary veteran that had gallantly survived a war.

She decided she would make one more attempt at survival. She would call Sabrina and ask her for help, if for no other reason than to perform her self-imposed role of caretaker and safeguard this ashram and its memories for Elias. Only if she failed would she accept the offer.

The night before her aunt was due to fly out, Afroz sat with Dorothy and Lindsay at the kitchen table. They had come to say their good-byes. Her aunt, vacant and tired, had gone to bed, and the three of them sat silently, immersed in their own thoughts.

Someone rapped on the patio doors, and looking up, they saw Junaid was standing outside, his face in shadow. As Afroz let him in, it occurred to her that this would have been any Thursday evening only a month ago. These people and this setting. But everything had changed.

'Afa,' Junaid said. 'I've got to move on; Mum's a bit sick so I've got something nearer London.'

Afroz nodded, pouring Junaid some tea.

'Keep in touch with Riaz, won't you?' she said. 'Make sure that he's okay?'

Junaid nodded.

'You've still got us,' Dorothy said suddenly. She spoke so rarely that they stared at her. 'We're here for you.'

Afroz felt the tears spring to her eyes, the hiccups skip out of her chest. She excused herself and went and sat on the stairs in the hallway.

'I didn't mean to make her upset,' she heard Dorothy say. 'I only meant, well, that we're here for her, aren't we?'

But no one replied. The sound of Afroz crying spread through the house, like the sea slapping the shore on an otherwise quiet night.

Upstairs, huddled against the radiator, on her prayer mat with suit-cases and boxes all about her, Jahanara listened to Afroz cry. She had spread Nasrin's hand fan in front of her and her fingers traced the coloured shital. The soft noises stirred in her the old urge to go to Afroz, to wipe away the tears with her fingers, to kiss away the pain with her lips pressed upon the child's head. The old urge stirred, but a newer fear vanquished it. And so, Jahanara listened and she prayed. Outside, flecks of white peppered the air. Jahanara stood and went to the window, her lips still moving. The flecks of white flew towards her haphazardly, glowing bright before melting on the windowpane. She watched, and she recited Surah ar-Rahman:

The sun and the moon move in celestial harmony
and the stars and trees all prostrate themselves,
and He has raised up the heaven and established the balance
that you may not transgress within the balance
and establish equability in justice and do not disturb the
balance.

One Summer Holiday

Sabrina is languishing in the afternoon heat. She sits on Afroz's knee, swaying from side to side. Afroz, who is only six years older than Sabrina, is still a child herself. Their bony legs swing together as Sabrina interlocks her fingers with Afroz's and examines them, taking in the differences, and also the similarities. Her fondness for her cousin Afroz is a source of entertainment for all the family.

'Afi!' Afroz's mother calls each morning. 'Your little puthol, your dolly, Sabrina is up and looking for you!'

'Afi, hurry home after your class, you know Sibby won't eat without you!'

'Afi, your puthol won't sleep until you recite Kajla Didi to her again!'

Around them, the house buzzes with activity: the servants scamper about, cleaning and cooking. There are raised voices in the garden where the workmen are erecting the marquee for the evening's party. In the far corner of the living room, Nasrin is reclined on the sofa, reading. Out on the veranda, the parents are taking their mid-morning tea and pastries. Sabrina's uncle is entertaining his sister with stories of the lemta fokir, the naked saint, who has been visiting the village house for alms this summer. He interrupts himself to throw instructions out to the workmen.

'Afi,' Sabrina says, bouncing with sudden impatience. 'Who is the lemta fokir?'

'He is a religious man.'

'But why doesn't he wear clothes?'

'Because he is so mad with love for Allah-ji, he has forgotten everything. Like food and clothes. Even underwear!' Afroz giggles. 'His hair and his beard touch the ground. There are ants and creepy-crawlies in his beard!'

Sabrina giggles at the thought, simultaneously scared and thrilled.

'Afi,' says Sabrina, bored of the fokir. 'Tell me a story.'

'Accha.'

'The one about the Jalal shab.'

'Shah Jalal's great teacher chose Shah Jalal as his favourite student. He said he would give him a great gift.'

'I love gifts!'

'I love gifts too.' Afroz kisses Sabrina's cheek. 'So, Shah Jalal's great teacher gave him a handful of soil.' Afroz takes Sabrina's tiny palm and presses down on it, closing the little girl's fingers around the imaginary sand. 'And his great teacher told him to wander the earth and to search for the land that has the exact matching colour of this soil.'

'And he found it here.'

'And he came to Sylhet, and he found the Sylhet soil was as golden as the soil in his hand. So, he spent the rest of his life here, in Sylhet, that's why it's known as Jalalabad, to spread the word of Islam.'

'But,' says Sabrina, 'why didn't he choose the Beacons?'

Afroz laughs, hugs Sabrina, her fingers finding tickle spots in the child's knees. 'Because he didn't go that far.'

'Where did he come from?'

'Yemen.'

'Are the Beacons far?'

'Very.'

'So why do we live so far from you?'

Afroz falls silent and shrugs. Sabrina watches her aunt and uncle, their profiles just visible on the veranda where they laugh with her Amma and Abba.

'Why,' Sabrina asks, turning to her cousin, 'did Shah Jalal's great teacher send him so far away? I mean, if he was his favourite?'

'Afi,' Nasrin calls out, throwing down her book, 'look, Taseen Bhai is here!'

Sabrina runs for her trainers as her cousin greets her best friend and neighbour, Taseen. In his hands he swings his cricket bat and a red ball.

'Sibby,' Taseen calls out to her, 'ready for some cricket?'

'Yes!' Sabrina squeals, as Afroz pulls the mess of her hair into a ponytail. 'Didi! Come quickly, Taseen Bhai is taking us to the matt for kirket!'

'Cricket!' corrects Afroz.

'Kirket!' scolds Sabrina. 'That's exactly what I said!'

They run out over the sleepy Baghbari Road, past the grey mass of the ugly orphanage building, and onto the patch of ground that the local children use for their games. Taseen sets up the game, and Sabrina is indulged with free hits and runs as the other children groan with displeasure. The sun steadily sinks into the horizon, freeing up their heads from the day's heat and colouring the reddish soil a deep sunset orange in its own image. It is an afternoon that is as blissful as those that have come before it.

On his turn to bat, Taseen hits the ball hard towards the orphanage building, and they all look into the cantaloupe-coloured sky to watch its progress. It comes down slow and then fast, and rolls into the orphanage's empty courtyard. Sabrina begins to run towards it, buoyed by the shouting behind her. 'Get it, Sibby, go get it!'

She comes to a stop when she turns into the courtyard, for there is something frightening in the moss-ridden furriness of the bricks and the barreness of the trees. She hears someone humming and looks about the courtyard. The courtyard is empty, though the swaying of the branches of the peepal trees and the shivering of its leaves make the courtyard seem inhabited. She braces herself and walks towards the ball, which has come to a stop behind a papaya tree. She crouches beneath the poking branches and reaches for it, when she hears the humming stop.

'Ey,' a voice says, 'look here.'

Sabrina looks up and stands slowly. She peeks through the window. A man with a chequered shirt and a green lungi lies on his bed. He gently reaches down and slides the green cotton up his legs. Sabrina wills herself to move, but suddenly she is rooted to that spot. The man puts one hand out to his nakedness and reaches the other towards Sabrina.

'Look, I said!'

Sabrina stands on tippy-toe, willing herself to move. The man's nakedness has paralysed her. She squeezes her eyes shut and then opens them again. There is something about the man's expression that makes her search his face – something about the angle in which he tugs at himself that makes Sabrina queasy. Sabrina covers her ears, shuts her eyes, but still she hears the man's urgent whispers, 'Look, ekhane dekh!'

Sabrina opens her mouth to scream, but a hand clamps firmly over it.

She struggles but the hand and the arm attached to it drag her away from the window, the papaya tree scratching her arms and legs on the way. Then the hand releases her, and she turns to find Afroz's eyes wide with fear. Afroz drags Sabrina out of the courtyard.

'Afi, that man!' Sabrina says, panting, her chest constricted with terror.

'No, we can't go back there!' Afroz holds her back.

'Afi, I want to tell Abba!'

'We can't, Sibby, listen to me!'

'We have to tell Amma and Abba!' Sabrina says, beginning to cry. Hot tears of anger that make her more flustered. 'Horrible, chi chi man!'

'No, Sibby, listen, promise me! We can't tell anyone? Do you understand? We can't tell anyone! It's not for us to see – not for us to say!'

Sabrina is furious. 'Why?' she asks. 'Why not?'

'Sibby, you don't understand how to live here, that's all. You can't talk about it. Just promise me? There are things you don't understand!'

'I'm going to tell!'

'Sibby, you will not! You will not, promise me!'

'Afi, let me go!'

Sabrina runs. Not towards the courtyard but onto the road opposite. She is angry at Afroz but she doesn't know why. She also knows that she will not tell Amma or Abba, because there is a fear in Afroz's face that commands her not to. Afroz's terror has overshadowed her own. This realisation makes Sabrina angrier. She does not see the car until it is before her.

It is white, and huge, and it is hurtling towards Sabrina. Sabrina is not afraid, but she is confused. Everyone is screaming at her. She is unable to move, perplexed as to which way to go. Suddenly she sees her darling Afroz running towards her and Sabrina is relieved. She holds up her arms, smiling. Afroz picks her up and throws her to the side.

Afterwards, Sabrina sits with Nasrin on the stairs with a plaster on her knee.

'Didi,' Sabrina tells her sister, her voice small and solemn. 'Silly, naughty Afi, she dropped me!'

'Chup! You're the one that is silly,' Nasrin chides, 'Afi didn't drop you, she saved you.'

The house is silent. The party has been cancelled and the servants move about listlessly. No one smiles. No one talks aloud, only in low voices. And when she tries to coax a story out of the houseboy, Sabrina is shouted at by her mother. Only her father is kind to her. He takes her for a walk and buys her an ice, even though it is almost bedtime. Sabrina tells her father, 'Abba, Amma will shout!'

'Your Afi has been badly hurt,' he tells her kindly. 'So Amma is looking after her. Amma won't shout.'

'I want to sleep with Afi, I want her to tell me about Kajla Didi.'

'Not today, re futh.'

Still, Sabrina tries. But no one will let her sleep next to Afroz.

'You will hurt her leg,' Amma scolds her. 'Her leg is broken, do you understand?' Amma tells her this, as though Sabrina is the one to blame. Sabrina lies down next to Nasrin, but when she thinks everyone is asleep, she slips out to look for Afroz. She wants to hear Afroz recite the Kajla Didi poem: *baansh bagaaner mathar opor chand utherche oi, Ma go amar sholok bola Kajla didi koi?* The moon has risen above the bamboo grove, where did my Kajla Didi go? It is a poem that makes Sabrina feel both reassured by the sisterhood of Afroz and Nasrin, and also anxious about its loss. She wants to ask Afroz, would Kajla Didi ever come back? She wants to ask Afroz about the man in the orphanage. Why is it they can't tell anyone?

But Afroz's door is closed. Sabrina hears voices inside. She crouches and peeks through the ventilator shaft. Amma is sitting on the bed next to the sleeping Afroz, in a pool of bluish light. Afroz's father, Amma's brother, stands by the table fan.

'I'm taking her with me,' Amma says.

'Don't be phagol.'

'I can't leave her. I've seen your wife with her, such a vicious, vicious—'

'Jani, don't be crazy. Think of what Sham Bhai—'

'I don't care! I don't care, I will take her.'

Sabrina turns. Someone has knelt beside her. It is her father. He smiles but stops short when he hears the voices inside the room. She opens her mouth to speak, but he frowns, and touches his finger to her lip.

'If you won't think of your husband,' Afroz's father is saying, 'think of Naju, think of Sibby. They need their mother!'

'And what about this daughter, Bhai? Doesn't she need her mother?' Sabrina's mother asks.

Sabrina's eyes are on her father's face.

'She has one. Amina looks after her well—'

'She beats her! So brutally—'

Sabrina tries to look away from her father's face, but it is as though her eyes are glued.

'Think of the daughters you do have, Jani,' says Afroz's Baba behind the door.

'No! Look at her – look how pale she looks, her leg—'

'Doctor said, didn't he? He said she will be fine. Take a hold of yourself.'

Sabrina watches her father and she is afraid. She has never seen an expression like this before. His face is like one of her pictures that she has crumpled up. Creased and folding in on itself. Quietly, he picks her up and takes her back to her bed.

'Abba,' she calls out as he turns to leave. 'I'm scared.'

Her father stares at her blankly for a few moments.

Then, as though he has not heard her, he switches off the light and leaves her in the darkness to picture the man in the orphanage, the lurid urgency in his face, the ugly thing in his hand. She blinks to erase the image, but instead of making it go away, the blinking conjures up the scene again and again. Sabrina begins to cry, angry at the prison of silence Afroz has forced upon her.

4

Towards the end of their very first month together, when they finished arranging the infrastructure required for their new lives (an apartment, a school and childcare), Sabrina and Elias were able to contemplate living their new life together. They stood before it like a pair of mountaineers, intimidated by the sheer scale of the journey before them, and for the first time, Sabrina wondered if it would not have been better to let her nephew stay in the Beacons with Afroz. The initial shock of his parents' death had worn off, and it was replaced in him by an attempt at courage that came across as a precocious aloofness. Sabrina winced each time he introduced himself to people with the peculiar phrase, 'My mummy and daddy died on Corn Du.'

Her own grief had regressed into something softer, and he heard her crying frequently in the shower. When she emerged, she was always distant, but in those moments, he followed her about, quick at her heels if she left the room, or waiting outside the bathroom door when she went inside. One morning, she slammed a coffee cup into the sink and shouted, 'Eli, just stop that! I'm not going anywhere!'

One Saturday morning she found herself stranded in the middle of Rockefeller State Park with him. Having insisted on taking his brand-new yellow scooter, Elias was halfway through their walk when he began to complain of being too tired to scoot. He wanted his aunt to carry him the rest of the way, and to leave the scooter on the path. They argued as people stepped around them. 'I can carry the scooter back, Eli,' she told him, 'but I'm not carrying you. You're a big boy.' Then she noticed him shifting from one foot to the other. 'Shit, Eli!' she cried. 'Do you need to use the toilet?'

And so, there they were, Sabrina and Elias, dragging themselves slowly through the Rockefeller estate, as other walkers edged passed them. 'I'm too tired!' he whinged every few minutes, sitting down on the path. 'Just a bit more, come on, Eli, the toilet's literally around the corner!' The sky's purple underbelly threatened to erupt at any moment, and as he added to the litany of his demands ('I need to pee … I need a drink … I need a snack'), so Sabrina's impatience and desperation grew. In the end, she hoisted him onto her hip and dragged herself back to the car, via the toilet, abandoning the scooter just a half mile or so from the gate. They sat in silence. Elias was all out of tears and she all out of words. Finally, just as the rain clouds burst open, she turned on the engine and drove them home.

When they reached the city, she parked at a grocery store to pick up milk and she tried to coax Elias out of the car. Still grouchy, he refused and she left him there while she ran into the store. As she returned, hugging the brown paper bag to her, she felt the shallow frustration of the afternoon leave her, and in the cold space it vacated, she felt a deep anger slip in. To do without her sister, without her father, without a career or the Peacock, only for the thankless task of raising a child when it had never been part of her life plans – was she up to the task? Was it a mistake?

But then she saw him, his face pressed against the car window, nose and palm splayed against the glass, a grotesque splat of pale flesh. She pressed her fingers against the window.

'Are you the idiot that left your kid locked in the car alone?'

Sabrina gaped at the woman, bathed in fluorescence on the steaming asphalt next to her cycle.

'Pardon me?' Sabrina said as she opened the car door and began to slide into her seat.

'I will not pardon you.' The woman glared, bending forward with barely concealed anger. 'You left a kid unattended in a locked car. I've got a good mind to call child protection services.'

As she drove off, Sabrina muttered under her breath. *Fucking ass. Fucking douchebag.* Her profanities filled the car, and after the initial shock, Elias began to giggle. Sabrina looked in the rear-view mirror. 'Your mother hated when I swore around you,' she told him. 'Fuck that.' He let out a hoot of glee, and Sabrina, keeping a straight face, turned into their apartment parking lot.

'Hi, Ms Sabrina, there's a gentleman, a Mr Ashok who would like to come up?'

'Ashok?'

She let him up, wishing she hadn't answered. She waited with the door open, heard the ding of the elevator, and then he was there, days of stubble on his stormy face, hands thrust into his jacket pockets. They stared at each other, she with some defiance, and he with angry recognition of it, before she finally stood aside and let him brush past her straight into the kitchen.

She watched him as he ran the cold tap. He let it run and banged the cupboard doors in search of a glass. She retrieved one and watched as he drank a glassful and began to fill another.

'My mummy and daddy died on Corn Du.'

Ashok switched the tap off and slowly lowered the glass. He turned to face the child standing quietly behind him. As he searched the small face, Sabrina saw Ashok's shoulders slump, the anger in his jaws soften.

'Eli,' she called, and Elias went to her. She picked him up and carried him back to his room, his arms locked behind her neck, his breath warming her earlobes.

When she returned to the living room, Ashok was standing outside on the balcony looking down at the traffic. The tarry night poured over him, and his shoulders seemed to bear the burden. She stood still at the door, waiting until he spoke. When he did not, she said, 'He tells everyone – about his parents dying on Corn Du – that's the summit where they were found, you know, in the Beacons? He keeps repeating it – almost to himself – at random times. Like to the doorman, or the guy at the grocery store.'

'Your sister's kid?'

'Yes,' she said.

He nodded. 'Fanni told me about what happened … I don't even know what to say.'

They stared out onto the street where two men were dragging a string of Christmas lights out of a van. Sabrina thought again of her father and her sister, their faces flushed by the lights of the Rockefeller tree. 'My sister loved Christmas,' she told Ashok softly. 'When we were little, she'd make us put cake and milk by the fireplace for Father Christmas. My mum was always against us adopting Western ways, but my sister, usually so compliant, well, she was so adamant about having Christmas.'

She stopped, searching his face for some understanding.

'Sab,' he said, 'I'm sorry. You adored her; I know.'

She nodded silently. Stepping out, she moved gently towards him, the cold damp of the balcony floor seeping through her tights.

'Your sister's kid?' he asked again, turning to her. He shook his head. 'Shit.'

For some moments they watched the men down below struggle to untangle the lights.

'Ash,' Sabrina hesitated. 'I'm … I don't know what to say.'

'Sorry? After what you did, "sorry" might be a good start.' He shrugged as though this was now futile.

'You would've done – you did do the same – you tried to throw me under the bus! I tried to ask you for help! It was going to be either you or me.'

'Sab, that was different,' Ashok said, his voice gentle. 'I told you

I'd look after you, I told you we'd make sure you made MD under my watch, didn't I? But what you did … I mean, do you understand the consequences? It wasn't just the job that I lost. Rachel threw me out. The rumours about you … about us. Ralph got wind.'

She took a deep breath. 'Ash—'

He turned to her. 'You of all people?' His chest shuddered, but he lapsed into silence. 'You know what, though? I sort of get it. The two of us … the way we were treating each other … no wonder you didn't believe me when I promised to look out for you.' He turned back to the night. 'I get it … I mean I hated the person I'd become, but you know, Sab, I've always had your back.'

Sabrina fought back angry tears. She realised she hated the person she had become too. But the defeat in his voice made her feel wretched, and she wished he would leave. Instead she said: 'We can't blame the job. We chose to become that way, elbows out, always out to win. You told me once, remember? When you stop needing to win, you're out.'

They watched a trickle of cars move through a green light.

'Does any of this matter now?' he asked. When she didn't respond, he continued, 'When Fanni told me, I had to google low cloud on mountains. I didn't even know that was a thing. I mean how does that even happen? Shit.' He tugged at his jacket as the wind picked up, and then looked at her. 'I didn't know you had your nephew here, though – I didn't know he was with you.'

'I brought him back because I think my sister would have wanted it.' She looked up at him. 'I've put in the paperwork to adopt him, officially I mean.'

'Wow, Sib.'

At that moment, in the gentle light from the streets, he was the old Ashok again. His eyes were pink, and his lips tense with some unfathomable emotion. She stepped forward, resisting the urge to rest the side of her face against his arm. Instead she whispered to him: 'Please, I need you to leave now.'

'I don't know what I'm going to do,' he whispered back.

'You'll know,' she said. 'I know you.'

'There are basically no jobs out there, right? It's like fucking Armageddon.'

'It's a total shit show.'

'I don't think I can do it, Sab. Fuck, I feel like a wreck.'

'*You* feel like a wreck?'

He stared at her and nodded. 'Is he going to be okay?'

'I don't know. But he's with me, and I'm not going anywhere without him.'

He frowned in that way he had that made him look like he was solving algebra. 'Are *you* going to be okay?'

She turned away, willing herself not to look at him again. After some minutes, he brushed past her, his coat rubbing her sweater in a gentle whisper, and Sabrina resisted the urge to run after him.

Almost a fortnight later, Sabrina and Elias sat on the sofa, clicking through the channels when the buzzer rang. Elias hovered at his aunt's elbow as she ushered Ashok in. Ashok's short, straggly beard glistened in the ochre light, and he glanced anxiously at Elias. He clutched a large box in his arms, wrapped in Christmas paper, and a paper bag from Magnolia Bakery.

'I thought the kid might want a Christmas present,' he told her. 'You've never been good with gifts.'

Sabrina was too surprised to respond.

'And some banana pudding from Magnolia.'

'I love banana pudding!' Elias cried, taking the small bag offered to him. 'How did you know?'

'I remember your aunt telling me that you liked it.'

Elias held out his hand for the larger box.

'What is it?'

'Go ahead,' Sabrina said. 'You can open it.'

Ashok licked his lips nervously. 'I actually just wanted to come and say hi.' He looked at Elias and then Sabrina. 'To you both.' He raised his hand, comically. 'Hi.'

'Hi,' Elias said.

Sabrina laughed.

'Do you want something to drink?' she asked, suddenly shy. 'No hard stuff, I'm staying away from the alcohol. I just did namaz.'

This elicited a chortle from Ashok. 'You know how?'

'I had to teach her,' Elias told him. 'She doesn't know. Do you know how?'

'Well,' said Ashok, shrugging out of his jacket, 'I'm a Hindu, but I'm not really religious.'

Elias nodded. 'Lalon was born a Hindu. But then he wasn't any religion either.'

They ordered pizza and cannelloni, and Elias sat between them, eating slice after slice and listening to them talk.

'You resigned,' Ashok said. 'Fanni told me.'

'You and Fanni are besties now?' Sabrina teased, but then she nodded, glancing pointedly in Elias's direction.

Ashok shook his head. 'I … I never in a million years would have seen that happening.'

'Things change.'

'People change. You're doing namaz.' He laughed.

Sabrina rolled her eyes, mouthing, 'I do it for him.'

Ashok nodded. 'They fired Fanni.'

'Ah, she had it coming. Rubs people up the wrong way.'

'Most of the old team is gone.'

'Fuck, I know!'

'Are you supposed to swear in front of the kid?'

'You should apply for the role. Build it up again.'

'Ha!'

'Anything out there yet?'

'Working on something. Let's see.'

'Will she take you back?'

Ashok didn't answer. Elias looked at him, pointed at the box he had given him. 'Can we play it now?'

'Sure.'

They began to set it up, a huge track looped around one end of the living room. Ashok inserted batteries into the car and stood to watch Elias control it over the course.

Sabrina stood up and cleared away the boxes, still surprised at Ashok turning up out of the blue, and more so at how natural it felt to have him here. The comfort of the last hour or so resembled the old days, and she found herself wanting to prolong his visit. She began to flip through her playlist.

'So who's this Lalon guy?' Ashok asked Elias.

'You don't know Lalon Fakir?'

'Is he a relative?'

Sabrina laughed at the look on Elias's face. 'He's a poet,' she explained, 'people sing his stuff and it's called Lalongeet.'

'I like the Lalon,' Elias told Ashok.

'You like Bengali folk songs?'

'Really? Why didn't you say, Eli? I have an album somewhere here!' Sabrina exclaimed, the excitement in her voice unmistakable. She began rummaging through her CD box.

'My favourite is "Bareer Kache Arshinogor".'

'Oh my God!' Sabrina stared at her nephew. 'Really?'

'And why do you like that one?' Ashok asked, picking up a piece of cheese from Elias's lap and putting it on his plate. Sabrina found the CD and the familiar and melancholic melody soared through the apartment.

Ashok considered it. 'I mean, it sounds like a lot of wailing.'

Sabrina laughed. 'It's just hard to translate, okay? He was very enlightened.'

'It's about how you're never alone,' Elias told him, talking through a mouthful of pizza. 'Nanabhai told me, it's about how your neighbour is always there when you can't see him. He lives in a city of mirrors, see? That's why you can't see him.'

'A city of mirrors, huh?' Ashok said. 'That's pretty profound. Is the neighbour a reflection of us?'

'The neighbour, see, is Allah-ji,' Elias explained to Ashok. 'But Nanabhai said to remember that even when we can't see Allah-ji, he is nearby.'

Ashok nodded.

After Ashok left that night, Sabrina stood on the balcony of her apartment and gazed out into the light-speckled city. The evening had been a short but necessary respite. She felt the lightness in her gut. She knew that the feeling that she was stranded far out at sea, with nothing but water around her, would return. But then Lalon's words revived her. *Shey aar Lalon ek khane roy, Tobu lokkho jojon fak re.* Though she herself was agnostic, she remembered how much she had appreciated her father's faith, that God, though unseen, was always near. She remembered how he believed that she was never a bad person, never selfish, like others thought her; that her goodness lived deep inside her, she just needed to dig deeper than others to find it. This ocean that she felt stranded in – perhaps it was a sort of liberation too? She could swim in any direction she pleased, towing her nephew along with her, with nothing to weigh them down.

She paced the apartment from room to room, gathering her thoughts. She went into her bedroom and sifted through a drawer full of her sister's old letters, many of them unopened. She found the photo she was looking for, held it up in the lamplight. The three of them, Afroz, Nasrin and herself standing beneath a betel nut tree during Eid morning. In it, their faces were small, and their grins huge. Sabrina sat on Afroz's lap, and Afroz's arm was looped around her neck, her cheek lowered to touch Sabrina's cheek. Sabrina remembered the downy softness of her cousin's skin, and the powdery smell of talc. Her sister, not cousin, but sister. Sabrina told herself this as she stood and walked slowly to her nephew's room. She watched his sleeping face in the gossamer shade of the night light.

She picked up her phone and dialled Afroz.

'I've wired the money,' she told her. 'It'll be in your account by Monday morning.'

There was a moment's silence.

'Thank you,' Afroz said.

'Do you remember,' Sabrina asked as though it had suddenly occurred to her, 'when you broke your leg, saving me from that car?'

Afroz didn't answer.

'Do you remember that poem you used to recite to me? Kajla Didi? Was it a Tagore poem?'

She heard a smile in Afroz's voice. 'No, it was Jatindramohan Bagchi, Sibby. You loved that poem.'

'I think Didi must have recited it to Eli, because he asked me for it too, but I can't bring myself to … I used to love it, but I was also so afraid of it … of that kid losing his Kajla Didi … and now …'

Sabrina waited for Afroz to respond but instead she heard soft sobs and felt her own eyes tearing up.

Sabrina said nothing more.

She understood that, despite their childhood attachment, she would never be close to her half-sister, or fully forgive her father. But she also understood that if she had done everything else to help her nephew brave this new world of his, then she would do this, too; she would allow him the possibility of three mothers on three different continents. She would help erect that troika of love.

Sabrina woke slowly on Christmas morning, then dozed and woke again as the light expanded throughout the room. Beside her, Elias stirred. She heard the cough from Elias's room, and for a moment was disorientated, before she remembered, and a small smile spread over her face. Ashok, after accompanying them to see the Met Christmas tree, had accepted her offer to stay the night.

'Khala?'

'Yes?'

'Is it Christmas Day?'

'Yes.'

She imagined he would ask if he could open his presents. She imagined there would be excitement. But her nephew lay still beside her.

She wanted to ask, what did Mummy and Daddy do on Christmas Day? But she did not. There would be no point in trying to replicate a parent she would never, could never be.

'Here's the plan for today,' she said, moving so she could see his face, 'let me know if you disagree, okay? First, we go down to Isabella's for a nice Christmas brunch. Then we're going down to the Rockefeller Center to ice skate. Then we can—'

'Can we speak with Nani?' he asked. 'Can we speak with Khala Afroz? And with Riaz?'

Sabrina sat up, irritation bubbling inside her.

'Sure.'

'Are you angry?'

'No.'

She walked to the kitchen, angry but unsure why.

'Hey.' Ashok stood at the sink, fully dressed. He was clearly on his way out. Sabrina felt herself stiffen. Why had she thought anything would be different?

'Morning,' she said, hating the tightness of her voice.

'I told Mom I'd come for Christmas lunch.'

'Of course! You're catching the train or driving?'

'If I drive, I'll have to go get the car. See *her*. Not sure I'm up for that.'

She nodded, moving towards the Nespresso machine.

'Are you okay?'

'Yeah.'

'Sab—'

'Everything's good! You should go. Elias and I have plans.'

Ashok bristled. 'Right.' He took his coat from the back of the chair. 'I'll get going.'

At the door, he looked back at her. 'I ... Monty called me. They're offering me my old job back.'

'What do you mean? How ...' She looked at him.

'I mean. To head up the new team—'

'I know what you mean!' Sabrina glared at him. 'But you're still under investigation, aren't you? They're just going to brush it under the carpet! Is that why you came over? To gloat? To get back at me?'

'Of course not! I came over to be with you. And with Eli. Why are you being like this?'

'You know what? Just leave.'

'Sabrina—'

'Just go!'

'You know what?' Ashok slammed the counter. 'I thought things were going to be different this time, but obviously I was wrong.'

The door banged and Sabrina stood watching it for the longest time, shaking with fury. Why was she angry? She had resigned. Why should Ashok lose out? Then she saw Elias standing by the bedroom door, watching her. His face was long with worry. She turned and put a capsule into the Nespresso machine. 'Come on, buddy,' she told him, hating the cold of her voice. 'Get ready.'

The morning wore on slowly. The restaurant was packed with tables of large families clucking over their young, the smell of pumpkins and cranberries in the air. The way Elias glanced at the table next to them dampened Sabrina's spirits and filled her with despair. She could imagine what he was thinking about. Of the Beacons. Of his Nani, Afroz, Riaz, the merry hubbub of her mother's kitchen. As they walked home, it began to rain, icy droplets that were sharp on their faces and the backs of their hands. The sky was a blank sheet of white, adding to the gloominess of the empty streets. When they finally reached the apartment, she peeled off his coat, and fetched a towel for his hair.

'How about a movie?'

'No.'

'Okay. Shall we play Monopoly?'

'No.'

'Do you want to take a nap?'

'No. I want to play with you.'

'Okay. But not Monopoly?' He shook his head. 'So, choose something. Let me go change, and then we'll play, all right?'

In the bathroom, she ran the water and washed her face. Her shoulders ached and her neck was so stiff it hurt to move. She was coming down with something. She couldn't remember the last time she had flu. She missed Abba. She wanted to hear her Didi's voice. Where was her mother? The world seemed so lonely and immense without them. Her only comfort was her nephew, but it hurt that he didn't want to be with just her and that, of all people, he missed Afroz. Afroz had been busily stacking up her wins against Sabrina's losses. Abba, then the restaurant and finally too, Nasrin's last days. *But she can't get Elias too*, Sabrina told herself. Not Elias.

She watched Elias taking out his box of Lego.

'I'll be there in a second,' she told him. She went into the kitchen and dialled her mother's number. She felt the weakness in her elbows, the throbbing in her head, and for a moment a panic engulfed her. Who would look after Eli if she became sick? Sabrina had spoken to her mother only a handful of times since her relocation to Sylhet, the nature of their conversations as short and abbreviated as they had been before – *are you well, have you eaten, are you sleeping okay?* Nasrin and Abba weighed heavily down on each of their exchanges but were never specifically mentioned. Sabrina did not dare bring them up, for her mother's grief had always had the ability to asphyxiate her. She remembered how, on her sister's wedding day, Amma had sat on Nasrin's bed as the make-up artist put the finishing touches on her Didi's beautiful face, and Sabrina's heart had twisted painfully as she watched her mother cry and cry, clutching Sabrina's hand to her chest. 'The two of you are my whole world,' Amma had said over and over again, 'and now you will leave and take my whole world with you,' and Sabrina had known she hadn't just meant Nasrin marrying and moving away, but also the fact that Sabrina had accepted a job in New York. The wretchedness of causing her mother this grief had made Sabrina run out of the house into the biting snow all the way to Llewid's Pond, ruining her juthis and the hem of her lengha and leaving her sister, as she always had, to console their mother. But now, there was just Sabrina and Amma.

She listened to the phone ring and ring.

'Sibby ni re futh?'

There was something newly contented in her mother's tone of voice, which made her seem all the more out of reach.

'Amma!' Sabrina said, and it came out as a half wail in the wintry dimness of the afternoon, and suddenly her nephew arrived at her elbow, and clung to her knees. She had frightened him, but she was fit to burst. 'Amma,' she said again, realising suddenly how much she needed her mother.

'Sibby? Everything is okay,' her mother soothed her. 'Cry. You can't cry it out of you, but you can cry as long as you want.'

'You feel so far away now! All the way in Sylhet,' Sabrina said after she had wiped her face. Her throat felt like it was covered in sandpaper. 'I didn't want you to leave.' But even as she said it, she realised it was a peculiar thing to say, to ask someone to stay in a place she herself had left behind. She tried to picture her mother in their childhood home, but without her father there, without Nasrin's intermittent presence, she found it a difficult vision to create. 'Why did you go?'

'I've been away a long time,' said her mother. 'All this time I have been in that cold country, just for my husband and children, and now my husband is gone … And Allah doesn't want me to be near my children. This is where I need to be.'

Afterwards, Sabrina would wonder at that last comment, but in that moment she merely sighed. 'Is the house up for sale?'

'Yes,' said her mother.

'Do you need anything, Amma?'

'I do. I want you to promise me two things.'

'What?'

'First, you make up with Afroz.'

'What's the second?'

'The second is that you send my grandson to me every summer holiday.'

'The second I will happily do.'

Her mother was silent for a moment.

'Don't you remember, Sibby,' her mother asked, 'don't you remember how much you loved her once? She carried you around like you were her doll. You did nothing without her. Don't you remember?'

'I do not,' Sabrina lied. 'I really do not.'

After she hung up, she followed Elias into his room. They sat with their backs to his bed and Sabrina emptied the Lego box out onto the floor.

'Shall we make the tallest tower in the world, Khala?'

'Yes. You do that.'

'I want to put the green ones at the bottom.'

'Good idea,' she said, picking out the green blocks and handing them to him. She picked up a balled-up piece of paper. 'What's this?'

She opened it. She felt Elias's eyes on her. She looked at the foreign scrawl and frowned. She recognised her father's handwriting.

'Don't read it,' Elias said, his voice quivering.

She looked at him, but he would not meet her gaze. He put

another piece of Lego on top of the short tower he had already constructed. 'Why, Eli?' she asked softly.

'It has bad things.'

'Can you read it? You can read Bengali?'

He shook his head. 'Mummy read it. Nani was angry. Very angry.'

Sabrina's hands shook as she laid the letter on the floor and smoothed out the edges. 'Because of this?'

'That's why I hid it.'

'In your Lego box?'

He nodded.

'When?'

He put the Lego down and looked at her.

'Oh,' she said. She moved his hair away from his face. 'I won't read it,' she said. 'What colour next? Red?'

She collected the reds and handed them to him.

'Just going to the bathroom, back in a minute.'

She walked into her room, dialling Riaz's number.

'Hey,' she said, 'sorry I woke you.'

'Sibby …' Riaz said, after a surprised pause. 'It's okay. I don't sleep much anyway.'

'Oh.' She sniffed, feeling tears of pity prick at her. 'How are you?'

'You know.' He was quiet for a moment. 'How are you?'

'You know.'

'Is Eli there?'

'Yes. He was asking after you.'

'I keep thinking of calling him.'

'You should.' She paused. 'Riaz, can you read Bengali?'

'Yes, why?'

'Can I send you a photo of something? In strictest confidence? Can you read and translate?'

After she sent it to him, Sabrina paced the small space in the bathroom.

'Khala-Amma?' Elias called.

'Coming, honey, have you finished your Lego?'

'Someone is at the door!'

Sabrina had not heard the buzzer. She ran to open the door.

Ashok stood outside, flicking the rain off his hair with his hands. She looked at his gleaming face, at the water dripping from his nose.

'Are you letting me in?'

Before she could answer, her phone rang. She left the door open and retreated to the bathroom to answer it.

'Riaz?'

His voice was eerily calm. 'Sibby,' he said, 'you'd better sit down.'

5

Jani,

If I were a braver man, I would have returned Afroz to you long ago when I saw a mother nursing her child's broken leg, afraid of showing the love that was bursting out of her.

But you've always been so afraid of how our community will judge you — and I understand because I've witnessed how complicit we are in forcing our women to be the cross-bearers of our honour and reputation. I've seen them suffer and be sacrificed to ward off shame and scandal. That bot gas in our Neel Bari; it's haunted by a girl not much older than you were when you left your home and came to mine. It was me she haunted; it was my dor she stoked with her prophecy. This is why I bought us shaath shomudhro paare, so we could stop looking over our shoulder, could live wihout dor. But I've learned that our fears follow us no matter how far we run away to shake ourselves free.

Now, Jani, I leave Afroz the Peacock as an apology for the years she has had to do without her mother, and I offer you this freedom to be with her without any scandal to your name, as an apology for the many years you have had to do without your firstborn. I pray this returns a mother to her daughter, and a daughter to her fold.

I know you will be reluctant — I have seen you punish yourself — suppressing your pleasure at seeing Afroz and worrying about Nasrin and Sabrina's every intransigence as though they were *your fault – but Jani, there is no absolute truth about sin and piety – there are only the small truths to be found in our love for one another and our faith that his most benevolent self loves us also. So, don't be afraid anymore, Jani re – your honour remains, as it has always been, unblemishable.*

Until we meet again across seven seas and thirteen rivers.
    Yours, Sham.

What Elias Saw Beneath
the Tamarind Tree

The sky is so big up here. Looking at the foamy uniformity of the cloud-drenched sky, Elias feels that the entire planet Earth, unfurled before his very eyes, could be home. He has been feeling homesick for so long but this realisation makes him feel elated. It is dampened a little by a fear that the homesickness will return. But it is a fleeting fear. He sits between Khala-Amma on his right and Khala Afroz on his left, and something tells him that he will always be able to find home, provided it is somewhere between these two.

Two days ago, Khala-Amma cried in his arms. She radiated heat, and her eyes shone in strange delirium. Elias doesn't know why she cried, but he felt something thaw inside her as she sobbed. A sort of hardness trickled out of her. Sitting on the cold bathroom floor, he gently wiped her face with his palms. She was like a cube of ice melting in the sun. She had held that dreaded letter in her hand, the one his mother had held before she died, and Khala-Amma looked at it again and again and had continued to weep. Then Ashok had come into the bathroom and carried Sabrina to her bed as he, Elias, cried inconsolably, worried that she was leaving him too. 'Your Khala-Amma has a bit of flu, Eli, let's give her a nap, and she'll be okay.'

The next morning, Khala-Amma seemed changed. Not just that her eyes were swollen, and that her skin was so pale. She somehow seemed softer. That hard thing had left her. All melted out. When Ashok arrived, she seemed to be invigorated by a sudden energy.

Khala-Amma handed Ashok a suitcase. 'Pack his bag for three weeks or so,' she said. 'Can you do that?' Then she went to her room and made a lot of phone calls. Some to Khala Afroz, some to Mustafa, some to Nani. Elias didn't understand the conversations: he seemed to be stuck in a tunnel, paralysed with fear, and the conversations were going on far away. What was happening? What was about to change? Who was he about to lose?

Then somehow, the next day, they were at the airport, and Ashok was heaving the suitcases onto the check-in conveyer belt. Elias gripped his aunt's hand, afraid he would lose her in the crowds of holiday travellers at JFK. She was on the phone to Khala Afroz. 'We'll change planes in Dubai – and then the next bit of the journey we'll sit together. Eli and I will wait at your gate.' Elias had never heard her talk in that tone to Khala Afroz before. Temporarily relieved, he soon grew fearful that the strange ceasefire could not last. And he is right to some extent, for his childhood is soon to be experienced between Afroz's Bangla and Sabrina's English; breakfasts of Afroz's aloo porotha and Sabrina's Manuka honey oatmeal; Sunday afternoons with Afroz's oil massages followed by carom board at the restaurant and Sabrina's brunches and boat rides in Central Park. They are to be the two ends of the river of his life: he will flow from one end to the other, but the two ends will refuse to meet. He will hear stories that a childhood love has bound them but will see little evidence of this in the years to come. Except for on this one trip.

The flight from Dubai to Sylhet is three hours, and Elias grips his aunts' fingers throughout the flight. He will not lose either of them. They are so easy with each other, he is afraid it will end.

'I'm sorry you had to resign.'

'It's a choice I had to make. No regrets. I'll find something when we're ready.' Sabrina ruffles Elias's hair.

'I was thinking about the money you lent. I can pay it back to you now. You see, Humayun has sold the shop.'

'Humayun Bhai sold the shop?' Sabrina asks. 'But what will he do now in Sylhet?'

'He is coming. To the Beacons,' Afroz says, suddenly shy.

Sabrina regards her. 'Is that good?'

'Yes, I think so. I think it is good.'

Sabrina chews her lip. 'Maybe, just leave it. I … I mean the money, only if you don't mind.'

'You mean like a partnership?' Khala Afroz's voice is so eager it makes Elias sick with trepidation, for what if Sabrina says no?

'Yes.' Sabrina said. 'Silent. I'll keep out of your way.'

'No, no, I'd like that.' Khala Afroz laughs. 'What do I know of business?'

'Well, no. I won't interfere. It's yours.'

'Ours,' Afroz says.

She nods. The stewardess arrives with water and juice.

'Sibby,' Afroz says, her voice suddenly tight. 'You said you wanted to talk?' There is fear in her voice, and it pricks at Elias.

'Let's wait until we're there. With Amma.'

There is a long silence as they drink their juices. Sabrina fiddles with a paperback on her lap.

'It's funny,' Afroz says suddenly, 'when bad things happen, I mean when they happen all at once, and we call them gordish? But why don't we have a word for when good things all happen at the same time? Ha?'

Sabrina bites her lip and when she finally looks up, Afroz is already reaching for a picture book and begins to flip through it with Elias leaning into her.

When the pilot instructs them to fasten their seatbelts, Khala-Amma leans over Elias and points through Khala Afroz's window to where Desh in all its watery emerald glory is spread before them. He will come to love this moment, as the plane lunges towards the land of golden hay and green rice paddies, and watery arteries, and as an adult, he will feel the pressure of his aunts on either side of him even when they are long gone.

When they land, Humayun and Mustafa are at the gates. Elias doesn't see them until he is picked up by Mustafa and embraced so tightly that he hears Sabrina say, 'Easy, Sasa, let him breathe.' Osmani Airport is bustling with people, and the air is tense with the joy of the homecomers and the grief of the homeleavers. For Elias this is a trip full of unfamiliar faces and manners. He grips Mustafa's hands, one more person to add to his list of potential losses. As they squeeze through the throngs, Elias keeps turning to make sure his khalas are behind him. 'It's okay, re Baba, we're here,' Khala Afroz says.

The car winds through a road lined with tall bushes coloured a deep, supple green. 'These are tea gardens,' Khala Afroz says, 'we came here all the time when we were small, Eli!' Elias hears the excitement in her voice, and he reaches up to touch her nose. 'Do you remember, Sibby?' Khala Afroz asks her, and Khala Sabrina swallows and gives a tight nod.

Soon Nirashapur comes into view: dots of turquoise blue amid a viridian landscape turning brown at the edges like a leaf approaching autumn. The pink crescent of the mosque and its Idgah jutts out of the feathery palms. They get out of the car and walk the remainder of the way – past the post office, and then the front ghat and the stables, and the guest house with its flat roof made with mosaic tiles in many shades of blue, and finally the three mango trees; these signposts will forever calm and thrill Elias, just as they do now. He steps through the newly painted gate of the outhouse, and there is Nani, clad in white cotton, with a little diamond nose stud, her white hair falling to her waist, drying in the sun. Nani's hands are so dear to him: tiny but perfectly formed, nails cut short and pale as the moon. Hands that touch his head and then pull him into an embrace. Hands that are never without her jade thasbih beads. Behind her is an entourage of curious adults and giggling children. They watch as Nani embraces Sabrina and Afroz and pushes them all towards the main house. One of the children takes Elias's hand, 'Ami thumar sasar goro bhai.' It means nothing to Elias, whose

Bangla does not extend to descriptions of cousinhood yet. But the adult Elias will come to understand that everyone in this village is a cousin in some way. This is the triangle of land where his history begins. If there is such a thing as mother earth, then this place here, where the very trees planted by his great-great-grandfather stand tall, bound on both sides by the compounds of his family, is where Elias will feel the maternal pull the strongest.

After lunch, Elias sits out on the veranda as Mustafa puffs at his hookah. At first, Elias is mesmerised by the water gurgling through the pipe, but gradually he becomes aware of something happening in Nani's room. He sees through the shutters that Sabrina sits with Nani on the bed. Khala Afroz stands by the door. The edge of her dupatta flutters a few yards from Elias, and he reaches for it, but Mustafa holds him back, lifts his stub of a finger to his lips. 'Shhhh.' Their voices are low, and the susurration, the jet lag and the afternoon sun make Elias drowsy.

Suddenly Khala Afroz runs out of the room, down the steps of the veranda, and out towards the tamarind tree. Once in its shade, she stops, she reaches out and puts her arms around its trunk. Elias is too anxious to move. Behind him in Nani's room, he hears Nani weeping. Sabrina is no longer whispering. 'Amma. You don't have to hide, not anymore. She deserves her mother. You deserve your daughter.' But Nani continues to cry.

Then the Asr adhan surges out over the horizon and Nani stirs. She shuffles past Elias and Mustafa and walks out to the tamarind tree. Sabrina comes out onto the veranda, and slowly follows her mother. Elias wants to go, too, but Mustafa raises his stub. 'Shhhh.' Mustafa makes his hookah, and lets Elias stoke the little coals. When they look up, the three women are perched on the bench beneath the tree. Elias notices the way the breeze lifts the hem of Afroz's dust-ridden shalwar, the way a piece of straw caught in a tendril of Sabrina's hair grapples its way to freedom again. Elias notices how their chests lift, how their shoulders sag, then straighten up again, like a sheet on a washing line being played by the wind. He will always remember watching the backs of his aunts and his Nani, Afroz's arm looped around Sabrina's shoulders, Nani's frail arm around Afroz's waist, the three of them cheek to cheek as they lean against each other beneath the old tamarind tree.

Glossary

Abagha: ill-fated.

Achol: this is the end of the saree that is worn over the shoulder and often covers the head.

Adda: the Oxford English Dictionary defines this as '*A place where people gather for conversation*,' which is rather understating the institution that adda has always been for Bengalis. The author's experience is that the very minimum requirements for adda is tea, fried savoury foods like daler bora or samosa and cerebral, erudite conversation among friends.

Adhan: in Islamic tradition, Muslims are called to the five scheduled daily prayers (salat) by a formal announcement made by a *muezzin*.

Afa: see *Didi* below.

Azrael: the angel of death in Islam, also known as Malak al-Maut, who separates the soul from the body and returns it to Allah.

Baba: this term is used in two different ways in this novel. Firstly, Afroz calls her father, Masoom, Baba, which along with *Abba* and *Abbo* is a term used to address one's father. Afroz also uses it to address Elias because it is also used by adults as a term of endearment for children.

Bebat: idiot.

Bhatiyali: a type of folk music sung by boatmen during his journey across the riverine districts of Bengal. The song begins with an endearing address to a person who remains at a distance.

Bidrohi Kobi: Bangladesh's national poet, Kazi Nazrul Islam was famous for his poem Bidrohi (The Rebel) and was an inspiration during the Liberation War.

Bilath: a foreign land, especially in reference to the United Kingdom. **Bidesh** is also used interchangeably. As an adjective **Bilayati** refers to Sylhetis who live abroad.

Bodmash: hooligan or mischievous person.

Bodna: a spouted vessel employed to cleanse oneself. Also known as a lota in other parts of the Indian subcontinent.

Bondhu: friend.

Boti: see **Da**.

Buzurg: an elder or senior person who, on account of his age, is deemed worthy of advising a community.

Chitol: a clown knife-fish, and a delicacy in Bangladeshi cuisine. Adult chital fish can grow up to five feet in length and weigh approximately 40 pounds. It is often used to prepare a delicious fishball stew.

Da: also know as boti, a cutting instrument used in the kitchen for chopping meat, fish and vegetables.

Dadu: term used to address paternal grandmother.

Daler bora: a mouth-watering fried lentil snack with onions, coriander and chilli.

Daroga: colloquial term for police official.

Didi and **Afa**: terms used to address an older sister.

Doodh bhat: this dessert of milk and rice with a sweetener such as sugar, banana or mango is often given to fussy young eaters who have skipped their dinner. Eaten in adulthood, it never fails to be both soothing and nostalgic.

Dor: fear.

Faristha: Angels.

Fufu: term used to address one's father's sister. A Fufu's husband is addressed, **Fufa**.

Futh: term of endearment used by Sylheti adults for their young.

Ghat: a series of steps leading down to large rectangular manmade ponds. The Neel Bari has one in the front for the use of male family members, and one at the back for the use of the female ones which is reputedly haunted by Manna.

Genda: marigold.

Gual: also known as Bengali Bual, a type of freshwater catfish native to Southeast Asia that is often cooked as mouth-watering stews with other ingredients such as **mukhi** (eddoes), **hutki/shutki** (fermented fish) and **uri bissi** (hyacinth beans).

Ghusl: in Islam, the 'major ablution' accompanied by a statement of intent and which entails washing the entire body in ritual fashion. It is required in specified cases for the living and all Muslims must undergo ghusl before burial.

Gordish: a time of great misfortune. The author's mother often spoke of *gordish* manifested as a woman: one who presided over ruin rather than one who induced ruinous actions by humankind.

Gunaah: sin.

Gur muri: puffed rice sweetened with date sugar and made into crispy small balls. This snack is featured in a Bengali nursery rhyme, 'Kaatberali', and beloved by all children.

Handesh: rice-based sweet treats made of *morcha gur* (date molasses) and rice flour. Afroz makes them so they are soft in the middle and crispy around the edges and serves them with tea.

Haram: means forbidden under Islamic jurisprudence.

Houris: sura 56 verses 12–39 of the Quran states that for the 'People on the Right' there will be a variety of divine rewards awaiting them in Jannah, including the houris, wide-eyed maidens, beautiful as pearls hidden in their shells.

Ibadath: acts of worship.

Idgah: a place, often mosque-like in structure, which has an open-air section used for public prayers during the Muslim festivals of Eid.

Ilish: the hilsa fish is the national fish of Bangladesh, but love for this *prince among fish* crosses borders and religions and it figures widely in the culinary traditions of east and west Bengalis alike.

Inna lillahi wa inna ilayhi raji'un: roughly translated as 'Indeed, to Allah we belong and to Allah we shall return' (Quran, Surah Baqarah ayah 156) and it is recited by Muslims upon receiving news of someone passing away.

Izzath: reputation.

Jalmuri chanasur: a delicious Bengali snack containing puffed rice, Bombay mix, tomatoes, onions, lemon, coriander and the mouth-wateringly aromatic mustard oil.

Jamdani: a type of textile where intricate designs are handwoven into a muslin fabric. Sarees made from jamdani are popular in Bangladesh.

Janamaz: Islamic prayer mat.

Janazah: Islamic funeral prayer performed in congregation to seek pardon for the deceased.

Jannah: Muslim concept of heaven or paradise.

Kafir: nonbeliever.

Kajla Didi: a popular poem by Jatindramohan Bagchi enjoyed by both Sabrina as a child and her nephew, Elias. Whereas Elias loved the poem for its delicious rhythm and the beauty of the Bengali lyrics, Sabrina was haunted by the protagonist's loss of his sister. The death of Nasrin triggers this memory in Sabrina, along with other memories of sisterhood, and some small part of her wonders at its prophetic nature.

Kala jam: black plum.

Katha and *Nokshi Katha (*also known as kantha): see *Shital* and *Shital Pati* below.

Keski: also known as the Ganges river sprat, this tiny fish is often eaten fried, or cooked with a sliver of the rind of a Bangladeshi bitter citrus fruit called *shatkora*.

Khala: term used to address one's mother's sister. *Khalamoni* is often reserved for one's mother's youngest sister, but Nasrin made Elias call Sabrina, Khala-Amma. *Khalu* is used to address a Khala's husband.

Khatm: recitation of the Holy Quran from the beginning to the end.

Kiraman Katibin: these are the two recording angels in Islamic tradition believed by Muslims to record a person's actions.

Kisuri: the customary fast breaking meal of Sylhetis is this porridge-like dish made from lentils, rice, onions, salt, ghee, fenugreek seeds and turmeric. The author's mother favoured adding a little ginger to it too, and it is served with fried chickpeas and daler bora.

Kuli: u-shaped tray made with shital or bamboo.

Kumro phul er bora: fritters prepared with pumpkin or courgette flowers.

Kuthor bacha: son of a dog.

Lalon: Fakir Lalon Shah, also known as Fakir Lalan Shah, a mystic, philosopher and composer, was probably born around 1774 in Kushtia. He was a celebrated Baul saint with a faithful following in Sylheti villages such as the one Shamsur was born into. As a child, Shamsur would watch Baul mystics singing Lalongeet, or songs composed and written by Lalon, as they journeyed through the village, and he was particularly drawn to the bard's resistance against religious bigotry and message of societal and interfaith harmony.

Mama or **Mamu**: term of address for mother's brother. **Mamani** is a Mama's wife.

Maulvi: also known as **Mulla**, a form of address for a learned Muslim who may minister to the religious needs of the Muslim community.

Mela: festival or fair. Also see **Pahela Baishakh**.

Mishti dhoi: this is a delicately flavoured curd sweetened with caramelised sugar or date jaggery (nolen gur) which gives the yoghurt a golden or reddish colour.

Moyna: common hill myna bird, popular as pets in Bangladesh. **Moyna** is also used as a term of affection used by adults for their youngsters.

Naath: poetry in praise of the prophet (pbuh).

Nali shag: a vegetable dish made with red jute leaves and jackfruit seeds, slightly bitter to the taste but considered nutritious.

Narikel kuruni: similar to a **Da** but used to grate coconut.

Nasheed: moral and/or religious songs sung in various melodies by Muslims usually without any musical instruments.

Nashta: formally, this term is used for breakfast, but Sylhetis often use it to describe snacks served with tea.

Nauka: riverboat.

Neel Bari: this is Shamsur's ancestral home in Nirashapur, famous in the district as the Blue House because of the turquoise roof tiles that glitter in the sunlight from a great distance. When his children were young, Shamsur taught them the address of their ancestral home, and always exclaimed as an afterthought, 'If you get lost, re futh, just ask someone the way to the Neel Bari! There's not a soul there that won't know it!'

Nikkah: a marriage contract under Sharia law which may only be conducted with full consent from both parties, and in the case of the female the approval of her wali (guardian) is also required.

Nozor: used by Sylhetis to denote the misfortune that befalls a person from the ill will or jealousy of an observer. Also known as the evil eye.

Paandan: also known as faandan, is a handcrafted receptacle (often in ornate silver) for storing paan (betel leaf), zarda, supari (or gua) and choona (also known as soon).

Pahela Baishakh: festival or fair celebrating the first day of the Bengali calendar.

Phitha: rice-based, fried snacks that can be sweet (such as handesh) or savoury. These are usually made during Eid.

Puthol: doll.

Rakkoshni: a human-eating, shapeshifting monster typically found in Bangladeshi folk tales.

Rehal: a foldable book rest used for placing the Quran during recitation.

Roshogolla: sweetmeat made from Indian cottage cheese and semolina dough, cooked in light syrup.

Ruza: fasting.

Sadka: a form of charitable giving.

Sehri: the breakfast consumed before dawn by fasting Muslims during Ramadan.

Shaath shomudhro, thero nodir paare: phrase literally meaning across seven seas and thirteen rivers.

Shaban: the eighth month of the Islamic lunar calendar called the hijri calendar. Shaban signals the coming of Ramadan and Muslims start spiritual preparation for Ramadan during Shaban.

Shabebarath: the Night of Forgiveness, celebrated on the 15th night of the month of Shaban, the eighth month of the Islamic calendar. It is observed by Muslims by a night of worship and salvation.

Shapla: waterlily. The white shapla is the national flower of Bangladesh and is ensconced between two rice sheaves in the national emblem to represent the country's many rivers. The national emblem is printed on the 50 poisha coin, and on the presidential standard.

Sharia: Islamic law.

Shemai: a sweet dessert made from vermicelli spiced with cardamom and cinnamon, milk and sugar.

Sheuli: night-flowering jasmine.

Shital and **Shital Pati:** the traditional art of weaving together strips of cane from the murta plant to make handcrafted mats or other domestic wares such as hand fans and baskets. The cane is dyed in vibrant hues to create mats with decorative designs, which are called *nakshi pati*. The art of nakshi itself (which loosely translated means artistically patterned) includes also the centuries-old Bengali art tradition of the ***nakshi katha***, where several layers of used or worn-out materials such as sarees, lungis and dhotis are stitched together to make a single katha, which is then embroidered. In his seminal poem, Jasim Uddin allegorised the Bengal landscape as *Nokshi Katha* in the poem *Nokshi Kathar Math* or the Field of Embroidered Quilt. Jahanara has been gifted many of these homewares as part of her trousseau and her attachment to them during her life in England is symbolic of her longing for a happier time in her childhood when she watched the katha art emerge out of the collective chatter, nostalgia and laughter of the village women.

Shobbonash: utter disaster.

Shobzi: sauteed vegetable dish.

Shomman: respect and honour.

Shongsar: family or household.

Shoror bacha: son of a pig.

Shoythan: the source of all evil according to Islamic mythology.

Shunamoni: term of endearment used by Sylheti adults for their young.

Shutki: dried or fermented fish and prawns. It has a distinctly umami flavour and a pungent smell. Shutki dishes are a delicacy in Bangladesh and an acquired taste.

Silan: promiscuous woman.

Sipara: each of the thirty parts of the Quran split into thirty sipara booklets for ease of communal readings.

SubhanAllah: usually translated as 'Glory be to Allah'.

Tarawih: special prayers conducted after every evening's last daily prayer (Isha) during the holy month of Ramadan. Tarawih is derived from the Arabic word meaning 'to rest and relax', as it is seen as a special form of Islamic meditation and can take up to an hour to perform.

Taweez: amulet worn for protection.

Thasbih: reciting the name of God using a string of ninety-nine prayer beads as a counting aid. Jahanara's jade beads were given to her by her father during her first pregnancy along with a reminder that the only comfort to be gained during times of difficulty, was by remembering God.

Tusha shinni: a halwa lightly spiced with cinnamon, cardamom and bay leaves that is often made to mark a religious ceremony of the anniversary of a loved one's death. This dish requires a strong arm for the continuous stirring, and the author's recollection is that the making of this dish was the only time her father was permitted into her mother's kitchen to help.

Zarda: a type of chewing tobacco flavoured with spices.

Zikr: Islamic prayers which are repeated on a set of prayer beads.

Acknowledgements

Special thanks to Manpreet Grewal for her passion for this book and to Anna Power for her unswerving belief and encouragement: without their support and editorial guidance, this book would not be in your hands. Thank you to Melanie Hayes and the entire HQ team for their enthusiastic assistance and support. Thank you to Jonathan Myerson and Clare Allan for their enthusiasm and tutelage during the earlier drafts and to Rachel Kerr for being a passionate and thoughtful reader.

Thank you to my daughters Ayesha Husain and Amna Husain, from whom I stole precious moments of childhood to write. Thank you to my parents, Rabea and Shofique Uddin to whom I owe everything and particularly the childhood memories from which I have shamelessly pillaged. Thank you to Nirupar Uddin and Shayaque Uddin with whom I shared the experiences that shaped these stories. Thank you to Rubina and Imdad Husain, for their steadfast support and love, and also thank you specifically to Imdad Husain for the plethora of advice relating to all things Islamic and aeronautical. Thank you, Tehmina Sheikh, for looking after my daughters so I could write.

Thank you to Richard Kretchmer and David Topham, whose passion for the written word still drives me two decades on. Thank you to Patrick Flood, my friend, fellow writer and sympathiser. Thank you to all my friends who provided support, love and encouragement – there are too many of you to mention, but especially Shireen Irani, Amana Humayun, Fatima Alquati, Joey Uppal, Dipali Sahni, Yi Tyng Tan and Penelope Mawson.

My last words belong to Ahmed Husain whose words, 'You should write a book' began this journey. Thank you, because without your love, belief and impatience, I would never have done it.

Permission Acknowledgement

Thank you for the permission granted by Hohm Press for the excerpt used in the epigraph, which is from Fakir Lalan Shah, Page 133, *The Mirror of the Sky: Songs of the Bards of Bengal*, Translated by Deben Bhattacharya, Revised Expanded Edition, 1999, 288 pages.

ONE PLACE. MANY STORIES

Bold, innovative and
empowering publishing.

FOLLOW US ON:

@HQStories